She was Vampire, used to being the hunter, not the prey . . .

Sophia smiled lazily, gliding her tongue along her upper lip as she lowered first one bra strap and then the other, feeling the heat of Colin's rapt attention as he watched her breasts slowly begin to overflow the lacy cups. She reached behind her and unfastened the clasp, letting it fall forward, feeling the accustomed rush of pleasure as her breasts were freed, glancing up and gasping as the hunger in Colin's eyes tightened her nipples and left her aching with need.

Her hands were trembling slightly when she tossed the bra to one side, shaken by what she saw when Colin looked at her. He wanted her. She knew that. But the strength of his lust, the sheer intensity of it . . . that rattled her. She had grown accustomed to her young men in Rio, the human toys she played with for a while and then cast aside, lovers who were completely dominated by her needs and wants. And she realized abruptly that Colin was not that kind of man. He was alpha down to his core, and he was eyeing her the way a lion eyes a particularly tasty gazelle.

Dedicated with love to my brother Stan.
even though he covers his eyes for the sex parts!

Other Books by D. B. Reynolds

Raphael
Jabril
Rajmund

Coming Soon
Duncan
Lucas

Sophia

***

D. B. Reynolds

ImaJinn Books

SOPHIA
Published by ImaJinn Books, Inc.

ISBN: 978-1-61026-049-7

10 9 8 7 6 5 4 3 2 1

PUBLISHER'S NOTE:
This book is a work of fiction. Names, characters, places and incidents are products of the author's imagination or are used fictitiously. Any resemblance to actual events or locales or persons, living or dead, is entirely coincidental.

Books are available at quantity discounts when used to promote products or services. For information please write to: Marketing Division, ImaJinn Books, Inc., P.O. Box 74274, Phoenix, AZ 85087, or call toll free 1-877-625-3592.

Cover design by Patricia Lazarus
Cover Credits:
Mans photo - Sophie Phelps - dreamstime.com
Sophies photo - Konradbak@dreamstime

ImaJinn Books, Inc.
P.O. Box 74274, Phoenix, AZ 85087
Toll Free: 1-877-625-3592
http://www.imajinnbooks.com

Prologue

Malibu, California

Raphael was drowning, trapped in a whirlpool of pain and loss . . . so much loss, sucking him down, icy shards swirling, slicing like razors into his soul. He raged at the bonds that held him trapped in this nightmare while his sweet Cyn wept, her tears warm against the skin of his chest, shredding what was left of his heart. The merciless sun forced him to lie dormant while he howled in silence, the voices of his dead children demanding vengeance against those who had destroyed them.

Five centuries old and the most powerful vampire on earth . . . and still he could only wait.

The hours ticked by, and then the minutes.

The sun was still a molten smear on the horizon when he shattered the chains of daylight that held him prisoner. He sat up, his arms circling Cyn, holding her close, pulling her onto his lap and murmuring meaningless words of reassurance. He reached out to his vampires, those still asleep and those just waking, but especially to Duncan who was near enough and strong enough to have felt the biting edge of Raphael's nightmare. A nightmare that was all too real.

Cyn jerked her head up, studying him in the lamplight, her eyes red and swollen, her lovely face streaked with tears. He kissed them away, knowing his own face was wet with blood.

"What was that?" she demanded. "You were in pain, Raphael. You're bleeding!"

"Tears, *lubimaya,* only tears. Two of mine have died, their lives stolen—"

Across the room his cell phone rang. Cyn jolted, twisting in his arms to stare at the intrusive device as if she'd never seen it before. "Who?" she asked fearfully.

"That will be Duncan," he said soothingly. "I need to speak with him. Come." He stood, still holding her tightly, sensing her fear for him, wanting to reassure her, but also needing the comfort for himself of having her pressed to his side, her heart beating strong and sure . . . and alive.

He crossed the room swiftly, one arm still holding onto Cyn as he picked up the cell on the third ring.

"Duncan. Marco and Preston are gone. Contact the Seattle compound and tell them we're coming."

Chapter One

Colin Murphy downshifted as he made the turn onto the narrow driveway. New gravel had been laid here a couple years back, but the rains had washed away much of it by now, leaving potholes big enough to swallow small animals. The truck dipped hard to one side and he gripped the wheel, his tires sliding on the uneven surface before the heavy 4X4 dug in and forged ahead. Say what you will about American-made cars, he thought to himself, but no one made a better truck. He gave the dashboard an affectionate pat as he leaned forward, squinting through the rain-spattered windshield.

Lillian Fremont had called to say she'd heard gunshots over here. Colin wasn't really a police officer—more like an overqualified private security guy—but the good people of Cooper's Rest paid him to deal with incidents just like this one, so he'd geared up and headed out. He didn't really know what to expect, though. Mrs. Fremont had been adamant about what she'd heard, but the woman was more than ninety years old and her house was a good two miles away. Granted, sound was a weird thing, and situated as she was on the opposite side of a shallow dip in the forest floor, it was just possible she could hear quite well over there. Especially if what she'd told him was true.

Of course, in his experience most people didn't know what real gunfire sounded like, expecting it to be like what they heard in movies and on television. But this wasn't the big city, either. Most people up here had guns of their own and knew firsthand about gunfire.

And screams pretty much sounded the same everywhere.

Jeremy's house came into view, a newer ranch style, single story with high ceilings and a fire-retardant shingled roof. The blinds were drawn behind the few windows, but then he'd expected that. Jeremy was a vampire, after all, so sunlight was hardly a priority. On the other hand, Jeremy's significant other, Mariane, was human, and Colin had seen her in town often enough during daytime to know that she didn't always sleep away the days with her lover.

Colin pulled up in front of the house, his eyes scanning the area as his fingers automatically switched off the ignition. He was getting a bad feeling about this. And if he'd learned one thing in twelve years as a Navy SEAL, it was to trust his feelings. Especially the bad ones.

He opened his door quietly and stepped outside, standing perfectly still for a moment to listen. There was no sound. None at all, except the patter of the ever-present rain.

He backed toward the rear of his vehicle, his gaze never leaving the silent house in front of him. He grabbed his Sig Sauer P228 from where it rode in a holster on his right hip and ejected the magazine, dropping his eyes just long enough to check it carefully before slapping it back in with the ease of long practice. Popping the hatch on his Tahoe, he leaned into the cargo area and brought out a Benelli M4 S90 shotgun, a combat shotgun designed to kill humans. Or vampires.

Colin pulled the cargo door down, leaning his weight against it so it closed with a muted click. And still not a sound from the house.

He didn't like this. Didn't like it at all. It had to be nearly sundown. It was difficult to tell sometimes with the heavy cloud cover, and he hadn't exactly checked his Farmer's Almanac this morning to find out the precise time of sunset. But it had to be close, and he sure as hell didn't want to be snooping around Jeremy's house when the vampire rose for the night, hungry and probably pissed if he found Colin lurking about uninvited.

But, he couldn't walk away, either. Not with those screams Mrs. Fremont had reported.

Shaking his head, Colin racked the shotgun and rounded his truck, circling slightly to the left of the house. Finding nothing amiss, he crossed to the right and maneuvered through crowded trees around to the back. The rear of the house came into view and his stomach muscles clenched as adrenaline flooded his system.

Goddamn if Mrs. Fremont wasn't right.

The back door, what was left of it, stood wide open, looking like someone had taken an ax to it. There was no other explanation. It was made from heavy, solid core construction without even a decorative window—or it had been. Nothing but shards and splinters of wood were left, hanging crookedly from those heavy duty hinges. Jeremy was serious about his security; all the vamps were. Someone else had known that and come prepared. But whoever it was, Colin was pretty sure they were long gone. There wasn't a sound coming from inside the house.

He approached carefully anyway, moving along the house's back wall, well below the high, narrow windows. When he reached the wooden porch, he darted his head out for a fast, oblique look inside before stepping up. A triangular pane high above the door had been destroyed, scattering glass all around. It crunched beneath his boots and he paused, waiting for a reaction. But there was none. Shotgun at the ready, he stepped quickly into the house and out of the doorway. A scan of the kitchen showed even more destruction—cabinets trashed, probably with the same ax, dishes broken, refrigerator hanging open and blood spattered over the floor in front of it. Seeing that blood sucked the air out of his lungs until he realized it was Jeremy's food supply, that among the litter were plastic donor bags, ripped and torn.

Did Jeremy need blood beyond what Mariane could provide? Apparently, he did. Or maybe it was for guests. Who the fuck knew?

Colin took a cautious step toward the archway on the other side of the kitchen, mindful of the slippery goo covering the floor. The next room was much bigger, with a high, angled ceiling and lots of furniture. A huge entertainment center took up one entire wall, now blasted to bits like everything else. Colin cleared the room carefully, aware of a sick feeling building in his gut. Where was Mariane?

He entered the back hallway. There were only three doors here, two of them open. One was a bathroom, obviously empty, but he cleared it anyway. The second was an office of some sort, the equipment trashed, files overturned in what was by now a familiar pattern of destruction. The trashed equipment in this room alone was worth thousands, which made him think this wasn't a simple case of breaking and entering. Either that or they'd been after something other than easily pawned electronics.

Colin stepped back and eyed the final door. "*Dammit,*" he mouthed soundlessly and made his way down the hall.

The door was pulled closed, but not latched. Colin paused for a moment, listening and hearing nothing. He stood back against the wall and pushed the door open with the fingers of one hand. A quick look showed more of the same, an almost random trashing of the room and everything in it. He stepped through the doorway and immediately put a wall at his back.

"Ah, shit," he swore softly.

Mariane lay in the middle of a big bed, blood soaking the sheets beneath her. Colin closed his eyes briefly, letting a wash of grief sweep over him before steeling himself for what had to be done. Every human instinct he possessed told him to rush to her side. Instead, he cleared the room, stepping into both the walk-in closet and attached bath before crossing to the bed and propping the shotgun within reach.

"Who did this to you, baby girl?" he murmured. She'd been beaten, tortured it appeared, her arms and legs covered with shallow knife cuts, designed to hurt like hell without killing the victim. None of the individual cuts would have been fatal, but the cumulative effect of so many . . . They'd left her lying naked, her legs spread wide. The blood and bruises on her thighs and vaginal area told him she'd been raped, and Colin gritted his teeth against a wave of anger so strong it nearly brought him to his knees.

If she was breathing, he couldn't see it, but he leaned over and placed two fingers against her neck, expecting to find nothing but confirmation of what he already believed to be true. Instead, he felt a weak pulse—barely there, but she was alive!

He straightened immediately, pulled the cell phone from his belt and speed dialed 911. The closest trauma center was a good sixty miles away, and most of that was twisting mountain roads, but he didn't know what else to do, who else to call. He knew battlefield medicine, had spent hundreds of hours in training sessions. He'd dealt with bodies torn apart by guns and explosives, but this . . . He forced himself to think clinically, to ignore the brutal nature of the attack. Okay. Shock was probably her greatest enemy right now. He cast about for something with which to cover her. He needed to raise her body temp and keep her warm. But all he could see were blankets as bloody as she was. Towels. He ran back into the bathroom as he waited for the 911 operator to come on the line. It would probably play hell with any forensic—

"Nine-one-one, what is your—"

The rest of her spiel was lost as the roar of an angry vampire filled the house.

Chapter Two

Colin backed two quick steps away from the bedside, grabbing up the shotgun as he went. In the blink of an eye, Jeremy was in the room, fangs fully distended, eyes flashing red fire as he confronted the invader.

"Jeremy," Colin said evenly. "You know me. You know I didn't do this."

The vampire stalked across the bedroom, his movements eerily graceful, gliding forward like a big hunting cat. He growled softly, threateningly, but his gaze kept flicking to Mariane, anguish replacing the rage on his face.

"I'm calling nine one one, Jeremy. Let me get some help for her."

The vampire's head snapped around at that, his gaze deadly cold despite the fires burning there. "You touch her and I'll kill you, human. I don't need your help."

Faster than Colin could follow, Jeremy was at the bedside, lifting Mariane in his arms, bloody tears rolling down his face as he saw what they'd done to her. A low keening rose from his throat, rising in volume until it became a furious howl.

"There will be justice for this," he snarled, his gaze once again pinning Colin in place. "Mark my words, human. This will not go unavenged."

And then he was gone, nothing more than a blur of movement and a slam of noise as the front door hit the wall in the living room.

"Well, shit," Colin whispered. He lowered his head and just breathed, letting his body recover from an adrenaline rush that dwarfed whatever he'd been feeling when he'd first entered the house.

"Jesus H. Christ." He sucked in a last deep breath and called 911 again, canceling the earlier call. Then he walked out to his truck and grabbed his gear. Jeremy might not want his help, but he was going to get it anyway. This was a crime scene and Colin was the closest thing they had to a police department in Cooper's Rest. Not that he was a real police officer. Legally, he was no more than private security, which meant this case fell under the jurisdiction of the County Sheriff. But the people around here didn't want the Sheriff or anyone else poking into their affairs, and that went double for the vampires who'd elevated privacy to a fine art. That's why the self-appointed town council had hired him in the first place. He hadn't been to any police academy; the nearest he'd come were a few criminology classes at the college down in the city. But he was qualified to handle just about every weapon that existed and could put a man, or a woman, on the ground in nothing flat, regardless of weight or training. He also had the ability to size up a situation and the confidence to deal with it. Which was what he intended to do with this one.

Cooper's Rest was his home now, the place he'd somehow ended up in after leaving the Navy. This tiny village in northern Washington state was about as far from where he'd grown up as it was possible to be, but it was a quiet, peaceful place, full of mostly good people who wanted to be left alone. And it suited him just fine.

But now someone had invaded this peaceful place, had invaded his home, and Colin wasn't the kind of man to sit back and wait for someone else to see justice done. He was going to find whoever had done this. And when he did, he wasn't going worry about reading anyone their Miranda rights.

Chapter Three

Vancouver, British Columbia

Sophia gripped the edges of the armrests, her nails gouging holes into the fine leather. She hated flying. She especially hated flying through the daylight hours, hated trusting her life to humans. She might be nearly three hundred years old, but that didn't mean she lived in the past. She watched CNN, went online and read the newspapers. She knew how often these planes fell out of the sky, right along with their human pilots and, maybe, vampire passengers.

It was possible, she mused, that a vampire could survive such a crash. Possible, but not certain. It was definitely not a theory she wished to test, nor did she want to learn whether a vampire could breathe underwater for however long it would take to reach land if the plane went down in the middle of the ocean.

Not that that particular outcome was a problem at this point. The ocean was no longer beneath her. Nor was the sun shining on the other side of the airplane's thin skin as it had been for much of the previous leg of her journey, which had taken her from her home in Rio de Janeiro to a stop in Toronto. She thanked whatever gods smiled on vampires that she at least had the resources to travel by private aircraft, one with a suitable sleep compartment for her daylight needs.

Of course, it would have been even *more* convenient if she'd been able to fly to Texas, or even Mexico, from Rio and gone on from there to Vancouver. She could have limited her flying time to the hours of darkness. But the North American vampires, unlike those in most of South America, were obsessively territorial. She couldn't even pass through one of their stupid airports without getting permission, something she wasn't willing to do. Not for this trip.

There were too many unknowns this time. She didn't know what her Sire, Lucien, wanted. Didn't know why he'd issued such an urgent summons and then disappeared on her before she could even get ahold of him. But there'd been an undeniable note of desperation to his mental call, a desperation reinforced by the fact that he'd contacted her at all. Lucien was her Sire, and her loyalty was his alone, but she hadn't even spoken to him in half a century. And now this. Whatever *this* was.

The ground rushed up to meet the plane and she closed her eyes, feeling every bump and skid as it finally came to rest. Sophia breathed a deep sigh of relief and whispered a superstitious prayer of thanks to the God of her childhood that she'd survived once again.

She only hoped she'd also survive whatever Lucien had waiting for her.

* * * *

"What do you mean, you don't know where he is?" Sophia

demanded darkly.

"Do we need a translator? Is that the problem, Sophia? I don't fucking know where he is, okay? He doesn't exactly check in with me."

Sophia leveled a flat stare at the vampire sitting across from her. Darren Yamanaka was Lucien's lieutenant. *In name only*, she thought viciously. She could squish him like a bug. She'd probably quite enjoy it, in fact. Her eyes narrowed appraisingly, but Darren met her gaze without flinching. He wasn't as powerful as she was, but he wasn't weak either. And he had courage. She'd give him that. What he didn't have was even the slightest clue as to the whereabouts of their mutual Sire.

"When did you last see him?" she asked with forced patience.

"I've already told you, and no matter how many times you ask, the answer will be the same. Lucien walked out that very door eight days ago." He pointed dramatically across the big conference room and through the open double doors to the heavy front door of Lucien's Vancouver headquarters. "He said he was off to meet another of his women. You, of all people, should remember how fond Lucien is of his women."

Sophia held back the snarl rising from her throat, forcing herself to remain calm. She hadn't flown halfway around the world, risking her long immortal life, to lose her temper with this pipsqueak of a male. *Everybody* knew Lucien loved women. Hell, Lucien loved men, too. But the fact that Sophia had once been his lover, and that he'd made her Vampire because he'd been unwilling to lose her to human age and frailty . . . that was *not* something everyone knew. Although, Darren clearly did. Lucien had been telling tales before he'd disappeared, the bastard.

"Was he alone when he left? Not even a bodyguard?"

"No," Darren admitted reluctantly. "He usually took someone with him, but not this time. He claimed the woman was someone he'd known a long time, that it was safe. And that he could defend himself if it came to it. I argued with him. But . . . you know Lucien."

She did know Lucien. He was handsome, brilliant, utterly charming, and sometimes a complete idiot. Especially if a woman was involved.

"Why do you think he called me?"

"I have no fucking idea. I don't even know if he really did. It's awfully convenient that Lucien disappears and now you show up. How long's it been, Sophia?"

"Not long enough, Darren," she said with saccharine sweetness, before her voice hardened. "But if you're suggesting I have in any way harmed our Sire, you should say good-bye to whoever is foolish enough to care for you because I will kill you where you stand."

He stood, leaning across the table, his eyes gleaming yellow. "You can try, bitch."

Sophia felt his power pressing against her, felt her own surging to meet his. She also stood, matching his aggressive stance, and pushed back just enough for him to feel the weight of it.

Darren's eyes widened in surprise, and he froze for a full minute before he slowly sank back into his chair. His gaze was riveted on her, like an animal that has just discovered a predator hiding in its nest.

Sophia smiled pleasantly and sat back down, satisfied for now. She didn't want to kill Darren. Not if she could avoid it. What she wanted was to find Lucien and discover what the hell was going on.

"Have you looked for him?" she asked in a mild voice.

Darren blinked, then said, "Of course I have. We all have. He's alive, but you know that already. It's odd, though—"

Sophia's gaze sharpened. "Odd? What's odd?"

"Have you searched for him since you've been in the city?"

She frowned, puzzled. "I haven't, no."

"Try. Then tell me what you find."

Sophia regarded the other vampire silently. Obviously, she couldn't trust him, but his concern for Lucien seemed real enough. And there was definitely something weird about all of this.

"Is there somewhere secure?" she asked abruptly. A thorough search for her Sire would require a level of consciousness that was almost a meditation. She would be vulnerable to attack, especially in this house.

Darren nodded. "I'll show you."

* * * *

Sophia waited until Darren had left, then shot the lock on the door and set her own barrier of power to secure it. She waited even longer, until the other vampire's footsteps had faded and she could no longer sense him nearby. Then she turned to regard what was clearly Lucien's private retreat. The sense of him was everywhere in here, and she was struck by a longing so sudden and so strong that it was a physical pain, as if her heart had stopped beating for a moment. What if the impossible had happened? What if someone had somehow taken down the powerful vampire lord who was her Sire? Was he dying even now, wasting away as she stood here squandering what little time he had left? She shook herself slightly and crossed the room, pulling open the French doors to the balcony beyond.

Bracing herself against the cold and wind, she stepped onto a balcony high above the city. Lucien's study was on the third floor of his manse, which was itself at the top of one of the steepest hills surrounding Vancouver. The skies were dark overhead, only the occasional star or glimpse of moon breaking the overcast. She longed for the warmth of her southern home, for the familiar pulse of life and vitality. She took in the lights twinkling down below. Although, she thought, Vancouver had a pulse of its own. Different, but no less alive.

Her gaze scanned the horizon. She had to give it to Darren. This was the perfect location from which to search for their master. Whatever the other vampire's feelings for her, he seemed genuine in his desire to help her find Lucien. Perhaps he loved their Sire as much as she did after all.

Drawing a deep breath, Sophia closed her eyes and set aside her dislike of Darren, set aside the cold and the wind, the strange scents and sounds of this foreign city. From somewhere deep inside herself, she touched the invisible, unbreakable bond she shared with Lucien. He was her Sire, the vampire who had ended her life three centuries ago and given it back to her as something more, something eternal and strong and beautiful. Sophia loved being Vampire, delighted in the power it gave her, in the exquisite heightening of her senses until she could hear the soft fall of an orchid's blossom on a dark night. Certainly she missed the feel of the sun against her face, the smell of her skin after a day at the beach. But it was a small price to pay for what she'd gained. And it was all because of Lucien who was missing and perhaps in trouble.

She stretched out her senses, drawing on all of her considerable power, and cast a net over the city

Hours later, she opened her eyes, exhaustion seeping through her pores, weakening every muscle in her body. She had searched through the night, had followed every trail, no matter how faint. And there were so many trails—the traces of Lucien were everywhere in this city. This had been his home, his lair for hundreds of years. If there was a single street or alley where he had not walked, she hadn't found it. But the very pervasiveness of his scent was somehow wrong. He was alive. She was certain of that. But it was almost as if he'd intentionally spread himself thin, so thin he barely existed in his own city anymore.

She shoved herself to her feet, shaking out legs gone almost numb from sitting in the same position for so long. Sunrise wasn't far off. She could feel it in the sluggishness of her blood, the dullness of her nerve endings. The time shift imposed by her rapid journey from South America only made it worse. Her body was telling her the sun had already risen, while her brain knew she still had an hour or so to get someplace safe and dark. Jet lag was hell on vampires, too.

She wondered if Darren was still about, or if she'd have to find her own lodgings somewhere in this massive house. It had been much smaller when she'd been here last, but she suspected some things hadn't changed. Either way, it hardly mattered. She'd been providing her own safe havens for hundreds of years; this morning would be no different.

She walked wearily back into Lucien's study, just in time to hear a timid knock on the door. She eyed the closed panel speculatively. It was a vampire; she knew that much. And it certainly wasn't Darren tapping so softly. She used power to release her personal shield and unlock the door. "Come," she called out as she sank into one of Lucien's chairs.

The vampire who entered was tiny but most definitely adult, her breasts amply displayed by a tight-bodiced gown which gave lie to her childlike stature. She had to be very old, harkening back to a time and place when her diminutive height would have been the norm among women. But whatever her age, she had little or no power. Sophia wondered what it would be like to live that long as Vampire, but to be so weak that she was forever frozen on the bottom rungs of power.

The vampire smiled gently, as if she knew what Sophia was thinking. "Lady Sophia, I am Larissa, Lord Lucien's secretary."

Something about the way she said the word *secretary* told Sophia, she meant it in the old way, an assistant and a confidante. Sophia had never met her before, so she'd probably come from one of Lucien's other cities sometime in the last hundred years, which was how long it had been since Sophia had been to Vancouver. But if Larissa had been close to Lucien, she just might know more about what went on with him than anyone else in the house.

Sophia didn't offer to shake hands. Judging by her manner and dress, Larissa would not be one of those who embraced the modern custom. "Larissa," she said, nodding, "How can I help you?"

Larissa again gave her that knowing smile. "You are kind, my lady, but I am here to assist *you*. You will want a place to rest, yes?"

Sophia breathed a tired sigh. "I will, thank you. And is there blood in the house?"

"Of course, my lady."

"Does Lucien still maintain the guest cottages? If so, is the smallest available, the one in the gardens?"

"The fire is already lit, my lady. Lucien was well familiar with your preferences. Shall I send the blood to the cottage, then?"

"That would be most appreciated. Thank you, Larissa." She stood and started to turn away, but then frowned as the meaning of Larissa's words penetrated her tired brain.

"Wait!" she called out. "Lucien told you I was coming to Vancouver?"

Larissa nodded. "Some weeks ago," she replied. "He told me you would be coming, my lady, and he left something for you. Only for you, he said."

Sophia stared at the tiny female. It had been *days* since Lucien had summoned her home, not weeks. "What . . ." She swallowed hard, suddenly certain that she didn't want to know the answer. "What did he leave for me?" she made herself ask anyway.

Larissa crossed to a bookshelf, pulling aside several volumes to reveal a hidden wall safe. It was the older kind with a numbered dial rather than a keypad. She spun the dial several times and pulled open the door, reaching in to withdraw a fine, white envelope. Setting it on the shelf, she carefully closed the safe and replaced the books before turning to face Sophia once again and holding the envelope out to her.

Sophia met and held the other vampire's gaze for several minutes, searching for any sign of betrayal or malice. Finding none, she accepted the envelope, glancing down to see her name written in Lucien's extravagant script. Judging by the weight and heft, it held several sheets of folded paper. She stared at it a moment, then asked, "Do you know what's in here?"

"Not all of it, but enough."

Sophia caught the note of sorrow in Larissa's voice and looked up, surprised and worried—very worried—to see the sheen of tears in her eyes. "Larissa?"

"Read what's there, Sophia," she whispered. She backed away and turned to leave, pausing by the door to say, "If you need anything, my lady, you have only to ask. I'm here . . . in this house. Always." She pulled open the door and was gone, leaving Sophia to fear that Lucien had gotten himself into a mess that even he could not get himself out of. She could only hope it was nothing more than that.

Chapter Four

North of Seattle, Washington

The sleek, black limo glided through the sturdy gates of the new Seattle compound. They still called it that, although, in truth, it was no longer in Seattle. That city, once a haven for those seeking to get away from the crowds and congestion of places like L.A. and San Francisco, had become the very thing they'd tried to escape.

For Raphael's vampires, that meant their old compound, which had once been located on ten acres of isolated countryside, had found itself in the middle of a crowded suburb. It had taken some time, but his people had finally located a suitable new site in the hills some distance from Seattle. They'd bought up adjoining parcels this time, until they had a hundred acres as a hedge against future expansion. The new compound had taken nearly as long to build as it had to find the site. There were no humans Raphael would trust with such a commission, and those few vampires who were both trustworthy and sufficiently skilled were in great demand. Of course, they were also his own children, which gave him a certain priority in requesting their services, but above everything else, Raphael was a businessman. He wasn't about to demand that any of his vampires sacrifice their businesses just to save him a bit of time. Not unless it was absolutely necessary.

The limo took the final curve of the driveway and the main building came into view from behind the trees. Wei Chen, head of the Seattle nest, emerged onto the steps along with several others, standing under the gray, concrete overhang, waiting to greet him.

Cyn sat next to him in the limo, her long leg warm against his, their fingers laced together. She'd been extra vigilant since his nightmare, almost obsessive about his security. She was armed, as always—a .9 mm Glock in a shoulder rig beneath her jacket—but she was also wearing a second identical weapon tucked against her lower back, into the waistband of her slacks. She hadn't even tried to hide it from him and had made clear her preference that he remain in the car until she'd checked out who and what waited for them. His woman, his very human mate, thought it appropriate to put herself in danger for his protection. As if the phalanx of vampire guards deployed around them weren't enough, as if he wasn't visiting one of his own nests where every vampire present was pledged to him personally . . . or as if he wasn't fully capable of protecting himself and her, as well.

A wisp of pain tugged at his awareness and he stared out the rain-darkened window at the new compound's stark gray concrete and redwood construction, at the solemn faces of his assembled vampires.

"What's wrong?" Cyn asked abruptly.

He turned his head to meet her gaze, her green eyes boring into his with a sure knowledge of his moods.

"I'm not certain," he admitted. "Something . . ." His voice trailed away as he tried to capture whatever it was that had caught his attention. But there was so much emotion among the vampires in that building— fear and grief, as well as pain at the terrible loss they'd suffered. Surely that was it, that two of their number had been wiped from the earth as if they'd never existed, their flames extinguished in seconds as their shocked cries bit into his soul. But that wasn't it. Or that wasn't everything. His gaze sharpened.

"Stop," he commanded. His driver hit the brakes, bringing the limo to a full stop before his conscious mind was aware of what he was doing. Raphael was only vaguely cognizant of the alarm spreading through the ranks of his security, of Cyn's voice calling his name as he opened the car door and stepped out into the wet night.

Wei Chen and the others hurried toward him, their faces creased with concern.

"My lord." Raphael's lieutenant, Duncan, appeared at his side, while his Security Chief, Juro, calmly deployed various personnel to accommodate this new development. There was very little that could rattle Juro; it was why Raphael had chosen him.

"Sire." Wei Chen was out of breath from the dash through the rain, testimony to his lack of any kind of routine physical activity.

Raphael lifted his head, his gaze searching the elegant face of the building, his heart aching at the pain he felt there. "Jeremy," he realized suddenly. He turned an inquiring gaze upon Wei Chen, his black eyes beginning to gleam silver with anger. "What's happened, Wei Chen? Where's Jeremy?"

The nest leader met Raphael's regard without flinching. "His house was attacked earlier, my lord. His mate, Mariane—"

Raphael had stopped listening. He was already moving, heading for the main entrance, following a trail of pain that was as clear as if it were painted on the ground before him.

Wei Chen hurried to keep up with him. "Jeremy is in the infirmary with her, Sire. He's sharing his blood—"

"It will not be enough," Raphael said, knowing it was true. He pushed through the heavy glass doors, heedless of everything but the need of his child pulling him down the hall. One turn and another, and he was striding into what passed for an infirmary on the vampire compound.

It was a smallish room. Vampires rarely required more than a donor's blood and a few hours rest, and only the youngest vampires or the most serious injuries demanded even that. But in the far corner, beneath the dim glow of a wall lamp, a young woman lay in a bed that seemed too big for her delicate frame. Her face was nearly as pale as the sheets she lay upon, the white bindings upon her legs and arms still soaked with her life's blood.

"Jeremy."

The vampire looked up at the sound of his Sire's voice, his face a mask of grief, streaked with the dried blood of his tears. "My lord," he said brokenly, falling to his knees. "It's not enough. My blood . . . It's not enough." His voice cracked as he began to sob, great wracking sounds that tore at Raphael's soul.

He went to the broken vampire, holding him as he would a child, his child, reborn as Vampire less than thirty years ago. Jeremy buried his face against his Sire's hip and Raphael stroked his head in comfort, examining the woman, Mariane, as he did so. He noted the shallow rise and fall of her chest, the sluggish beat of her heart, which was barely managing to push the blood through her body. The flesh of her fingers was already pale and cold, as her body shut down her extremities in favor of saving what vital organs it could.

"It is not too late, Jeremy," Raphael said for his vampire's ears only. "Let me help her."

Jeremy's head came up, hope warring with possessiveness for a brief moment before he nodded. "I would beg you, my lord, if it would help her."

Raphael shook his head chidingly. "You are my own, blood of my blood. And Mariane is yours."

He gently disengaged from Jeremy and shrugged out of his suit jacket, letting the expensive garment fall heedlessly. He was aware of Cyn standing close behind him, aware of her hands catching the jacket as it fell, handing it off to someone else as he walked around to the opposite side of the bed. She followed, staying close by his side, and his heart wrenched at the thought of her lying in this sterile bed instead of poor Mariane.

Without pausing, he rolled up his sleeve and used his fangs to slice through the skin of his wrist and open a vein. Sitting on the bed and bending over the young woman, he placed his wrist over her mouth, letting the first few drops fall through her open lips. Jeremy hovered across from him, holding his mate's hand, whispering in her ear of his love for her, encouraging her to drink, to live for him.

Mariane's throat moved spasmodically, her body forcing her to swallow before the blood choked her. Something stirred behind her closed eyelids and she swallowed again, and then again, before her thin, pale hands came up to hold Raphael's life-giving wrist to her mouth. She began to suck greedily at the bounty that was his blood—the blood of a vampire lord, more powerful than anything produced in centuries of human medical research.

She was suckling like a hungry child, and Jeremy's avid gaze was fixed on the physical connection between his Sire and his mate. His stress over that contact was growing with every second. Vampires were possessive creatures, even one so new as Jeremy. Raphael pulled his wrist away carefully, letting Jeremy take the woman's hands when she would have grabbed for more. She mewed unhappily at the loss, and Jeremy covered her lips with a kiss, licking the blood from her mouth and feeding it back to her as their tongues twined.

Duncan handed Raphael a warm, wet towel to clean the blood from his arm. He remained seated on the bed, absently wiping the towel over his wrist as he watched Jeremy kiss Mariane's hungry mouth. He handed the towel back to Duncan and held out his hand to Cyn. She came to him, placing her hand on his shoulder, dropping her cheek briefly to brush against his head.

"Jeremy."

The other vampire looked up, his eyes wary, his fingers tightening anxiously on Mariane's pale hands.

Raphael rolled down his shirt sleeve casually, the self-inflicted wound already healing. He stood, taking Cyn's hand and pulling her into the circle of light. "My mate," he said for Jeremy's benefit. He lifted Cyn's fingers to his lips. "Cynthia."

Jeremy's entire body relaxed at those words. If Raphael had a mate of his own, he could not be interested in stealing Mariane. Raphael understood. "She will be well, Jeremy. And if you need me further, I am here."

As Raphael prepared to leave, Jeremy fell to his knees, taking his Sire's hand and kissing it in gratitude. "My lord . . ." His voice broke with emotion. "Sire. Thank you."

Raphael disengaged his hand lightly, resting it instead on Jeremy's bent head. "You are my child," he murmured. There was nothing else that needed saying.

He looked up and met his lieutenant's eyes, letting a little bit of his anger show for the first time since arriving. "Duncan."

"Yes, my lord." Duncan turned and began hustling the gathered vampires from the room, murmuring orders via a throat mike to Juro and the others. Cynthia held out Raphael's jacket, holding it as he slipped it over his arms and up onto his shoulders, her hands smoothing it across his back before he turned to face her. Unshed tears filled her eyes and he smiled. His Cyn wore a mask of toughness, a shield against a world that had shown her little love for most of her life. But there was a soft spot that only he could touch. He pulled her close, kissing her gently.

"*Lubimaya,*" he whispered.

Her warm fingers lingered on his jaw, then slipped behind his neck to tug him closer and press her forehead against his. "When do we go after the bastards who did this?" she murmured.

He pulled back to meet her fierce gaze with one of his own. "Very soon, my Cyn." He urged her out of the room, his hand resting low on her back. "We will hunt them to the ends of the earth."

Chapter Five

Raphael allowed Wei Chen to lead the way from the infirmary. He'd seen enough blueprints of this new compound that he didn't need a guide, but this was the first time he'd been here since its completion. A visit had been planned for the near future, albeit under very different circumstances. Who could have foreseen the murder of two of his own, the attempted murder of a third and . . . His jaw tightened at what had been done to Mariane. She had been defenseless against them. She wasn't a warrior, not like his Cyn. But he was all too aware that even Cyn could be overwhelmed when faced with that sort of brutality.

He pulled her closer with the slight pressure of his fingers. She obliged, but glanced up at him, questioning. He gave her a faint smile meant to be reassuring, although he knew it didn't succeed. It would have been easier, he thought, if he'd fallen in love with a stupid woman, or at least one willing to ignore the more troublesome aspects of life. Cyn was none of those things. She was smart and intuitive, especially, it seemed, when it came to him, and her preferred method of dealing with trouble was to confront it head on. It was precisely those qualities that had drawn him to her in the first place—the first time they'd met, when she'd been smart enough to fear him, but too stubborn to give in to that fear.

He admired that about her. But it also terrified him when he thought about all the things in the world that could rip through that stubbornness and tear her apart. Like they had Mariane.

Their group moved into the gathering room of the compound's main building, a spacious living space with high ceilings and a wall of glass granting a spectacular view down the hillside, across the city far below and on to the distant bay. It was early enough that the city was still full of light, but the ocean was a black, empty space, too remote for the tiny running lights from the boats anchored there to be seen.

The room was furnished casually, with leather couches and armchairs scattered about in an almost random pattern. Since only vampires lived here, the heavy furniture was moved about to suit whoever was using the room at any given time.

Taking Cyn with him, he made his way to a collection of several large armchairs positioned directly in front of the window, but facing inward. His security people spread throughout the room, with a couple stationed behind him, between his chair and the empty window. The windows were bulletproof, of course, and the possibility of an attack negligible within the compound, but it was a risk Juro would not be willing to take.

He sat down, nodding for Wei Chen and the others to sit with him. Duncan took up his usual station to his master's left, while Cyn slouched on the wide arm of the chair to his right, leaning in to rest her arm on his near shoulder. She still wore her weapons, despite the fact they were now safely within not just the compound, but the building itself with its formidable security. She and Duncan had joined forces in urging him not to make this trip, saying it was too dangerous. What if it was a trap? What if the humans were killing his vampires one by one to lure in the biggest prize of all—not just a vampire, but a vampire lord? He forced back a growl at the memory of their arguments, all of which he'd rejected. He had to be here. These were *his* vampires who were dying.

"My lord."

Raphael was jerked out of his thoughts by Wei Chen's soft voice. He speared the nest leader with a fierce gaze. "I want details, Wei Chen. Everything you've discovered about these murders and who's behind them."

"Of course, my lord." He gestured at a vampire sitting next to him. "Loren is our security—"

"I am aware of who Loren is," Raphael interrupted coldly.

Wei Chen's lips trembled slightly. "Forgive me, my lord. Would you prefer Loren to—"

"I don't care who gives the report, as long as *someone* starts talking."

The nest leader paled so badly that Raphael feared he would topple over where he sat. As a vampire, Wei Chen's power was greater than any other vampire in the nest, although not nearly as strong as most of Raphael's closest security staff. However, Wei Chen was not a fighter, which was why he lived here. The Seattle compound reflected its environs. This had never been a high risk area before the recent murders. The vampires here maintained a fairly low profile. They were mostly professionals, many of them computer experts of one sort or another— vampire geeks Cyn called them in private. Most worked exclusively via computer or phone, rarely if ever meeting in person with their clients and/or human counterparts. Wei Chen was a financial consultant, chosen to lead the compound because of his corporate mentality and a natural ability to manage others.

"Loren, perhaps you could give us the specific details of what has happened thus far," Duncan, ever the diplomat, said, easing the tension which had been sucking the air out of the room.

Loren glanced at Duncan, then met Raphael's gaze and gave a self-assured nod. He opened a folder on his lap and began speaking. "Sire, as you know there have been two previous attacks, three now, after this vicious assault on Jeremy's mate. I think it probable that the target of this latest atrocity was, in fact, Jeremy himself, that—"

"It was." They all looked up as Jeremy walked slowly into the room, his exhaustion obvious, but his face full of determination. "They tortured Mariane, trying to force her to reveal my location. She refused."

"Jeremy," Raphael acknowledged. "Your mate?"

"She is well, my lord, thanks to you. I bless whatever chance of fate brought you here this evening. A human doctor from your retinue is examining her—"

"Peter Saephan," Raphael confirmed. "He is an excellent healer, and I have trusted him with the life of my own mate on more than one occasion." He twisted his mouth in a wry smile, acknowledging to himself if to no one else, the reality that repeatedly drew Cyn into situations requiring Dr. Saephan's skilled care.

"I will tell Mariane. Thank you, my lord."

Raphael nodded a silent acknowledgment, but Jeremy lingered, his thin frame vibrating with the effort of maintaining his dignity in the face of tonight's terrible trauma. He seemed to be warring with himself over some internal debate, until finally he approached Raphael and dropped to his knees.

"I was with her, my lord," Jeremy whispered. "I was there." His eyes, when they met Raphael's, were full of guilt. "But I couldn't reach her. I tried," he said desperately, more to convince himself, Raphael thought, than anyone else.

Jeremy drew a deep breath and seemed to gather himself. His back stiffened and when he spoke next, his voice with firm with resolve, "I am not a soldier, my lord. I know this. But I wish to join you in bringing down these animals. The blood of my mate has earned me a place in the hunt."

Raphael heard the unvoiced desperation in his plea. Jeremy's blood had not been enough to save Mariane's life. That it was Raphael's blood which saved her lessened the pain of his failure, because Raphael was master to every vampire in this compound, his power so far beyond theirs that it transcended description. But still, his failure to save his mate himself would sting. He could, however, avenge this attack on her.

"Your assistance will be invaluable, Jeremy. You know the area and you know the people. And through you, your mate can tell us much about these creatures who dared attack her. On my word, Jeremy, they will pay the ultimate price."

Jeremy's head fell to his chest, his long, dark hair covering his face before he raised eyes now brimming with gratitude. "Thank you, Sire."

Raphael studied his child carefully, noting the tension in his stiff gait as he climbed to his feet and took a chair nearby. He ached for Jeremy and would rather have spared him the retelling of the night's awful events, but it was necessary. And far better that Jeremy tell him, than ask Mariane to relive it.

Loren moved to sit next to Jeremy and began a low-voiced conversation. Cyn took the opportunity to lean close to Raphael's ear and whisper, "Will he know what happened?" Her question was voiced softly enough that, even in a room full of vampires, it was for him only.

Raphael responded in kind, saying, "Jeremy is young, but they've been mated a few years. His connection to her should be strong enough for him to have seen most of what happened. It will be enough." He felt Cyn breathe out a sigh of relief next to him.

"Jeremy," Raphael said more loudly.

The vampire immediately cut off whatever he'd been saying to Loren and faced Raphael.

"My mate, Cynthia, will begin the questioning. She is a trained and experienced investigator, quite skilled in these matters, especially when it comes to humans. Her insight will be particularly helpful."

Cyn sat up straight, leaving a cool spot on his arm as she withdrew the warmth of her body. Raphael glanced up at her and caught a frown of concentration, followed by a gentle smile for Jeremy.

"I'll start with some questions about the events of that afternoon," she said. "It will be painful for you, and I'm sorry. I wouldn't ask if it wasn't absolutely necessary, please believe that. But every detail matters. You never know what might be the one thing that gives them away."

Jeremy nodded, swallowing nervously.

Cyn leaned forward, her posture and gaze intent. "Okay, let's start with the basics. Was Mariane home when these guys broke into the house?"

He shook his head, his gaze haunted. "She was out. Our house is very secure, but they smashed through the back door with an ax. They must have hidden their vehicles and waited for her to return. I knew when she arrived home, I felt her presence—she always enters through the front door—and then I felt her terror. They grabbed her before she even realized they were there."

"Is Mariane normally awake during the day?" Cyn asked. "Forgive me if this is private, but . . . she doesn't sleep with you?"

"Most days she does, yes. But on some days, she remains awake to run errands. She shops in Cooper's Rest, which is the small town near here, and on rare occasions she drives down to the city below. She buys food for herself and does whatever else needs doing. There's the mail to be picked up, of course. And sometimes . . . sometimes Mariane simply wants to enjoy the sunlight."

Cyn nodded, and Raphael knew she would understand Mariane's need for sunlight. It was the same reason Cyn kept her condo just down the beach from his estate. She didn't live there anymore, but she still spent time there on occasion, sitting in the sunlight, walking along the water in the warm sand.

Cyn spoke again, drawing Raphael out of his reverie. "Does she follow a routine? Maybe certain days of the week, every other Monday or something?"

Jeremy frowned, concentrating. "Perhaps. Not specific days, but she does go into town at least twice a month. Usually in the morning. And when she comes home, she remains awake—cleaning, making phone calls, sometimes sitting on the porch if the weather is nice."

"Who would know about this besides you?" Cyn asked. "Does she have any friends here? Maybe someone she meets for coffee? Does she go anyplace in particular?"

Raphael saw Jeremy's brow lower in a troubled frown. He was a very young vampire and his relationship with Mariane even newer. The suggestion that she could be meeting anyone, possibly even another male, while Jeremy slept would rouse his possessive instincts. And unlike Raphael, who was old enough and powerful enough to sense whatever Cyn was doing at all times, Jeremy would not usually have a link strong enough to follow his mate through a normal, uneventful few hours. It was only the traumatic nature of the attack that had forced their link into full-blown awareness for the duration. That and the fact that, while Jeremy had probably been sleeping in a vault below ground, he would not have been far from where Mariane was being brutally assaulted.

"She goes to the post office," Jeremy was repeating. "And the grocery store. I've never gone with her. I don't generally go into town at all. My business is at home, mostly via computer or phone. The truth is, unless they're Vampire, I very rarely meet anyone in person, not even my clients."

"What is your business?" she asked. Raphael had seen her do this before, using routine questions to relax the subject.

"I'm an accountant, a CPA. I do taxes mostly."

"How well did you know Marco? Or Preston?" Cyn asked, naming the two dead vampires.

Jeremy shook his head. "I knew them, naturally. We'd met a handful of times, I suppose, here at the compound. I didn't do their taxes or anything, if that's what you're asking. They did their own. Computer geeks, you know," he gave a half smile. "They've got a program for everything." His smile fled. "Or they did."

"Okay." Cyn was still sitting next to him, close enough that Raphael felt her draw a fortifying breath before continuing. She was no more eager to hear the details of this outrage than Jeremy was to tell them, but she would do what needed to be done. He rested his hand lightly against her back, offering his support.

"I need you to tell me what happened during the attack, Jeremy. I'm going to ask that you leave nothing out, no matter how ugly, no matter how painful. I'll try not to interrupt you with questions; I'll save those for later. Just take your time."

Jeremy glanced from Cyn to Raphael and back, then nodded and began talking.

* * * *

By the time the story had been told in full, with Jeremy's voice breaking over and over again as he was forced to remember his mate's agony, the anger of Raphael's vampires was a sharp, bitter tide of emotion in the room. He scanned them slowly, sharing their outrage, but mindful, too, of the potential for disaster. Their anger would be useful once they began hunting their prey, but that would not happen tonight. He was aware of Duncan standing next to him, hyperalert and as watchful as Raphael himself. From across the room, Juro met his gaze silently, shifting slightly to block the closed doors.

And sitting beside him, tears overflowing her eyes as she listened to the story, her hands fisted in a frustrated anger of her own, was his Cyn.

"I'd recognize their voices," Jeremy was saying, his voice all but a whisper now. "But I didn't see any of their faces. They kept those black ski masks on the whole time. And when I woke at last, they were gone. When I saw her . . . I was nearly mad with grief. The only thing keeping me sane was the need to get help for her. I knew she was alive, barely, but alive. Colin was trying to help when I—"

Cyn straightened abruptly. "Colin?" she repeated. "Who's Colin?"

Jeremy blinked. "He's, I guess—"

"Colin Murphy," Loren provided. "He's sort of the police in Cooper's Rest."

Cyn scowled. "Sort of? How can someone be sort of the police? I thought you guys were under the County Sheriff's jurisdiction."

"We are," the security chief agreed reluctantly. "But we're a long way from the nearest Sheriff's station. They're not eager to drive all the way out here, and frankly, we're not that eager to call them. And it's not just us either," he added, indicating his fellow vampires. "The human locals here about tend to be loners for the most part. There's probably more than a few survivalists among them, although not all will admit to it.

"Colin Murphy's a former Navy SEAL. He did more than ten years before he decided to get out while he still had a few bones intact. The stories he tells . . ." Loren shook his head admiringly, before looking around and cleaning his throat. "That is, he's a skillful guy. Knows weapons, martial arts, tactics, and a bunch of other stuff I'm sure he can't talk about. He came here with a buddy when he got out, a guy named Garry McWaters. McWaters grew up here, but he didn't stay long. His family were all dead or moved away, and he couldn't take the weather anymore.

"But for some reason, Colin stuck. He's a good guy. Takes care of nuisance calls, checks on the old ladies, hustles the drunks out of town, that sort of thing. If someone suspected something bad was going on over at Jeremy's that day, Colin would be the one they'd call."

Cyn returned her attention to Jeremy. "So this Colin was there when you woke up?"

Jeremy nodded. "I think he was calling an ambulance or something. He had his phone out, and I knew even then that he was trying to help, but . . . I kind of went off on him anyway." He looked away uncomfortably, still young enough to be embarrassed by what he saw as a loss of control.

"Your mate was under attack," Raphael reassured him. "You lay there for hours, knowing what was happening, and unable to come to her aid. And then you woke to find a human with his hands on her." He shook his head slightly. "This Colin Murphy is lucky to be alive. I don't know if I could have shown such restraint."

Jeremy flushed with pleasure at Raphael's praise, then drew a breath and continued more strongly. "Colin backed away as soon as he saw me. I picked up Mariane and brought her here."

"I should talk to him," Cyn said, turning to Raphael. It was more of a statement than a suggestion, but Raphael hesitated. "I need to know what he found when he got there, Raphael," she added in a low, urgent voice. "It's possible he arrived soon after the attackers left. He might have seen something more, something Jeremy didn't notice because he was so focused on Mariane. Besides, if he's the law in town, it might be useful to have him on board with our investigation. If nothing else, he knows the people and that gives our own hunt the imprimatur of the local authorities, such as they are."

Loren was watching Raphael, waiting for his decision.

"Arrange a meeting for tomorrow night," Raphael told him.

"I'll see to it," Loren said immediately.

Raphael stood and everyone stood with him. "Thank you, Jeremy. I know this was painful. Return to your mate, now. She needs you."

Jeremy bowed briefly. "Thank you, Sire." The vampire was visibly exhausted. Even with Raphael's assistance, the depletion of Jeremy's strength would be severe, his mate's need a constant drain. He paused for a few seconds, long enough to steady himself before walking slowly out of the room.

Raphael raked his gaze over the remaining vampires. "An outrage has been perpetrated on us, and it will not stand. No one . . . no one touches what is mine and lives. Prepare yourselves, gentlemen. Tomorrow, we hunt."

Chapter Six

Vancouver, British Columbia

True to Larissa's word, the cottage was already warm by the time Sophia made her way through the garden. Given the size of Lucien's manse, she was certain there were plenty of guest rooms in its basement. But she preferred the privacy of these old cottages, and this one in particular. Although spacious enough for comfort, it was nonetheless the smallest of the three guest houses and the farthest from the main building. But it was also the most secure. Like all the others, the windows were for show only, completely blocked by sealed metal shutters inside. That alone made it safe enough for most vampires. But this particular cottage also had a basement level, accessed through a hidden door beneath the floor of the generous closet. Decades ago, Lucien had shown it to her, the last time she'd visited him here in Vancouver.

Sophia opened her suitcase and began hanging up the few clothes she'd brought with her, delaying the inevitable moment when she'd have to open Lucien's envelope. She held up a wrinkled silk blouse, wondered if it was worth getting the thing cleaned and pressed, when there was a knock on the cottage door. She listened carefully first, then reached out with her vampiric senses. It was a human male, probably one of the servants with her blood.

She dropped the blouse and crossed the room, verifying before opening the door that no one but the single human waited on the other side. The cottage's low light cast a yellow square of illumination on the man who stood on the narrow porch step. He was taller than she was—most men were anymore—although this one was not by much. She judged him to be in his late twenties, pretty, slender and boyish in the way she liked her men to be these days. His dark good looks and soft brown eyes reminded her of the lovely young men so common to the cafes and clubs she frequented in Rio de Janeiro. She eyed him appreciatively, up and down, frowning when she saw that his hands were empty. Maybe this wasn't her blood delivery, after all.

"Mistress," he whispered, those big eyes lingering briefly on her face before dropping submissively.

Sophia barely managed to hide her grimace of distaste. She'd forgotten Lucien's penchant for blood slaves, which meant he rarely had bagged blood on hand. Not that his slaves weren't willing donors— Lucien didn't keep any other kind. And it wasn't that she objected to taking blood from the vein. Quite the contrary. All of her young men in Rio were very much aware of what she was and more than willing to spend a night, or longer, with her. It was a rare thing that she resorted to bagged blood anymore.

But none of her lovers were blood slaves, either, those men and women who existed solely to be used by their vampire masters, humans who hungered for the sexual release that such use provided. It was an addiction every bit as powerful as the drugs sold in dark alleys all over the world. And like any addiction, it could be used as a weapon against the addict, forcing them to perform unspeakable acts, to endure horrific treatment that too frequently crossed the line into torture.

Lucien's slaves were all well cared for, however. She gave him that much. Abuse was never tolerated, not in this house. Even so, his slaves were so . . . pathetically eager. With an emphasis on the pathetic.

She sighed. It was too late to arrange for something less personal, so it was either this lovely young man or she'd have to wait until tomorrow night. She suspected tomorrow would be even worse than today because the one thing she knew, there would be nothing good in that elegant envelope of Lucien's.

She stepped back. "Come in, *gato*."

* * * *

The slave was certainly skilled. Sophia wondered if Lucien had perhaps trained this one himself. Her Sire was quite the hedonist when it came to his lovers, choosing men and women equally. And always the pretty ones.

Aurelio—probably not his real name, but one chosen to appeal to her—moaned softly as she pulled him away from her naked breast, fisting a hand in his dark hair and tugging lazily. He twisted his head away obediently, baring his neck in a fine, taut line of golden skin. There wasn't time for a true seduction, but she had played with him a bit, letting him earn his pleasure, building the anticipation. She might not keep any blood slaves of her own, but she understood them, understood their need to *earn* their reward. An odd sort of reward in her mind, but, as the French were wont to say, *chacun ses goûts*. Although she was fairly certain that not even the most esoteric of gourmands had actual blood drinking in mind.

Pretty Aurelio whimpered when she teased him, rolling him over until he was beneath her, licking a long line down his neck and breathing against it softly, smiling when the skin prickled with goose bumps. Her fangs punctured the soft velvet of his vein without warning. He groaned, a guttural sound of pure pleasure as his already stiff cock hardened even further against her thigh. Sophia drank deeply, relishing that first hot rush of blood down her throat, feeling it spread throughout her body, replenishing tissues dehydrated by the long flight and the stress of everything that had happened since. She was suddenly glad Lucien kept his stable of blood slaves. She'd needed this; no bagged blood could have nourished her so completely.

One more long draught and she began to slow, careful to take only what she needed, only what the human male could afford. A few more delicate sips, savoring the bouquet of his blood, untainted as it was by alcohol or drugs, and she withdrew her fangs slowly, pausing to nip playfully as his flesh before licking his skin clean and closing the small wounds.

Sophia closed her eyes, sated and ready to rest, the long journey catching up with her at last. But there was Aurelio to tend to. He lay perfectly still beneath her, so careful to make no demand for his own completion, but she could feel his heart pounding, could hear the heated thrumming of his blood as it headed in a single direction. Toward that ever hardening shaft between his legs.

Sophia let her gaze travel along his sweat-sheened body, always willing to admire a beautiful male form. She trailed her hand slowly over the curve of his collarbones, down past the flat, hairless planes of his solid chest until she encountered the silky line of hair arrowing straight to his groin. She purred quietly in approval as her fingers closed around his straining erection, feeling him tremble beneath her as he struggled to remain still.

She stroked him slowly at first, admiring his discipline, admiring even more the fine piece of flesh she held in her hand. As hard as marble, it was satiny smooth and elegantly shaped. Long and thick with a well-formed head, the narrow scar of his circumcision so exquisitely sensitive that he shivered every time she touched it, which she did again, delighting in his moan of entreaty, begging her wordlessly to release him.

"Sssshh, Aurelito," she bent to murmur against his ear. "Are you ready to come for me?"

His eyelids fluttered, his cock jumping in her hand. "Yes, please, mistress," he whispered.

Sophia tightened her hold on him, squeezing and releasing as she played her fingers over the warm, golden skin. "Then, come for me, *gato*. Come now."

Aurelio's eyes flew open, rolling back in his skull until only the whites were visible, grunting low in his throat as he thrust uncontrollably against her hand, his long-delayed orgasm spurting between her fingers, onto his thighs and belly until he was spent.

Sophia remained still, giving him time to recover, letting his heart and breathing slow to something approaching normal. She waited as long as she could, but the sun was very close now and she wanted to be underground before it arrived.

"Aurelio," she said softly.

His eyes opened, cheeks flaming red with embarrassment. "Forgive me, my lady," he said immediately. "I didn't mean—"

"Be calm. You served me well."

"Thank you, my lady," he said fervently. He grabbed the loose, linen pants he'd worn to the door and wiped himself quickly before standing and pulling the now sticky garment up his legs and tightening the drawstring closure.

Sophia eyed his tight ass appreciatively as he did so, wishing she'd had longer to play tonight.

But it was not to be.

She stood, barefoot, but still fully dressed, except for her shirt, which gaped open, her breasts displayed, the nipples flushed and hard after Aurelio's dedicated attention. The blood slave cast surreptitious glances at her, but Sophia made no move to cover herself. She took pleasure in the knowledge of her body's appeal to males, whether human or vampire.

"Thank you, Aurelio," she said, opening the door to the garden. "I am very pleased."

"Thank you, mistress. It was my honor."

Sophia watched him hurry into the cold night, shivering in sympathy of the few clothes he wore. Perhaps one became used to these temperatures if one lived here long enough. Closing the door quickly, she locked and bolted it, then turned and stared at Lucien's envelope where it sat on a charming antique bureau.

Sighing impatiently, she shook off a curious sense of foreboding and crossed immediately to the bureau. She picked up the letter, taking it with her as she hurried to the closet and its secret entrance. Taking the few steep stairs downward, she closed and locked the door behind her, then sank onto the thick mattress which served as a bed in the tight quarters.

Legs crossed beneath her, she slid a scarlet fingernail beneath the seal and sliced it open, withdrawing a single, folded sheet of paper. A photograph tumbled to the floor and she bent over to pick it up, frowning at the three people pictured there. Two men and a woman. None of whom she knew.

Laying the photograph aside, she unfolded the piece of heavy linen writing paper and found it covered in Lucien's handwriting. Sophia's heart sank as she began to read.

Chapter Seven

Raphael sighed as the vault door closed behind him and he listened as Cyn locked them in with a series of muted thuds. This room was below ground, accessed by a private elevator and reserved for his exclusive use when visiting the Seattle compound. All of his vampires here slept their days underground, secure in a state-of-the-art vault like this one, which, once closed, could be opened only from the inside, except by Raphael or the nest's leader or security chief. Within the larger vault, each vampire had a private sleeping chamber. Raphael's private room was in a separate wing, more spacious and better appointed, but it was no more or less secure than those of the other vampires in the compound.

Cyn threw her leather jacket over a chair, slipped off the shoulder holster and popped the magazine from her Glock before coming close enough to lean into him and wrap her arms around his waist. "I'm sorry about Marco and Preston," she said. "They were with you a long time."

Raphael circled her slender shoulders and pulled her against his chest, taking comfort from her presence. "I'm glad you're here," he admitted.

"I told you," she teased gently. "Besides, after that last New Mexico trip of yours, I swore I'd never let you leave me behind again. I was miserable the whole time you were gone."

Raphael smiled into her sweet-smelling hair and let himself be distracted from the horrible night. "Were you?" he asked.

She jabbed him in the side. "Like you weren't. Besides, who will take care of you if I'm not here?"

"Duncan? Juro, perhaps?"

"Don't be obtuse."

"Obtuse. I suppose that's better than your usual epithet."

"Which one would that be?"

Raphael snorted dismissively. "I'm hardly going to provide ammunition for my own execution."

"Don't be a baby."

"Hmmm," he murmured, gliding his hands down over her back to cup her ass. "Not what I had in mind, no."

Cyn pressed herself closer, rising up onto her toes to reach his mouth. "How long before sunrise?"

"More than an hour, sweet Cyn."

"We'll have to hurry then."

Raphael laughed, and it felt good. He swept her up in his arms, crossed to the bed in a few strides and dropped her onto its wide expanse. "Clothes, *lubimaya*," he said. "Off."

"You're such a romantic," she murmured as she kicked off her boots, then lay back on the bed to unbutton and unzip her slacks, shimmying them under her sweet ass and down her legs in a way that had his cock growing heavy against his thighs. He tore off his own clothing, tossing it to one side as he watched Cyn tug her sweater over her head, leaving her in nothing but a sheer bra that enticed more than it covered and a matching bit of lace between her legs.

Raphael eyed that bit of lace and growled as he shed the last of his own clothing, prowling over to the bed and tugging her closer, until her hips rode the very edge. "Off," he repeated with a snarl. He snapped the two thin bits of satin holding the triangle of lace in place and tossed it over his shoulder. He reached for the bra, but Cyn was already there, freeing her beautiful breasts as he spread her legs around his hips and slipped his hands beneath her ass, holding her open to him.

"Raphael," she said breathlessly.

Scenting her arousal, he plunged into her tight sheath without warning, pushing himself in as deep as he could go. She was ready for him, as he'd known she would be, and she hummed with pleasure as his penetration stretched her open around his cock, her muscles straining against his thickness. She shivered with desire, growing wetter, slicker and hotter, warming his cock, welcoming him home.

He wanted to fuck her, to slam his cock over and over into the human heat of her until he forgot everything but the sheer sensuous pleasure of her luscious body pulsing around him. Until he was coated in her creamy juices as she screamed his name.

She looked up, her green eyes narrow and sparking with desire, her gaze never leaving his as she deliberately began caressing her own breasts, cupping them provocatively, squeezing and releasing. She took a nipple between her thumb and fingers, rolling until it was hard and full, and then moved to the other breast. She raised her fingers to her mouth and licked them thoroughly, until they glistened with moisture. Raphael watched, his cock throbbing as he began to move slowly, in and out of her silken body.

Cyn blinked lazily, rubbing those wet fingers over her breasts, trailing down the flat span of her belly to slip between the plump folds of her sex. Holding herself open, she began to circle her clit, her breath catching as he thrust harder, faster, his arms stretched taut and stiff to either side of her, so he could watch her play with herself, watch her sensitive pearl swell with desire, flushing pink with blood as it responded eagerly to the stimulation of her fingers.

Cyn's breath shuddered from her lungs and she leaned back, eyes closed, face gleaming with sweat as she fought her orgasm.

"Come for me, sweet Cyn. Let me feel you shudder around my cock."

She gave a small moan, trembling as she whispered, "Raphael."

He stretched forward and took her breast into his mouth, sucking hard, letting his teeth graze along the soft flesh and lapping up the small trickle of blood. Cyn's breath grew fast and shallow, her fingers tangled in his hair now, holding him close, urging him to grant her other breast the same treatment. He obliged willingly, swirling his tongue over the engorged nipple and sucking hard, biting just enough to release a taste of her succulent blood.

"Oh, God, God. Raphael, please."

"Please what, my Cyn?" he crooned, laving her breast and driving himself deeper into her body, feeling her growing even hotter and slicker with every new thrust.

Her eyes flashed open, her nails scraping down his back as she nearly screamed her demand. "Raphael!"

He bit her nipple, eliciting a fresh sob of pleasure as he licked his way between her breasts and over her tender collarbone, closing his teeth on the taut tendons of her shoulder before moving up to rub his lips over the swell of her jugular. He inhaled deeply, smelling the delicious scent of her blood, the tantalizing aroma of her arousal.

Cyn moaned, tightening her arms around his shoulders, crushing his chest against the hard mounds of her nipples, the heavy fullness of her breasts. Her hips were moving in time with his now, shoving against him, the muscles of her stomach clenching as her womb convulsed, sending tremors rippling along his cock deep inside her.

He licked her neck one last time, blowing on the wet skin, feeling her shiver. "I love you, my Cyn," he whispered against her heated flesh. As he sank his teeth into her jugular, her body arched beneath him, the orgasm seizing her hard and tumbling her into ecstasy. She gasped his name, her breath stolen away, tears streaming down her cheeks as pleasure overwhelmed her and she convulsed helplessly in climax.

Raphael let the sweet flow of her blood fill his mouth and roll down his throat like warm honey, hardening his cock until he groaned with the need to come. He threw his head back and roared as he found his own orgasm, pumping his release deep into his mate's trembling body, feeling her legs tighten around him, holding him, caressing him, draining him dry.

Chapter Eight

Lucien's words were still with Sophia when she woke the next night, sitting like a weight on her chest. She threw aside the many down-filled blankets, suddenly feeling suffocated instead of warmed by their presence. A small exertion of her will and candles flared, lighting the dreary little dungeon where she'd spent the day.

She folded the letter carefully, touching the single pink tear staining one corner, evidence of Lucien's regret. Then, slipping the sheet of paper back into its envelope, she picked up the photograph of three vampires she'd never known and now never would. All three of them were dead, destroyed by human hatred and Lucien's foolishness. But now his stupidity had reached out to touch others. Dangerous others whom he somehow expected her to placate and what? Save his worthless hide while he hid in safety? Typical Lucien, she thought angrily. Never thinking of anyone but himself—his pleasure, his curiosity, his damnable sexuality.

Dashing away the remnants of her own tears—not for Lucien, but for the innocent vampires he'd given over to death—Sophia stood, shivering as the cold air hit her bare breasts. She had a momentary flashback of the lovely Aurelio, with his long, sleek body, and then she set it aside. She might enjoy her sensual interludes, but she was at heart a woman of discipline and purpose. Yet another thing she and her Sire had always disagreed upon.

Taking the few steps to the trap door, she paused long enough to ascertain the emptiness of the room above her before pushing upward and climbing into the cottage proper. A quick glance assured her nothing had changed in her absence, that no one had been there while she'd slept defenseless beneath their feet. She shivered again, with an entirely different sort of chill, hating the circumstances which had forced her to be here, hating Lucien for his persistent self-indulgence which would one day get him killed.

She crossed to the bureau, picked up the old-fashioned telephone and waited for someone to answer. It didn't take long.

"My lady?" a smooth male voice responded.

"I need to speak to Larissa."

"Shall I send her, my lady, or—"

"The phone will be fine."

"One moment only."

It was more like ten seconds before she heard Larissa's delicate voice. "Lady Sophia, how may I serve you?"

"I need to contact Lord Raphael's office, Larissa. Do you have a number?"

"Of course, my lady. Do you wish to speak with him personally, or shall I—"

"No," Sophia interrupted quickly. "Someone from his staff will do. I just need some information from them." Possibly the *last* person she wanted to speak to directly at this point was Raphael. The news she had to deliver was bad. Very bad. Far better to talk to whoever was heading up his Seattle nest these days.

"Perhaps his lieutenant, Duncan, then?" Larissa prompted her.

Duncan, Sophia thought glumly. She'd never met either the vampire lord or his lieutenant, but Duncan was reputed to be as powerful as any member of the Vampire Council, excepting only Raphael himself. She snorted softly. Only Raphael could hold a vampire as strong as Duncan as his number two.

"My lady?" Larissa inquired.

"Whoever answers the phone will probably suffice, Larissa. Thank you."

Sophia hung up the phone and waited, her gaze returning once again to the photograph. It was a casual shot, taken with a personal camera. The three of them sat close together, the woman in the middle with the men's arms entwined around her in easy affection. The woman was smiling, her head tilted against the shoulder of one male, her hand resting on the thigh of the other. But there was wariness in her eyes as she looked at the camera, a distrustfulness that told Sophia this woman was probably an older vampire, one used to living in the shadows and not quite comfortable having her photo taken. The men had no such reservations, their expressions were wide open and laughing happily, an evening spent among friends.

Sophia's heart clenched. Gone. They were all gone. How old had they been, how many years had they walked the earth, and what had they witnessed in those years?

"Damn you, Lucien," she whispered again. The phone rang and she snatched it up, wanting to get this over with.

"Sophia," a cool, male voice said. "I am Duncan. How may we help you?"

Sophia froze. Duncan? Why would Raphael's formidable lieutenant be the one to take her call? She was nobody. Powerful, yes, but nobody knew about her. She'd never been to a Council meeting, had never even been seen at Lucien's side outside of Canada, and that was decades ago.

So why would Duncan pick up the phone when she called out of the blue?

Maybe because Raphael already suspected what Lucien had done, and now Sophia was going to be the one to suffer for it.

Chapter Nine

North of Seattle, Washington

Raphael woke, filled with a cold and deadly intent. Yesterday had been for grieving. Tonight was for vengeance. Cyn stirred slightly beside him, and he looked down at her where she still slept, curled against him. His arm tightened over her hip. He'd exhausted her last night. More correctly, they'd exhausted each other in the ages-old remedy when confronted with the face of death. A reaffirmation of life, even if their joining would never produce anything but mutual joy.

He leaned over and kissed her softly awake. Her eyes flashed open, a smile lighting their mossy depths even as her expression firmed with purpose. "We have work to do," she said.

Raphael grinned viciously. They were well matched, he and his mate.

"We do," he said. "The shower is big enough for two."

Cyn sat up, running her fingers through her tangled hair, causing her breasts to push forward eagerly. He gave a low growl of appreciation. Her eyes, when she met his gaze, were filled with heat. "I've always been a big believer in multi-tasking," she breathed.

* * * *

Raphael found Wei Chen and Loren waiting for him upstairs, deep in conversation with Duncan and Juro. Duncan crossed the room as soon as Raphael and Cyn entered.

"My lord. Cynthia," he said in greeting. "We received an unusual request just moments ago. The call was forwarded from Malibu, and I do not believe the caller realizes you are here in Seattle."

Raphael gave him an inquiring look.

"One of Lucien's children, Sophia . . ." Duncan's voice trailed off and he shook his head. "Her formal name is quite lengthy, one of those aristocratic, lineage-revealing titles from old Spain. I don't know that you've met her before, my lord. I have not."

Raphael frowned thoughtfully, paging back through the thousands of vampires he'd met over his long life, some only briefly, others he'd spent decades or more with. He shook his head. "I don't cross paths with Lucien that often, other than our annual Council meetings. But his lieutenant is male, so this Sophia holds no formal position with him that I know of. What does she want?"

"She has requested permission to enter your territory from Vancouver. In point of fact, to journey here to the Seattle area and secure guest privileges at the compound."

Duncan turned and beckoned to Juro.

"I don't like it," Cyn said flatly, as Juro joined them.

All three vampires looked at her with carefully blank faces.

"Oh, cut the inscrutable vampire crap, you guys. Someone's killing vamps, and now suddenly this chick shows up from nowhere and wants to drop in for a visit? You don't find that even slightly suspicious?"

"More than slightly, I would say," Duncan agreed. "But knowing what she wants could be helpful, whether she means ill or not. She claims to be on an errand for Lucien, so perhaps they've had similar problems in Canada."

"When would she like to arrive?" Raphael asked.

"This evening, my lord. She is already at the border. If we grant permission, she is prepared to cross immediately, which speaks to a certain urgency on her part."

Cyn stirred unhappily, but Raphael said, "Let her come, Duncan. Juro, arrange for two of our people to meet her with transportation. I want her here as soon as possible, but she enters alone, on my terms, or not at all. I will guarantee her safety, but no one else's."

Juro nodded. "A team was dispatched as soon as she called, my lord, to save time in the event you granted her passage. I will advise them of your permission and arrange a rendezvous with Sophia." He pulled out his cell phone and was already punching in a number as he walked away.

"How long before she arrives?" Raphael asked.

"I would think an hour or two, my lord. If Sophia crosses the border and meets our team partway . . ." He shrugged. "It's only the mountain roads that will slow them somewhat."

Raphael considered this. Vampires had superior reflexes and far better night sight than humans. The roads wouldn't slow them much.

"Very well. When she arrives, I will speak with her myself—"

Cyn spoke up immediately. "Raphael, what if—"

He raised a hand to stop the predictable objection. "We will take all necessary precautions, my Cyn."

She flushed, but her eyes were full of rebellion when they met his. "Is there coffee around somewhere, Duncan?" she asked, not bothering to hide her irritation.

Duncan glanced at Raphael before saying, "There is a dining room across the way. Wei Chen houses a full shift of daylight guards on the compound, and there are one or two vampire mates who live here as well."

"Thanks," she said to Duncan, then shifted her attention to Raphael. "Since I'm not needed here, I'm going to get some caffeine. And then I'd like to ask Wei Chen and others a few questions . . . if that's all right with you, *my lord,*" she added sarcastically. And with that, she spun on her heel and left.

Raphael watched her go, enjoying the sway of her hips, even though she was irritated with him. He turned back to Duncan with a wry twist of his mouth. "I think she worries even more than you do, Duncan."

Duncan grinned. "Impossible, my lord," he commented, adding,

"She loves you deeply."

"She wants to *protect* me."

"Speaking of which, if you permit this Sophia to meet with you—"

Raphael blinked slowly and gave his lieutenant a patient look.

"Ah, that is, *when* you meet with her, my lord, I believe you should permit Juro and myself to greet her first. I'd like a better sense of her purpose before we admit her to the building, at least, and certainly before she is permitted into your presence."

"You're as bad as Cyn."

"No doubt. And for somewhat the same reasons."

Raphael arched an eyebrow at him.

"I did say *somewhat*," Duncan said dryly.

Raphael flashed a quick grin, sobering almost immediately.

"Very well." Raphael heard Cyn's footsteps and looked over his shoulder to see her heading for their private quarters. "I think I'll have a word with my mate."

* * * *

Cyn was coming out the large bathroom when Raphael entered their suite. She had a towel in her hands and her face was still damp from a recent wash. She didn't say anything, just tossed the towel onto a rack, then walked over to the side table and began refastening her shoulder holster, her back to him once more.

Raphael crossed the room silently, taking selfish pleasure from her gasp of surprise as his hand snatched the gun from her fingers before she could slide it into the holster. Sliding the weapon across the table out of her reach, he spun her around to face him. Not that she was cowed by his show of strength. The look she gave him all but dared him to try anything.

"Sweet, sweet Cyn," he said silkily. He felt her grow perfectly still, saw her eyes flare in alarm as she recognized the danger simmering beneath his quiet voice. The stubbornness fled, replaced by a wary watchfulness. He growled soft and low in his chest. "You are angry because I value your life too much to hide behind you? You are human, my Cyn, and I am Vampire. Which of us do you think more likely to survive an attack by my enemies?"

"Well, thank you very much, oh great one. I won't trouble you with my useless human efforts on your behalf any longer."

Raphael tightened his grip, pulling her closer, forcing her up onto her toes. "I don't *need* you to protect me," he insisted, only inches away from her face. "I have hundreds of vampires specifically trained to do that. You *know* this."

"And what about all the others?" she snapped back at him, raising her hands between them and pushing ineffectively at his chest. "The *thousands* of vampires who depend on you for their lives, the thousands who will *die* if anything happens to you. What about *me*? How would I live without you?" Her voice cracked with emotion as she fisted one hand and punched his shoulder. "You're irreplaceable, damn you!"

He stared at her, loosening his hold until he could run gentle hands up and down her arms. "And do you think you're not?" he asked, his impatience replaced by stunned disbelief. "Do you think I could go on if something happened to you? Do you think I would *want* to?"

Cyn looked away, a flush of embarrassment staining her lovely cheeks.

"Sweet Cyn," he murmured, pulling her into his arms. "*Lubimaya,*" he whispered against her fragrant hair. "I would sooner die at your side than live without you."

"Me, too" she whispered, tears filling her voice.

"Then there is nothing for it. We shall *both* have to live, my Cyn."

He placed a finger under her chin and raised her face to his, kissing her long and slowly, savoring the luscious, warm taste of her mouth, lingering to twine his tongue around hers until she softened against him at last, her arms snaking beneath his jacket and around his back.

"I love you, my Cyn," he said, breaking away from the kiss and holding her close. "And I need you always. Never doubt that."

"Ditto, fang boy," she muttered against his chest.

Raphael laughed. "Put on your gun, then. We'll have a visitor to question soon.

"Sophia can't be here already." She dashed back into the bathroom, checking her face in the mirror and splashing it with cool water to erase the signs of her tears.

He followed her, leaning against the door frame and watching her in the mirror.

"No, but Juro's team won't take long. Vampires drive fast."

"While we wait, I want to clear up a few things with Wei Chen, and there are the reports from Juro's team on the two crime scenes. They went out there the first night and secured the houses."

She crossed to the table and snapped her gun into the shoulder rig, then slipped on her jacket, concealing the gun from casual inspection. A vampire wouldn't need to see the weapon, of course. The scent alone would betray its presence. Cyn knew this, but she'd carried her gun in this fashion for years, she'd told him, and saw no reason to change. She looked over her shoulder, meeting his gaze with eyes filled with anticipation. "So, we meet this chick from Canada, and then we can start tracking these guys, right?"

"So eager, *lubimaya*. I approve."

She blew out a dismissive breath and he grabbed her, swinging her around and claiming her mouth in a hard kiss. Then he raised his head and said, "Soon, my Cyn, very soon we hunt."

Chapter Ten

Sophia surveyed the Seattle compound as the big gate rolled shut behind her, nearly silent despite its obvious heft. She was reluctantly impressed by the Western vampires' security, from the careful scrutiny of the two who'd been dispatched to escort her, to the watchful gaze of the guards as she was passed through the gate and into the compound proper. Lucien had nothing like this in his territory, not even in his own lair, which she'd found almost alarmingly unguarded. Of course, that might be because Lucien himself was not in residence. Surely, if their lord had been present, his guards would have been more alert? On the other hand, if they'd been doing their job properly, he never would have gone missing in the first place.

Although, having read his letter, it now seemed more likely he was in hiding, rather than missing.

The truck—and regardless of what the makers called it, this behemoth vehicle could be considered nothing but a truck—drove into the compound, winding through more of the ever-present trees as they rounded the curved driveway and headed for a quite elegant concrete and steel structure. There was a surprisingly strong hum of power coming from the building, and Sophia wondered just how many vampires were inside. It had to be considerable to produce that strong a power signature.

The truck came to a halt and she remained still, waiting for some sort of signal from her escort. The big Asian vampire driving hadn't said a word the entire journey, so she looked to the other, a dark-skinned male whose Caribbean accent flowed cheerfully over her ears. She could hear him murmuring from his seat in front and realized he was wearing a communication device on his wrist of the type used by high-level security personnel around the world. *Even more impressive*, she thought. If they observed this much caution for a visit to the local compound, imagine the gauntlet one would have to run for a visit with Raphael himself.

Two vampires emerged from the building and made their way down the stairs, clearly heading her way. Between the light cast from the building's interior and the generously lit landscaping, she could see their faces clearly and at first glance didn't recognize either of them. But that wasn't a surprise. Vampires tended not to mingle, and especially not across territorial boundaries. Larissa had produced a file on the Seattle compound which had contained a few photographs, but beyond that, Sophia had little information on whom to expect here. Darren, who'd attended years of Council meetings with Lucien, would have been able to describe the Council members themselves, and perhaps their vampire lieutenants, but Sophia didn't expect to run into any of them here in Seattle, so she hadn't bothered to ask him.

She studied the two males as they approached the vehicle. The first was an eerily accurate match for her humongous driver. He was at least a brother, if not a twin, which was fascinating—she didn't think she'd ever seen the like. The other Seattle vampire was a good-looking male, tall and well-built, with long blond hair tied back into a neat queue. He said something to the twin, who walked over to the truck and opened her door.

"Step out, please," the giant said in a deep, rumbling voice that matched his impressive stature perfectly.

Sophia swung her legs through the open door and scooted forward. The male held out a huge paw, offering his assistance, and she took it gratefully, noting as she did so the deep hum of power beneath his skin. It wasn't a deliberate show on his part. If he'd wanted to test her, he would have been far more blatant about it. This was simply the power that lived inside him, and it was considerable. Sophia knew he was receiving a similar trace of her own power, which was just as firmly banked. They were all being very carefully polite this evening. ·

She reached the ground and disengaged her hand, watching from the corner of her eye as the blond vampire approached.

"Sophia," he said in a cool, uninflected tone. "Welcome to Seattle. I am Duncan."

Sophia froze and fought not to show it. This was Duncan? When she'd spoken with him earlier, she'd assumed he was in Malibu. But, of course, her call could have been forwarded anywhere. Clearly it *had* been forwarded right here to Seattle. But if Duncan was in Seattle—

Suddenly everything made terrible sense. The security, the impossibly strong power signature. Aware of the knowing brown eyes watching her ever so closely, Sophia forced herself to take a step forward, to accept the hand Duncan was offering. Many of the older vampires didn't shake hands, especially those who eschewed human contact. Sophia was not one of those. Her life in Rio was filled with far more humans than vampires.

"The inestimable Duncan," she acknowledged. She shook his hand firmly, surprised that he, at least, hadn't tested her power with that handshake. Many vampires in his position would have. But then, if what she'd heard about him was true, he probably didn't feel the need to. But at the same time, she wondered how much they had discovered about *her* in the short time since that phone call. Not much, probably. She'd kept an intentionally low profile down in South America, and before that she'd been just one more of Lucien's playmates, not worthy of any notice at all.

Duncan smiled slightly. "Just Duncan will do. And this is Juro," he added, indicating the giant vampire next to him. "What brings you to Seattle, Sophia?"

Well, she thought, at least they didn't waste any time on chitchat. "As we discussed on the phone, I'm here on behalf of my Sire," she said smoothly. It was close enough to the truth that it would pass, and, besides, she had more than enough power of her own to conceal her thoughts. "I'm searching for someone, a vampire who has gone missing. The trail led me here, where I hoped to secure permission to continue my search and a safe haven for the duration."

Duncan regarded her steadily, giving away nothing of his thoughts. "For whom do you search?"

Sophia met his cool stare, her expression calm despite her exquisite awareness of the building behind him, and far more importantly, of who she now knew had to be waiting *inside* that building. She sent out a thin thread of inquiry and snapped it back almost painfully, very nearly singed by the raw, unimaginable depth of power that could only be Raphael. A shiver of dread crept along her spine and she steeled herself against it. She could not afford to show weakness. Not anymore, not with Raphael here in Seattle and her own Sire mysteriously absent. Was it possible that Raphael had something to do with Lucien's disappearance? Or, *meu Deus*, might her Sire be Raphael's prisoner? Maybe right here in this compound?

Duncan was regarding her patiently, seeming willing to stand in the cold damp of a Pacific Northwest night for as long as it took to get a response to his query. She frowned and drew a deep fortifying breath. "I am looking for Lucien," she said at last, knowing she'd never get past the front door otherwise. "I have reason to believe he's nearby. I had even thought he might be visiting here, but I now think that unlikely."

Is he here? Do you know where he is? She choked back the questions she was desperate to ask.

Duncan raised one eyebrow quizzically, the most reaction she'd seen from him so far. He went very still and she knew he was mentally speaking to someone inside. Raphael, probably. He would take direction from no one else.

He smiled at her then, just a slight upward curve of his lips as he turned and gestured with one hand toward the warmly lit building. "My Sire will speak with you."

Seeing no alternative, Sophia started up the concrete stairway toward the front door, irritated by the awkwardness of the individual steps, too long and too shallow, so that she felt like an overgrown child scurrying along a giant's staircase. But even as she swallowed her irritation, she recognized it for what it was—a distraction from the fear pooling in her belly, something she hadn't felt in longer than she could remember. Not since her earliest nights alone, after Lucien had cast her out of his nest and forced her to find a home of her own.

Duncan strode along next to her, with Juro slightly ahead of them. Neither of the two said anything, but Duncan at least seemed friendly in a reserved sort of way. Not terribly forthcoming, but not hostile either. More curious than anything else, she thought.

Juro pulled open the heavy, glass front door and went through first.

Duncan caught the door and held it for her, with a slight bow. She acknowledged the courtesy with a smile, nodding her head as she stepped through. All of that courtesy didn't keep her from noticing the heavy steel shutters hanging over her head, however. Shutters she had no doubt were lowered every day before sunrise and could probably be dropped at the touch of a button, if necessary. Just beyond the front doors was a "great room." Rooms like this were used for many things in modern houses, but this one was a large, casual sitting room, with a pair of long, heavy couches facing each other across a thick glass coffee table. A pair of matching chairs stood to either end, making a square seating area, with an enormous area rug framing the entire thing. The ceiling was high, two stories at least, with windows on the far wall that nearly met the roof line. And like the door, automatic shutters framed every window. This building had been constructed for vampires. The door was the only real vulnerability and by the time an intruder reached it, the shutters would be deployed and it, too, would be pretty much impregnable.

Halfway across the great room, Duncan quickened his pace, stepping out in front of her and heading straight for a pair of tall wooden doors. At the same time, Juro slowed to flank her, even as his twin and the Jamaican closed in behind, herding her in Duncan's wake as he opened the doors and disappeared into the room beyond.

Juro slowed further, glancing once at his twin before pausing in front of the open doors and indicating with a sweep of his broad palm that she should enter ahead of him.

Sophia met his flat stare, then tossed her long hair over her shoulder and entered the lion's den.

She took two steps into the room, her gaze sweeping quickly from side to side, taking note of the small group of vampires. The Seattle nest leader, Wei Chen, was there. He was one of those she recognized from a photo the efficient Larissa had included in her file. There were three others, none of whom she knew, but all of them, including Wei Chen were watching her closely, their power simmering just below the point of challenge, ready to defend their Sire. Letting her gaze travel farther, she saw Duncan crossing to the far side of the room, toward a huge bank of glass overlooking the valley below. As she entered, he turned to take up a position next to a vampire who could only be Raphael.

Sophia couldn't help it. She sucked in a breath, her gaze riveted on the big vampire sitting in the place of honor. Why had no one warned her of his sheer *presence*? He fairly vibrated with power. It distorted the air around him and zinged painfully along her nerve endings as she fought to keep up a cool front. She'd thought her master Lucien was powerful, and he was. But he'd never had power like this, had never sought to hone his strength to anything beyond what it took for the loose governance of his territory, spending most of his time and energy on pleasure and foolish games. Sophia wasted a few precious seconds regretting her *own* foolishness in spending so many years dancing through the hot, humid streets of Rio, instead of cultivating her power. And she cursed Lucien yet again for encouraging his children to do nothing but play during their long lives.

Raphael, she knew instantly, did not play at life. He was power in its truest form, power whetted to the finest edge and knowing no equal.

But while the vampire part of her took note of his power—and kept her own carefully tamped down to avoid even a breath of offense— the woman she still was took note of his beauty. Even as a human, he must have been formidable, well over six feet and broad of shoulder, with short cut black hair and unusual black eyes. There was the slightest flicker of silver in those eyes, evidence of his ready power. As if he'd need it, surrounded as he was by so many of his own powerful children.

Sophia was abruptly thankful she'd taken care with her appearance. Knowing her figure-hugging sweater and black leggings highlighted what were very feminine curves, and that the knee-high boots with their stiletto heels added attractive length to her legs. She swept her long coat behind her and dropped into the graceful curtsey she'd learned hundreds of years ago at her nanny's knee.

"Lord Raphael," she said, pitching her voice deliberately into a low, sensuous purr. "Sophia Micaela Angelina de Sandoval y Rojas, in loyal service to my Sire, Lucien Guiscard, Lord of the Canadian Territories."

She looked up, meeting his gaze intentionally. "But between us, my lord," she said. "Sophia will suffice."

Raphael eyed her dispassionately, giving no indication that he considered her anything but a nuisance. The skinny human woman draped over his shoulder was another matter. She was studying Sophia with undisguised dislike, her right hand dipping briefly beneath her short leather jacket where ... *Meu Deus*, the woman was carrying a weapon! Sophia shifted her gaze back to Raphael, who had clearly noticed the human's reaction and would no doubt chastise her for it.

But instead, the vampire lord slid his hand off the chair arm and onto the woman's leg in a clear signal that was not lost on Sophia. Nor was the smug look in the human's green gaze or her tiny smile of victory. Bitch.

Sophia shifted her attention away from the human, meeting Raphael's eyes and letting her own register a polite disappointment, even as she bowed her head in respect.

"Where is Lucien, Sophia?" Raphael asked, his voice a burr of velvet-sheathed power against her skin.

Sophia's head came up, her gaze meeting his once again. "My lord, I had hoped to find him here."

She saw Duncan shift slightly, heard the intake of breath from the vampires behind her, and knew with cold certainty that her Sire was not in Seattle. Or if he was, none of them knew about it.

Raphael continued to study her, his expression devoid of any emotion. Of them all, only he had shown no reaction to her response and the information it conveyed—not the tiniest bit, not surprise, not puzzlement, and certainly not alarm.

"Lucien has not entered my territory," he said bluntly, clearly having no doubts and feeling no need to elaborate.

"Why would you expect to find him here?" Duncan asked from his position to Raphael's left.

Abruptly aware she was still bent into the uncomfortable curtsey, Sophia rose to her full, modest height. She shifted her gaze from Duncan to Raphael and back again. How much should she tell them? Lucien's letter had sent her here, but had he meant for her to confide to anyone the details of the Vancouver deaths?

In general, the vampire lords did not share information—or anything else—with each other. They were viciously territorial and quite openly hostile, at least in North America. It wasn't unheard of for a stronger lord to push the territorial boundaries in an attempt to enrich his own power at the expense of another, and frequent disputes erupted, sometimes violently. Lucien's Canadian territory was vast, but largely unsettled, both in terms of people and vampires, and rarely the object of any other lord's ambition. This was a good thing for Lucien since, as he'd told her many times, he was a lover not a fighter. Sophia wasn't aware of any open conflict between her Sire and Raphael, or any of the other North American lords, for that matter. But then, she'd been gone so long, and had paid so little attention.

An unwelcome thought sent tendrils of nausea twisting into her gut. Had Lucien known Raphael would be here when he'd sent her on this errand? Or if not known, had he at least suspected it? Could there be a connection between the Vancouver deaths and whatever business had drawn the Western vampire lord away from Malibu and up to this concrete and steel compound?

Sophia sighed and turned her unwilling gaze on Raphael, who blinked lazily, letting his eyelids drop slowly over the silvery sheen of power. She almost laughed. What was she thinking? He didn't need to *ask* for the information he wanted; he could rip her mind open like a tin can and simply take it.

"Lucien summoned me home several days ago," she said bitterly. "It was our first contact in years." She shook her head. "Decades," she amended. "I've been living in Brazil. The lords down there are lax in their enforcement, to say the least. As long as a vampire observes a few basic rules, they don't care who sired you or whom you call master."

"How did Lucien contact you?" Duncan asked.

Sophia glanced at Raphael before answering, but the vampire lord seemed content to let his lieutenant take the lead. "Directly," she said simply. "He spoke in my mind just as I woke for the evening. He gave me no reason, simply summoned me home to him with an indication of urgency."

"Do you know why?"

Sophia shook her head, letting some of her frustration show. "No," she admitted. "I only arrived in Vancouver yesterday evening. I went straight to his main estate above the city, expecting to find him waiting, but he wasn't there. And no one I spoke with knows where he is."

"What made you think you'd find him here in Seattle, then?"

"A letter. He left me a letter with details of certain recent and very troubling events. And then he told me to come here."

"What events?" Raphael spoke at last, the question a whiplash of power demanding an answer.

Sophia drew a deep breath and forged ahead. Lucien had left this matter to her. She had only her instincts to guide her, and those instincts were telling her to come clean with what she knew. Any other path would only lead to more killing.

"Death, my lord," she said bluntly. "Three vampires in Vancouver have been destroyed. I do not know how or by whose hand, but the killers may now be in your territory, and . . . I believe Lucien is somehow at the heart of this."

Chapter Eleven

Thinking of his own dead, Raphael felt a renewed surge of rage. Next to him, Cyn shifted, resting her fingers against the back of his neck.

"Who died?" he demanded of Sophia.

He saw her blink in reaction as his anger washed outward, felt her power push back briefly. She had surprising strength for one of Lucien's children. Perhaps that was why she'd been the one Lucien had called when he got into trouble over his head.

"I have their images, my lord," she said with admirable calm. "And their names, although I've never met them."

"Who?" Raphael insisted.

"Giselle," she said softly.

Wei Chen gasped audibly when she said the name. Sophia shot him a quick glance over her shoulder before turning back to Raphael. "Along with Damon and Benjamin," she said. "It is my understanding the three lived together and died on the same night."

"My lord," Wei Chen started to say, but Raphael raised his hand for silence. Giselle wasn't one of his, but he'd known her. She was old and canny, but with very little power. And because of that, she'd chosen to live in Vancouver after Lucien and Raphael had matched the boundaries of their two territories to the international border between the U.S. and Canada. She'd wanted a quiet life and had trusted the easygoing Lucien to give her that. Unwisely, it turned out.

"How do you know these three are dead?" Raphael asked Sophia.

"Their names were in Lucien's letter, along with a photograph. I have both of those with me, my lord, if you'd like to see them."

Raphael signaled Duncan who stepped forward to accept a folded envelope Sophia drew out of her coat pocket. Duncan opened the letter slowly, shaking out the photograph and studying it carefully before handing both photo and letter to Raphael.

Raphael only glanced at the photograph, handing it off to Cyn almost immediately. He turned his attention instead to Lucien's letter. If he'd had any doubts before about what Sophia had told him, he had them no longer. The handwriting was Lucien's, but more than that, the vampire lord's power was imbued in the parchment itself, the regret and sadness he'd experienced while writing it was as vivid as the tear drop staining the fine linen paper. But rather than sympathy, Raphael was revolted by the words of his fellow vampire lord.

Lucien and Raphael were nearly the same age, but the other vampire had set himself up in America decades before Raphael arrived in the New World. At first, Lucien had confined himself to the eastern provinces of what would become Canada. When he decided to expand westward, he and Raphael had easily agreed on a territorial line, moving it as events warranted and the humans expanded their settlements. Lucien had always been a poor protector of his people and a lax guardian of his territory, but he'd been just powerful enough to hold onto it, especially given the lack of any serious takeover bids.

But the current situation was a new low, even for Lucien. His people were dead, murdered as they slept, and he was gone, leaving nothing but an urgent summons to Sophia and this pathetic letter in which Lucien confessed his own complicity in leading the killers right to Giselle's door.

And now, the animals who'd murdered Giselle and her lovers clearly had moved southward into Raphael's territory to continue their killing spree. Was it coincidence that Lucien had directed Sophia to follow in their wake? That his letter connected the two sets of murders? Raphael didn't believe in coincidence, especially not when it came wrapped in Lucien's words of self-pity.

But Raphael was not Lucien. He would not cower in hiding while his people died. He would find these killers and eliminate the threat once and for all.

And after that . . . perhaps it was time to find a new lord for the Canadian Territories.

* * * *

Sophia stood silently, watching Raphael read Lucien's letter. She knew how incriminating it was, knew her own anger upon reading it. She could only imagine Raphael's rage. It was his vampires whom Lucien had put at risk by hiding instead of dealing with the tragedy he created.

She jumped when Raphael suddenly barked out an order.

"Wei Chen," he said. "Have someone show Sophia to the guest quarters."

"But my lord—" Sophia's protest died on her lips when the powerful lord turned his black gaze upon her. She felt her heartbeat speed up, felt her own power trying to rise to the surface as every defensive instinct she possessed screamed to the fore all at once. She squelched the reaction brutally, nearly passing out with the effort, but knowing she would be dead in seconds if Raphael willed it. And he was in a temper. She didn't need to know him to see that. His rage was like a separate entity in the room, a creature of heat and fury.

She dropped to her knees, willing to beg for what she wanted, what she needed—to be a part of the hunt for these killers. Because there had to be more than one of them. Probably a whole murderous pack. No single human could have taken down three vampires and sent Lucien scurrying for cover. She wanted to see these humans brought to justice—*Vampire* justice. For reasons she couldn't explain, it mattered more to her than anything had in centuries—with one exception, and that was something, someone, she never permitted herself to think about.

"Lord Raphael," she said, trying to keep the pleading out of her voice. "Permit me to be a part of this. These were Lucien's children who were murdered, and yes, it was at least partly his fault," she hurried to add. "But my Sire is alive, my lord. I *know* this."

Her voice died, her throat suddenly dry as a desert as Raphael's already chilly expression turned absolutely frigid. Sophia knew in that moment that Lucien's remaining nights would be counted on one finger if Raphael found him alive.

Hot tears pressed against the back of her eyes, a wrenching grief that squeezed her heart painfully. She loved Lucien. In spite of his many faults, he'd given her the greatest gift of life when he'd turned her, and they'd shared so much joy together. It would *hurt* her if he died, even if he had brought it on himself.

She bowed her head, unwilling to let Raphael or any of the others witness her pain. Clenching her jaw and forcing her sorrow aside, she raised her eyes to meet his once again. "I know you don't *need* my help, Lord Raphael, but I beg you to let me offer it. For the sake of Lucien's people, who do not deserve to suffer for his misdeeds."

Raphael just stared at her with no expression. "Wei Chen, have someone see Sophia to her room," he said.

"Yes, my lord," the Seattle nest leader said from behind her.

Sophia came gracefully to her feet, turning in time to see a slender, young vampire conferring with Wei Chen, who looked up and caught her gaze. "Sophia," he said. "This is Lukas. He'll show you to the room you'll be using during your stay."

Sophia nodded, then dared to turn back to face Raphael once more. "My lord?" she asked. He still said nothing, regarding her with a flat expression that gave no clue as to what he was thinking. She drew a deep breath and made her way toward the waiting Lukas, aware of everyone watching her as she wound through the cluster of furniture and across the echoing space.

At least he hadn't sent her back home immediately. That was something. And if he tried . . . she had power of her own. Far more than she let on. It wasn't enough to take on Raphael, but it was enough to challenge anyone who thought they could set her aside like an unwelcome puppy. She *would* hunt for the killers. With Raphael's help or without it.

Chapter Twelve

"She's telling the truth," Duncan said once the doors had closed securely behind their visitor.

"What she knows of it," Wei Chen clarified, taking his seat again. "I had our people do some checking. Like she said, she's been living down in South and Central America for nearly a century, most recently in Rio. For all purposes, she's been without a master, flying under the radar. You know how relaxed they are about those things down there."

Raphael sat back, content to let his people talk it out.

"She flew in yesterday, my lord," Juro provided. "It was a private flight, but the distance necessitated several stops and took some time. At least part of her travel was in daylight, however, which lends credence to her claim of urgency."

It was Cyn who asked the question they were all thinking. "So where is this Lucien guy? Is he dead?"

All of Raphael's people looked to him for the answer. He thought about it, his fingers stroking Cyn's leg absently. "No, he's not. Lucien was never the most powerful among us, but his strength was still considerable. His death would certainly have been detectable to you here in Seattle, Wei Chen, and probably even to most of us in Malibu. Particularly if the death was unexpected. Even he was taken out by one of his own in a *coup d'état,* there would have been at least some losses among his children, and that many deaths would definitely have been felt. Unless Lucien has a child we don't know about. Someone strong enough to eliminate his Sire and seize power without a ripple."

Duncan snorted softly, circling around to take the chair next to Cyn. "Highly unlikely, my lord. Lucien has always chosen playmates as his children, not players."

"*Sophia* could do it," Wei Chen observed. "She's hiding her power, but it's there."

"She probably could," Duncan agreed thoughtfully. "But she's spent the last hundred years following in her Sire's hedonist footsteps, so her strength remains mostly potential. And if she'd eliminated him, she'd hardly risk coming here on a pretense of looking for him. There would be no point. Plus, she seems to genuinely care for Lucien, which makes her an unlikely candidate to have killed him."

"Perhaps," Wei Chen conceded. "My lord," he continued, turning to Raphael. "Would it be possible for Lucien to mask his signature well enough that he couldn't be found?"

Raphael shrugged. "Not from me. He is not within my territory, but he *is* alive and I *will* find him."

Cyn moved restlessly. "But finding him isn't our first priority, is it? If he's not here, he doesn't matter, except that now we know the killers started up there and traveled here."

"Why?" Wei Chen asked. "That's what I'd like to know. And how did they decide on who their targets would be? Jeremy," he said, turning to the vampire sitting quietly next to him. "Did *you* know Giselle or her nest mates? Did you do any work for them, by chance?"

Jeremy shook his head right away. "All of my clients are U.S. based. And I didn't do any work for Marco or Preston, so that can't be the link."

Wei Chen blew out a frustrated breath. "So, why them? How did they come to the attention of these killers?"

"They didn't," Cyn said suddenly. She leaned forward intently. "I'm betting the humans never saw any of their vampire targets before the day they hit them."

The Seattle vampires were staring at her with matched expressions of doubt. Despite what Raphael had told them earlier, they'd expected his Cyn to be nothing more than arm candy. Duncan and Juro knew better and were regarding her with thoughtful expressions, but Cyn ignored all of them.

"We need to talk to that local guy," she said, halfway to herself, before shifting her gaze to Loren. "Colin Murphy."

Loren nodded. "I figured we wouldn't have time tonight. He'll be here an hour after sunset tomorrow. But why is that important? Surely those of us in this room are better qualified to find and destroy these people. Frankly, the last thing we need is the interference of human authorities who will only get in the way."

"Maybe," Cyn conceded with little conviction. "But consider this. We know Lucien betrayed his peoples' location to the killers. I'm willing to give him the benefit of the doubt and assume he didn't do it knowing what would happen to them. But that means whoever he told was someone he knew and trusted. Probably not the killers, but someone working with them."

"Why do you say that?" Loren asked.

"Lucien's a vampire lord. Even if he isn't the strongest one around, he has at least enough juice to read humans. Wouldn't he know if the person he was talking to hated him enough to commit murder?"

"Assuming he bothered to look for it," Duncan observed. "If it was someone he trusted, someone he'd known for years . . ." He shook his head. "He might never have noticed a shift in sympathies."

"But see, that's why we need the cooperation of this guy Colin. I don't know the humans around here. I don't know who might hate vampires enough to want them gone, or who has the stomach and the organization to commit multiple murders. Do you?" she asked Loren.

He opened his mouth to speak, then closed it and frowned, clearly considering Cyn's question. He shook his head. "No, I don't, and you're right, I should. But if this started in Vancouver, there might not be anyone local involved, either."

Cyn shrugged. "That brings us back to how they knew where Marco and Preston lived. Jeremy, too, but especially Marco and Preston. Mariane went into town. Anyone could have followed her home and she never would have known."

"Such a possibility would never have occurred to her, and why should it?" Jeremy said, somewhat defensively.

"It shouldn't," Cyn agreed. "And no one's blaming Mariane. My point is it would have been easy to know where *you* lived, Jeremy, but not Marco and Preston. They didn't get out much and when they did it was mostly with other vampires. And it's not like you live in the suburbs here. Their houses were miles from the highway. If you didn't know to look for them, you wouldn't have known they were there."

"But most of us live within the compound now, even the ones who lived separately before," Loren objected. "How would someone know the few of us who live outside and where to find them?"

"Exactly," Cyn said. "Do you have a database somewhere, addresses, phone numbers, that sort of thing?"

"We maintain a database, of course. But it doesn't include the details of their security arrangements. I'm not certain I would have known if someone had asked me what Marco or Preston's private quarters looked like."

"But both of them lived in this area before you built this compound, right?"

"They did, yes. It was Marco who suggested we move here to Cooper's Rest in the first place."

Cyn considered that, her mouth twisting as she bit the inside of her lower lip. "How many vampires do you have living outside?" she asked.

Wei Chen raised his eyes to Raphael's in silent query. Cyn caught the exchange and scowled, but Raphael rested his hand against her lower back, rubbing gently. He nodded his permission to the Seattle nest leader.

"We have a total of forty-seven vampires affiliated with what we call the Seattle nest, although there are only a few still living in the city itself. Most live here on this estate. It's safer and, frankly, more comfortable to be around our own. Fewer than ten maintain separate residences, including those who still live in the city, although most of those spend at least some time here on a regular basis. Marco and Preston were among those who lived apart, and they were the ones who'd been in this area longest. Jeremy lived in the Seattle nest until he bonded with Mariane and they built their own house."

"She wanted a place of our own," Jeremy confirmed softly. "We bought up here to be close to the new compound."

Cyn tapped her fingers restlessly against her thigh, and Raphael knew what her next question would be. He also knew why she hesitated to ask it.

"What were your daytime sleeping arrangements, Jeremy?" Raphael asked for her.

Jeremy looked briefly surprised at the question, but since it came from his Sire, he answered quickly enough. "A vault, my lord. Like what we have here. Much smaller, of course, but just as secure."

Cyn leaned forward. "You built your house from scratch then?"

"We did."

Cyn rocked herself slightly and nodded. "But they didn't know that," she said thoughtfully. "They knew where you lived, but they didn't know about the extra security."

"No," Jeremy said bitterly. "So, they tortured Mariane instead."

Raphael felt Cyn freeze, heard her sharp intake of breath at the implicit suggestion that she was somehow ignoring what had happened to Mariane. Which she surely had not intended. His Cyn was many things, but insensitive, especially to another's pain, she was not.

"My mate and I," Raphael said emphatically, "are wholly focused on finding justice for those who died, and those who lived, Jeremy. Especially Mariane. Cyn's methods may seem abrupt to you, but she is far more skilled than either of us at uncovering human criminals of this sort."

Jeremy flushed at his Sire's gentle reprimand. "My apologies, my lord. It is difficult to think straight."

"I understand. Cyn?"

She leaned back hard against his comforting hand. "Okay," she said on a deep breath. "We know Lucien gave away Giselle and her nest, but he couldn't have revealed where Marco or Preston lived. Or Jeremy and Mariane, either. So, who gave them away? I know you guys, and I know Raphael's security. You don't exactly take out ads in the yellow pages advertising your presence. And yet, somehow the killers knew not only where the other two lived, but where they slept, because I'm assuming it wasn't in a back bedroom with blackout shades. Marco and Preston had survived a long time. They must have had some sort of hideaway they thought was secure. Someplace in or near their houses, but hard to find, am I right?"

Wei Chen gave Cyn an uncomfortable look, clearly unwilling to give out those kinds of details. Cyn huffed impatiently. "They're dead, Wei Chen. Whatever arrangements they had didn't work."

He sighed. "You're right, of course. I apologize. It's an automatic response. Marco and Preston each had a safe room beneath his home. Not as secure as what we have here, but certainly safe enough, we thought. The entrances were concealed and the rooms heavily reinforced."

"How'd the killers get inside?" She turned to look over her shoulder at Raphael. "I really need to examine their houses. In daytime, when I can see what I'm looking at."

Raphael frowned, unhappy at the idea of her running around unprotected while a gang of human vigilantes ran free, especially given what they'd already done to Mariane. But Cyn didn't see his frown;

she'd already turned back to address Loren.

"I want to meet up with Colin Murphy during the day tomorrow. If you give me his number, I'll—"

"No."

Cyn's head whipped around and she stared at Raphael.

"I will meet this human tomorrow night and decide *then* what course we will follow."

Her jaw tightened irritably, but again he knew she would not argue with him in front of his vampires. Besides which, she was shrewd enough to know when he would not be budged, and he would *not* change his mind on this one point. Until he met this local policeman, he was not trusting Cyn alone with him. For that matter, he wouldn't trust the man even then. If his mate felt it necessary to pursue some part of her investigation during the daylight hours, he would detail a bodyguard to go with her. One of his own, someone he trusted absolutely.

He stood, sliding his hand up to Cyn's shoulder, then down her arm, linking his fingers with hers and pulling her to her feet while cursing the still short Spring nights. "The sun is near. We will meet again tomorrow evening and determine how to proceed. Duncan, get Maxime here from Malibu. I want to know if our security has been breached electronically or otherwise. Wei Chen, I want all of my vampires within the walls of this compound by next sunrise."

"My lord," Loren said quickly. "We sent out a warning as soon as Marco and Preston were slain. Most of our people have already come in, but some have lovers outside—"

"Everyone," Raphael stated. "No exceptions or they answer to me."

* * * *

Cyn was out of the elevator almost before the doors were fully open, discarding her jacket on a chair and getting rid of her shoulder rig with jerky, agitated movements. Raphael watched her through half-lidded eyes. She hated being told what she couldn't do. She'd been on her own for too long. Even as a child, when her only supervision had been hired nannies who cared mostly that she entertain herself and not bother them. He shrugged inwardly. He didn't care if his restrictions chafed her overdeveloped sense of freedom. He'd much rather deal with her anger than her death. She checked her weapon, ejecting the magazine and working the slide to verify its status—something she never neglected to do, no matter how angry she was.

Raphael slipped out of his clothes, taking the time to hang them in the closet. These quarters were nothing like those in his Malibu estate, just a single large room, which served as both bedroom and sitting area, with a generous-sized bath. They were, however, completely private and secure, which was what mattered. The elevator had a coded lockout, which engaged automatically every morning, and no one had the code except for Cyn and himself. And neither of them would have a reason to go out during daytime while visiting. An opinion he was certain Cyn would disagree with.

Finished with her nightly gun routine, Cyn strode over to the closet and began undressing, still avoiding him, not meeting his eyes as she kicked off her boots and stripped off her clothes, brushing against him only inadvertently when she leaned over to snatch up her jacket and hang it up. Raphael's cock hardened at the sight of all that lovely skin, tightened further as she opened the front closure on her bra and removed it, then bent over to strip away the lacy bit of underwear she wore. Making no effort to conceal the reaction of his now naked body, he let his eyes roam along her curves, pausing to admire her delicious breasts with their rosy tips already swelling beneath his gaze. He growled hungrily and looked up to find her watching him, hands resting on slender hips, eyes sparking. She looked quite irresistibly seductive, although he doubted that was the effect she was going for. He suppressed the smile trying to curve his lips and met her gaze, waiting.

"You trust her?" she asked suddenly.

Raphael's eyebrows rose in surprise. "Sophia?" he verified.

"Of course Sophia," she snapped. "Was there some other fat Spaniard chick in that room tonight?"

Raphael almost choked trying not to laugh, and he had the brief thought that it was a good thing she'd unloaded her weapon already. "Why Spaniard?" he asked. "She flew here from Brazil."

"And I spent a summer in Paris when I was eighteen. Doesn't make me French. She was spitting all over the carpet when she reeled off that list of names. Trust me, her first language is Castilian Spanish." Her eyes narrowed, studying his response. "And she sure as hell liked you."

Raphael shrugged his dismissal. "She's an attractive woman who's used to manipulating men with her looks."

"She'd have gone down on her knees and sucked you off in front of everyone if you'd crooked a finger," she snarled.

Raphael lost the effort not to laugh, capturing her in his arms before she could explode. He pushed her up against the wall, trapping her there with his greater bulk, letting his erection play between her silky thighs. "An exaggeration, my Cyn. Are you jealous?"

"In your dreams, fang boy."

"In my dreams," he purred next to her ear. "There is no one between my legs but you, *lubimaya*."

"Smart move since I'm the one lying next to you while you sleep."

"It's late, sweet Cyn, or I'd give you a demonstration of my dreams," he said, pretending exhaustion, leaning heavily against her, maneuvering them both away from the wall until they tumbled onto the bed. And then, with a quick, sure move, he looped a big hand over her hip and snugged her beneath him, leaning down to nuzzle her soft neck.

"I thought you were tired," she murmured, as his fingers found their way over the smooth skin of her flat belly and pushed her thighs open to delve into the velvet folds between them.

"I seem to have caught a second wind," he teased.

Her heart was pounding against his chest, her breath warm puffs of air as she gripped his shoulders and her nails dug into his flesh. "Raphael," she gasped, arching up against him as he slipped one finger, then two, deep inside her. She lifted her hips, thrusting against his hand and spreading her legs wider, urging him deeper into her sweet, hot center, smooth as satin and soaking wet—eager for his touch, for his invasion. He groaned, knowing there was, in truth, too little time, though his cock strained painfully, eager to bury itself in the volcanic heat of her luscious body.

Cyn mewed softly, wanting more, rubbing herself against his hand, tightening her fingers in his hair and holding his mouth against her neck in invitation. Raphael pressed his tongue against the juicy swell of her jugular, but didn't take her, not yet. Grinning at her groan of frustration, he licked his way downward, dipping into the arch of her collar bone and down further until he captured her nipple in his mouth, biting gently. She cried out, hooking her leg around his hip, fucking herself against his fingers. Without warning, he slid a third finger inside her and began plunging in and out, mimicking the action his cock was hungry for, taking pleasure in the slick heat of her, in the trembling of her muscles, the small, hungry noises she was making as her hips pumped up and down, her breath coming in gasps as she whispered his name over and over again, a prayer for release.

And still he waited, waited until she was all but screaming his name, until she was clenched so tight around his fingers that he could barely move his hand. He scraped his thumb lightly across her clit, circling it once, twice and a third time before caressing it fully, rubbing back and forth until her entire body spasmed beneath him, her silken walls convulsing, her nipples so hard he could feel them like warm, smooth stones against his chest. She sucked in a keening breath, the air trapped in her lungs by the sheer magnitude of her orgasm. He lifted his head and sank his fangs into her neck, the rush of warm, sweet blood filling his mouth as she climaxed again and her scream of passion filled his ears. He held her tightly, reveling in the taste of her as she shuddered beneath him, her inner muscles trembling around his fingers as he stroked her over and over again, her body jolting as if shocked every time his thumb caressed her swollen clit.

When at last she lay limp, her arms clinging to him weakly, he retracted his fangs and licked the small wound closed. Crooning wordless sounds of comfort, he pulled his fingers gently from within the still trembling depths of her body, the juices of her orgasm coating his fingers and trailing across her abdomen as he wrapped his hand around her bare hip and tucked her closer in the safety of his arms.

"I owe you a blow job," she murmured, already half asleep as she curled into his embrace. His arms closed around her, her bare breasts pressed against his chest, the thudding of her heart a comforting metronome as he drifted closer to his daytime sleep.

As the sun's glow lit the horizon, he smiled, thinking his next awakening would be a sweet one. His final thought as the sun crept fully into the morning sky and stole away both his smile and his consciousness was that the night had ended all too easily. And Cyn hadn't said a word about his forbidding her to go into town without him.

* * * *

Raphael knew when Cyn slipped out of the bed they shared. He watched in his dreams as she dressed quickly and donned her weapon before kneeling on the bed next to him. She leaned over and touched her lips to his in a good-bye kiss. Raphael raged at her, their connection through the mate bond strong enough that her eyes widened when his anger struck hard at her consciousness. For a moment he thought he read indecision on her face. But then, she drew a breath and whispered, "I'll be fine. I promise."

And she was gone.

Chapter Thirteen

Colin sat in front of his office, the cheap plastic chair tilted back on two legs, a weathered, wooden overhang protecting him from a drizzle that threatened to turn into rain as he leaned against the wall and contemplated his town. The office wasn't much. A single room with a small holding cell and piss poor insulation that left it icy cold most of the time. The only exception was the rare occasion when the sun managed to come out from behind the clouds long enough to warm the place up a bit. Most days he didn't even bother to come in here unless he had a drunk or two locked up overnight, something that didn't happen all that often. Most of the drunks he collared winding through town had more or less sober friends who were happy to take the offender off his hands rather than travel back for him, or her, the next day.

But this morning he'd made a point of showing his face in the few establishments sprinkled around town. People had heard about Mariane. It was inevitable, really. The smaller the town the more active the gossip mill, and Mrs. Fremont had no doubt primed the pump on this particular story. His cell phone had been ringing almost nonstop since the attack. Some were worried about their own safety or the safety of their women. Others just wanted the news firsthand. And still others had the facts all wrong and were calling him nearly hysterical with fear about some vampire invasion.

Not that the latter was completely off base. Colin hadn't missed the parade of big, black SUVs that had zipped down the highway the other night with a limo snug between them. They'd driven right past him on his way home from Jeremy's. And then this morning, there'd been a message waiting for him from Loren. Apparently, some big honcho had arrived and wanted to meet what passed for the local law. Colin could hardly wait.

He frowned, rocking the chair against the wall behind him. He could understand Jeremy's anger. Hell, he shared it, although he was smart enough to know that no matter how angry he might be, it couldn't come close to what the vampire was feeling. But why would a single attack—as vicious as it had been—bring out the big guns like this? And how had they managed to arrive so quickly, virtually on the heels of the crime itself?

His attention was drawn down the block as one of the SUVs he'd just been thinking about pulled to a stop in front of Emma's, the local answer to Seattle's coffee shops. Colin let the chair drop to all fours and leaned forward, forearms resting on his thighs as he studied the new arrival. The truck's windows were all but blacked out, so he couldn't see anyone inside, but the meager sun still rode the sky somewhere behind the thick clouds, so he knew whoever it was had to be human, at least. And human he could deal with.

The truck door opened and Colin stood. A black clad leg emerged wearing thick-soled combat-style boots. He took a half step forward and tripped to a halt when the leg turned out to be that of a tall, slender woman. Closing the truck door behind her, she stood for a moment surveying downtown Cooper's Rest. It wasn't much, he admitted, and she seemed to agree, if the frown on her face was any indication.

Her gaze fell on him where he stood under the porch overhang, then lifted to read the sign identifying the office as the local police station. Eyeing him once more, she gave a small shrug and headed his way.

Colin watched her approach. She was wearing clothes that very nearly matched his own outfit—black combat pants tucked into sensible, lace-up boots, and a black t-shirt, although she wore hers considerably better than he did. His smile of appreciation didn't last long as he registered the existence of a shoulder rig beneath her short, all-weather jacket, its presence in stark contrast to her graceful walk and the way she filled out that t-shirt. He took a step forward when she reached the stairs in front of him, stretching to his full six-foot-four height, his hands grabbing the overhang before dropping to rest on his hips.

She smiled slightly, as if acknowledging his dominance display, before climbing the three stairs to stand on a level with him. "Colin Murphy?" she asked, tall enough that she very nearly met his eyes without raising her head.

Colin tipped his head. "The very same, darlin'" he responded, enjoying a bit of satisfaction when her mouth tightened at the endearment.

"My *name*," she said. "Is Cynthia Leighton. Cyn, if you prefer."

"Pleased to make your acquaintance, Ms. Leighton," he drawled, letting every ounce of his Georgian upbringing play with the syllables. He found most Northerners assumed anyone with a drawl was dimwitted, and he wasn't above using it to his advantage.

The Leighton woman's mouth curved up slightly. "Don't bother, Murphy," she said dryly. "I've got friends in the South. Good friends. And besides, I know who you are."

Colin looked her up and down, narrowing his eyes. She probably played that killer body the same way he played his accent, and to a hell of a lot better effect, too. So who the hell was she? "What can I do for you, Leighton?" he asked bluntly, his accent still present, but considerably less so.

"I'm a private investigator. Very private. In fact, I have only one client, and he's sleeping at a compound not far from here."

Colin let his surprise show on his face. "You're with the vampires?"

"I am. And I'm sure you know why I'm here."

"I know a whole bunch of trucks drove through this town two nights ago."

"And you were there when Mariane was attacked."

"Afterward," he amended sharply. "By the time I arrived, whoever had attacked her was gone."

"Forgive me," she said, and seemed to mean it. "I didn't mean to imply anything. Wei Chen and Loren have both vouched for you and your honesty."

"Is Mariane okay? I wanted to call an ambulance, but Jeremy—"

"Mariane's doing well, considering. Jeremy taking her to the compound really was the best course, Mister Murphy."

"Colin," he said. "No need for formality between us, is there?"

She grinned, the first honest, uncalculated thing she'd done so far. "Formalities aside, then. I'm here because I need to see the crime scenes—all three of them—in daylight."

Colin frowned. "Crime scenes?"

She tilted her head at him. "I thought we'd moved past this, Murphy."

He shook his head, puzzled. "No, I mean, I understand you want to see Jeremy's place. I don't think he's been back there since it happened, but, crime scenes, as in plural?"

She studied him intently. "You don't know," she said, making it a statement not a question.

"Know what?" he snapped.

"About Marco and Preston."

"Marco? What about Marco?"

"You knew him?"

"*Knew* him? Why are you talking in past tense? Has something happened to Marco?"

He saw a flash of sympathy in her eyes. "Marco's dead," she said quietly. "And so's Preston. Both of them murdered, presumably by the same people who attacked Mariane the other night."

Colin felt a hard stab of grief, his jaw tightening as he stared at her. "When?"

"Two days before Mariane was attacked. Both Marco and Preston on the same night. I'm sorry. I thought you knew."

"No." He inhaled deeply, looking away from her too perceptive gaze.

"You were friends?"

"With Marco, not Preston. He had horses and my dad's a trainer back in Georgia. Marco ordered some equipment from a tack shop a while back, and I saw him loading the stuff into his truck. We rode together sometimes." He shook his head. "Dammit. Are you sure he's dead?"

"Very," she said, nodding once. "There's no mistaking something like this."

"Fuck."

"What about Preston?"

"I didn't know him," he repeated. "Marco mentioned him once or twice, but that's it."

"Did you know where they lived?"

"Marco, for sure. Like I said, we rode together—his horses, I don't have any here. Wait, what happened to the horses? He loved those animals."

"They've been taken care of. They were sent to a ranch in Wyoming," she added at his skeptical look. "Vampires have no interest in horse flesh or blood."

Colin shrugged unapologetically. "What I know about vampires wouldn't fill a single page, Leighton."

She gave him a half smile. "My knowledge is somewhat more extensive. I'd like to see all three crime scenes. Can you take me there?"

"Sure. I've got a roster inside. Let me look up Preston's address and we'll get going."

"A roster? It lists everyone?"

"Everyone I know of," he said over his shoulder as he strode into the small office.

"Who has access to something like that?"

Colin stopped and looked at her. "No one but me, I guess. It's on a computer, a laptop I take home with me every night. Why?"

"From what Jeremy's said, the two of them were pretty open about where they lived. They were new to the area, and Mariane even shopped here in town. But Marco and Preston shouldn't have been that easy to find. If someone got hold of your roster there—"

"Darlin', this is a small town. Everyone knows everything," he muttered, not looking at her as he brought up the file on his computer.

"Apparently not, *stud*, since *you* didn't even know Marco and Preston were dead."

Colin looked up, his eyes narrowing in irritation. "You're right," he agreed finally. "And I'm sorry about the *darlin.* It's a habit."

"Yeah, okay. Truce. We've got bigger fish to fry anyway."

Colin stood and grabbed his windbreaker from the back of the chair. "Damn right. There's something going on in this town, and I intend to find out what it is."

* * * *

They took his Tahoe and headed for Jeremy's place first. It was closest to town and they passed right by Colin's house on the way, which meant he had the chance to stop and grab some more firepower.

"Planning to invade a small country there, Murphy?" Leighton asked, eyeing the Benelli as he laid it on the backseat. He'd invited her into his house, but she'd chosen to wait by the car, muttering something about "throwing fuel on the fire." Whatever the hell that meant.

"I don't know about you, Leighton." He closed the back door of the truck and opened the front. "But when I'm dealing with vamps, I like to go armed for bear."

"No argument from me," she said easily. "Although my personal choice of weapon focuses more on the load rather than the delivery system."

He gave her a puzzled look as he slid back into the driver's seat and turned the ignition key. "I thought you worked with these guys."

"I do."

"Yeah, so?" He whipped into a fast 180 turn and headed up his driveway to the main road.

She gave him a sideways smile. "Not all vampires are created equal, Murphy. There are all different kinds, just like the rest of us."

Colin shrugged and turned onto the highway toward Jeremy's. "Makes sense, I suppose, since they all *started* the same way as the rest of us, right?"

"That's very enlightened of you."

"Yeah, well, I do what I can, ma'am," he said with an exaggerated drawl.

She laughed, but sobered almost immediately, fingers tapping nervously on the door frame next to her. "Vamps didn't do this, though," she said thoughtfully. "It happened in daylight, for beginners. You have any idea which of your fellow citizens might be a little less enlightened than you are?"

Colin shook his head, frowning. "When this thing with Mariane happened, I figured it had to be someone from outside. We get a lot of people passing through—tourists, people looking to commune with nature, loggers. This is a small town and it just doesn't sit right that someone I know could have done what was done to that little girl. Besides, judging by what I saw in that house and . . . well, Mariane's condition, I'm pretty sure there was more than one of them there that day. To my way of thinking, that makes it even less likely that it was locals. People around here know Mariane and they like her." He slowed slightly, making the turn onto Jeremy's drive. "But now you tell me that Marco and this other guy Preston were killed, and it makes me wonder how well I really know the folks I live with."

"This is a pretty wild area," Leighton offered. "Could be all sorts of people hanging around in the woods and you'd never know it."

He gave her a sharp look as he pulled up in front of Jeremy's house. "You know something I don't?"

She scoffed lightly and gave him a toothy grin. "Probably all sorts of things." She showed him both hands and said, "I'm going to check my weapon. Don't panic, okay?"

It was his turn to scoff as she pulled a Glock 17 from her shoulder rig, checked the magazine and worked the slide before securing it back beneath her jacket.

"Panic isn't a word in my vocabulary, dar' ... Leighton," he said with a shit-eating grin of his own.

"Good to know," she said, opening her door. "That might come in handy in the next few days."

Walking around to the back of the house, he saw that someone had boarded up the broken windows and replaced the shattered door with a makeshift replacement and a heavy padlock. Leighton produced a key to the lock, which told him it was probably Jeremy who'd arranged the temporary repairs, or at least someone who cared about him and Mariane.

Inside, she barely looked at the room where Mariane had been savaged, heading instead for Jeremy's office, where she looked around, carefully examining what to his eye was the utter destruction left behind. Furniture had been tossed or tipped over, computers smashed and paper was strewn everywhere.

"You looking for something in particular?" he asked finally.

She gave him an absent look. "Hmm? No, just looking. More curiosity than anything else." She turned her hands over, scowling at the grime clinging to them. "Let me wash my hands, and then I'm done here, if you are."

Colin watched as she washed at the kitchen sink. "Jeremy's daytime hiding place, right?"

She turned off the water and grabbed some paper towels before turning to give him a careful look. "What?"

He smiled knowingly. "Whoever did this tore the house apart. There was equipment they could have fenced for good money, but instead they trashed everything. And Mariane—" His lip curled. "I found her, Leighton. She wasn't just raped; she was tortured. They wanted something from her, and I'm guessing that something was Jeremy. They didn't find him, even though he was close enough to scare the shit out of me within minutes of sundown. Now, we're either working together, or we're not. I'm not asking for any deep vampire secrets, but I like to know I can trust the person I'm working with."

Leighton stared at him for a long minute, then drew a thoughtful breath and exhaled noisily. "You have a point," she said slowly. "So, yes, Jeremy's daytime resting place is under that floor. I'm guessing the vamps who boarded up the house moved some stuff around to conceal its location, since the house isn't really secure anymore. But, truthfully, even knowing where it was, I can't get inside. Which is why Jeremy's still alive."

"What about Marco?" he asked, as they locked the door once again and headed for his truck.

"He and Preston both built their houses a while ago, and I'm betting neither one of them had updated their security."

Colin shook his head, then stopped, eyeing the ground around his truck. "There've been a lot of vehicles here recently. Your guys?"

Leighton nodded. "Lord Raphael's security team was out here night before last, and some others came out last night to pick up some things for Jeremy. They're also the ones who boarded the place up," she added, gesturing toward the house.

"*Lord* Raphael?" he repeated, not bothering to hide his skepticism.

She gave him a sidelong glance. "You better believe it. In the vampire world, he controls all of the U.S. west of the Rockies, plus a big chunk of the mountains themselves."

"What the hell does that mean, *controls*? I've never ever heard of him. How powerful can he be?"

She shrugged, unconcerned. "That's because you're not a vampire. If you were, believe me, you'd know about him, because, living here, he'd be the only thing between you and instant death."

Colin frowned.

"Trust me on this one. He's scary powerful. But you can judge for yourself tonight. You've got that meeting at the compound. He'll be there."

"Fantastic," he muttered, as they climbed back into the truck.

Neither of them said much on the way to Marco's. For his part, Colin was not looking forward to seeing the place with Marco gone. Not that they'd been close, not like his friends from back home, and sure as hell nothing like his buddies from the SEAL teams. But they'd both loved horses—not just riding them, but the simple beauty of the animal. Marco had been so pleased to find someone he could talk to, someone who understood the fine points of horse breeding and training the way Colin did. Colin may not have taken up his father's business, but he'd been raised on the family's ranch, had worked in the barns almost from the day he took his first step until he'd walked away and joined the Navy. He'd gone into the service partly because it was the last thing anyone expected of a boy from Georgia who'd been nothing but trouble all through high school. But he'd also done it to escape his father's determination to control every aspect of his youngest son's life.

It had been a surprise for Colin to discover he could still enjoy talking about the family business and he would miss those conversations with Marco.

"You said a security team was out at Jeremy's," he said, breaking the silence. They visit Marco's place too?

She nodded. "Night before last, same as Jeremy's and Preston's."

"So, why—"

"I need to see for myself in daylight so I can tell what I'm looking at."

Colin nodded. Made sense to him. Although, to be honest, he still didn't know what to make of Leighton. She seemed to be just what she claimed, a private investigator hired by the vamps to look into these crimes. She didn't swarm all over his crime scene like some sort of drama queen pretender, and she didn't wave her gun around like an amateur. Neither one of her guns. He'd noted the backup piece in the small of her back before they'd left town.

And his confusion wasn't just because she was a woman, either.

He'd served with plenty of females in the military, some good, some not, just like the men. But none of them had looked like a fucking fashion model or wore a diamond wedding ring that even his untutored eye knew was worth more than most people's annual salary. Not to mention showing up and claiming to work as a private investigator for vampires. How did one get a gig like that anyway?

He drove around the final curve to Marco's house, tree branches skimming the roof of his truck. Marco had valued his privacy. He'd never bothered to make his house anymore approachable than absolutely necessary.

Colin stopped the truck and switched off the key, staring through the windshield. The place looked abandoned already. The paddock was empty, the doors open on the small barn's vacant stalls. Even the house looked diminished somehow.

"You're sure the horses are safe."

"Absolutely," she assured him.

He drew a deep breath and shoved open the truck door. "All right, let's do this."

A few minutes later, they were in the basement of Marco's house— a basement Colin hadn't even known existed until Leighton had led him to it. All the times he'd been in Marco's place and he'd never noticed the door concealed by the den's paneling. But then, why would he?

Leighton had cruised the walls, running her hands along the joints, as if she knew what to look for. And clearly she did, because she'd given a satisfied grunt and popped the door right open to reveal a rough stairway under the house. A chain pull had turned on the overhead light, but Leighton had augmented it with a couple of halogen lamps from the duffle bag she'd thrown in the back of his Tahoe. It was bright as daylight in the basement now, which made what they were looking at even more of a surprise.

"You're a Navy SEAL, right, Murphy?" Leighton asked thoughtfully.

"Retired, but yeah."

She glanced back at him. "That makes you the expert as far as I'm concerned. What do *you* think happened here?"

Someone had blown a hell of a hole in Marco's basement wall, *that's* what had happened. Or not precisely in the wall. The target had been the reinforced door which now lay halfway on its side, warped and hanging from a single lower hinge, exposing a small insulated room beyond.

Apparently, this was Marco's daylight place, and it wasn't anything like they showed in movies. There was no coffin filled with dirt, no wax-draped wall sconces with cobwebbed candles. It was a modern, pleasant and simple bedroom with a queen-size bed and a single nightstand with a reading lamp. Or it had been before someone had trashed the place. Presumably after murdering Marco.

"Murphy?" she jogged him out of his thoughts.

"Yeah, okay. The door was heavy enough, and it had interior hinges, but it was old, and these walls . . ." He slapped one of the crumbling structures. ". . . are older than dirt and breaking up. There was probably just enough of a seam to shove some plastic explosive—I can't say what kind without chem tests—into the gap. Set the fuse and scurry back upstairs until it goes boom. A controlled explosion, blow the door off its hinges and . . . that's it." He sucked a breath through his nose and surveyed the damage. "I'm guessing Marco was pretty much helpless since they came at him during the day, right?"

"Pretty much. And he lived out here all alone, so there was no one to defend him."

"Damn waste."

"Yes, it is. Who around here had the knowledge to do something like this?"

"A lot of people. But, yeah, to answer your real question. Anyone with my kind of training sure as hell could have done it."

"Any former military besides you live in Cooper's Rest?"

"Not active, not anymore."

She raised her eyebrows, questioning.

"My buddy grew up in Coop's. It's how I ended up here, but he left a while back. He's living down in San Diego and making big bucks working for a private contractor to the Pentagon. We've got a couple of older guys who were in Vietnam back in the day. I suppose it's possible they'd have the skills for this, but I'm pretty sure they were regular infantry. Plus they stick to themselves and, from what I've heard, they're both more concerned with getting stoned than killing anyone. Whoever did this wasn't stoned."

"No," she agreed. "Whoever did this was very focused and knew exactly what he was doing."

She sighed, then checked her watch, which was an expensive but unshowy sports model. The lights caught her wedding ring again, and he tried unsuccessfully to imagine letting his wife work for vampires. Even as he thought it, he knew it wasn't a terribly modern attitude to have. Somehow, he didn't think Leighton cared much about what her husband *let* her do.

"If there's nothing else you want to see here," she said, already moving toward the first halogen lamp. "I'd like to get over to Preston's before heading back to town." She doused the light without waiting for his answer, sending half the basement into deep shadow. The second lamp quickly followed until there was only the weak gleam of the overhead bulb, turning the wreckage of Marco's hideaway into nothing more than a black chasm of darkness beyond the dim, yellow glow.

Colin took a last look around the place where Marco had died and pulled the chain on the overhead, dropping the basement into darkness once again.

A short drive took them to Preston's house, which was more of the same. Different on the outside, there was no paddock or barn, but the basement could have been Marco's, right down to the method used to destroy the nearly identical safe room.

"It's like the same guy built both places," Colin remarked, as they walked around to the back of his truck.

"Maybe he did," Leighton said. She watched while he opened the cargo hatch, then hoisted her duffle inside. "The two of them moved up here at pretty much the same time. They never lived together, the way some vamps do, but they were friends. So, it's very possible they had the same contractor build their daylight rooms. Probably a vampire, since they wouldn't trust a human with that kind of knowledge. Either that or they killed the human as soon as he finished."

Colin stopped with his hand still on the open hatch overhead. "You're joking, right?"

"Sure, if that makes you feel better." She stepped back, so he could close the cargo door.

He studied her narrowly, trying to figure out if she was serious.

She saw him watching her and smiled. "Don't worry, Murphy. It was probably a vamp builder, anyway. Come on, I need to get back to town and pick up my car."

Colin walked down his side of the truck and slid behind the wheel. "You gonna be at the big meeting tonight with this guy Raphael?" he asked as Leighton settled into the passenger's seat and reached for her seat belt.

"Wouldn't miss it for the world," she said. "I don't think he's going to be too happy with me, though." She clicked the seat belt home. "Or you, either."

Colin paused in the act of turning the ignition to stare at her. *What the hell did that mean?*

Chapter Fourteen

Raphael woke to the scent of Cyn, warm and fresh from the shower, still smelling of soap and water and the light scent of her shampoo. Her skin was satiny smooth as she curved her body around his, her soft, full breasts a delightful weight against his bare chest, and her legs caressing his. She lay on top of him, kissing his closed eyes, her mouth lingering on his lips in invitation.

He stroked his fingers through her silky hair and down over her back. She hummed with pleasure, arching against his touch. Without warning, he tightened his hold and reversed their positions, so she was beneath him.

She smiled, raising her eyes to meet his . . . and sucked in a breath, freezing to stillness at the anger he knew she had found there.

"Did you think I wouldn't know?" he asked with a deceptive calm.

Her expression flashed through a series of emotions—surprise, guilt, even defeat briefly—before finally settling on her usual angry defiance. "I needed to see for myself, dammit."

He pushed away from her and rolled off the bed, heading toward the shower.

"Where are you going?" she called after him, her tone conveying both disbelief and outrage.

He spun around at the bathroom door, his eyes flashing silver sparks in the darkened room. "Does it ever occur to you that I have good reasons for what I ask of you, Cyn? That perhaps I understand certain dangers better, that there might be enemies who would use you against me?"

"Of course, but—"

"But. There is always a *but*, isn't there? Always an excuse to do what you want, regardless of my wishes."

She jumped out of bed and strode across the room to confront him. "I'm not one of your vampires, Raphael. I don't have to follow your rules. Besides, I'm fully capable of defending myself, and I wasn't alone. That local police guy, Colin Murphy, was with me."

"Is that supposed to make me feel better? To know that my mate is spending the day with another male while I sleep alone? As you would say, fan-fucking-tastic."

"Don't be childish. You know perfectly well—"

"Childish? Perhaps you should look up the definition." He took a step back into the bathroom and closed the door, securing it with a small jolt of his power to keep her from trying to continue their argument in the shower. Her body was far too appealing and he didn't feel like being coaxed out of his temper tonight.

Raphael lingered in the shower longer than usual, just to make her wait. Even through the closed door, he could hear her muttering dire threats against him the entire time. He found it amusing overall and returned her angry glare with a bland smile when he finally surrendered the bathroom. He dressed while she showered and was knotting his tie when she finally came out, wrapped in a modestly big towel, as if she hadn't been naked in bed with him less than an hour before.

"The towel's a good look for you," he commented. She flipped him the finger over her shoulder and he laughed.

"Asshole," she hissed.

He crossed to the bedside and picked up his watch, fastening it over his wrist as he watched her across the width of the bed. "How much longer will I be forced to endure these little power plays of yours, Cyn?" he asked. "How much longer before you no longer feel the need to set yourself apart from me, to prove that you can do without me?"

She spun around, and he could read the truth in her eyes before she drew a breath to deny it.

"Be honest with yourself, if not with me, *lubimaya*. I'll see you upstairs."

* * * *

Duncan was waiting for him when he emerged from the private corridor, standing with his back to Raphael, his attention seemingly on Wei Chen who was deep in conversation with a human woman near the front doors. Juro was looming over the pair, looking very unhappy and increasingly impatient. The woman's presence violated one of the basic rules for Raphael's security on this trip—no humans were permitted within the compound after sunset unless they were mated to one of the vampires, or their presence was specifically cleared by Juro or Duncan.

As Raphael came up to Duncan, the woman glanced up, said something to Wei Chen and departed, shouldering a backpack not unlike what Cyn frequently carried.

Duncan spun around smoothly and greeted him. "Good evening, my lord."

"Duncan." Raphael said absently, frowning at the trio near the door. "Who was that?"

"She works for Wei Chen, I believe."

Raphael stared at the woman's departing back as Juro and two of his vampires escorted her down the outside stairs and toward the parking area.

"What's the status on the security system check?" he asked, turning his attention back to Duncan.

"Maxime is already on the ground, my lord," Duncan replied, referring to Raphael's computer security specialist. "She left L.A. just before dawn and daylighted on the tarmac in Seattle." He checked his watch. "She's too young to be awake yet, but soon. The extra guards you requested flew in with her. By the end of tonight, we'll have tripled

Wei Chen's human and vampire guard presence around the clock."

"Elke is with them?" As the only female member of Raphael's personal security team, Elke was frequently assigned to guard Cyn, and he wanted her here as an added precaution.

Duncan nodded. "Under protest, of course. You know how she feels about flying during the day."

"She can protest all she wants. I want her here." He paused briefly at the sound of the elevator coming up. The hallway doors opened behind him and Cyn stomped across the room toward the dining hall without a word. He smiled grimly at Duncan's look of surprise. "Cynthia went exploring earlier today," he said dryly.

Duncan raised his eyebrows expressively. "Alone?"

"No. Apparently, she rendezvoused with the local police force."

"I see."

Raphael saw Wei Chen approaching over Duncan's shoulder and nodded for him to join them.

"Good evening, Sire," Wei Chen said in his quiet voice. "I thought you'd want to know that all of our people will be within the compound shortly. The last few from Seattle are leaving their homes as we speak. Once your presence was known, everyone came immediately. It was only the distance that kept the Seattle people holding until this evening."

"Understood."

"When is this police person due to arrive?" he asked Wei Chen.

"At any moment, my lord. Loren told him—"

Duncan interrupted Wei Chen's account by nodding and holding a hand to his earpiece to indicate someone was calling him. Raphael watched expectantly.

"He just arrived at the gate, my lord," Duncan murmured, still listening to the voice in his ear. "Juro will escort him in."

Raphael bared his teeth in a shark's grin. "Excellent. Invite Sophia to join us, but give us a few moments with Mister Murphy first. I'm eager to meet the man who spent the entire day alone with my Cyn."

Chapter Fifteen

Colin lowered his window and eyed the hulking security guards who rushed to surround the truck. These weren't the usual compound guards. He didn't know the regular guys personally, but he'd been here a time or two and this wasn't them. In fact, he didn't recognize a single face. The guard at his window—vampire, obviously, given the bright red gleam of his eyes in the reflected glow of the gate lights—studied his license photo carefully, checking it more than once as the others flashed lights into the backseat of his truck and lifted the cargo hatch door. Under any other circumstances, Colin would have objected to the search. But not tonight. These boys were deadly serious and he had a feeling they wouldn't bother with fine distinctions if it came right down to it.

The vamp at his window barked something in a language other than English and two of the others dropped out of sight as they checked his undercarriage. They were all using dim flashlights with a yellowish glow like a fog light, and they covered the lenses with their fingers, so only the tiniest sliver of light leaked out. Night sight, he realized. He knew vamps were supposed to have unparalleled night vision—in fact, Leighton had said something about it earlier—but he'd never seen it used like this before.

The two vamps checking his undercarriage popped back into sight and snapped something in that same language. The guard at his window shoved his ID back at him and told him in heavily accented English to pull through the gate and park, indicating a small paved area a ways up the driveway and to the right.

Colin took his time, sliding his license into his wallet and his wallet into the zippered inside pocket of his windbreaker. He nodded politely, put the truck in gear and rolled slowly through the gate. Usually, he drove right up to the main building and parked there. But apparently there were new security measures for the big honcho's visit. So he pulled into the designated area, noting as he did so that his was the only vehicle there. So, not a lot of visitors. Or maybe it was just not a lot of human visitors, because he could see the main building from here and there was plenty of activity inside. Every light seemed to be lit and there were quite a few people moving around behind the big glass doors. Even the upstairs windows showed movement, the people there little more than shadow shapes behind the heavily frosted glass.

Turning off the engine, he grabbed the keys and opened the truck door, assuming someone would—

"Mister Murphy."

Colin considered himself a big man. At six, four and two-hundred thirty pounds, he outclassed most people he encountered, even in the military. But the giant standing in front of him was huge. Sumo wrestler huge, but without the flab, and wearing a three thousand dollar suit. Seven feet of hard muscle and black, unflinching eyes which held a faint golden glow as they regarded Colin.

"Yes," Colin answered, although it hadn't been a question.

"Are you armed?" the Japanese vampire rumbled.

"Yes, I am. I'm a licensed security consultant for the town of Cooper's Rest and, as such, authorized to carry at all times."

He thought he saw a slight softening of the giant's mouth, as if something Colin said was amusing. "That may be, Mister Murphy. But you are no longer *in* Cooper's Rest and you will not be permitted to carry a weapon into my master's presence."

Colin kept his face carefully blank. *Master?* Neither Loren nor Wei Chen had ever called anyone "master." He seriously considered— for about two seconds—throwing his hands up on the whole deal and walking away. He didn't need this shit. He certainly didn't need to walk into a building full of vampires without even his sidearm for protection. But he really wanted to know who was behind the attack on Mariane, and he honestly doubted that, whoever this "master" was, he intended to serve Colin up as a light supper.

Colin sighed. "Can I leave it in my truck then?" he asked.

"Certainly."

Holding up his empty hands, he slowly pushed his windbreaker off his right hip, unsnapped his holster and gun from his belt and, opening the truck door, leaned in and deposited it in the console compartment.

"No other weapons?" The giant vamp asked, eyeing him up and down with that remarkable night vision. "No backup piece?" he added.

Colin jolted a bit at the colloquialism coming out of the Sumo wrestler's mouth, but he shook his head. "Didn't think I'd need one," he said, waiting calmly beneath the vamp's scrutiny.

"Very well. Follow me."

As they started up the curved driveway, the vampire spoke into a throat mike that Colin hadn't noticed before. He didn't catch the words, but he didn't have to. The giant had just told someone inside that they were on their way.

Loren was waiting for them just inside the door. He stepped forward immediately and shook Colin's hand. "Colin, good of you to come."

Colin gave the security chief a bemused smile. "I could hardly refuse, could I? Besides, I'm sure we all want the same thing. To stop whoever's doing this."

"Absolutely."

"I notice you've got a lot more security out there tonight. Have there been more attacks?"

"No, no. Nothing like that," Loren assured him, glancing at the vampire hulking behind Colin. "Just a precaution."

"Leighton told me about Marco, Loren. And Preston. I was kind of surprised no one thought to let me know. Especially about Marco."

Loren had the grace to look uncomfortable. He'd known that Colin and Marco were friends. "My apologies, Colin. We weren't certain what was happening and—"

A cool voice interrupted. "Loren was told not to share that information, Mister Murphy."

Loren stiffened to attention like a sailor fresh out of RTC, twitching visibly as he spun around to face the speaker. "Duncan," he said. "This is—"

"Colin Murphy," Colin interrupted, holding out a hand, even as he studied the newcomer—Duncan—curiously. He was broad-shouldered, but shorter than Colin, an even six feet, maybe six-one, and he wore the same sort of tailored suit the Sumo wrestler was wearing. Obviously a uniform of sorts.

The vampire noticed Colin's open appraisal and smiled crookedly, his brown eyes lighting up with a very human warmth. But he was definitely a vampire for all that. And judging by Loren's reaction, not just any vampire either. This guy Duncan was *somebody*.

He gave Colin's hand a friendly shake, using enough pressure to make it felt, but not enough to intimidate. *Careful, calculated*, Colin thought.

"My name is Duncan," the blond vamp said unnecessarily.

No last name, no title, Colin noted and shrugged inwardly.

Duncan turned slightly and gestured across the great room to where he saw Cynthia Leighton disappearing between a huge set of open double doors.

"Lord Raphael is waiting for us," Duncan explained.

Well, okay. Apparently, Colin was about to meet the head honcho. What was it Leighton had said this afternoon? That this guy ruled most of the Western United States? Including part of the Rockies. Mustn't forget the Rockies. He frowned when he remembered what else she'd said. That the big honcho wasn't going to be happy with her . . . or with Colin either.

Chapter Sixteen

Raphael sat in the same chair as the night before, well aware of the dramatic setting created by the panoramic wall of glass behind him. The moon was full tonight and for once in this perpetually rainy place, the clouds were only scattered, so the moon's silver glow lit the sky, making it seem more blue than black.

With his own people securing the gate and grounds, there was no need for additional security inside the room, so there was nothing between him and the wall of glass but empty space.

He settled back into the big chair, watching as Cyn entered and remained standing against the far wall, regarding him narrowly. He met her gaze and raised a single eyebrow in question. She rolled her eyes in response, but pushed away from the wall and strode across the room, standing in her usual place to his right, but far enough away that he couldn't touch her easily.

She held her position, stiff and unyielding, for a few minutes, then sighed audibly and sidled nearer, speaking in a voice meant only for his ears. "He didn't know about Marco and Preston until I told him. He said he and Marco were friends."

"Do you believe him?"

She thought about it a moment, then said, "Yes."

"Thank you, my Cyn," he murmured and stroked one finger down the back of her thigh, closer now that she'd shifted in order to talk with him.

The muscle beneath his finger tightened and she huffed out a disgusted breath. But she didn't move away.

He bit back a smile, looking up when he heard footsteps approaching the room. His smile had disappeared altogether by the time Duncan appeared between the doors with Colin Murphy in tow.

* * * *

Colin followed Duncan into a really large and nearly empty room. The far wall was nothing but glass with a million dollar view down across the valley and probably all the way to the bay. It was spectacular, but his gaze quickly fell instead to the black-haired vampire sitting in a big chair in front of the window. Every nerve in his body jolted straight into the classic fight or flight reaction. Years of training, of experience on the deadliest battlegrounds in the world, were screaming at him to defend himself, to draw the fucking gun he didn't have, put a wall at his back and get the hell gone. Forget the big Sumo wrestler behind him, forget Cynthia Leighton with her guns and Duncan with his watchful, human eyes. Lord Raphael, and it *had* to be him, gave off a vibe so strong it crushed against Colin's chest like three hundred pounds of iron on a bench press. Some instinct deep inside his hindbrain, maybe something left over from his primitive ancestors who'd looked to the gods for protection from the natural world, wanted him to drop to his knees and pledge undying fealty.

But Colin Murphy didn't kneel to anyone, and he'd pledged his loyalty to his country and his team long ago. It was everything he could do to hold that cold, black stare, but he did it, forcing himself to stay cool. No problem here. Just a meeting with the local vamps. *Like hell.*

The pressure dropped away and Colin breathed what he hoped was a subtle sigh of relief. The damn vampire was regarding him with veiled amusement and Colin knew it could have been much, much worse. He felt a surge of anger at the knowledge he'd been toyed with, but gritted his teeth and said nothing. That was another lesson he'd learned in the military. There were times when you just had to grin and bear it.

Like when you were facing down a vampire who could squash you like a bug. Come to think of it, now that the games were over, that was pretty much the look Raphael was giving him, like he was something unpleasant that had ended up smashed against his windshield.

With the pressure more or less off, Colin took the opportunity to check out the surroundings, which was what he should have been doing instead of staring at the view. Lord Raphael was sitting in a huge chair placed right in front of that spectacular wall of glass. Was it arrogance that put him there where a good sniper's bullet could take him out? Hell, maybe bullets couldn't touch this guy. But bulletproof or not, Colin was going with arrogance, because this guy had it in spades. Colin had faced down some tough assholes in his time—drug dealers, tribal leaders, hell, even a terrorist or two. But none of them held a candle to the vampire sitting in front of him.

He gave the rest of the room a quick scan. There were clusters of furniture scattered throughout, but only the area directly around Raphael was occupied. Wei Chen sat on a short, leather couch to Colin's left, along with Loren. Jeremy was present, too, sitting on one of three matching chairs to the right. The other two chairs were empty.

Colin nodded at Jeremy. "Jeremy, how's Mariane?"

"She's recovering," the vampire said stiffly. "Thank you."

Colin shifted his gaze back to Raphael. Duncan had taken up a position to the big guy's left; Cynthia Leighton stood on his right, close enough that her leg brushed up against the chair arm where . . . *Ah shit.* No wonder Leighton had said Raphael wouldn't be happy with him. They were an item. *Hell, no,* he thought, remembering the ring on her finger. Not just an item. They were fucking married or whatever it was vampires did. And Colin had spent the whole day alone with her.

He raised his eyes to meet Raphael's again. The vampire lord curled his lips into a smug smile, clearly having noticed Colin's *ah shit* moment. Raphael blinked lazily and said, "My Cyn tells me you knew Marco."

Colin didn't miss the possessive pronoun. A potted plant wouldn't have missed the fucking possessive pronoun.

"We were friends," he said, nodding.

"Indeed. An interesting man, Marco. His family was Spanish aristocracy, you know. A direct lineage to Queen Isabella."

"*Very* interesting," Colin agreed, "since Marco was Italian and his family were merchants. He had a genealogical chart hanging in his living room, said it reminded him of where he came from."

The smile was more genuine this time. "You were right, my Cyn," Raphael said to Leighton, although he never stopped looking at Colin. "Have a seat, Mister Murphy." He indicated the empty chair next to Jeremy. "Loren, ask Sophia to join us."

Colin headed for the chair closest to the door, leaving the one between him and Jeremy vacant. It was a classic guy move, but that wasn't why he'd done it. It was just good tactics to get as far away from Raphael and as close to the door as possible.

His ass had just hit the chair when the doors opened and Loren returned, followed by a dark-haired woman. She was short and curvy, her dark head turned toward Juro, murmuring her thanks as he held the door open until she was through, then pulled it closed behind her. She took a graceful step into the room, her gaze going left, skimming over Wei Chen and Loren, before turning large brown eyes toward Colin where they widened into a disbelieving stare.

Colin stood, his heart slamming against his chest wall.

"Sophie?" he whispered.

Chapter Seventeen

Sophia stared at Colin Murphy, the last man she'd ever expected to see again. He was her one and only regret, the only human she'd truly loved through her centuries as a vampire. And what the hell was he doing here? He was from the South somewhere. She couldn't remember where exactly, but she did remember that slow, lazy drawl in his deep voice, the way he whispered delicious things to her as his hands did . . . She snapped herself back to the present, shocked at her reaction after all this time. She was aware of everyone in the room watching them, could feel Raphael's stare all but drilling a hole in her head. This was the last thing she needed.

"Colin," she managed. "How are you?"

He just stared at her, anger replacing disbelief, darkening those striking blue eyes of his. She remembered that, too. The way his eyes darkened with emotion as he thrust deep inside her, filling more than just her body, filling her soul, making her feel so alive, so treasured, so . . . loved. *Meu Deus*, she couldn't do this now. She tore her gaze away from him, taking the two steps forward that would take him out of her sight, out of temptation. She bowed from the waist to Lord Raphael, feeling too unsteady to achieve anything close to the grace required for a curtsey.

"My lord," she said.

Raphael was studying her with shrewd eyes that saw everything. He had already been suspicious of her, wary that she'd shown up out of nowhere claiming to be searching for Lucien. And now there was Colin, who was apparently the local sheriff they'd been talking about. This could only make Raphael suspect her even more. She met his gaze evenly, having nothing to hide. He tilted his head toward her in silent query.

"Colin . . . that is Mister Murphy and I knew each other several years ago, my lord. In another country. I didn't know he was living in this area now." *Or, Lucien be damned, I never would have come here*, she thought to herself.

Raphael watched her a silent moment longer, then said, "We're going to Vancouver tonight, Sophia."

Sophia blinked in surprise, taken aback enough that all thoughts of the man standing behind her fled. Raphael was going to Vancouver? Crossing into Lucien's territory without invitation? Her back stiffened in outrage. Who the hell did he think he was? She glared at him, not bothering to conceal her anger, but fighting against the instinctive desire to lash out with her power, to slap him down for such an insult to her master. Because to do so would have been suicide, and Sophia was not ready to die. Not for this, and not before she knew what had happened to Lucien.

And not before she had a chance to talk to Colin.

She bowed her head slightly to Raphael. "I will accompany you, my lord," she said, as if he hadn't pretty much ordered her to do so.

A smile played around his lips. "Excellent. We leave in half an hour. First, however—" He paused as Duncan leaned down and whispered something in his ear. "A minor change of plans. We'll leave for Vancouver as planned. For the rest, however . . . please excuse us, Mister Murphy. Some business has arisen which I must take care of. We do appreciate your cooperation in this investigation, however. Cyn will contact you later regarding our mutual efforts to locate the killers."

Raphael stood, gesturing to the human woman who, Sophia had discovered, was far more than the vampire lord's arm candy; she was his mate. Vampires frequently took mates, but it was unusual for a vampire lord to do so. Or maybe that was just her experience with Lucien.

Everyone had risen when Raphael did, and now there was a general movement in the direction of the doors. Sophia looked around quickly and saw that Colin was already gone. She held back until Raphael had cleared the doors, then shoved her way past Loren and Jeremy, emerging into the great room in time to see Colin slam open the big glass door and head down the outside stairs. Rushing after him, she waited until she too was outside before calling his name.

"Colin!" His shoulders tensed, but he kept going. "Colin!" she repeated and put on a burst of vampire speed to catch up with him. She considered grabbing his arm, but circled him instead, planting herself in his path.

"Colin," she said again, meeting his furious gaze. "I'm sorry."

"Sorry?" he growled. "Sorry, Sophie? Is that the best you can do?"

"What do you want—"

"I thought you were dead," he ground out.

"I know. It was necessary."

"Necessary? What was fucking necessary about it? It's not like I put any demands on you. We weren't married. Hell, for all I know I wasn't even the only guy you were doing—"

"Colin," she protested, letting her pain show, even though she knew she had no right.

"Then why, Sophie? I went through hell, thinking I'd left you there to die. I'd like to know why."

"Because I'm a vampire! Don't you understand? What was I supposed to say?"

"How about the truth?"

"You make it sound so simple. What would you have said, Colin? What would you have done if I'd told you all those years ago that I was Vampire?"

"I guess we'll never know, will we?"

"It was impossible, what we had. Human and vampire. It would never have worked."

"It doesn't seem to stop your friend Raphael in there."

Sophia laughed bitterly. "He's not my friend. He's . . . Ai Jesus, he's the most powerful vampire I've ever met. If he wanted you dead, your heart would be nothing but pulp in his fist before you ever saw him move. Don't take him lightly, Colin. Or his mate either."

"Thanks for the advice."

He sidestepped her and started to leave, but Sophia put herself in front of him once more. "Colin."

He stared at her impatiently.

"I'm sorry. I didn't mean—"

He didn't let her finish. "Yeah, whatever. I'll see you around, *Sophia.*"

Sophia watched him walk away and knew it was the right thing to do. Again. She'd survived this long by not caring about anyone, a lesson learned from Lucien. They were two of a kind, she and her Sire. Dancing their way through life, never caring too much about anyone or anything, no strings to bind them, no untidy emotions to tug at their hearts and hold them in any one place for too long.

Colin was the only one who'd ever tempted her, with his deep voice and warm hands, his big body wrapped around her against the night's chill. He was a warrior born. It was in his bones and blood, every instinct he had drove him to protect those he cared about. And he'd cared about her. He'd loved her. And she'd loved him back. She'd gone to that café to save him. And she'd lost him instead.

She rubbed her hands up and down arms gone suddenly cold and sighed, turning back toward the main building. That long ago night was history, where it belonged. She had problems enough with Lucien and his infernal games. And apparently she was going back to Vancouver tonight. Raphael had decided it would be, and so it would. He didn't need her to cross the border, but her presence would give him the appearance of propriety. Lucien might still be alive, but he'd pretty much ceded control of his territory to her for the duration. If she invited Raphael across the border, it would serve well enough. And who was there to protest it, in any event? Not Lucien, curse his black soul.

She shivered again and hurried up the stairs, telling herself it was the damp night air making her feel so cold. It had nothing to do with the ice around her heart. Ice that had begun to crack the moment she'd seen Colin Murphy again.

Chapter Eighteen

Raphael and his people followed Loren through a nondescript metal door and down an unadorned stairway, with its flat painted walls and ordinary metal pipe handrail. The compound had an extensive basement which included the vampires' sleeping quarters, but this particular stairway had only one destination, and that was a state-of-the-art computer room, which was also the heart and soul of the security network. Raphael kept Cyn just ahead of him, with Juro between her and Loren. Duncan was behind him, just over his left shoulder, as always. The rest of his security team remained upstairs.

Maxime, his computer specialist and the vampire who had designed this particular system, had arrived from L.A. earlier and begun her assessment immediately, searching for possible breaches. Raphael wanted a minimal audience for this particular briefing, just in case.

Loren reached the bottom of the stairs and turned right down a truncated hallway. "This way, my lord," he directed.

Not that Raphael needed direction. There was nowhere else to go down here. He touched Cyn's shoulder, more for the sake of touching her than for guidance. She would be very unhappy with him again later. He'd put plans into motion to ensure her safety and he doubted she'd go along with it easily. But he wasn't going to change his mind, and he would not apologize for wanting her safe.

Ahead of him, Loren entered a nine digit code and pressed his thumb against a biometric scanner. The locking device buzzed loudly and opened with the thunk of retracting bolts. Maxime was already there, her spiky blond head bent, as always, over a keyboard, her gaze riveted to the lines of computer code rolling down the screen in front of her.

"Maxime," Raphael said.

She finished whatever she was typing and spun around with a somewhat dazed look, blinking rapidly before managing an awkward smile. "Pardon, my lord. I was—"

Raphael shook his head. "What have you discovered?" He pulled out a chair from the long table running the length of the room and offered it to Cyn, before seating himself on the one next to it.

Maxime grabbed a pad of paper covered with notes and rolled her chair up to the table backwards, spinning it around at the last moment to face them. "My lord. A primer on the nature of this system first, if I may?"

Raphael nodded his permission.

"This—" she indicated the banks of computers, monitors and security video displays around her, "—is the heart of the compound. Its main function is security, but to that end, it controls every aspect of the environmental system, from lights to air quality. Every lock on every door or window can be monitored from here, as well as the various stations on the perimeter. With a single key stroke, the entire compound can be locked down if desired. It is, and this is vital, my lord, a closed system. There is no, and I mean absolutely no, contact with the outside world. No Internet access, no outgoing line of any kind. There is a separate server, maintained in a separate office, which provides Internet access for the residents here, but there is nothing else on that server. All information of a sensitive nature, and that is defined in the broadest terms, is stored here in this room."

"Which means what?" Raphael asked, urging her along. Maxime loved her work. It was what made her so good at it, that and a truly brilliant mind. But she would go on a bit if not nudged in the right direction.

"It means no one can access the information stored here from outside the compound, or even from outside this room. It also means," she hurried on, "the database on our vampires, including names and addresses, could not be accessed by anyone who did not have authorization to enter here."

"Or someone who got into this room, whether authorized or not," Cyn qualified.

Maxime stared at Cyn blankly for a few seconds, as if trying to compute what she'd just heard. "Correct," she said finally. "But the security here—"

"Is not infallible, Max. No one's is," Cyn interrupted.

Maxime frowned. "Theoretically, that's true."

"You've checked for unauthorized access, of course," Raphael said, bringing them back to the purpose of their briefing.

"Yes, my lord. There has been none. No one not authorized entered this room. I have digital video if you would like to see it, archived for the last year, which covers virtually the entire period this compound has been functional."

"Do you have a record of who accessed the database, even if they were authorized?" Cyn asked.

"Of course. And I've checked it, as well. But I'm running a deeper scan now. It is possible, again theoretically, for a highly skilled operator, to cover his or her tracks. But not completely. If someone has illegally invaded this system, I will know within twenty-four hours. However, at this time, I would say there has been no breach of security. Your leak is somewhere else. I have the data, my lord—"

Raphael shook his head as Maxime spun back to her computer station, retrieved a thick stack of papers covered with data and spun around again, offering them to him. "No, thank you, Maxime. I trust your skills completely."

Maxime gave Cyn a triumphant look that had Cyn turning to meet his eyes with an expression of supreme annoyance. Raphael winked at her and stood. "We'll leave you to it, Maxime. Advise Duncan the moment you have anything new."

The stairs up from the basement security center left them on the first floor in a back hallway of the main building. As they headed toward the great room once again, Raphael turned to Duncan.

"Make sure Sophia is ready. And find out what you can about her history with Colin Murphy. I suspect the answer will lie in his background, not hers."

"He's a former SEAL," Cyn said, turning around and walking slowly backwards. "His records will be hard to come by."

"We'll see," Duncan said with a grin.

Cyn shook her head, smiling at Raphael's lieutenant. "Are there no secrets—"

"My lord."

Cyn spun around at the familiar voice, staring at Elke who was waiting for them at the end of the hallway. She was dressed in the typical uniform of his security forces, her pale hair and even paler skin a sharp contrast to the dark charcoal suit.

"Elke?" Cyn said in obvious surprise. "When did you get in?"

"Who knows?" the female vampire said, obviously disgruntled. "I only know the sun was shining, which means I wasn't."

Cyn shot Raphael a suspicious glance over her shoulder, clearly anticipating the reason for Elke's sudden appearance. "Well," Cyn said to Elke. "Welcome to Seattle. Have fun." She strode away quickly without looking back.

Elke watched her go, before turning to Raphael with a puzzled expression. "Was I not supposed to be here, my lord? Duncan said—"

"You are where you belong, Elke. Duncan, find Sophia and get someone started on tracing her history with Colin Murphy. I'll return shortly."

Raphael strode across the great room and down the corridor, stopping the elevator doors from closing when he was still several steps away. It took only a small exertion of his will, holding them back until he entered. He released the doors and they closed immediately. Cyn was leaning against the far wall, both hands behind her. She waited until the elevator was moving before saying quietly, "I don't need a babysitter."

"No, you don't," he agreed.

She frowned in confusion. "But Elke—"

The doors opened on their darkened suite, the vault door standing open for the night. Raphael gestured for Cyn to go ahead of him. She did so, but not without a distrustful, sideways glance as she passed in front of him.

"So why send for Elke specifically?" she asked, stopping halfway across the room to confront him.

"I asked Duncan to reinforce the security on the compound with some of our own people. Not that I don't trust Wei Chen or his guards, but mine are better."

"So, Elke's just part of that?"

Raphael closed the distance between them, brushing her body with his and cupping her face in both hands. He whispered a kiss against her forehead, her eyes, traced the soft fullness of her lips with his tongue before claiming her mouth with a long, slow kiss. She responded automatically, lifting herself onto her toes to meet him, her arms sliding beneath his jacket and curling around his back.

He gave up her mouth reluctantly, swirling his tongue over her lips and dropping several gentle, swift kisses on her mouth. "I love you, my Cyn."

Her eyes were bright with emotion when they met his. "I love you, too. You know that."

"I do."

She blinked, suddenly recognizing she should be worried. "But?"

He smiled to reassure her. "No but, *lubimaya.*"

"Don't *lubimaya* me, you sneaky bastard. I know a 'but' when I hear one."

Raphael laughed. "I told you, I've decided you're right."

"About what?" she demanded.

"About your need to move about more freely while we uncover whoever's behind these murders. I brought you here, after all, not just because I wanted you with me—"

Cyn scoffed noisily and he smiled.

"I *would* miss you, my Cyn," he chided.

"Uh huh. Go on."

"I *also* brought you with me to make use of your investigative skills. Skills which you cannot employ fully if you're pinned to my side all night and day."

She was listening to every word, clearly trying to find the catch. And there was a catch, Raphael knew. He just hadn't gotten to it yet.

"On the other hand—" he began.

"I *knew* it."

"—because your safety is far more important to me than your investigative skills—"

"I am *not* going to hide out here in the basement while you and everyone else get to—"

"I've brought in the appropriate personnel," Raphael continued, talking over her protest, "to serve as your bodyguards."

She stared at him open-mouthed. "Fuck that! That's the real reason Elke's here, isn't it? You lied to me. She *is* my babysitter."

"She is one of your *bodyguards*, just as Juro and the others are mine. You're the one who insists I need protecting. Surely one could argue the same of you?"

"It's not the same. You're the damn vampire lord! Everyone wants to take you out. No one up here even knows who I am. They—"

"Of course they do." Raphael's temper finally snapped. "Three minutes after you walked down that poor excuse for a main street, every soul in this misbegotten village knew *exactly* who you were and what you were doing here. You're being unreasonable."

"*I'm* being unreasonable? Fine. Elke can sit and watch me read all fucking night long, then. I'll just wait until the sun comes up and then go about my business. Unless you're planning on chaining me to your bed every morning, too?"

Raphael fought for patience. If any of his vampires had spoken to him thus, they'd have been groveling on the floor by now, begging for their foolish lives. But, as she pointed out to him over and over again, Cyn was not one of his vampires. And the last thing he wanted was to see her hurt. Which was why they were having this damn argument in the first place.

"I would not require anything so crude as chains to keep you here if I chose," he said at last. "However, when you leave the compound in daylight, a human guard will accompany you."

"No."

"Yes, my Cyn."

"You can't do that."

"I can."

"Fine. You go ahead, assign your little watchdog. I'll just ditch him," she retorted childishly.

"Oh, no, *lubimaya.* I know you far too well to trust your cooperation. If you *ditch* your assigned guard, there will be a price."

"I'm terrified," she drawled.

Raphael gave her a slow, satisfied smile. She saw it and gasped softly. "What?" she breathed.

"There *will* be a price, my Cyn, but you will not be the one to pay it. Your human bodyguard will. And I think we both know the price I would exact for a failure of this nature."

"You can't do that."

"Of course, I can."

"There are rules, Raphael. You can't just—"

"Ah, but, my Cyn, I am Vampire. I don't follow *your* rules."

She glared at him, hearing her earlier words thrown back at her. "Fine," she snapped, ripping off her jacket and starting on her shoulder harness. "Have fun in Vancouver. I'm not going."

"I didn't think you would," he said mildly. "Should you decide to go out later this evening, Elke will be waiting for you upstairs."

He pulled her toward him as she slipped out of her shoulder holster, drawing her in for an entirely different sort of kiss, this one hard and proprietary. She kissed him back, giving as good as she got, and finally bit his lower lip until he laughed and stepped away. He watched her lick his blood from her mouth, seeing the flush it brought to her cheeks, and felt his groin grow heavy in response.

He met her gaze, which was half angry and half aroused. "Be safe, *lubimaya,*" he said and left her there, not looking back until he was inside the elevator and the doors were almost closed. He met her eyes at the last moment and saw her lips move almost silently.

"You, too," she said.

Chapter Nineteen

Raphael came out of the elevator, locking it behind him. It wouldn't lock Cyn in, but it would keep anyone else out. Elke was waiting for him, standing in the open doors between the elevator hallway and the great room where she could see anyone coming or going from either area.

"My lord."

"She doesn't go anywhere alone," he ordered. "Nowhere, Elke."

"Yes, my lord."

Raphael met her eyes with a flat stare, emphasizing the seriousness of his order. He knew all too well Cyn's ability to talk people into things they wouldn't do otherwise, and she and Elke were friends of a sort. But he was Elke's Sire and his will would trump or heads would roll.

He put all of this into a single glance that had Elke stiffening to attention. "I will protect her, my lord. On my life."

Raphael nodded and turned his attention to Duncan, who'd crossed to his side. "Sophia is waiting outside, Sire. And our people are working on ferreting out Colin Murphy's record. Maxime insisted on doing it herself. She seemed to feel cracking the Defense Department's records would be an enjoyable exercise of her skill."

"I'd rather she focus on the possible breach of security."

"I said as much to her, but she indicated the diagnostics will run without her intervention for several hours, while the records search on Murphy would take, in her words, a fun few minutes."

"Tell her to keep in touch, Duncan. This little trip to Vancouver will probably take up most of the night."

"I've already instructed her to call as soon as she has anything."

Their conversation had taken them across the great room to where Juro waited near the entrance. At a nod from Raphael, the big vampire opened one of the heavy glass doors to admit a blast of wet, cold air.

"Lovely weather," Raphael commented.

"Yes," Duncan agreed. "Perhaps we should consider relocating from the Malibu estate."

Raphael grunted and climbed through the open door of the waiting SUV, sliding across the bench seat to make room for Duncan. "I shall give the idea all due consideration," Raphael replied.

The journey to the border was surprisingly quick. The three SUVs slowed as they neared the boundary between the U.S. and Canada, and Raphael waited to feel the press of Lucien's power against his own. It struck him that he should have sensed the first trickles of the other vampire lord's power long ago, leaking across their territorial lines. He knew with certainty that Lucien could detect *his* power from well inside the Canadian side of the border, even within his own lair. Try as they might to respect each other's sovereignty, power was not something that could be cut with a knife. There was always leakage.

But tonight, there was nothing of Lucien to be felt, not even within the border checkpoint, where they waited while the Canadian agents verified their identification. Sophia's Brazilian passport caused a small delay, but only because it was unexpected. Raphael and his people were all perfectly legal citizens of the U.S. and carried valid passports to prove it. Vampires might not consider themselves subject to human law, but neither did they flaunt it unnecessarily.

As they waited, Raphael sent out feelers, searching for Lucien, but he still felt nothing at all. He frowned, concentrating harder as they crossed the territorial line and headed toward the lights of nearby Vancouver.

"We'll go to Lucien's headquarters, Juro," he said, suddenly. "Have Sophia call ahead to prepare his staff. I don't want any pointless shows of defiance."

"Yes, my lord," Juro said and gave directions over the radio to the SUV in front of them.

Raphael paid little attention to the city as they sped through. The clouds had closed in again, cloaking everything in darkness, but the general impression was one of a typical big city, with its brightly lit business and residential towers marching right up to the water's edge. Streets and highways were full of cars and trucks, and even at this hour, they had to slow several times for traffic. There were occasional flashes of the bay, but that too was crowded, with fishing boats and warehouses.

Raphael was certain the humans who lived here were fond of their city, and he knew it had a deserved reputation for sophistication and charm. He also knew that Los Angeles was a far more crowded city. But then, he rarely had to deal with L.A.'s suburban sprawl or its packed freeways. When he thought of L.A., it was only of his estate in Malibu with the endless, empty sea stretching beyond the cliffs below his home.

As they neared the city center, Raphael finally felt the first stirring of power, so faint he would never have credited it as coming from the Canadian lord if he didn't know better. Sitting quietly in the backseat, he tried to reach out, to grab hold of the weak tendril and follow it to its origin, but it was gone, lost in a wash of general vampiric power. Most of Lucien's Canadian vampires lived here in Vancouver, and most were concentrated in the downtown area. There was a large contingent in Toronto and a smaller one in Montreal, with the rest scattered throughout the vast Canadian territory. But none of those equaled the Vancouver nest in size, simply because this was the city where Lucien spent most of his time.

Even so, it shouldn't have been possible for a vampire lord's signature to be lost among those of his subjects. Something was seriously wrong with Lucien, and Raphael was beginning to suspect he knew what it was. But first, he would have to deal with Lucien's people, who would not welcome his intrusion into their master's domain.

* * * *

Raphael studied Lucien's Vancouver headquarters when it came into view. It was a stately home, perched in the hills high above the city. Almost Victorian in appearance, it had been built just after World War I to Lucien's specifications, and it boasted balconies and gables at every turn of its three stories. Every window and door was blazing with light when the SUVs pulled up in front, as if Lucien's people were shining a beacon to guide their Sire home.

The passenger door on the front SUV popped open as soon as they came to a stop, and Sophia jumped out, hurrying through the gate and up the long walkway. The front door opened before she reached it, white light pouring out briefly before the door filled to overflowing with vampires who surged out onto the porch and down the stairs. One of the males stepped ahead of the rest, stalking toward Sophia angrily.

"Darren Yamanaka, my lord," Duncan provided. "Lucien's lieutenant."

Raphael watched the two of them arguing. Yamanaka was only average in height, but he was thickly built and trying to use his size to his advantage. Not that it seemed to be working, since Sophia didn't appear the least bit intimidated by the larger male. But then her power exceeded Yamanaka's by a considerable margin, which was all that really mattered. Raphael let the argument continue for a few moments, then shifted irritably.

"We don't have time for this," he said. Reaching to his left, he yanked the latch and shoved the truck door open on his side. Rounding the front of the truck, he pushed through the gate and came up behind Sophia in time to hear Yamanaka accusing her of betraying their master, of inviting the enemy into the heart of his territory, that enemy being Raphael himself, of course.

"Enough," Raphael said quietly, putting sufficient power into it that every vampire present heard him and obeyed.

Darren shot Sophia a killing glare before turning it on Raphael. "We will not surrender without a fight, my lord. You may kill us all, but you will pay some price at least for the theft of our Sire's life and sovereignty."

Raphael studied Darren, admiring the vampire's courage, even as he disdained the foolishness of it. "Don't be an ass, Yamanaka. If I wanted your master's territory, you'd be dead already."

The vampire's eyes flared briefly, but as he was not, in truth, suicidal, he turned his anger on Sophia, instead. "Is this how you help our Sire, Sophia? You bring his enemy to his doorstep?"

"Shut up, Darren," Sophia hissed. "I slapped you down once, and I can do it again. If you read Lucien's letter, you know—"

"What letter?" Darren asked, his anger disappearing.

Sophia opened her mouth to respond, but Raphael intervened. "Perhaps we should take this inside," he suggested. "Or is it your intent to entertain the neighbors?"

Sophia looked smug, but Yamanaka jolted at his words, darting glances at the other houses up and down the street. Granted none was closer than a hundred yards, but sound carried unexpectedly in hills like these.

"We will use Lucien's study," Sophia announced serenely and gestured toward the house in invitation.

"Excellent," Raphael agreed. He started up the walkway, his security forming a tight cordon around him, effectively brushing aside any last ditch objections by Lucien's people. Yamanaka watched broodingly as they passed and Raphael was aware of Lucien's lieutenant falling in behind as they reached the stairs.

He felt a brush of Sophia's power and heard her chide the other vampire, "Don't be a fool, Darren."

Raphael smiled grimly without looking back. He hadn't come here looking for conquest, but if Lucien was truly gone, it might not hurt to winnow the field of contenders before he left. After all, Raphael didn't want a fool sitting on his northern border.

Once inside, Sophia directed them to a narrow staircase and up to the third floor. She strode around Raphael and his security at that point, leading the way down a short hallway to a pair of closed doors. Like everything else in the house, they were old and much narrower than those found in more modern homes. But they were also well cared for and carved in beautiful detail. Sophia pushed the doors open and crossed the room, pulling aside a pair of heavy curtains to reveal the lights of Vancouver behind a set of French doors leading to the balcony beyond.

The room itself was large and filled with Lucien's papers and possessions, as well as a strong sense of the vampire lord's powerful presence. Drinking in that essence, as if Lucien himself stood in the room, Raphael went directly to the glass doors on the opposite wall and stepped out onto the balcony. Walking right up to the blackened iron railing, he gripped the cold metal and opened his senses to the unique signature that was Lucien.

What he found didn't surprise him. He'd suspected as much from the moment he'd crossed the border with its weakened defenses. But the expectation did nothing to lessen the concern that confirmation brought. He'd known Lucien wasn't dead, but this might be worse.

He felt Duncan's presence behind him. "Do you feel it?" he asked.

Duncan moved up next to him and shook his head slowly. "It's odd, my lord. I feel a definite presence, but it's . . . weakened somehow. I don't know what it is."

"No," Raphael said. "I doubt you'd recognize it. I myself have experienced it only once before, hundreds of years and thousands of miles from here."

"What is it?" Sophia's voice came from the doorway behind them.

"Fading," Raphael said.

"What does that mean?" she demanded. "I've never heard—"

Raphael spun around to face her. "Lucien is dying."

* * * *

Sophia heard Raphael's words and saw the absolute certainty in his black eyes. And she felt her heart squeeze nearly dry in her chest. Lucien couldn't die. She wouldn't allow it.

"You will find him, then," she said, not asking but telling. "If you can feel him dying, you can—"

"No," he said, pushing her back inside by the simple expedient of walking forward himself. "I'm afraid Lucien does not want to be found."

"Of course, he wants to be found. My Sire would *never* accept death that easily. He loves life far too much."

"I admit it's unlike him," Raphael agreed with an irritating calm. "Perhaps he's overcome with guilt."

He was moving around Lucien's study, picking up objects and studying them before putting them back down in the precise position he'd found them. Sophia watched him roam about as if measuring the place for new furniture—his furniture—and suddenly regretted letting him in here at all. Maybe Darren had been right.

"Tell me, Sophia," Raphael said, turning that emotionless gaze on her. "Why do you suppose Lucien sent for you?"

Sophia stared at him, not expecting the question, but keeping her own gaze every bit as flat as his. "I would assume he wanted me to find whoever had done this and avenge his people." It sounded weak, even as she said it.

Raphael gave her a patronizing smile. "Why you? Why not Darren? He *is* Lucien's lieutenant, after all, and he's already here. He knows the city better than you, and probably the people, as well. For that matter, he's far more likely to have contacts among my own vampires, something Lucien would have known to be useful. So why you?"

Sophia bristled with anger that he persisted in quizzing her, as if he knew some secret that she didn't. Or maybe she was just angry at being forced to confront the truth. No longer. She drew herself up and met his gaze directly.

"I'm more powerful than Darren," she said bluntly. "To my knowledge, I'm the strongest of Lucien's children."

Raphael shrugged. "Is that significant here?"

Sophia glared at Raphael with something close to hatred. Only a strong sense of self-preservation kept her from lashing out at him as she snarled, "Lucien intended me to be his successor. If he dies, I need to be here."

That smug smile of his grew, but there was no humor in his voice when he pinned her with those silver-struck eyes and said, "Then I suggest you act. Lucien's fading is already weakening his borders.

Before long, you'll have contenders from across the continent descending to fill the vacuum left by his absence. You are fortunate in your neighbors for now. I have no desire to expand my territory and Rajmund in the Northeast is still consolidating his power. He has no energy to spare for anyone else. But that won't last forever. And as the vulnerability grows, the signs of it will spread."

He glanced around the room, as if surveying the territory's invisible boundaries. "Someone needs to reinforce Lucien's defenses before it's too late. For now, several of you can work together, if you can get along well enough. But eventually, one person will have to step into the breach. If it is not to be you, it will certainly be someone from outside, because Darren Yamanaka is not up to the task. He'll fall to the first contender."

Raphael signaled his security people and headed for the doors to the hallway.

"Wait," Sophia demanded. She wanted answers from the big vampire lord, not lectures.

He stopped just inside the room, turning back to regard her with one eyebrow raised at her preemptory command.

"Could Lucien be a prisoner? Could someone be starving him, holding him captive?"

Raphael tilted his head to one side, as if considering her question. "It is possible," he conceded. "Lucien was ever too trusting."

Sophia expelled a long breath, part relief that Lucien might yet live, and part agony that her Sire could be starving, tortured by his captors.

"Will you be returning with us?" Raphael asked.

Sophia stared blindly for a moment, her mind struggling to take in his question on top of everything else she'd just had dumped on her. She blinked and swallowed hard, then nodded once.

"Yes," she said. "The key to finding Lucien lies in solving these crimes."

Raphael signaled to someone. "One of my vehicles will wait, so that you may confer with your fellow house members before you leave."

Sophia sank into the chair behind Lucien's desk as Raphael strode from the room, her head sinking into her hands. She didn't want this. Not the mysterious deaths of Giselle and the others, not Lucien's cryptic letter or his sudden disappearance, and sure as hell not the almost certain battle with Darren over control of Lucien's territory. She gasped out loud as the thought made itself known. There would *be* no battle for control, because Lucien was not dead, and he wasn't going to be. She didn't for one minute believe he was trying to kill himself over some ridiculous sense of guilt. The idea was laughable. Lucien had clearly been saddened by the deaths of Giselle and her young men. His letter was proof of that. But the greatest portion of his sadness was probably reserved for himself, that he had to suffer their loss and deal with the consequences.

No, she would find whoever was doing this, and she would find Lucien, too. He might need her help for a few months, maybe even a year, while he regained his strength. But then things would return to normal.

At the same time, she was forced to admit that Raphael had a point. If her Sire was to have a territory to come back to, something would have to be done right now to secure it. Somehow she and Darren—

"He's gone."

Darren's unwelcome voice announced his presence, as if he'd known she was thinking about him.

"He wasn't here very long," he said, frowning as he noticed she was sitting behind Lucien's desk . . . on Lucien's chair. "What'd he do here?"

"Nothing you and I haven't tried already, but he did it with greater success," she admitted. "I suppose that's not much of a surprise, given who he is."

Darren came around the desk, choosing to perch on its edge next to her, rather than take any of the chairs in the supplicant position in front of it. "What does that mean, greater success? Did he find Lucien?"

"No, unfortunately." She proceeded to tell Darren pretty much word for word what Raphael had explained to her.

"Fuck that," he exploded, standing up and pacing over to a book shelf and back again. "Lucien would never do anything to hurt himself. I know him."

"I agree," Sophia said, relieved to hear someone else say it out loud. "But what Raphael said about the territorial borders is true. I felt it when we came over here tonight. At first, I thought it was just because Raphael was in the vehicle right behind me, but it was more than that. And if we don't want a bunch of vultures moving in, you and I need to figure out a way to hold things together until Lucien gets back. Either that, or fight them off one by one."

Darren stopped pacing and stared at her. She could see him sizing her up, trying to decide if their earlier spur-of-the-moment contest truly reflected their relative power, or if he could take her in a straight up fight. She knew he would never have challenged Lucien. Even if their Sire came out of this greatly weakened, Darren would never go against him.

But the possibility that Lucien might die . . . that changed everything. Darren was loyal to Lucien, but he was also Vampire. And vampires were, at their core, territorial and aggressive. And if Lucien died, there was absolutely no reason to honor his preference for Sophia as successor.

Sophia stood, favoring her fellow vampire with a cool look. "I won't fight you over this, Darren." His eyes blazed with triumph and Sophia chuckled. "Not now," she added deliberately. "I believe Lucien is coming back. But if he doesn't—" She let her own power swell, let it spill into her eyes until their glow drowned out the dim lighting.

"If he doesn't," she repeated softly, meeting Darren's gaze directly. "I will fight you to the death before I let you have this territory."

Chapter Twenty

The SUVs rolled through the now deserted night, the streets quiet, but for the occasional vehicle sharing the road with them. In the distance, Raphael could hear a far away foghorn bellowing its desolate warning over and over again.

His mind was quiet, too, mulling over the night's events, but without any particular urgency. Lucien's situation was intriguing, but it no longer seemed relevant to his own hunt. There remained a simmering fury against the Canadian lord, lurking just below the surface of his thoughts. But that was for later—after he'd tracked down the killers Lucien had left on his doorstep, after their blood had fed his soldiers and their bones been reduced to ash and ground into dirt. Lucien could wait until then. He wasn't going anywhere.

Next to him, Duncan lifted a hand to his earpiece as up front Juro did the same. Raphael glanced at Duncan, who turned to him and said quietly, "Sophia is an hour behind us, my lord. They are traveling quickly and should catch up by the time we reach the compound."

"Tell them not to bother with speed limits, Duncan. I want all of my people inside and safe." And he was confident that if by chance they were stopped by the human authorities, his vampires had the skill to persuade the officer to look the other way. The ability was a requirement for every vampire included in his personal security detail.

"What are your orders regarding Lucien, my lord?" Duncan asked carefully. What he really wanted to know, Raphael thought, was what Raphael intended to do next.

"Lucien will wait, Duncan," he said. "First we avenge our own."

They met no policemen on their way home, and very few other travelers, either. The lights of the compound soon came into view, a bright spot in the otherwise dark forest.

Raphael spent a few moments conferring with Duncan and the others, but the night was already fleeing and he wanted some time alone with Cyn before sunrise.

She was asleep when he finally made it to their bed. He'd spoken to Elke before coming downstairs. She'd reported that Cyn had kept her word, that she had indeed spent the night in their quarters, not even emerging for something to eat. Raphael would have been relieved if he hadn't known her as well as he did. She'd probably been online the entire time, searching out ways to endanger herself during the day tomorrow.

He sighed as he stripped out of his suit and tie, unbuttoning his fine Egyptian cotton shirt and tossing them all into the hamper for dirty clothes. He wouldn't be wearing any of these things for the rest of this journey. Until the killers were caught and punished, his plans would not involve anything as tidy as a proper suit and tie.

Cyn had left a soft light burning on the bureau top. She'd left it for him, even though she knew he didn't need it. It had more to do with her heart than her head, which was the same reason he left it on when he secured the vault and headed for their bed. He might not need the light tonight, but she would in the morning. There was no natural light in their underground suite, no windows to announce the rising sun. But he didn't need that either. He knew the sun's progress across the sky better than any astronomer.

He approached the big bed, smiling when he saw that she slept clothed, rather than naked as they usually did. Although she was not wearing clothes so much as underwear—a tank top which clung to her breasts, outlining them in exquisite detail, and a pair of tiny panties that only served to heighten his desire. If she'd intended these things to repel his advances, she'd failed miserably.

Raphael slipped beneath the covers, wrapping an arm around her slender body and pulling her close, curling himself around her sleepy, human warmth. She murmured softly, too deeply asleep to remember her anger, and too accustomed to his presence to wake because of it. Grinning, he slid one hand along her silky skin, beneath the stretchy tank top, filling his hand with a full breast and his fingers with a plump nipple. Cyn smiled in her sleep, pushing her pretty ass into his groin and rubbing gently against his rapidly hardening cock. He growled low in his throat as his hunger for her surged along with his erection. It had been a long night and they had not parted on the best of terms. He wanted to bury himself inside her, wanted to mark her as his, to replace their anger with possession. He was Vampire and she was his mate.

Bending his head, he kissed her temple, her jaw, but softly so as not to wake her. Not yet. She stirred slightly, but only to cuddle deeper into his embrace. Raphael bared his teeth, his fangs already splitting his gums as the scent of her blood, flowing beneath her fragile skin, hit him like an anvil. She was his. She would always be his and no other's.

He sank his teeth into the satin flesh of her neck, reveling in the fleeting resistance of her vein as it popped beneath his fangs, in the first taste of her blood flowing down his throat.

Finally awakened by the rush of euphoric released into her bloodstream along with his fangs, Cyn moaned softly, whispering his name. "Raphael." She reached back to caress him, holding his head against her neck as he fed.

He rolled her nipple between his thumb and forefinger, palming her breast in a gentle embrace before stroking his hand down across her flat belly to the velvety smooth skin between her legs. The tiny bit of lace she'd worn in a halfhearted attempt to dissuade him tore easily and he shoved it out of his way, pushing it down to lay tangled against one thigh. He changed his attack then, slipping his fingers into her from behind, feeling the shiver race along her skin as he slid them in and out until she was wet and ready for him.

But Cyn didn't wait for him to take the initiative. She lifted her thigh forward in invitation, spreading her legs and pressing her ass against him, eager for the feel of his cock inside her. She whispered his name again, but full of need this time, a demand rather than a caress. her slender fingers reaching back to grasp his cock. rousing him to an even greater hunger.

Raphael brushed her hand aside, taking hold of his shaft and positioning it at the very entrance to her plush. heated core. sliding forward until he was just inside her, feeling the grip of her inner walls as she flexed against him, trying to draw him deeper.

Cyn groaned a protest, stirring fitfully within his arms. trying to force the pace of their lovemaking.

Raphael chuckled deep in his chest, the vibration traveling along his fangs, still buried in her neck, and making her shudder with renewed desire. He took his time, no longer drawing on her blood. but holding her motionless with his bite, placing his hand over her abdomen and holding her still there as well, as he teased her, sliding his cock an inch into her wetness and then out again, never leaving her completely. but never filling her either.

"Raphael, please," she whispered.

He lifted his head and growled in response. plunging into her with a long, powerful thrust, slamming deep inside her and out again, only to do it once more. Her inner walls clenched around him so tightly it was almost difficult to force his way through when she climaxed. her cries filling his ears with sweet sound, her fingers tightening in his hair and holding him close. Her orgasm finally diminished. becoming no more than a trembling of her limbs, the random convulsions of her womb rippling down and around his cock as he continued to pound into her. knowing the ecstasy of his bite was still raging in her body and she would not rest for long.

He slid his fingers over her abdomen and deep into her slick folds once more, spreading the swollen lips of her pussy and baring the eager nub of her clit, suffused with blood and hard as a pearl. He began circling it, gliding over its sensitive surface and away until she was thrusting against his hand in time with his cock. making soft. mewling noises as she sought her release yet again.

His fingers closed on her clit, squeezing softly. rubbing his thumb where it swelled eagerly begging for attention. "Oh. Jesus," she whispered. Her abdomen clenched first. and then her entire body spasmed against him. He held her tightly as the second orgasm took her and she screamed his name.

Deep inside her, his cock surged in response to her orgasm. his release boiling from his balls, racing down his cock and splashing out to fill her, marking her, claiming her as his, inside and out.

"You cheat," she muttered, when she had finally stopping shaking. when he'd covered her sweat cooled body with the blankets and kissed away the tears of her overwrought emotions.

"I was hungry," he offered.

"Bullshit. You were horny."

"That, too," he chuckled. "But only for you, *lubimaya*."

She breathed deeply, snuggling back against him and holding his hand between her breasts, burrowing deeper into his embrace. "I love you, you know," she murmured, already half asleep.

"I know," he said, feeling the sun's burning heat emerge over the horizon. "I love you, too, my Cyn."

He fought as the sun began its journey into the morning sky, wanting to warn her of what he'd learned in Vancouver. To remind her that the killers had been set on their path by Lucien, that they were targeting those most important to Raphael. And no one was more important to Raphael than Cyn. But the sunrise stole his words and fear chased him into sleep.

Chapter Twenty-One

2000, Central America

Colin strolled down the dark, narrow street, the cobbles hard and uneven beneath the sandals he wore to blend in. The sun had set hours ago, and they weren't much on street lights in these parts. The brilliant colors of the walls rising around him were mostly muted by the darkness, with the occasional ribbon of color in the light of a doorway or window. People crowded the streets around him, taking advantage of the slightly cooler evening air. The daytime temperatures were intense around here. Even he found it hot and he'd grown up in south Georgia where if the heat didn't kill you, the humidity would.

But he was feeling good tonight. Better than good, he felt great. Young, strong and healthy, an alpha male in his prime on his way to meet the most beautiful woman he'd ever met. But Sophie wasn't just beautiful, she was sexy and mysterious and smart, too. Just about everything Colin had ever wanted in a woman wrapped up in a delicious package that curved and swelled in all the right places. He picked up his pace, eager to get to the café where he knew she was waiting for him.

"Yo, Murphy." His buddy, Garry McWaters, grabbed his arm. "Slow it down there, stud. The lady will wait. Let's not call attention, all right?"

"Yeah, sorry," Colin said, somewhat sheepishly. "It's these hot nights. They always get to me."

"Reminds you of high school, huh? All those sweet, little Southern girls just dying to drop their panties for the football hero?"

Colin laughed. He was only six years younger than Garry, but in the SEALS that made a world of difference.

"Not as many panties dropped as you think, Mac," he said, using McWaters nickname. "Most of the girls in my hometown were holding out for a ring, just like their mommas taught them."

"You keep talking, Murphy. Somebody'll buy it. Here we go."

They rounded the last corner, bringing the café into sight across the public square. Despite the open space, the weekly marketplace was set up and if anything, the crowds were thicker here. He and Mac slowed even further. No one hurried in this town, and, like Mac said, they didn't want to call attention to themselves. They weren't supposed to be here. Hell, they *weren't* here. Not officially. Only a couple more days and they'd be gone for real. Back to the States. For awhile anyway.

Which was why it was so important he talk to Sophie tonight. He didn't want to lose her just because he was going home. It might take a few weeks, or even months, but he'd arrange an American visa for her, a tourist visa or whatever else he could get. She'd love it in California, where he was based with the SEALs. He knew she would.

They finally broke through enough to see the café, still halfway across the square. He searched the patio and balconies, looking for Sophie. Sometimes she waited for him there, waving through the crowds when he came into sight. But not tonight. Tonight—

He stopped, frowning. "Mac?" he said softly.

Next to him, his buddy edged away slightly, giving them each plenty of room to draw the weapons tucked into their waistbands in back. "Yeah. Looks kinda empty, don't it?"

"Shit," Colin swore softly. "I've gotta get in there, Mac. If Sophie's wait—"

The rest of his sentence was lost as the world exploded around them. Burning debris was everywhere, flying through the air like shrapnel, landing on the tables of the merchants, starting new fires among the wares displayed there. Flames were shooting out of the small café, reminding him of a Roman candle on 4th of July.

And the screams. People racing around the square almost mindlessly, like pinballs in an arcade game, knowing only that they had to escape, but not knowing how to get there. Others running from the burning building, from the torched merchandise tables, some of them on fire, some chased by friends trying desperately to help.

"We're outta here, buddy." Mac grabbed Colin's arm, tugging him back the way they'd come.

He allowed himself to be pulled a few feet, staring in disbelief, before reality crashed in on him. "Sophie!" he roared. He yanked his arm away from Mac and raced toward the burning building, jumping over injured people on the ground, their faces and limbs bloodied and burned, their clothing little more than blackened shreds.

"Sophie!" he shouted again, feeling the heat of the flames before he'd gotten within thirty yards of the cafe, sweat dripping down his face.

"Murphy!" Mac's voice was right behind him, the snap of command slowing Colin's headlong charge, but not stopping it. Not when the woman he loved—ah, Jesus, he *loved* her. Colin bent over his knees, the pain in his chest so great he thought he'd die from it. He lifted his face to the conflagration and knew no one was alive in there. Had she been inside? Had she arrived ahead of him like she always did?

"We're gone." Mac's voice was hard, no room for discussion, no arguments. He grabbed Colin by the back of the neck, bending over to talk into his ear. "I'm sorry, bud, but we're leaving. Right now."

He tugged Colin upright, turning him with brute force until they joined the rest of the people streaming out of the square. Slinging an arm over Colin's shoulders, he pulled him along, just one more walking wounded from what had surely been some drug cartel payback, a hit on someone or a message to someone else, and who cared how many innocent civilians died in the process?

Sophie! Colin dug in his heels. "I've gotta check, Mac. I gotta know—"

"You don't gotta do nothin' except keep walking. You'll call her later, check to see if she's okay, say all those sweet, Southern things. But right now, we're leaving."

Colin kept walking, putting one foot in the front of the other, Mac's presence the only thing that kept him moving. They reached another street finally, a narrow alley that led who knew where. But it was dark and cool, a welcome relief from the overwhelming heat behind them. Mac would have hustled him into its safety, but Colin turned at the last minute and saw the flames, saw someone stagger out of the building, a black corpse of a figure, screaming when rescuers rushed to help. He stopped and stared. Was that Sophie? Was she somewhere in that flaming wreckage waiting for him to save her, waiting for—

* * * *

The phone rang, jarring Colin out of the nightmare he hadn't had in years. He wiped a hand over his face and found it soaked with sweat, just like the rest of him. He grimaced, shoved aside the damp sheets and climbed out of bed, naked as the day he was born. And the damn phone kept ringing. Who the hell was calling him so early? He went into the bathroom and splashed water on his face, trying to wake up, listening to the phone ring, and in between the rings—

"Fuck." He spat the word out with feeling. That damn hound dog of Art Collard's was barking again. It drove the neighbors nuts, which was probably why his phone was ringing. Art went down into the city every once in a while and the dog didn't like being left alone. And every time it happened, his phone rang off the hook with complaints.

Oh, right, ma'am, sir. I'll get right on that. Let's slit the dog's throat and barbeque it for dinner, how's that? No more barking then, huh?

Colin smiled in spite of himself, imagining the look on the neighbors' faces if he actually said that to any of them. They all had dogs of their own. Everybody up here did. But somehow the only barking that ever bothered anyone was that big blue tick hound of Art's. Although, Colin had to admit that old John Henry's deep bellow did sound like the voice of doom.

He found his jacket lying on a chair in the living room where he'd left it and dug his cell phone out of the pocket, catching it just before it went to voice mail. "Murphy," he droned, checking his watch where it lay on the table. Okay, so it wasn't actually that early in the day, after all.

"Good afternoon to you, too, Murphy."

He pulled the phone away from his ear and checked caller ID. Cynthia Leighton. Perfect.

"What do you want, Leighton?"

"Goodness, you're in a mood. I thought maybe you'd like to help me investigate a couple of murders here roundabouts, Sheriff."

"I'm not the damn sheriff, and what do you need me for anyway? I'm sure all your super vampires can handle it just fine."

"Stop sulking, Murphy."

"I have no idea—"

"I'm coming over, so put some clothes on."

"Don't—" But she was gone already. "Son of a bitch!" he swore loudly, catching himself at the last minute from throwing the damn phone against the wall. It was a nice phone, and besides, it was a pain in the ass to replace those things.

He dropped the phone on the bar next to his watch and stood, hands on his hips, looking around his house. He'd put a lot of work into this place. The air still had that fresh wood scent from when he'd installed new kitchen cabinets just a month ago. Granted, there was a lot more to be done, but it was coming along. He liked it here. He wanted to stay here. Which meant he probably had to play along with that damn Leighton and do what he could to solve these murders. Not that he didn't want to find whoever had done in Marco and make him pay. He just didn't want to do it with vampires looking over his shoulder.

Or maybe it was one particular vampire he wanted to avoid. One who came in a curvy package with big brown eyes.

Yeah, he definitely should avoid that damn compound altogether until this was done.

"Coward," he muttered.

"Damn right," he answered his own accusation and went to take a shower.

* * * *

Colin pulled a black t-shirt over his head and slicked back his wet hair, grabbing a towel when water dripped down his back. He told himself he should get a haircut, but he'd gotten used to having it longer, especially during his last years in the Navy when they'd been out of the country more than not, and in places where a man with short hair and a bare face stood out. He'd shaved the beard as soon as he got back, but the hair was convenient.

A knock on the door drew his thoughts away from his hair. *Thank God.* Maybe he'd been lost in the woods up here just a bit too long if that's all he had to think about.

He tucked his shirt into his camos, his combat boots making a racket as he crossed the hardwood floor to his front door. He saw the black SUV outside and pulled open the door.

"Leighton," he said and looked over her shoulder where a big black guy was giving him an appraising look right back. "Who's the muscle?" he asked.

"Robbie Shields, meet Colin Murphy," she said briefly, pushing her way into his house. Apparently she was no longer worried about appearances now that her fucking *vampire* husband had sent someone along to bodyguard her. "You two have a lot in common," she added.

"How's that?" Colin asked, eyeing the bodyguard. *Robbie* was an inch or two shorter than Colin, but made up for it in sheer muscle mass. The guy's muscles had muscles.

Leighton spoke without turning, too busy scoping out his house. "Special Forces, rah, rah, all that shit. Robbie was a Ranger. Robbie the Ranger."

Colin shared a long-suffering look with his fellow warrior and gestured for the man to come in. "Rangers?"

"Yeah, man," Robbie said. He took two steps inside and they shook hands.

"I worked with a lot of Rangers during my time in. Good men."

"Leading the way," Robbie said with a big grin. "Someone's gotta clear the field for you Navy pussies."

"Well, isn't this nice?" They both turned to regard Leighton who was eyeing them sourly. "Bonding over our bullets?" she asked sweetly.

"Don't mind her," Robbie said. "She's just pissed 'cuz the big man won't let her roam around and get killed."

"As if," she dismissed. "I've got plenty of hours in the field when it comes to police work."

"Yeah? You gonna read your vamp killer his Miranda rights?" Colin asked, "Because I hadn't planned to."

She winked at him. "I knew there was a reason I liked you, Murphy."

"So, why'd you quit the LAPD?"

"You Googled me. I'm touched," she said absently, wandering into his kitchen and looking around. "Police work is too much of a boy's club, despite all the equal opportunity crap. Being a P.I. suited me better, let me work on my own. I'm not much of a team player."

"No kidding," Robbie muttered.

"You be nice, Robbie, or I'll report you to Irina," Leighton said, coming back into the living room.

"Like that'll work. Irina had nothin' but sympathy for me when she heard about this assignment."

Leighton grinned and punched him in the arm, not lightly.

Colin grimaced. "Speaking of significant others, Leighton. Raphael's your husband?"

Her smile disappeared. "Strictly speaking, he's my mate. It's a vampire thing. Kind of like a husband, though. Bossy like one, anyway. But I like to think of him as my boyfriend. It sounds cuter."

Her smile returned in full force, but Robbie started choking suddenly, covering it with a cough while Leighton pounded him on the back helpfully. Colin figured poor Robbie would have plenty of bruises to show for his bodyguard effort today. He also noticed Leighton had switched out the expensive diamond ring on her finger for a simple platinum band. Maybe she really did have some field experience, after all.

"Besides," she continued, brushing her hands together and propping them on her hips. "I like a person's first impression of me to be of *me,* not him. So . . . I've been thinking about how someone—someone human, that is—could find out where Marco and the others lived. They didn't exactly advertise their whereabouts and you're all pretty spread out here. It's not like a person could just drive down streets until they found a house. You can't even see most of these places from the main highway and half the roads go nowhere."

"Yeah, Coop's just one of several unincorporated towns up here. There's a few thousand people spread out over a couple *hundred* thousand square miles of territory. But property records are public in Washington state. Anyone with online access or a lot of time to kill could search to their heart's content."

Leighton nodded. "But that would only tell them the owner of record, not who actually lives there. Plus—and I'm trusting you to be discreet with this, Murphy—most vamps own their property under an alias, or even several different ones. When you live a few hundred years, it's sometimes necessary to make it look like the property's been sold, or the owner's died and the heirs have taken over or whatever. If nothing else, these recent murders prove the wisdom of that kind of subterfuge."

"I can see that," Colin agreed. "But if we scratch property records, I don't need to tell you that means there's most likely a leak somewhere."

"Yeah, I know. Raphael's got someone following up on that, too."

"And you'll share what you find," Colin said, giving her a flat look.

"We'll share," she assured him. "Raphael's not big on Miranda rights, either."

"Can't say I blame him. Not in this case, anyway. On a separate track," Colin continued, "Loren gave me a list of things missing from Marco and Preston's places. Electronics mostly. Jeremy says nothing was taken from their place, but I figure that's because they trashed everything looking for him, and then it got too late and they ran before the sun went down. I don't think they'd been gone all that long when I showed up."

"Pawn shops?" Leighton asked.

"Not here in town, but I've already got feelers out down in the city. A couple of guys on the force down there are former military. We get together once in a while, play poker, talk about old times."

"See? That's what I'm talking about. Nobody ever invites me to play poker." She sighed.

"Aw," Robbie crooned sympathetically. "We'll invite you to our game, won't we, Murphy?"

"Depends," Colin said thoughtfully. "Does she cheat?"

Leighton grinned. "Only when I have to."

"You're in."

"What about hate groups?" Leighton said, picking up the previous conversation thread. "You guys have any homegrown Nazis around?"

"You're thinking maybe they've added vampires to their list of *Untermenschen,*" Colin commented. "That's certainly possible. Mostly, they're over the state line, but we're close enough to get a few outliers."

He walked over and picked up his Sig, checking the chamber and magazine before snapping it onto his belt. "Let's go talk to some people, shall we?"

* * * *

They took Colin's Tahoe. It was a familiar enough vehicle that the man they were going out to visit wouldn't disappear at the sight of it. Everyone in Coop's knew there was a big contingent of vampires in town. If someone involved in these killings saw that big, black SUV of Leighton's pull up, they'd either take off into the woods or start shooting. Either way, it wouldn't get Colin the answers he was looking for.

Hugh Pulaski's place was buttoned up as tight as a drum when they finally maneuvered their way past the several gates he'd installed to block traffic along his mile and a half of private road. None of the gates were locked. That would have been pretty pointless, since a determined visitor could simply walk around. But they were an inconvenience, requiring a driver, or a passenger if he had one, to get out of the vehicle at every gate and find something to prop it open, since they were spring-loaded to close automatically. Hugh liked people to believe he had motion sensors and cameras all over the place, too. But Colin had firsthand knowledge of those kinds of devices, and he was pretty sure they only existed in Hugh's survivalist fantasies.

"Doesn't look like anyone's home," Robbie commented from the back seat. He'd been the one who'd gotten out at each of the four gates, complaining that he felt like he had a bull's eye painted on his back after each one.

"He's home," Colin said, jerking his head at a beat-up old pickup off to one side.

"That?" Leighton said, disbelieving. "I thought you good ol' boys took care of your trucks."

"We do," Colin agreed, pulling up next to the pickup. "But Hugh isn't exactly a good ol' boy. He's a trust fund baby—or old man now—with a BS in chemistry from Harvard. You might be wondering if we have ourselves another Ted Kaczynski, but I don't think Hugh graduated anywhere near the top of his class."

"So why are we here?"

"Hugh's not a danger by himself, but he is clued into the white supremacist movement. Hangs around the fringes mostly. Anything else would take too much effort. If something's going on, he'll probably know about it, though."

"Think he'll talk to us?" Leighton asked, climbing out of the truck.

"I think he can hardly wait," Colin said, lifting his chin in the direction of the house where he could already hear the rattle of multiple locks sliding open. As they came closer, the heavy door swung inward to reveal a skinny figure in khakis and a flannel shirt, both of which were brand new and a size too big. But what caught Colin's eye was not Hugh's version of woodsman apparel, but the shotgun he was aiming straight at the three of them through the screen door.

Leighton stopped in her tracks, snarling at Robbie when he stepped in front of her, placing himself between the shotgun and his primary, just like he was supposed to do.

"Put the damn gun down, Hugh," Colin said, letting his impatience show, even as his hand drifted over to the Sig Sauer .9 mm on his right hip.

"What're you doing here, Murphy? And who the hell are they?"

"Put the gun down," Colin repeated. "And we'll talk."

Hugh lowered the gun, but didn't put it down. Staring at Leighton and Robbie, he pushed open the screen and stepped out of his house, taking the two steps down to the ground, which still left several feet between him and his visitors. "Don't want those people in my house," he said, spitting to one side.

"I'm crushed," Leighton muttered, coming out from behind Robbie. She would have stepped closer to Hugh, but the bodyguard touched her arm in warning. She frowned, but took his advice.

Hugh couldn't have heard what she said, as far away as he was, but he narrowed his eyes at her anyway, before addressing Colin. "I'm asking you again, Murphy, what do you want?"

Colin eyed the other man. Hugh was mostly posture and bluff, pretending he was some sort of survivalist living out here in the woods with his rickety truck. The truth was his so-called rustic cabin boasted every amenity modern life could offer and the trust fund checks just kept coming.

"You heard about the murders." Colin made it a statement, not a question.

"A'course," Hugh responded, puffing his chest out a bit. "Good riddance to bad trash if you ask me."

Leighton didn't like that. She stiffened, one hand easing aside her jacket to give clear access to her own weapon. Colin held out his hand toward her, low and open, in a placating gesture.

"Why would you say something like that?" he asked Pulaski. "What'd Marco or Preston ever do to you?"

"Fuck," the old man said slowly, dragging out the word. "They're vampires, ain't they? Unnatural. Can't even walk under God's good sunlight."

"You do a lot sunbathing, Mister Pulaski?" Leighton asked, eyeing him up and down. "Looking a little pale to me."

"That's 'cuz I'm a white person, missy. Not like that gorilla you're hiding behind there."

"Enough, Hugh," Colin snapped. "I'm sure we're all very impressed by your bullshit attitude and what a tough guy you are. Now, answer a couple of questions for me, and we'll be on our way."

"Ask then. Can't get rid of you soon enough."

Leighton turned her head to give Colin a disgusted look. He just shrugged and looked back at Pulaski. "Word is you're familiar with any white supremacist groups operating in these parts," he said.

"A'course," Pulaski said again. "Ain't much I don't know."

"You know if they had anything to do with these murders?"

"Like I'd tell you if they did?"

"Well, I'll tell *you*, Mister Pulaski," Leighton snapped suddenly. "This is a murder investigation. You might not care for vampires, but they've got rights whether you like it or not. And if you know something about what happened out there and don't tell us, that's called conspiracy after the fact . . . or maybe you did a little conspiring before the fact? Maybe Murphy here should snap some handcuffs on those skinny, white wrists of yours and haul you into town. Shouldn't take too long for the County boys to arrive, make a proper arrest. *A'course*," she said, mimicking him, " . . . it might take a bit more than a day, don't you think? Might get dark in the meantime, and I don't think that jail I saw at Murphy's office would do much to keep the vampires out. What do you think, Robbie?"

"Hard to say, Miz Cynthia," Robbie drawled. "But them vampires are hellacious strong. Why I've seen 'em rip iron bars like that right out the walls. Hell, they probably won't bother with the bars a'tall. Probably just bust right through them walls." He paused, as if thinking about it. "Yep, that's what they'd do, all right."

"So what's it gonna be, Mister Pulaski? You want to answer a few questions for us? Or wait until after dark?" She regarded him lazily, a smug smile playing around her mouth. "Personally, I'm hoping you wait."

Pulaski gave her a hate-filled glare, but not before Colin caught the flash of fear on his face.

"Just tell me what you know, Hugh," Colin said patiently. "It'll go no further than the four of us here."

Hugh shifted his gaze to Colin, back to Leighton and over to Colin again. He took a step back and away from Leighton, his fingers tightening on the gun at his side. Robbie saw it, too. "Cyn," he said sharply, touching her arm and stepping in front of her again.

The bodyguard's reaction pleased Hugh and he had a sly smile on his face when he looked back at Colin. "The ones doing this aren't from around here," he said abruptly. "Outsiders barging in and taking over like they belong. Shoved aside those of us who've lived here all our lives like we were nothing. Brought lots of money and guns, all kinds of equipment and shit I've never seen before."

"You didn't recognize anyone? Why would they choose Cooper's Rest, if they're not from around here?"

"Wouldn't tell you if I did know 'em. But I didn't. As for why

Coop's? Hell, Murphy, it's 'cuz of those damn vampires moving in with their big, fancy house and their fucking fancy whores." He looked at Leighton when he said those last words, giving her a sneering up and down appraisal. "You be careful there, missy," he said. "A looker like you whoring yourself out, those righteous men might just do to you what they did to Mariane. Woman'll take it from a vampire, she'll take it from just about anyone."

Leighton didn't even flinch. She just met old Hugh's gaze and bared her teeth, her eyes going cold and flat. Colin had seen that look on a lot of faces before, but never from a woman.

Not trusting what might happen next, he said, "Fine, we're outta here. You watch who you keep company with, Hugh. This is gonna go badly for anyone involved with what went down out there."

Robbie was already hustling Leighton back to the truck, opening the door to the backseat and urging her inside. He slammed the door and waited until Colin was behind the wheel before holstering his weapon and sliding into the truck himself. "Let's get the fuck out of here," he snarled.

Colin reversed out of the clearing in front of Hugh's house, not willing to take his eyes off the old man until they had some distance between them. Once he hit the narrow private road, he backed off the road enough to get some turn around room, then headed out toward the highway.

"So how'd white boy back there know about Mariane?" Leighton said. She had scooted to the edge of the back bench and was leaning between the two front seats.

"This is a small town," Colin said, turning off Hugh's drive and onto the highway. "Everyone knew everything there was to know about the attack on Mariane and Jeremy within hours. Maybe not every little detail, but a rough idea of what had happened and who was involved. What's more curious is that Hugh didn't even flinch when I mentioned Marco and Preston. He already knew they were dead, but I didn't even know it until you told me yesterday and I've told no one else. He might not be directly involved in these crimes, but he knows what they're doing. Maybe—probably—he's just sitting at a table in the shadows and eavesdropping."

She made an exasperated noise and pushed herself back against the seat behind her. "So, you've got some white supremacists operating in your back yard. But how the hell does that tie in to what happened up in Vancouver?"

"What happened in Vancouver?"

Leighton just looked at him.

"Come on, Leighton," he said, eyeing her in the rear view mirror. "You want cooperation from me, it's a two-way street. What happened in Vancouver?"

She met his reflected gaze. "Your girlfriend Sophia didn't tell you?"

Colin gave her a cold stare. "She's not my girlfriend," he said evenly. "And you're avoiding the question."

Leighton shrugged, stretching out her legs before answering. "Three more vampires were killed," she said. "That's why Sophia's here. She thinks, and I tend to agree, that whoever killed the vamps up there has decided to spread the joy southward."

"Shit."

"That doesn't begin to cover it. You've never seen what happens when a vampire gets really pissed, Colin. I have. They don't believe in trial by jury and they don't give second chances. These killers, whoever they are, sealed their fates the minute they decided to cross into Raphael's territory. This isn't going to be pretty, no matter how you look at it."

"Yeah? Well, I'll *tell* you how I look at it, Leighton. I *saw* what they did to Mariane. So, as long as the only ones getting bloodied are the animals who did that, I say let the bloodletting begin."

Chapter Twenty-Two

Sophia checked herself in the mirror critically, using both hands to pull her hair out of the high-necked sweater she'd chosen for tonight's hunt. It seemed foolish to think of it as a hunt, especially in this day and age, but she didn't have any other word for it. Raphael's vampires were going to hunt down the humans who'd crossed the line of civility and started the killing. It seemed clear, to Sophia at least, that the motive for these crimes was simple hatred. The things they'd done to that child Mariane were proof of that, if any further proof was necessary. She thought Raphael agreed with her, although it was difficult to know for sure since she was still frozen out of any serious discussions.

The western vampire lord didn't trust her, not even after last night when she'd shown her *own* trust by admitting him not just to Lucien's territory, but to the heart of his nest. Trust came hard to vampires. She had to remind herself of that now that she was back in Vancouver. She'd spent too many years down in Brazil, a country ruled by a vampire lord so laid back he barely qualified for the title.

She should have remembered, though. Should have remembered that village in Central America and the night she'd been given a choice—leave now or swear loyalty to a new master. *That* region's vampire lord hadn't been laid back. He'd been unwilling to tolerate her presence in his territory as long as she was sworn to Lucien. And Sophia had had no intention of forsaking her Sire, not when there were so many other places in the world she could live peacefully.

Of course, leaving the hostile vampire lord's territory had meant leaving Colin, too. She'd rationalized the decision in her head a million times over the years. That he was human, that he wouldn't understand, that he wouldn't *want* her if he knew what she was. Or that he'd have left her soon, anyway, called away by his own masters in the United States military. But every one of those excuses still left a bad taste in her mouth. She could have handled it differently. *Should* have handled it differently. But when the fire had struck, it had seemed like a gift, a sign from the Fates that this was the right path for her to take.

But then, she'd never expected to see him again, never expected to feel that punch in the gut when she'd walked into the room upstairs and seen those blue eyes accusing her.

She turned away from the mirror, no longer willing to see the accusation in her own reflection. Maybe she should talk to him again. Try to make him understand. She snorted delicately. As if Colin hadn't made his own feelings on the subject perfectly clear already.

Heavy footsteps sounded in the hallway outside, reminding her of the night's coming festivities. She ran her hands over her hips, pulling the sweater into place. Thank God she'd thought to pick up some clothes in Vancouver last night. She'd never planned on being in Raphael's territory this long, but it looked as if she'd be staying here at least a couple more nights. She didn't think they could wrap this up before then, not even with Raphael's power and resources on their side.

She'd worn casual clothes tonight—jeans, flat-soled boots and a thick sweater. The hunt was likely to involve a lot of tramping through the woods, especially since there wasn't much *other* than woods around here. The clothes made her look much younger—something she usually avoided in her never-ending quest to be taken seriously in the male dominated world of vampires.

And it was definitely male dominated. Witness the thumping footsteps outside her door just a moment ago. For centuries vampire lords had chosen their minions with physical defense in mind, which meant the bigger the better, and that equaled male. Modern times made that less necessary, but the tradition continued, because the vampire lords controlled who got turned and the lords were mostly old traditionalists. Raphael's people were a very good example of the testosterone-laden ranks of Vampire. Sophia had seen only one female among all the vampires he'd brought with him from California.

For her part, Sophia was more powerful than most of the vampires she met, but female still equaled weak in most vampires' eyes. She could have gone the route of Raphael's lone female, Elke, who appeared to be every bit as muscled as the males she worked with. But Sophia had grown up in a culture where beauty was a woman's best, and sometimes only, weapon. And she knew she was beautiful, just like she knew it fed the males' misperception of her weakness. But then her beauty was something she'd learned to wield long before she'd ever become Vampire. And she'd never enjoyed lifting weights.

But tonight, she'd forgone appearances in favor of practicality. She had no intention of trudging through the underbrush in four inch heels and a silk blouse. Her only concession was her hair, which she'd left hanging down her back instead of the more practical braid she usually adopted in such situations. She told herself it had nothing to do with the possibility that Colin would be around, that he'd remember how much he'd loved her long hair when they were together.

She was usually very good at lying when it served her purposes. But she'd never been very good at lying to herself. She soothed her vanity with a final glance in the mirror, then opened her door to an empty hallway. Apparently Raphael's vampires were all upstairs already.

Climbing the steep stairs from the basement level, Sophia admired again the degree of security in the compound and the comfort afforded even a visiting vampire like herself. Raphael took good care of his people. That was his reputation, so she shouldn't have been surprised. But the reality had exceeded even the reputation. She was impressed in spite of herself and feeling slightly disloyal to Lucien because of it.

She heard laughter as she came around the corner, the sound chased into the building on a wash of cold air. Recognizing Colin's deep voice, she looked up eagerly . . . and frowned. Colin was there all right, but he was with Raphael's woman, the two of them laughing and talking like old friends, as if they hadn't just met two days ago. Sophia's eyes narrowed in displeasure, but she quickly erased the expression. If Colin wanted to waste his time on Raphael's woman, that was his choice.

Listening carefully, while pretending not to, Sophia heard the woman Cynthia bid Colin a good night and head across the wide expanse of the great room, accompanied by another one of Raphael's hulking bodyguards, this one human. They were met by the pale, blond Elke, who was dressed in a suit just like the males wore. Sophia watched somewhat enviously as Cynthia and the black bodyguard greeted Elke, spending a few minutes more in cheerful conversation. Did she have any friends like that? Sophia wondered. Or even acquaintances? Anyone with whom she could exchange a few moments of lighthearted conversation? The answer was no. Not in Vancouver, not even in Rio which had been her home for years. She had no one. What startled her was that she had never noticed the lack until now.

She studied the small grouping. Raphael's mate was beautiful. Sophia had never minded acknowledging beauty in other women. She had her own beauty, after all, and so recognized it in others. But this Cynthia used her beauty differently than Sophia did, less consciously, perhaps, but she used it all the same. It gave her a breezy confidence that made others accept her more readily, that let her take chances a less self-assured person would never have dared.

Sophia glanced around, noting the number of eyes watching the exchange. Eyes which included Colin's. She frowned, feeling the jagged edge of jealousy scrape across her gut, something she rarely experienced. As if aware of her reaction, Colin glanced over, his gaze meeting hers for a long moment. Sophia started toward him with a smile, but before she'd taken two steps, he shook his head in disgust and spun away from her, pushing through the doors and admitting another gust of cold, damp air to swirl around the sparsely furnished room.

Sophia's mouth tightened in irritation. So he could spend an entire day with this Cynthia, who was clearly off limits, but he couldn't spare a moment's greeting for Sophia? As Raphael's Cynthia had been heard to say . . . *Fuck that!*

She scanned the great room and spied Wei Chen heading toward the winding stairs up to the second floor. With a burst of speed, she cut him off before he reached the first step.

He recoiled a bit at her abrupt appearance, but then acknowledged her politely enough. "Sophia," he said. "Is there something you require?"

"A car," she said simply. "Not one of those enormous trucks, but a simple sedan will do."

The Seattle compound leader seemed confused. "It was my impression you would be accompanying the others on the hunt tonight. The trucks are unwieldy but—"

"Later," she interrupted. "I need to run an errand first. Your Sheriff Murphy and I are old acquaintances."

Wei Chen's eyebrows shot up. He couldn't have missed the obvious tension between her and Colin the other night. No doubt, he'd already had his people searching out every detail of her history and relationships, as well as Colin's. By now he, and by extension Raphael, knew more about her former lover than she did.

"Of course," Wei Chen said amiably, recovering from his surprise. "Would you like someone to drive you—"

"No," she said quickly. The last thing she needed was more witnesses. "Although, I am unfamiliar with the roads here. If you have a car with a GPS device, that would be helpful, and perhaps someone to program the relevant addresses?"

Wei Chen's already small mouth pursed tightly. "You do know how to drive?"

Sophia gave him a flat stare. "Of course," she said in as patronizing a tone as she could muster. "We do have cars in Brazil." Not that she actually *drove* them, but he didn't need to know that, the supercilious little prig. In truth, she couldn't remember the last time she'd driven a car. But there wasn't that much traffic here in the woods and the darkness would be no impediment. How hard could it be?

"Very well." Wei Chen took a cell phone out of his pocket and spoke rapid Chinese for several minutes before hanging up. "One of my people will have a car waiting for you on the ground level of the garages just outside to the left. He'll program Mister Murphy's address, as well as that of this compound for your return. You have a cell phone, of course, so if you get lost, give us a call and someone will guide you in."

Sophia narrowed her gaze, feeling a streak of familiar resentment. Wei Chen was an officious little bastard. Probably very good at what he did, but his attitude was typical in its paternalism. She kept her face carefully blank, while imagining all the ways she could make the little prick pay. Not the least of which would be to seduce him and then leave him with a handful of hard dick. She smiled at the thought, letting him see it. He blushed as red as a schoolgirl, which made her feel far better than it should have. He was her host, after all. So, she thanked him prettily and headed for the garages.

Colin Murphy might think he could avoid her. But Sophia hadn't survived this long by letting others dictate to her. Not prissy, little Wei Chen and not Colin Murphy either.

Chapter Twenty-Three

Raphael felt Cyn's arrival back in the compound, knew when she entered the building and when she lingered outside the elevator upstairs speaking with Elke and the others. He was egotistical enough—and he knew it was ego—that it irritated him to have her gone when he woke for the night, to have her chatting upstairs rather than coming down directly to greet him. His mouth quirked in a half smile as he considered her probable reaction to his irritation.

The elevator doors opened behind him. He didn't turn around, but continued dressing, pulling a black long-sleeved t-shirt over his head. Her arms around his waist kept him from pulling it down further, her hands still chilled from outside.

"I'm sorry I wasn't here when you woke up," she said, kissing his bare back. "A big rig truck jackknifed, blocking the road. We eventually went off-road and around, but it took time."

"You weren't involved in the accident?" he said, eyeing the ruffle of her dark hair over his shoulder, which was all he could see in the mirror.

"No," she said, looking around to meet his reflected gaze. "It happened before we got there."

He turned and kissed the top of her head, pulling his shirt down and tucking it into his denims before buttoning the fly. She made a small, exasperated noise at his cool greeting, then flopped down in a chair, watching as he sat on the bed to pull on his boots.

"You're changing clothes?" she asked, stating the obvious.

"Duncan and I met with the others earlier. Maxime continues to examine the records on the local server, though she's found nothing and I suspect she won't. I'm breaking my people into three teams and letting them hunt in the old way for now. Each team will begin at one of the crime scenes and circle out, ending with the town itself. We can cover far more territory far more effectively than any human search team. My vampires are getting restless with this interminable waiting, and angry because of it. This search will give them something to do. I don't suppose you and your friend Colin discovered anything useful?"

He looked up and caught her eyeing him warily. He met her gaze with a questioning look, eyebrows raised, but she just rolled her eyes briefly and said, "Murphy's put out feelers on the stolen electronics. That might turn up something. In the meantime, though, we questioned a few locals. It was pretty boring. I felt bad for Robbie, having to hang around. But it did give me some ideas to follow up on the computer tonight. You're going out with the hunts?"

"Yes."

"You should let Elke go with you. I'll just get in the way out there, so I'll stay here and work. There's a lot of ordinance and equipment coming into this area. That's going to show up somewhere. I just have to find the right thread and tug it."

Raphael stood, stomping his feet lightly to seat his boots. "I don't expect much from tonight. The real hunt will begin when we have something more to go on, perhaps from Maxime's work, or yours. But until then, we'll hunt the only way we can." He donned his long, leather coat and started toward the elevator.

"Raphael," she protested from behind him.

He turned to regard her, noting the brightness of her eyes even in the dim light.

"Aren't you even going to kiss me?" she asked.

He studied her silently, then held out a hand. He nearly smiled at the flash of stubbornness that crossed her face. But he kept his amusement to himself, waiting for her to come to him.

She did so, sighing heavily. "Why I ever fell in love with a damned arrogant vampire lord, I will never know," she muttered, coming into his arms.

He hugged her, smiling against her silky hair. "I have often asked myself the same thing," he said. "Although, my own question is somewhat different than yours."

She slapped him lightly and raised her face to his for the long-delayed kiss.

"Good evening, *lubimaya*," he said, then pulled her into a long, simmering kiss, putting just enough power into it to forcibly remind her of their lovemaking. Her nipples had hardened against his chest and her heart was pounding as she pressed her long, lean body against his.

"Damn you," she whispered when he lifted his lips from hers. "That's just mean."

He chuckled softly. "It was you who asked for a kiss, my Cyn."

"How late will you be?" she asked breathlessly.

"That will depend on many things." He took her hand and headed for the elevator again. "Traffic accidents and such," he added blandly.

Elke was at her post in the hallway outside the elevator when he and Cyn emerged. He knew Cyn was right, that Elke would rather have joined the hunt tonight, but regardless of what Cyn might say about her intentions to remain tied to the computer, he didn't trust her. If something caught her fancy, if her computer search turned up something intriguing, she'd be gone into the night without a thought for her own safety or her promises to him.

He saw Duncan and the others waiting across the great room. Before he could head that way, however, Robbie Fields, the human bodyguard he'd entrusted with Cyn's daytime safety, signaled him from near the dining room door. Raphael left Cyn to her teasing of Elke—she was engaging the female vampire in a serious discussion of which board game they should occupy their time with this evening—and joined Robbie, who had ducked into the dining room out of sight.

"My lord," Robbie said as soon as he saw him.

"Robbie," Raphael greeted him. "Cyn tells me you had an uneventful day."

The human's surprise was obvious and all too predictable. "Not exactly, my lord."

"Ah. So, tell me then, what exactly *did* happen?"

A short, but informative conversation later, Raphael left the dining room and headed straight to the couches where Cyn sat talking to Elke and some of the others. He'd already assured Robbie that he'd done the right thing, both in the performance of his duty and in reporting the details to Raphael. Not that there'd been any question of that last. Raphael had made it clear that he wanted a full report on Cyn's activities, knowing well her tendency to gloss over the fine points. She claimed it was to avoiding upsetting him unnecessarily, but even she no longer believed he fell for that excuse.

"A moment, my Cyn," he said, taking her hand and pulling her off the couch and back down the hall to the elevator. Vampire hearing was excellent and he didn't want the entire compound to hear the coming conversation.

She spun around as soon as they were downstairs, her mouth tight with irritation. "Robbie finked, didn't he?"

"Finked? Robbie did his duty, which is first to protect you, but second to inform me of any danger incurred during his watch."

"There was never any—"

"Then why did I have to hear it from him instead of you? White supremacists? Vampire hate groups? You didn't think this was relevant? And what about the clear threat to *you* made by a man with enough connections to know the men who savaged Mariane?"

"I knew you'd freak out like this," she mumbled.

He looked down at her impatiently. "I am tempted to lock you in this room—"

"You just try!"

"But, as you so often remind me, you are who you are. So I will content myself with warning my security people to be extra vigilant." He turned on his heel and entered the elevator once again, eyeing her dispassionately from within its depths.

"I am disappointed, my Cyn." The doors closed seconds before he heard something hard hit their surface. He laughed loud enough for her to hear as the elevator started upward.

He was still grinning when he emerged upstairs, meeting Duncan halfway across the nearly empty great room.

"My lord," Duncan said somewhat warily.

"We'll be taking a short detour this evening, Duncan. Let the others go ahead."

"Yes, my lord. Juro will accompany us, of course. Will you want anyone—"

"No others. We'll join the hunt later."

Raphael strode out into the wet night, for once not noticing the weather. It was time these humans learned there was a price to pay for threatening that which was Raphael's. And he intended to begin their instruction tonight.

Chapter Twenty-Four

Sophia drove slowly down the narrow lane to Colin's house. She'd nearly missed the turnoff, had only caught it at all because of the GPS's melodious female voice urging her to turn right. As it was, she'd passed right by it and had to back up to make the turn. The lane seemed barely wide enough for the luxury sedan Wei Chen's people had provided for her, but she thought that might be due more to her lack of driving experience than anything else. After all, she remembered that Colin drove one of those oversized American alpha-mobiles, as if a man's courage was somehow tied to the size of his truck. Or perhaps it was something else, something more intrinsic to being a man? She laughed out loud at the thought. As she recalled, Colin had no worries in that regard.

All thoughts of laughter died as Colin's house finally came into sight. She saw the lights first, shining through the ubiquitous trees which gathered closely around and above the narrow lane. Before too long, she entered a large clearing and saw the house itself. It was a big A-frame, all wood and glass, with light beaming from every one of the many windows, including the entire top half of the A itself. Short wings tucked out to the left and right, but only the one on the right had any lights showing.

At least she could be fairly certain Colin was home. Either that or he didn't like to come back to a dark house. But, no, his truck was there, parked off to the right in front of a detached garage.

Sophia half expected him to hear her arrival. Not that the car she drove was noisy, quite the opposite, but it was so quiet here, especially compared to the cities she was used to. She turned off the engine and sat for a moment, waiting for the house door to open. When it didn't, she opened her car door, closing it gently and walking up onto the porch. There was no bell, so she knocked . . . and knocked again. She frowned and sent a narrow thread of power past the door and into the house. There. A human heartbeat. And running water, which probably explained why he hadn't heard her knock.

There were few times that Sophia regretted being Vampire. This was one of them. Had she been human, she would have simply opened the door and walked in, surprising Colin when he finally emerged from his shower, or whatever washing up he was doing. Unfortunately, as a vampire, that wasn't an option. So she waited until the sound of running water ceased, and she knocked again.

Footsteps came from inside and she repeated her knocking. The footsteps drew closer, the heavy tread of a big man and her heart beat a little faster.

The door opened and Colin stood there. He was only half-dressed, his broad chest completely bare, a pair of low-slung sweat pants hanging on narrow hips, revealing a flat abdomen ridged with muscle. He had a towel draped around his neck, and his hair was still damp.

"Sophia. What do you want?"

His voice startled her into meeting his sapphire blue eyes, so striking in contrast with his black hair, and she realized she'd been staring. But oh, he was so stare worthy. If anything, he was more delicious now than he'd been when she'd met him nearly a decade ago. He'd held the promise of a man back then, young and strong and fit. But now he was a man fully grown, with thickly muscled shoulders and arms and a man's deep chest. A light sprinkling of dark hair across his chest arrowed downward, teasing her eye as it disappeared beneath the loose, drawstring waist. There were slices and puckers of shiny scar tissue across his torso and down his arms, but they only made him seem more fearsome, a warrior in his prime.

And suddenly Sophia remembered why she'd taken him as her lover. Men had always wanted her, some for the bragging rights of claiming her, others for the things she could give them. But no one had ever wanted her for herself. Until she'd met Colin Murphy. He hadn't wanted Lady Sophia Micaela Angelina, her father's only child and heir, or Sophia, vampire and favored child of Lucien. Colin had only wanted Sophie, a peasant girl from the Central American countryside.

"Sophie?" Colin said again, his brow creased in concern. "Is something wrong? Did something happen?"

"No," she dragged herself back to the present, to this place of perpetual rain and towering trees. "I just wanted to talk."

He studied her for a few minutes, then stood back from the door, inviting her in. She felt a blush heating her face and neck.

"You need to invite me in."

"What?"

"You need to say the words," she snapped, embarrassed and angry about it. "I'm a vampire, Colin."

"That part's true?" he asked in disbelief. "You really can't come in without an invitation?"

"It's true. And it's cold out here."

"All right, all right," he said. "Come on in, Sophie. Or do I have to call you Sophia?"

"Sophie will do," she muttered and stepped into the warmth of his house.

* * * *

Colin closed the door, watching Sophie—no, *Sophia*, he reminded himself—scope out his home. She was polite about it—more polite than Leighton had been the other morning—sticking mostly to the front room, poking her head into the kitchen and glancing down the hallway. She lingered there and he could read in her body language that she was dying to explore further. But she didn't, looking over at him, before walking back into the living room where he stood waiting.

He didn't sit. Didn't invite her to sit. It was bad enough that she was here in this house with him, looking pretty much the same as she had when he met her ten years ago. In fact, she looked *exactly* the same tonight with her hair hanging loose and those tight denims hugging her plump thighs and that fine, high ass of hers that had once made him hard just looking at it and thinking about what they'd do later. He'd dreamt about that ass when he was out in the jungle, had awakened too many times hard and aching, and counting the days until he'd see her again. And damn if he wasn't getting hard just thinking about it again.

This was the Sophie he'd fallen in love with. He'd stopped kidding himself about that a long time ago. He'd loved her, had never loved anyone since and figured he never would. When she'd died—or when he'd thought she'd died—he'd mourned for a long time. And now he'd discovered it was all a lie. He had to remember that. That he'd wasted all those years mourning a lie.

"So, what is it, Sophie?" he asked impatiently. "Why are you here?"

She looked up at him, her chocolate brown eyes boring into his soul, searching. For what? What did she want from him this time?

"You can't have her, you know," she said abruptly.

He scowled at her in confusion. "Who?"

"Raphael's woman. Cynthia. She's in love with him, and even if she wasn't, she belongs to him. He won't let her go."

"You're out of your fucking vampire mind, Soph."

"I saw you with her at the compound tonight, laughing and talking."

Colin chuckled bitterly. "Jealous, Sophie? You're a little late to that game, aren't you? You've been dead for ten years."

She jerked a little at his words. He felt bad about hurting her and then immediately called himself twenty kinds of fool. She'd torn his heart open and left it bleeding on the jungle floor and he was worried about hurting *her*?

"We're working together," he said finally. "She's kind of like my partner. We watch each other's backs. It's a matter of loyalty. Something I wouldn't expect you to understand."

"What does that mean?" she demanded, bristling.

"It means your idea of loyalty is letting me think you'd been burned to death in a fire instead of just telling me to take a hike," he snarled. "If you wanted to end it, Sophie, you could have bought me a glass of *chicha* and just *told* me."

"I didn't want to end it," she said, still giving him those big eyes. "I didn't have a choice."

"Sure you did. Everyone has a choice."

"It wasn't that simple," she insisted. "There was a lot going on back then, Colin. More than you know."

"And clearly more than you're going to tell me. So why are you here, then? You working for Raphael?"

"I am *not* working for Raphael and I never will. My master is

Lucien. Raphael rules the west, but Lucien rules all of Canada. He's the one who made me Vampire, which was . . ." She stopped talking suddenly, giving him an almost frightened look.

"What were you going to say?" he asked her intently. "This Lucien guy made you a vampire, which was what?" He was still staring at her, but she'd shifted her gaze away, refusing to meet his eyes any longer. He tilted his head thoughtfully, repeating her words in his head. The thought hit him and he jolted in surprise.

"Not what, but when. Isn't that right, Sophie?" He put his hand on her arm when she would have moved away. "When did you become a vampire, Soph? How old *are* you?"

She raised her gaze to his, her pupils so big her eyes were nearly black. "I was born in seventeen thirty three," she said defiantly. "Lucien made me Vampire just prior to my twenty second birthday."

Colin stared at her. He'd known what it meant to be Vampire, knew they lived a long time, that they didn't age, but he'd never . . .

"Christ," he said in sudden realization. "That means you were—"

"Nearly two hundred sixty-eight years old when you met me."

Not just when he'd met her, but when he'd fucked her. When he'd fallen in love with her!

"Colin?"

"I need a drink," he growled and headed around the kitchen counter, grabbing the bottle of whiskey he kept on hand for emergencies. If this didn't qualify as an emergency, he didn't know what did.

Three hundred years, give or take a few decades. His Sophie, the sweet girl from the village he'd been so careful with, was a centuries-old vampire who had probably seen and done things he could only imagine. And after twelve years on the teams, he could imagine an awful lot.

He poured a healthy three fingers of whiskey into a glass, then took a long sip, closing his eyes and letting the whiskey roll down his throat, its warmth spreading into every muscle and nerve.

He leaned back toward the living room and called to Sophie. "You want a—"

The words froze in his throat at the sight of Sophia bending over to pull off her boots, her long, dark hair tossed over one shoulder. Her faded jeans stretched lovingly over her pretty ass as she slipped off first one boot and then the next, revealing small, delicate feet with bright red nail polish.

He stifled a groan, his gaze traveling over her curvaceous body. This was a bad idea.

Chapter Twenty-Five

Raphael climbed out of the SUV while it was still rolling. Duncan joined him immediately, giving him an enigmatic look he ignored, while Juro swore softly in rare surprise. Raphael wasn't worried. There was nothing here that could threaten him.

He gazed around the clearing, noting the battered truck to one side and the untidy pile of wood next to a metal tool shed in the back. The dwelling was more of a cabin than a house, small enough that he suspected it had just one room, the wood in desperate need of refinishing and the windows taped over or painted. He couldn't tell for certain. Perhaps it was both. The lone door looked like it cost more than the entire cabin around it, which told him the owner didn't know much about security.

Next to him, Duncan was doing his own survey of the surroundings. "There is a single human male inside the house, my lord. Who is he?"

"Hugh Pulaski."

Duncan tipped his head curiously.

"A very foolish man," Raphael added.

Duncan shrugged. "The *door* appears rather sturdy. The walls on the other hand . . ."

Raphael bared his teeth. "I thought we'd try knocking first. I have a few questions for him."

Duncan nodded, leapt onto the rickety porch and knocked loudly. Raphael could hear movement inside. Hell, he could hear the man's racing heart and panting breath. The human might not know it was vampires in his yard, but he certainly knew it wasn't a friend.

"Hugh Pulaski," Raphael called. "We know you're there."

The door swung open suddenly and a shotgun shoved the screen door open, the man behind it already flexing his finger on the trigger. Juro leapt in front of Raphael, while Duncan used his inhuman speed to grab the gun's barrel and whip it upward before the human could finish squeezing the trigger. He jerked the shotgun away from Pulaski with enough force that the human stumbled out of the safety of his house. Realizing what he'd done Pulaski screeched frantically and tried to turn around, but Duncan had already closed his fingers around the man's throat.

"I should kill you for that," Duncan said intently, throwing the shotgun into the yard.

Raphael strolled closer. "Not yet, Duncan. Questions first."

"I don't know who the fuck you people are," Pulaski tried to yell, "but I don't have to—"

Duncan bared his fangs, stopping the man's words. The pungent scent of human sweat on an unwashed body filled his nostrils and Raphael sniffed. "If you would, Duncan."

Pulaski screamed as he was thrown through the air to land with a grunt at Raphael's feet.

"What do you want?" he whined shakily. "I don't know nothin' more about them murders. I swear."

Raphael looked down on the sniveling piece of humanity. "You're lying. And we'll get to that later. But first—" He crouched down, letting his power rise until the dirt around them was dancing with electricity, until the human worm was cringing beneath the silvery glow of his eyes. "You threatened my mate this afternoon. Tall, beautiful, dark-haired? You remember her?"

"Nuh, no! I never saw—" He screamed as Raphael's power closed around his heart just enough to hurt . . . badly.

Raphael tsked softly. "Didn't your murdering friends teach you anything about vampires? After all, a good hunter always knows his prey. And I know all about you, Hugh Pulaski."

Tears were streaming down the man's face, carving a path through the oily sweat. He was mumbling something beneath his breath. It sounded like a prayer.

Raphael laughed. "You would do better to pray to me, human. Your life is in my hands tonight, not your God's. Now—" He drilled into Pulaski's brain, forcing him to look up. "I believe you wanted to apologize, didn't you?"

Pulaski nodded desperately, his eyes rolling white with fear. "I'm sorry, I'm sorry."

Raphael shrugged. "Of course, it would be better if you apologized directly to my mate, but that won't happen. In fact, I think it would be best if you left this area altogether. You're not the kind of neighbor I had in mind for my people."

"I'll leave. I will. I'll go tomorrow."

Raphael frowned and Pulaski screamed again. "Tonight," he sobbed. "I'll go tonight. I promise. I will. Just, please don't hurt me anymore."

"Hurt you? Oh, Hugh. You don't know what pain is yet."

Raphael ignored the human's pathetic whimpering and began rummaging through Hugh Pulaski's brain, his mouth pursed with distaste. The man was nobody. A rich man pretending to be poor, a small man pretending to be big. A liar and a cheat. And this, this *slug* had dared insult his Cyn, dared threaten her with violence? Raphael should do the world a favor and rid it of bad trash. But that wasn't his purpose tonight.

Cyn's bodyguard, Robbie, had been certain Pulaski knew more than what he'd been willing to tell Colin Murphy this afternoon. But it was also possible that Pulaski knew more than he realized he did. Raphael sent a suggestion to the human's mind, directing him to the recent vampire murders, to the people behind it.

Pulaski twitched where he lay on the ground, his eyes rolled back in his head, drool dripping from his mouth. He looked like the idiot he was, but he wasn't permanently damaged. Not yet.

Raphael followed the human's twisting thoughts, the vicarious thrill when he'd heard about Marco and Preston being murdered, the sick twist of perverted arousal at the news of Mariane's brutal rape. Raphael growled and dug deeper, going farther back in time. Pulaski was in a tavern of some sort. It was small and dark, with no lights except over the bar and only a few tables cloaked in heavy smoke and deep shadow. It smelled of beer and sweat and old cigarettes, with the lingering scent of a toilet that had run over in the not too distant past. The only noise was a low hum of conversation, too low to hear. A few words popped out, though. Enough to know they were going to hunt some vamps, going to hit 'em in daytime while they slept. No one would know a thing until it was too late and they'd be long gone by then.

Raphael forced Hugh to look deeper, to see details, things he passed over without paying conscious attention. Details about the bar—the sign advertising some beer, the brand indistinguishable because half the bulbs were burned out, the dusty deer head above the cash register, a plastic lei twisted in its antlers. Details about the conspirators—men Hugh knew well, and others he didn't. But it was the men he knew that Raphael was interested in. He dug further, pushing until an involuntary whine rose from the human's throat and his back bowed from the ground with effort.

Raphael released him.

A stench filled the air as Pulaski wet himself. He rolled over in the dirt and curled up into a ball, weeping piteously for his own suffering.

Raphael stepped away, shaking dirt from his coat. "Don't forget, Hugh Pulaski," he said, watching dispassionately as the human froze, listening. "You're leaving this area tonight. And make it permanent. I'll know if you come back."

Duncan walked with him back to the SUV, while Juro waited, standing over the whimpering human. Once Raphael was in the truck with the door closed, Juro followed, climbing into the driver's seat without the slightest reaction to the human or his suffering.

He looked up, meeting Raphael's gaze in the rear view mirror. "Sire?"

Raphael considered how much time was left before morning.

"Locate Wei Chen and Loren," he told Juro. "Tell them to meet us at the compound."

Juro spun the SUV in a tight circle, the tires coming close enough to Pulaski that he was pelted with bits of dirt, close enough that he screamed, cringing away from the big truck. Raphael glanced at his security chief and caught a slight upward twinge of the big vampire's mouth. Juro was very fond of Cyn. He respected her, which was saying something. There weren't very many beings Juro respected, human or vampire.

As they drove back to the main road, Raphael considered everything he'd learned from Pulaski's muddled brain. There was useful information there, but it would require interpretation. He'd originally wanted to meet Wei Chen and Loren, because they were local. But what he really needed for this was someone local *and human*. Someone like Colin Murphy.

* * * *

Raphael spotted Elke as soon as he came through the glass doors. She was standing on guard in the precise position she'd occupied when he'd left earlier.

"My lord," she said upon sighting him.

Raphael tilted his head in question.

"She came up for a few hours earlier. We played *cards*," she added disparagingly. "I think she did it on purpose."

"No doubt," Raphael agreed. "But it won't work. How long ago?"

Elke didn't have to check her watch. Like all vampires she measured time by the sun's next arrival and knew exactly how much time had passed, because she knew how much time was *left*. "An hour, my lord. A few moments more."

He nodded, turning when he heard more vehicles pulling through the gates. Standing near the doors, Juro turned and said, "Wei Chen, Sire. Loren is not with him."

Raphael paused in taking off his coat. "Where is he?"

Duncan was already on his cell. He said a few words, hung up and turned to Raphael. "He was checking out a lead, my lord. He's on his way back now."

Raphael and Duncan shared a skeptical look. Loren was Raphael's own child. The vampire couldn't lie to him, not successfully. Still, the situation bore watching. He finished removing his coat and threw it across the long couch not far from Elke before crossing to the meeting room. "We'll be in here," he told her, signaling Duncan to accompany him.

They settled to one side of the big doors, Raphael sitting at the end of a huge, antique sofa, his legs crossed at the knee, his arm stretched out along the back.

Duncan sat at the other end. "Other than Mister Pulaski's close affiliation with his tree-dwelling ancestors," he said, "did his brain reveal any reliable information?"

Raphael smiled slightly. "The man's a worm. He sat within a few feet of the humans who planned these murders and was too terrified to even look over his shoulder. Instead, he eavesdropped like an old woman in a marketplace." He shrugged dismissively. "Unfortunately, the music was loud and the conspirators careful."

Duncan met his gaze knowingly and Raphael's smile grew.

"I know your skill, my lord, and your determination. If it had been necessary to tear Pulaski's meager brain out through his ears and spread it on the ground to examine it, you would have done so."

"Colorful. But accurate. The worm knew two of the people involved. One he called by a nickname. *Junior*. It was a taunt of sorts, something the conspirator had been called as a child and apparently hated. The other is Curtis. I don't know if that's a first or last name. And I don't think our people will be too helpful on this."

Duncan eyed him thoughtfully. "But Colin Murphy would be."

"Exactly. Let's give him everything I got from Pulaski, not just the names, but the description of the local bar where they met. Pulaski spent a fair amount of time there, so anyone familiar with the place should be able to ID it from what I got."

"And Cynthia?"

"What about her?"

"Will you also inform her of these new findings?"

Raphael drummed his fingers on the tufted back of the sofa. "I don't want her anywhere near this, but she'll be well and truly pissed if she finds out from someone else. And we both know she will. So, send her the same info, but copy Robbie on everything. At least she won't be able to pull a fast one on him and go after it herself. And tell Robbie if anything happens to her, he'd better be dead before I know about it."

Chapter Twenty-Six

Colin watched Sophia walk toward him, laughter warring with desire in her deep brown eyes. Her hips swayed as she crossed the room, one long curl of hair falling over her shoulder to caress her breast. She looked terrific. Sexy as hell. Just looking at her made his dick hurt. It always had. Nothing had managed to change his reaction to her—not the years, not the lies, not even the knowledge that she drank blood to stay alive. He tried to imagine what it would be like to have her licking his skin, to feel her teeth sinking into his neck, drinking his blood. His erection grew harder.

Fuck that! He forced himself to remember the months he'd grieved for her, the guilt and pain he'd endured, thinking she was dead.

He looked away and took a good, long draught of whiskey, hoping it would wash away the taste of her, still so fresh despite the years.

Sophia slid gracefully onto the couch to sit facing him, her feet tucked under her thighs. She reached for his glass and he let her take it, watching as she drank, her plush lips closing around the rim, her tongue slipping out to taste before she let the whiskey roll into her mouth. *Christ, what was wrong with him?* He looked away, desperately trying to think of something, anything except what it would feel like to have that tongue licking other things.

She offered the glass back to him and he took it, careful to sip from the opposite side of the glass, not wanting to feel the warm residue of her mouth. He drank, glancing up to meet her eyes, seeing her awareness of his arousal in their chocolate depths. Not that she'd need any special powers for that one. His cock was so stiff, he was afraid it would break if he didn't move soon.

"So," he said, clearing his throat when his voice came out as scratchy as a thirteen-year-old's. "Vampires drink? I mean, other than blood."

"We can," Sophia agreed. "Some do. I don't usually, although I do enjoy the taste of a good wine."

"No wine here, darlin'," he drawled, relieved to have something to think about besides her effect on his libido. "Just beer and whiskey."

"The whiskey is fine. Quite nice, actually," she murmured. She moved closer, until her breasts were brushing against his shoulder, her hand resting high on his thigh, so close to his throbbing cock, he would have sworn he could feel the heat of her fingers caressing its aching stiffness. She ran her other hand up his arm to his shoulder, her fingers playing lightly in his hair. She reached for the whiskey again and he released it, thinking she wanted another drink.

Instead, she set the tumbler on the coffee table, the remaining liquid sloshing slightly against the sides of the glass. Colin watched the gentle amber waves move back and forth, closing his eyes when her fingers closed over his erection. He grabbed her hand.

"Don't," he said.

"No?" Sophia purred confidently, pressing her breasts harder against his shoulder.

"No," Colin confirmed. He stood suddenly, dislodging her so that she fell against the back cushions of the leather couch.

She rose to her feet slowly, anger in every movement, her eyes literally throwing off sparks of bright amber, reminding him illogically of the whiskey they'd been drinking moments before. "How dare you?" she demanded.

"How *dare* I?" Colin repeated sharply, grateful for the anger that washed away the last vestiges of desire. "Who the fuck *are* you? This is America, darlin'. The U.S. of A. I'll dare anything I damn well please, including choosing the women I want to fuck. And you know what, Sophia? That doesn't include you, because I don't fuck dead women."

She gasped, her hand flashing out with incredible speed. He grabbed her wrist. "Ah, ah. No hitting, remember? Besides, I didn't mean it like that," he added, grudgingly. "I know you vamps aren't dead. But you died for me ten years ago, Soph, and you made damn sure I knew it. I see no reason to change that now."

She looked up at him, all of her anger gone, replaced by a look so lost, so full of sadness . . . Shit. He felt like an ass. And he was pissed that she'd made him feel that way.

But before he could figure out what he wanted to say, her expression changed again, like a mask suddenly covering her face—a mask of pure, cold arrogance. Without looking away from him, she stretched her arm toward her boots where she'd left them beneath the counter. They came whipping across the room, passing so close to his head that he felt the air move, so close that he knew it had been on purpose. He narrowed his eyes at her, and she flashed a look of smug satisfaction in his direction, before tucking the boots under her arm and opening the door.

Before he knew what was happening, she was out of the house and inside the car, which was already gunning for the highway. Colin swore softly. He hadn't seen her move, hadn't even seen the damn car door open and close. She zipped by so fast, his front door was still swinging slightly in the breeze.

"Son of bitch," he muttered. He shook his head and turned to go back inside, wondering why his dick had grown hard all over again.

Chapter Twenty-Seven

Raphael waited while the elevator made its smooth descent, his leather coat hanging over one arm. It was late. By the time he'd finished briefing Duncan and the Seattle vampires, his hunt teams had begun arriving back at the compound. Duncan could have handled those reports, but he'd chosen to sit in on them, to show his people that this matter was important to him, that his need for revenge burned as hotly as any of theirs. The truth was his desire for retribution was greater than they could possibly understand. It was his vampires who'd been taken, his children. Blood of his blood.

But vengeance would have to wait a few more hours. The sun was looming just below the horizon. He felt it in his blood and bones. It infuriated him. It wearied him.

The doors opened on a nearly dark room, only a small light near the bed playing across the nearly still form of his beloved Cyn. He secured the vault doors and crossed to the bed, watching her breathe for a few minutes and wishing he had the courage to send her back to Malibu, to brave her anger and her protests and keep her safe. But he couldn't do that to her. *Wouldn't* do that to her. Wouldn't trap her in a cage of his making, a cage she would never leave because she loved him too much. But a cage that would eventually leave nothing but hate between them.

He sighed and stripped off his clothes, wondering at such dismal thoughts. He must be more tired than he thought. He lifted the covers carefully and slid into bed next to Cyn. She stirred, turning toward him instinctively, draping a leg and arm across his body without ever waking. He wrapped his arms around her, holding her tightly, wishing he could protect her from . . . His heart stuttered in his chest as an alarming foreboding suddenly darkened his thoughts and a final, terrifying question filled his mind before the sun took him. Protect her from what?

Chapter Twenty-Eight

Colin stood at the counter between his kitchen and living room the next morning, sipping his first cup of coffee and trying not to think about Sophia or her visit the night before. He scanned the list of e-mails that had come in during the night, studying it as if he expected anything to be there but junk. Holding the cup in one hand, he deleted one after the other until he came to a message from Loren. His fingers paused over the touch pad and he frowned. He didn't think he'd ever received an e-mail from the vamps before. If asked, he wouldn't have been certain they had his e-mail address. Not that it was a secret. Pretty much everyone in town had it, and it was printed on his business cards, too.

With a mental shrug, he clicked the file open and began to read the e-mail from Loren, swearing under his breath as he read the first few lines. Lord fucking Raphael had paid a visit to Hugh Pulaski last night. Not that Hugh was a model citizen or even a particularly decent one, but, damn, if even half of what Sophia had told him about Raphael was true, Hugh must have had a rough time of it. Colin was thinking he should probably take a trip out there, to make sure the aging woodsman wannabe had survived the encounter, but then he read the rest of the e-mail and decided Hugh could wait. The bastard had held out on him. Son of a bitch.

He checked his watch. It was just barely nine o'clock, probably too early for Leighton. He called anyway, waiting while the number switched over to voice mail.

"Leighton, Colin Murphy here. Check your e-mail. Your boyfriend apparently got us some new leads last night. I know the bar Hugh described. It's a fair distance out of town, on a two-lane road that connects to the main highway eventually. We'll probably find Curtis Jenkins there, too. He's on disability right now—broken arm or something that hasn't healed right—spends most of his time there. Anyway, I'm guessing he's the "Curtis" Hugh talked about. Don't know anyone who goes by "Junior," though.

I'm gonna check out the bar later and thought you might want to come join in the fun. Robbie's welcome, too, even if he is just a pussy Ranger. Can't hurt to have some extra muscle on hand.

So, call me when you get this. I'm going to make some calls myself, see if I can't figure out who "Junior" is. Could be an old nickname. Hugh's been around a lot longer than I have. I'll try to track it down before we hook up."

He started to disconnect, then added, "And I meant hook up in a completely nonsexual way, so don't get all riled up and tell your boyfriend on me. Later."

He poured himself a second cup of coffee before making the next call. He and Garry McWaters went back a long way. Back to BUD/S when Garry had been an old man with several years seniority and Colin had been a raw recruit. It had been Garry who'd pulled him out of that town in South America, who'd dragged him back to base camp and made sure he made their pickup out of the country the next night.

Cooper's Rest was Garry's hometown. He'd been raised here by his grandparents, and *they'd* been among the first founders of the independent community. His grandmother had died while their SEAL team had been out of country. Garry hadn't even been able to attend her funeral. His grandfather had lasted longer, dying less than a year after Garry and Colin had shown up in Coop with little more than their duffels and their Navy regulation haircuts.

The old man's death took something out of Garry. He didn't want to hang around after that, even though Colin had decided to stay. Garry headed back to California and signed up with a corporation that provided private armies to the U. S. Government. It was lucrative work, especially for someone with SEAL training and experience. He'd tried more than once since then to recruit Colin into it, but the money wasn't enough to make up for a job that was too much like the one he'd left behind. Besides, Colin had discovered he kind of liked the laid back lifestyle he'd found in Cooper's Rest.

He pulled up Garry's number on his contact list and hoped his buddy was in-country. If not, Colin would have to—"

"Yo, Colin!" Garry's voice boomed loud enough that Colin pulled the phone away from his ear by a few inches. "What's up, dude? Ready to make some money at last?"

"Sorry, Mac, you'll have to find some other sap to bail your ass out."

Garry made a dismissive sound. "Think you got that a little backwards. Must be all the rain up there. Speaking of which, how's old Coop doing?"

"Same as always, slow and easy, just the way I like it." Dead silence greeted this announcement and Colin frowned, wondering if they'd been disconnected. "Garry? You there?"

"What? Oh, yeah, Colin. Sorry, I dozed off."

"Fuck you," Colin drawled.

"In your dreams, my man. So what's up?"

"We've had some trouble up here and a name's come up. One I've never heard before. I figure since you're old as dirt—" He kept talking over Garry's profane reaction. "—and know just about everyone around here, maybe you could help me out."

"What kind of trouble?"

"Vampire trouble."

"Vamps? We never had any problems with—"

"It's not the vamps causing the problem. Someone's killed a couple of 'em—"

"Fuck me. Who?"

"I'm not sure you knew them. Marco and Preston? Don't think they had last names, not that I knew anyway."

"Marco's the guy with the horses, right? On the short side, dark hair? He was living there when I was just a kid. Man, he's dead? How?"

"Someone broke in, blew off the door to his . . . bedroom, I guess you'd say. More like a vault. But they killed him. It was daytime, so no resistance. Happened maybe a week ago. I didn't even know about it until some vampire big shot showed up to investigate. They killed Preston the same day and hit Jeremy and Mariane two days later. Couldn't find Jeremy, so they savaged Mariane instead."

"Jesus. I've got the next month free. You need me to come back and give you a hand?"

"I appreciate the offer, but the vamps brought in their own army to hunt down the killers. I'm not big on vigilantes, but in this case, I'm not inclined to protest too hard."

"I see your point." He breathed deeply. "So what's the name you got?"

"Junior."

"Junior? That's it?"

"That what I got. Supposedly a nickname, but not one the person particularly liked to be called. I don't know any juniors. You?"

"Junior," Hugh repeated. "I'm thinking back to grade school, maybe? High school?"

"That is a *long* way back," Colin said with mock seriousness.

"Damn you, Murphy. There's only something like six years between us."

"Yeah. Let's see, when you were doing BUD/S, I was in eighth grade."

"Fuck you. And I don't remember any juniors off hand, but I'll think on it. Anything else?"

"Nah. I'm going out to Babe's later this afternoon, following another lead."

"Rough place."

"There's a human P.I. in town, a woman who works for the vamps. Former cop. She's not military, but she knows her stuff. She'll be with me."

Garry laughed. "Better than nothing."

"I get the feeling she's tougher than she looks."

"I'll let you get to it, then. And I'll get back to you on that name, maybe drag out my old yearbooks or something."

"Jesus, Chief, you've still got your high school yearbooks?"

"I keep flowers from freshman homecoming pressed in the pages, memories of my first lay."

"Didn't get any until then, huh? I'm sorry."

The silence on Garry's end was complete. His friend had hung up on him. Colin laughed briefly, already thinking about the trip out to Babe's when the phone rang.

"Leighton," he answered after checking caller ID. "I wasn't sure you'd be up."

"Up is a relative term. I'm vertical, if that's what you mean, but *awake* will take a couple more cups of coffee. So what's going on?"

"You check your e-mail yet?"

"I'm doing it now. I'm guessing you mean the one from Loren. Let's see . . . Oh shit."

"You didn't know Raphael was going out there?"

"No. Robbie the fink told him about visiting Pulaski in all its gory detail." She sighed audibly. "What can I say, Raphael's a very protective guy."

"I'm not complaining. He got more out of Hugh than we did. Like I said, I know the bar and I know Curtis. I'm going out there today. You wanna come with?"

"Sure, sounds fun."

"And Robbie?"

Leighton made a dismissive sound. "Like they'd let me out of this place without him. We'll come by your house. Give me an hour."

"Bring all your guns, Leighton. You'll need 'em."

* * * *

Colin was loading the magazine for his Benelli when he heard the truck coming down the drive to his house. He secured the shotgun in its combat sling, set the whole thing down and pulled open his front door. Leighton was standing next to one of the big Suburbans, talking on her cell phone, while Robbie walked around back and reached into the cargo compartment, emerging with a huge, black duffel bag. He slung it over his shoulder, strolled over to Colin's Tahoe and dumped the bag on the ground.

Colin nodded to Robbie and leaned back inside to grab his keys. Beeping the locks open on his truck, he grabbed his gear and walked out onto the porch, closing the house door behind him. Robbie had already tossed the black duffel into the Tahoe. Colin eyed it curiously as he dropped his own gear next to it, but Robbie didn't offer and Colin didn't ask.

The two men leaned against the truck, watching Leighton on the phone. Colin didn't know with whom she was talking, but he was pretty sure it wasn't girl chat. She was listening carefully and responding with short, terse sentences he couldn't hear.

Colin wondered again about the duality that was Leighton, with her model's good looks and her concealed weapons. He wondered if she'd always been this way, or if Raphael had somehow molded her into what he needed.

"What do you think it's like?" he asked Robbie thoughtfully.

"What's that?"

He nodded in Leighton's direction. "Having a vampire lover."

Robbie's dark eyes crinkled with amusement. "You've never . . . *indulged* with a vamp?"

Colin frowned and shook his head. "Hell, no." *Not intentionally*, he added to himself. After all, he hadn't known Sophia was a vampire back then.

Robbie laughed, teeth flashing. "Once they draw blood, the sex is terrific, man. But it's more than sex if you're actually mated to someone, like Cyn." He gave Colin a challenging look. "Or like me," he added.

Colin drew up in surprise. "You? Shit. I didn't mean anything. I was just curious."

"*De nada*," Robbie said casually. "My wife Irina is Vampire. A tiny little thing who runs Raphael's household with an iron fist."

"She runs you pretty much the same way," Cyn interjected, having joined them without either of them noticing.

Robbie grunted in agreement, looking like a very satisfied man. "You hear me complaining? So, what'd you find out?"

Colin quirked his eyebrows in question.

"That was an old contact of mine. A gun seller. Not altogether legal, but not a bad guy either. His business gives him a certain amount of access to his customer's activities. Sometimes he has a problem with those activities and he's willing to talk, including the white supremacist groups operating out of Idaho and parts west. He tells me there's a whole lot of ordinance being trucked this way, along with the people to use it."

"Damn. Let's hope they haven't arrived yet," Colin muttered. "I hope you guys came prepared. What's in the duffel?"

Robbie grinned and unzipped the black bag, pulling the two sides wide. He reached inside and pulled out an Uzi submachine gun, tossing it to Colin. He then dug farther in the bag and produced a Point Blank ballistic vest for Leighton, handing it to her with orders to "put it on."

Colin inspected the matte black Uzi. He was familiar with the weapon, but preferred his Benelli. He handed it back to Robbie who was watching a grumbling Leighton don her vest. It was a concealable model, the same thing worn by most police departments in the country. It was also probably the only kind she'd be willing to wear. Anything heavier would weigh her down and restrict her movements.

"Where's yours?" she asked Robbie, giving him a narrow look.

"In the bag. I'll put it on if I need it."

"Why can't I—"

"Cuz I promised Raphael I'd take care of you. But mostly because you've got a piss poor sense of self-preservation."

"I do not," Leighton objected, but she was laughing when she said it.

Colin shook his head. He wasn't even going to *try* to figure that one out. "Let's roll," he said out loud. "We've got a fair drive ahead of us."

* * * *

"Colin here's a virgin." Robbie was leaning forward from his seat in the back, his substantial presence inserted between the two front bucket seats.

"I am not," Colin protested immediately.

"Not like that," Leighton clarified with a sideways grin. "Robbie's talking vampire virgin. You've never been bit?"

"No," he snapped.

"Really? I would have sworn there were sparks flying between you and that Sophia chick. Definite *sexual* tension," she added, drawing out the word.

"That was a long time ago," he responded stiffly. "And she never told me she was a vampire."

Next to him, Leighton raised her eyebrows, but didn't make any further comment about Sophia. "So what's this place we're going to?" she asked instead.

"Babe's. It's what we'd call a good ol' boy bar back home. Sits just off the highway, the other side of the forest. It's open five, sometimes six, days a week, but Friday and Saturday are the big nights, just like everywhere else. There's at least one fight every weekend, and that's just counting the ones where someone gets arrested or someone else ends up in the hospital. It's a pain in the butt, but it's been here a while, since back in the sixties. Strictly speaking, it's not a part of Cooper's Rest, but we're the closest town to it.

He spotted the break in the trees signaling the bar's parking lot. "Here ya go," he told her.

The parking lot was full, or nearly so, when they pulled even with the bar. It wasn't a big lot—just two rows in front, perpendicular to the highway. The rows had just enough room between them to maneuver, with spaces for four or five trucks to park side by side. And trucks were just about the only kind of vehicle anyone ever parked here. Colin surveyed the crowded lot and frowned. It looked more like a Friday night, than a weekday afternoon. One of the logging crews must have shut down early.

He drove past and made a U-turn, then parked his Tahoe in the last space next to the highway, driving right into to it with the front of his truck facing outward, so that he could make a fast exit, if it came to it. It probably wasn't necessary, but it wouldn't be the first time he'd wanted a quick departure from Babe's either. Fights were as common as the beer here, and the patrons played rough.

His tires were barely off the highway asphalt, his door opening right into traffic, if there'd been any. A Dodge Ram dually—a big truck with four wheels on the rear axle—was parked next to him, nose in to his tail. A scant few inches separated the two trucks, with the other guy's passenger side squeezed right up against his.

He checked the highway and slid out of the truck. He went to close the door, but stopped when he realized Leighton was climbing over to his side from the passenger seat, rather than attempting the narrow space on the other side. His momma having raised him to be a gentleman, Colin held the door open while she levered herself onto the console and over with a surprising amount of ease, finally sliding across his seat and out onto the dusty roadside.

She grinned at him as she stepped out, then stood staring up at the rusted and bullet-pocked sign that hung from the top of a lodge pole pine at the edge of the parking lot.

"Paul Bunyan?" she asked, eyeing what had once been a fairly decent rendering of the huge lumberjack in his red plaid shirt, arm draped over the wide shoulders of his blue ox, Babe. She glanced over at the bar and back again, giving him a skeptical look.

Colin grimaced. "Yeah, well. The couple who opened the place back in the day were university professors from down south somewhere. They retired up here and opened this place. You'd think they'd know better, being professors and all. But while they were expecting the bar from Cheers, what they got was a lot closer to Cops. When Leon's dad bought the place off of them—pretty much for a song, I'm told—he kept the sign. It was cheaper than buying a new one, and the name's okay. This is lumber country, you know."

"Who's Leon?"

"Leon Pettijohn. He and his wife Ellen took over from his dad a few years back. That was before I got here, but word is the old man retired to Mexico for the weather. Leon's here most nights, but Ellen works at the grocery in town. Far as I know, she never comes to the bar. Most women don't."

Leighton shifted her attention, her eyes scanning the nearly full parking lot before moving on to the bar itself. Not that there was much to see. Babe's was a small, single story, concrete block building, with a satellite dish on the roof. The whole thing was painted black, and Colin knew if you got close enough it looked like the paint had been rolled on thick by someone more interested in getting it done than getting it done right. The only window was a tiny triangle of filthy glass set in the front door. The bar was set well back into the woods, with thick tree trunks crowding around the three sides that didn't face the parking lot. Those trees blocked out what sunlight there was, leaving the whole building surrounded by bluish-gray shadows. When combined with the black paint job, they gave the whole thing a rather sinister feel.

Colin took another look at the trucks crowding the lot. "Fuck it," he said and followed Robbie to the back of the Tahoe. Yanking open the cargo hatch, he grabbed his vest and pulled it on with a few swift movements. Robbie met his gaze and Colin shrugged. "Too many trucks in this lot. Could be nothin', one of the logging crews shut down early.

But could be our guys are having an impromptu meeting in there."

Robbie frowned, then turned to look at Leighton and shook his head. Swearing under his breath, he pulled over the huge duffel, unzipped it and dug out his own vest. Leighton wandered back, her gaze sharpening when she saw what they were doing.

"What're you thinking?" she asked Colin. Her right hand was resting at her waist, just inside her jacket. Not touching her weapon, but close enough that she could get to it. She felt it, too. Something not quite right.

"I think maybe you should wait here," he said. "This isn't exactly a place for ladies."

Robbie coughed and Leighton gave him a dirty look before saying, "I didn't come all this way to sit in the car. Besides, you're the one who said to bring my guns. I'm guessing that's because you thought they might come in handy."

Colin shot a quick look at Robbie, who shrugged. "Don't look at me, man. I've seen her shoot." He reached into the duffle and handed Leighton one of the Uzis, along with three thirty-two round magazines, taking the second gun and some ammo for himself.

Leighton tucked two magazines into the thigh pockets of her black combats and slapped the other into the weapon with a practiced ease Colin hadn't expected, despite her claims of experience and Robbie the Ranger's endorsement. She glanced up and saw him staring.

"I'm pretty sure that weapon's illegal," he observed blandly.

"I'm licensed as a private bodyguard for Lord Raphael in every state in the Union," she said, grinning. "I can show you my permits back at the compound, if you'd like."

"I bet. I'll go in first. You two hang back a couple steps. Most likely, I'll know everyone in there, or they'll know me, anyway. I hope you're not shocked by foul language, Leighton."

Robbie laughed out loud at that and Leighton muttered darkly, "Yeah, fuck you, Robbie. You fink."

Colin shook his head at the two of them. Despite their sniping at one another, he got a clear sense of friendship between them. It reminded him of the relationships he'd had with the guys on his SEAL team. Guys like Garry McWaters. He had a moment's regret that Garry had chosen to leave Cooper's Rest. Times like this, he could have used someone he trusted. Not that he didn't trust Leighton and Robbie. But he didn't really know them either. It just wasn't the same as working with someone who'd walked into hell with you and come out the other side.

He pulled the combat sling over his head, secured his Benelli and closed the cargo hatch, clicking the locks closed. He'd taken three strides toward the bar when some instinct made him stop and click the remote again, unlocking the Tahoe's doors. Maybe it was all these trucks making him nervous, he thought, or maybe it was just the Uzis and the level of violence they brought with them. But whatever it was, he went with his instincts.

Leighton had moved ahead of him into the parking lot. She had her cell phone out and was snapping pictures of license plates as she passed them. She looked up as he walked around her, giving him a quick grin before slipping the cell phone back into her pocket.

Colin approached the door, Leighton and Robbie a few feet behind him, and spread out to the right. Robbie was standing slightly ahead of Leighton, his much larger body blocking hers, as if he expected something awful to come boiling out as soon as the door opened. Colin hoped it wouldn't come to that, hoped he was wrong and there was nothing in there but some hard drinking men taking advantage of an early break from a dangerous job.

Standing slightly left of the door, Colin reached out and closed his fingers over the door handle, pushing against the door first, and then tightening to pull. He caught movement from the corner of his eye as Leighton crossed out of Robbie's shadow and took two careful sidesteps to the right. Robbie turned to follow her and Colin opened the door.

And all hell broke loose.

Robbie bellowed a warning, "Murphy!" as he grabbed Leighton and shoved her between the nearest trucks on the right. A shaft of sunlight hit the opening door and Colin saw the black barrel of a gun just inside.

"Gun!" he yelled, as the boom of heavy shotguns roared from the trees around the right side the bar.

Colin felt the shock of bullets hitting the thick wood of the door before he rolled to one side, shielded by the solid block walls. The door crashed open and a hail of gunfire spewed out from the dark interior. Leighton and Robbie had taken cover behind a big two-ton rig, and they popped up now, both Uzis firing full auto as Colin scrambled away from his now exposed position next to the building wall and ducked between two trucks on the left side of the lot.

From the open door of the bar came the distinct rat-tat-tat of an M4 carbine on full auto, and all three of them ducked down as bullets sprayed the parking lot full of trucks, zinging off metal and shattering glass. The oily stinky of diesel fuel snuck into the air and then the hollow boom of a big tire deflating punctuated the racket.

Colin saw Robbie swivel around the two-ton's long bed and fire a quick burst. Someone screamed inside the building and the door slammed shut once again. But the steady barrage of fire from the right side of the building continued, the shooters using the trees and the bar itself for cover. They were concentrating all of their fire on Leighton and Robbie's position, which made Colin suspect they didn't know he was across the parking lot by himself.

He considered maneuvering quietly down the left of the building and around the back to come up behind the shooters, but ruled it out almost as soon as he thought of it. There was a back door to the bar. The guys who'd been waiting for him inside seemed to have given up on the front door, but that probably meant they were on their way out the back to join their buddies, and those boys were shooting to kill.

Judging purely by the amount of fire they were taking, the three of them were vastly outnumbered, and this was not a fight they could win. What he, Leighton and Robbie needed to do was get the hell out of Dodge. But how to do that without becoming even more of a target than they already were?

While Leighton and Robbie were right in the middle of a firefight, Colin was taking no fire and had no targets from his current position. He crouched over, maneuvering down the narrow space between the trucks and the trees on the left side of the parking lot. He kept glancing over his shoulder. The parking lot was wider than the bar, which meant he was exposed if someone realized where he was and came around behind him. He stayed as close to the trucks as he could, taking advantage of their bulk. He was hoping to get an angle on the shooters and provide cover for Leighton and Robbie to withdraw back to the Tahoe. He'd then have to cross the open parking lot to join them, but that was for later.

He cast a fleeting look as he ran along the tree line and saw Robbie go down. His stomach twisted and he paused, slipping alongside a beat-up F-150, but he quickly realized the big Ranger hadn't been shot. He had dropped into a combat crawl and was using the vehicles and ground for protection as he maneuvered closer to Leighton who was no longer sheltering behind the two-ton rig. While Colin had been positioning himself to join the fight, she'd managed to get away from the two-ton and was now crouched alongside a big Century wrecker, which was probably the heaviest thing in the lot and only two trucks away from Colin's Tahoe. If she could hold there until Colin got into position, he could provide covering fire while she retreated safely to—

He swore softly as Leighton pulled herself up onto the back of the wrecker and started firing, using the body of the tow arm for protection.

He heard Robbie cursing, heard the splintering crack of safety glass and the sharp ricochet of bullets as they struck the heavy metal of the wrecker's body. But Leighton stuck to her position like a tick on a hound, her slender frame tucked in behind the thick tow arm as she kept up a steady hail of fire.

Robbie caught Colin's attention, holding up a hand with five fingers. Colin nodded, watching as the fingers dropped one by one. When the countdown ended, Robbie stood up and started shooting, joining his fire power with Leighton's, pinning their attackers beneath a wave of death.

Colin dashed across the lot and dove beneath the dually which was snugged up against his Tahoe, belly crawling under the dually first and then his own truck. His back scraped on the Tahoe's skid plate, but he blew out a breath and came out on the other side, right next to the highway. He stepped up onto his truck's running board.

"Leighton," he yelled. "Fall back."

He thought she shouted an acknowledgment, but couldn't be sure as she ducked down and the back window of the wrecker blew out when someone cut a line of fire right across where her head used to be. Colin held his breath as she seemed to fall off the big wrecker, swearing in relief as she appeared next to Robbie who dragged her to the ground and shoved her under the next truck in line.

Colin pulled the Benelli up and fired a couple of rounds into the trees. He couldn't see anyone, but someone gave a cry of pain, far enough away that he knew it wasn't from the Benelli's fire. Shotgun in hand, he crouched down, back-stepped along the side of his truck and opened the rear passenger door.

"Robbie," he shouted. "Let's go!" Moving back to the hood, using the engine block for cover, he swung the Benelli away and took up his .9 mm, firing steadily. The sound of a second .9 mm joined in and he glanced over to see Leighton had rolled out from under the Tahoe and taken up a position near the rear end of the Tahoe. As he looked over, she ejected the magazine from her Glock 17, slapped in a replacement and resumed a steady, methodical rate of fire with a speed that spoke of a hell of a lot more than just target practice.

Robbie dropped to the ground on the far side of the dually, but he was too big and the truck was too close to the ground for him to crawl under, even if he blew out every ounce of air in his lungs. The front end of the dually was snug up against the trees and fully in the line of fire from that side. He duck walked his way to the back end instead, pausing long enough to slap the spare magazine into his Uzi.

Colin saw what the big man had planned and yanked his Benelli up again, stepping up on the Tahoe's running board and firing over the roof. It wouldn't hit anyone at this distance, but it would keep their heads down. Robbie took the advantage offered, rushing out of cover and backing toward the road, his Uzi spitting fire all the way. He reached the relative safety of the Tahoe, ducked beneath the windows and ran toward Leighton who was still shooting her Glock in a steady double tap rhythm—bang bang, bang bang.

"Leighton!" Colin shouted. He glanced worriedly at the open highway behind them. It was time to leave. Leighton nodded and kept firing.

The Tahoe tilted as Robbie jumped onto the running board behind the passenger compartment, putting Leighton between the two of them. Firing his Uzi on semi-auto in the general direction of their assailants, he roared at Leighton, "In the truck, Cyn. Now!"

Fresh gunfire erupted suddenly from a new direction, coming from the other side of the parking lot, where Colin had been hiding earlier. Colin dropped to the ground as Leighton stepped out and began firing, covering his back while he yanked the front door of his truck open, and began to return fire. He felt more than saw Robbie drop off the running board and glanced over to see him reaching for Leighton, trying to pull her out of her exposed position and into the protection of the truck.

Colin heard a soft grunt and a gasp of breath, heard Robbie's horrified shout of denial.

He spun around, a wordless protest choking him as ice water filled his veins. *"Goddammit!"* he swore. Leighton was slumped on the ground, blood already drenching the front of her combats and soaking into the dirt.

"Get her in the truck, Robbie. Get her in the fucking truck!"

"Last magazine," Robbie shouted and threw his Uzi at Colin who caught it one-handed. He tucked the .9 mm into its holster and started firing the Uzi on full auto, not even trying to hit anything. His only thought was to force their enemies to take cover long enough for Robbie to get Leighton in the truck so they could get the hell out of here.

He shot another glance over his shoulder and saw Robbie scoop Leighton up like she weighed nothing. Bullets were whizzing through the air, carving into the dirt parking lot and gouging chunks out of the trees. Someone got lucky and shot out all the windows on the Tahoe, spidering the safety glass. Robbie curved his body around Leighton and kept moving, crawling into the backseat and staying low.

Colin reached over and slammed the back door. Lying almost flat on the front seat, he shoved the keys into the ignition and jammed the truck into gear. He started to sit up, his foot reaching for the gas, when he heard a voice shouting orders, a voice almost as familiar to him as his own. His stomach clenched in denial. That was impossible. The gunfire died abruptly and he heard his name called. He closed his eyes against a wave of sick betrayal.

He slammed his truck door and hit the gas, his tires spitting dirt before catching on the asphalt with a scream of burning rubber.

Colin didn't think about anything for the first few miles. The windshield was cracked, but he could still see, so he concentrated on driving, on getting Leighton some help, on putting distance between them and goddamn Babe's. The Benelli sat on the passenger seat, along with Robbie's Uzi, the .9 mm was in his hand. His attention veered from the road in front to his rear view mirror and back again, over and over until he was convinced no one was following.

"How bad is it?" he asked Robbie, risking a quick look over his shoulder.

"You got a first aid kit or something in this truck?" Robbie asked tightly.

"Yeah, it's in the back, but it might be better if we—"

"Pull over, *goddammit,"* Robbie demanded. "I need something besides my hands to stop this bleeding," he added more quietly, his voice rough with emotion.

"Fuck." Colin checked the mirror quickly and turned down an old logging road, not stopping until the highway had disappeared into the trees behind him. He threw himself out of the truck, raced around back, lifted the cargo hatch and grabbed the first aid kid, slamming the hatch down.

Hurrying back, he yanked the back door open and swore viciously at what he found there.

Blood. Too much blood for one person to lose. Her pants were black with it, the gray carpet splotched with bright red. Robbie was cradling Leighton in his arms, one big hand stroking her hair back off her face over and over again. "Cyn, baby," he begged softly. "Hang on for me, sweetheart. Hang on."

"How bad is it?" Colin asked grimly.

Robbie looked up and met Colin's gaze. He didn't need to say anything. The grief was written all over his face.

"We're not giving up," Colin said in a hard voice. "The hospital's a good sixty miles, but I can make it in—"

"No." Leighton's voice was unexpected, terrifying in its frailty. Her eyes opened, fogged with pain as she searched Robbie's face. She fumbled for his hand with bloodless fingers. "Raphael. Robbie, you've got to get me to—" She groaned, vomited to one side, and then screamed with pain.

Colin automatically grabbed a wet wipe from the first aid kit, staring at it in his hand before throwing it onto the floor. What the fuck did it matter if her face was dirty?

Leighton's cries subsided into soft moans, and she sobbed suddenly, her hand falling away where she'd been clinging to Robbie's arm. "It hurts so bad, Robbie." Tears were flowing down her cheeks, choking her words. "Promise me, Rob," she said in a barely there whisper.

"I promise, sweetheart. I will. You know I will. Just take it easy now."

Colin was grabbing packages almost at random from the first aid kit, tearing them open, shoving the contents into Robbie's hand and ripping open some more. Bandages, wraps, gauze, anything he thought might help. The floor was littered with paper wrappings on top of the blood and vomit. Robbie was holding the makeshift compress over Leighton's bloody gut, keeping it in place even when she cried out, whispering apologies to her over and over again.

He looked up, suddenly intent. "Let's go," he said tersely. "She's right. We've got to get her to the compound before sunset."

"The compound?" Colin said. "Man, what the fuck's that—"

"Just do it," Robbie said in a hard voice. "Or I'll shoot you and drive the damn truck myself."

"Shit. I'll fucking drive. You take care of her."

Colin slammed back into the driver's seat and reversed into a three-point turn. He headed back to the highway, stopping only to check the road carefully before pulling out and starting back toward Cooper's

Rest and the vampire compound. He crushed the gas pedal beneath his boot, demanding every bit of speed the Tahoe had to give him.

"Stay with me, Cyn," he heard Robbie plead softly. Colin glanced in the rear view mirror. The big man's face was streaked with tears, his eyes closed as his mouth moved in a silent prayer.

"Ten minutes," Colin called over his shoulder what seemed like a lifetime later. He made a sharp turn onto the narrow road where the vamps had their compound. "Maybe less."

"You got a cell phone?" Robbie asked tautly. "Mine got fried back there."

"You shot?" Colin demanded, risking a backward glance.

"Nothing that won't hold. Cell phone," he repeated.

"Yeah, yeah. Here." Colin fished it out of his pocket and held it back over his shoulder, but Robbie didn't take it.

"Call this number," he said instead, rattling off an L.A. area code and phone number.

Colin punched it in, heard it ring. "It's ringing. What now?"

"Hand it over."

Robbie's hand was covered with blood as he took the phone. "Doc Saephan, it's Cyn. She's—" His voice broke and Colin heard him draw a deep breath. "Yeah," he continued. "It's bad. Gut shot. She's bleeding . . . She's bleeding a lot, man. Murphy says ten minutes tops." He paused a moment, then said, "Fuck me, you think I don't know that? Right, sorry. Okay. See you there."

Colin watched in his rearview mirror as Robbie wiped a bloody forearm across his brow. The big Ranger looked up and met his gaze. "You want this back?" he asked, holding out the phone.

Colin reached for the phone which was sticky with blood. He dropped it in the center console. "Who was that?"

"Doc Saephan. He's a trauma surgeon, one of the best in the country. His partner is one of Raphael's soldiers and he travels with us a lot, especially if Cyn's along. How long 'til sunset?"

It took Colin a minute to process the shift in subject. "Uh," he glanced around at the darkening trees. "I don't know exactly. Half hour, maybe? The light's deceptive around here."

"That's good," Robbie breathed. "You hear that, Cyn sweetheart. It's almost sunset."

Colin was pretty sure Leighton wasn't hearing much of anything. But she was still alive and that was something. And if this surgeon was as good as Robbie claimed, maybe he could save her life. And, okay, so it was nearly sunset and Raphael and the other vamps would be awake soon.

But other than Raphael holding her hand while she suffered, what the hell difference would that make?

He looked up as the compound came into sight. The guards were ready for them and had the big gate rolling out of the way before they got there. Colin barely slowed as he made the turn, hitting the brakes all the way around the curve of the driveway and up to the big building.

He'd never been here in daylight before. Every window in the place was shuttered on the inside, presenting a nearly uniform gray façade with the concrete front. The shutter over one of the big glass doors was rolling upward as he skidded to a stop by the broad stairs. The door flew open and a slender, dark-haired man rushed out, carrying a folded, portable stretcher. He hurried down the stairs and yanked open the back door before the Tahoe had stopped moving.

He took one look at Leighton in Robbie's arms, cursed fluently and snapped into doctor mode, which told Colin this was the Doc Saephan Robbie had talked about. Two of the gate guards had followed the truck up to the house and one of them was already deploying the stretcher, snapping it rigid as his buddy grabbed the other end.

"You," Saephan ordered Colin, "get around here and give them a hand. I don't want that dressing disturbed anymore than necessary right now. Robbie, we've got maybe twenty minutes before the shit hits the fan. I can't do much in that time, but I can make her look better than this. You ready?" he asked over his shoulder.

The two gate guards nodded. "Ready, Doc."

"All right, let's go."

Robbie scooted across the seat, holding Leighton to his chest, using his legs to control the slide. When he reached the door, he turned slightly and Colin was there with Saephan, taking her weight and transferring her to the stretcher. Leighton cried out as they moved her, but she didn't regain consciousness. Her face was deathly pale beneath the dirt and sweat, her hands lying limply over her chest where Saephan had put them.

The guards were already moving up the stairs, the stretcher held carefully between them, Saephan running alongside. A woman stood at the top of the stairs, holding the door open, her eyes wide with shock.

"Who the fuck is that?" Robbie demanded.

Saephan glanced over hurriedly. "She works here." He turned back, drawing Robbie's attention. "You've got to get out of here, Rob. Just for the night. I'll call you."

Robbie opened his mouth to protest, but Saephan held up a hand, his gaze following Leighton's stretcher through the doors.

"I don't have time to argue and you know I'm right. I don't need two patients. I'm sure this gentleman will let you sleep on his couch. Now I've got to help Cyn."

Saephan spun around, taking the last few steps and dashing through the open door, shouting orders as he went. The woman appeared again. She pushed the door closed, her fingers resting on the handle for a moment as she studied Colin and Robbie through the glass. Then she stepped back and the heavy shutter rolled down, closing them off completely.

Colin turned on Robbie, his anger a fire in his gut. He'd been forced to wait more times than he could count while his buddies fought for their lives, but he'd never been shut out like this. "What the fuck? Look, I get it, Raphael's gonna be pissed. But why can't we go in there with her? What kind of—"

"He's right," Robbie said dully, his gaze still riveted on the now-shuttered door. He lowered his head, sighing deeply. "Doc's trying to save my life. Yours, too."

Colin stared at him. "You know, somebody better start talking and I don't see anyone here but you. You got a trauma surgeon here, fantastic. So why aren't we life flighting the doc and Leighton to a hospital? And who the fuck cares if Raphael's awake yet or not? The woman needs medical care, not handholding. And why the *hell* are we standing out here like yesterday's trash?"

Robbie met his stare wearily, despite Colin's anger. "You've seen wounds like that before, Murphy. You know the odds. But you don't know much about vampires, so you'll have to trust me when I say her best chance of surviving is asleep in that building. That's why she's here and that's why I care what time the damn sun goes down, all right? As for the other—"

His words chopped off, his eyes going wide with shock as a huge roar thundered through the air, shaking the ground beneath their feet and sending dust flying everywhere as the concrete building trembled on its foundation.

"What the fuck?" Colin breathed.

"Raphael," Robbie whispered.

Chapter Twenty-Nine

Raphael came awake with a howl of rage. Cyn's pain was like a knife in his belly. He could smell her blood, could feel the weakening beat of her heart, her lungs struggling to breathe. For the first time in centuries, true terror struck him at the thought of losing her.

He didn't bother with clothes, striding across the room, cursing at the time it took to open the vault door, then the elevator door, waiting for the doors to close, for the elevator to rise the short distance to where she lay dying without him.

The doors opened and he sprang down the hallway and into the great room, snarling at the two human guards who stood huddled near the front doors.

"They carried her from the car, my lord," a man's familiar voice said. "They can't leave until the shutters open for the night."

Raphael's head swung to the human kneeling next to his Cyn. He growled, but the human had already turned away and was leaning over her, doing something that Raphael couldn't see. Raphael reached out, intending to pick the man up and throw him across the room for daring to touch her. But the human looked up at the last moment and Raphael had just enough presence of mind left to recognize Peter Saephan.

"Move," Raphael ground out.

Saephan did so, rolling away without standing.

Raphael sank to his knees in front of her and ripped open his wrist. He touched it to her mouth, but she was too weak to drink. He howled and raked a fang over his lip instead, bending over to press his lips to her unresponsive mouth, sliding his tongue between her teeth. Her breath hitched and then eased, as if she'd been waiting for him, as if she knew he was finally here.

Raphael closed his eyes and lifted his mouth away from hers, nearly crushed by the pain rolling off her in waves. He fisted his hands and rolled his head back on his shoulders, letting out an anguished roar that filled the building, shattering glass behind the heavy shutters.

Gathering Cyn into his arms, he stood and, holding her tightly against his chest, he moved with lightning speed back to the elevator.

Footsteps clattered behind him and he could hear Saephan speaking quickly. "She needs blood, my lord. Human blood to replace what she's lost."

Raphael ignored him. He knew only one thing. He was taking her down to his lair where no one could touch her, where she was safe. With him.

Raphael leaned against the back of the elevator, his head next to Cyn's, whispering words of reassurance, of love, of entreaty, begging her to stay alive. He barely noticed the doors opening downstairs, barely registered his own movement as he crossed the room and laid her on the bed with exquisite care. He sank his fangs into his wrist, tearing open the vein which had already begun to close. Blood poured out and he held it over her mouth, urging her to drink. He reached out to her mind, but she was too weak, too far gone. He felt a wave of despair and shoved it ruthlessly aside.

Dragging his fingers through his own blood, he rubbed it over her lips, sliding his fingers into her mouth and massaging her gums. Her tongue touched his fingers instinctively, taking in even more of his blood. She swallowed at last, feebly, then coughed, and cried out in pain, tears leaking from beneath her closed eyelids.

Raphael felt his own face wet with tears. "A little more, *lubimaya*," he whispered encouragingly. He widened the tear in his wrist, letting a few drops fall into her mouth and rubbing her throat gently. She swallowed again, more easily, her mouth opening eagerly as if some part of her understood, even in her unconscious state, that his blood would save her.

She swallowed once more, strongly this time, and he fed her a few more drops, murmuring to her the whole time, slipping into the fluid rhythms of his native Russian. Her chest rose in a deep breath and his heart soared . . . only to crash again when he began to remove her clothing and saw the true extent of her injuries.

Her ribs were broken along her right side, her chest black and blue where the vest had protected her. But the vest could do only so much, and its protection had not extended below her waist. The assassin's bullets had torn into her stomach and belly, ripping apart her intestines, damaging so many vital organs. Saephan had been worried about blood loss, but Raphael knew that was the least of it. Infection was already spreading through her damaged body, its heat like a malicious beacon taunting him.

Anyone else would have been dead already. Only her connection to him, fortified by the blood she took from him almost daily, had given her the strength to survive this long.

But his Cyn was not immortal. The blood they shared made her seem so to those who didn't understand. But for all their closeness, for all that she was life itself to him, the reality was they had not been together for long—less than a year, which was not long enough for her to have more than a minimal healing ability. A hundred years from now, she would be virtually immortal, but even then she would still need his assistance to heal something this devastating.

A spike of pristine fury stabbed him in the gut. He wanted to tear down the walls of his so-called civilized existence, to destroy every human who had dared to harm her, to lay waste to their foolish little town and leave every one of them bleeding and broken for the buzzards to feast upon.

Cyn moaned softly and Raphael jerked back to awareness, cursing himself. She had felt the strength of his anger and reacted to it. It had *hurt* her. *He* had hurt her. He wiped the tears from her eyes and lay down next to her, pulling her gently into the curve of his body, tugging the covers up around them. Ignoring everything else, everyone else, he sank into the depths of his power and pulled Cyn in with him. He would heal her. She would survive. Or they would die together.

Chapter Thirty

Sophia woke with a start, a howl of raw power still thundering in her head. She sat up, heart pounding with adrenaline, her own power roiling just beneath her skin. The sun wasn't down yet. She could feel it clinging to the horizon and yet she was awake. And she wasn't alone. Doors slammed open down the hall and footsteps pounded past. Voices were raised everywhere, shouting orders, demanding information.

Sophia closed her eyes and listened. Not to the voices of panic and confusion outside her door, but beyond to that ephemeral something which was the aura of power, the gift of Vampire.

She stretched out her senses as much as she dared in this unfamiliar place. She was a guest here, not welcome but tolerated. She had to be careful. A second wave of fury shook the walls, silencing the noise outside her door, sucking the breath from her lungs. She pressed a hand to her chest, drawing on her own power to insulate her from the anger and the pain that was all but oozing from the walls. Something had happened. Something terrible. Raphael was raging, his unbound wrath waking every vampire in the building, threatening to tear the walls down around them and causing the very air to vibrate for those with senses to feel it. She'd never experienced such raw pain from one so powerful. And she dreaded to discover what could have caused it.

She dressed quickly, pulling a t-shirt and sweater over her head, stepping into her denims and jamming her feet into low boots. She yanked open her door, braiding her long hair as she ran, joining the guards and others who were hurrying in the same direction.

The great room upstairs was controlled chaos. She smelled blood, a lot of it. She turned her head, tracking the scent to a location on the far side of the room, near the hallway to Lord Raphael's private lair. Two of his vampire guards were removing a couch soaked in blood, another rolling up the rug which had lain before it. Across the way, a door stood open to the large room where she'd met Raphael that first night and she saw Duncan standing just inside, talking to someone out of sight.

She headed that way. Whatever it was that had happened, Duncan would know. No doubt her presence would be unwelcome, but at worst, he'd ask her to leave. And at best, she would find out who was dead. Sophia hurried, determined to find out what had happened before Raphael's people had a chance to shut her out. This had to be connected somehow to the recent murders and to Lucien's disappearance. And she wanted to know whose blood had stained the couch red. She could think of no one but Raphael's mate who could trigger an outpouring of such agonized rage from the powerful vampire lord. But if Cynthia had been injured or if, God forbid, she was dying, how had it happened? And had Colin been with her?

She slowed down when she reached the tall double doors and slipped quietly inside the room. Duncan was there with his back to her, the mountainous Juro by his side. For the first time since she'd arrived, the two were dressed in something less than sartorial perfection. Duncan had clearly pulled on the first thing at hand, a pair of worn sweatpants and a t-shirt, his feet still bare. Juro had managed shoes and a pair of dark slacks, but his plain white shirt was untucked and only half buttoned.

Neither acknowledged her presence, focusing instead on the third person in the room—a human male who was speaking rapidly.

"It was bad, Duncan, as bad as I've seen. I don't know if even Raphael can heal something like that."

"What happened, do you know?" Duncan asked intently.

The human shook his head, clearly frustrated. "I didn't ask. Robbie called ahead, warning me they were coming in with her. When they arrived—"

"Who's they?"

"Ah, I think it was that local policeman—"

"Colin?" The name slipped out before Sophia could stop herself. She froze as everyone turned to stare at her.

"Sophia," Duncan said in a cool voice. He paused, then tilted his head slightly. "Join us. This is Doctor Peter Saephan, a valued member of Lord Raphael's staff." He gestured in her direction. "Sophia, Lucien's representative."

Sophia strode forward, nodding an acknowledgment. "What about Colin?" she demanded. "Was he injured?"

"No," Saephan said, shaking his head. "Well, not that I could see," he amended. "I mean, he and Robbie were both scratched and bloodied, but I think most of the blood was Cyn's. Murphy was driving. Robbie was in the backseat with Cyn and . . . Ah, God, Duncan, when I opened that door and saw them . . ."

When he looked up, his eyes were full of misery. "There was nothing I could do for her. Even with a full trauma unit, I don't know if I—"

"You did what you could, Peter," Duncan reassured him. "And so did Robbie by bringing her directly here. Where's Robbie now?"

"I sent him away. I was afraid of what Raphael would do when he saw her. I don't know—"

"They're still at the gate," Juro interrupted. "Murphy refuses to leave until he knows her condition."

"I'll talk to him," Sophia said, keeping her voice every bit as emotionless as Duncan's.

Duncan turned that impersonal gaze on her once again, his face completely expressionless. "Very well," he said. "Juro will walk you to the gate."

Sophia wanted to protest, to say she didn't need anyone walking her the hundred yards to the damn gate, but decided it wasn't worth arguing over. This was their compound and she'd only lose.

"As you wish," she responded impassively.

* * * *

Colin forced himself to remain still, aware of the hostile gazes of the vampire guards who had poured out of the building right after Raphael went ballistic and now seemed to have doubled in number over the last few minutes. Robbie was crouched a few feet away, next to the wall, his head lowered into his hands. He'd washed off most of the blood, using a garden hose near the garage. He'd all but forced Colin to do the same, turning the water on him almost without warning. Colin had thought it inappropriate, a waste of time and effort. Until the vampire guards had shown up to replace their human counterparts. Until every one of them had stared hard at Robbie, nostrils flaring. They'd paid less attention to Colin, but then he'd had less blood to wash away. Robbie had been almost bathed in it.

Colin strode over to his Tahoe just for something to do. It was pretty much wrecked—there were no windows left, except the windshield which was cracked, the body was riddled with bullet holes and the inside was soaking wet from the water they'd used to wash away Leighton's blood. Not that it mattered. He didn't care about the damn truck. The only thing that mattered was whether she was dead or alive. And no one seemed able, or maybe willing, to tell him that.

He tightened his hands into impotent fists. It was hard standing around here when what he wanted to do was start looking for the person who'd done this. That voice kept coming back, haunting him. He had to be wrong. It couldn't have been—

The vampire guards suddenly stiffened to attention. Colin spun around as Raphael's huge Japanese security chief appeared out of the darkness, followed by—

"Hello, Colin," Sophia said. Her face was utterly calm, her voice devoid of any emotion.

Colin just stared. This wasn't Sophie from the village. This wasn't even the seductress Sophia who'd shown up at his house the other night. This was Sophia in her true vampire visage. Her usually warm brown eyes were frigid pools of black in the low light, her body held haughtily upright. He turned his gaze away, wondering which was her real face, or if any of them were.

Robbie had risen from his misery-soaked crouch as soon as they appeared. He was standing in front of the big Sumo guy now, hands fisted tightly on his hips, as if to keep them from grabbing the vampire and shaking the truth out of him. "How is she, Juro? Is she alive?"

"She's with Raphael," Juro responded. "That's all we know."

"She's alive," Sophia said with certainty. "None of us would be standing here if she'd died."

That made no sense to Colin, but it seemed to satisfy Robbie. He nodded and looked longingly up at the big house.

"There's no need for you to leave, Rob," Juro's deep voice rumbled with surprising compassion. "We know you did all you could. Lord Raphael will know it, too."

Robbie looked up, his face filled with gratitude, but he shook his head. "She shouldn't have been there at all, Juro. It wasn't—"

"We both know her better than that," Juro insisted. And for the first time, Colin saw real emotion cross the huge vampire's face. It was the same expression he'd seen on Robbie's face in that bloody car. The same thing he'd seen on the faces of his buddies as they paced the sterile halls of military hospitals, waiting for word on whether they'd be attending another funeral or cheating death one more time. It was a look he'd seen on his own face in the mirror. They loved Leighton. Not as a lover, but as a friend, as a comrade-in-arms.

"Colin." Sophia's voice jerked him out of his contemplation of this new idea.

"Yeah?"

Her lip curled slightly, acknowledging his rudeness. "If I could have a word with you?"

He studied her for a moment, then shrugged. "Sure, why not."

* * * *

Sophia gazed up into Colin's eyes. They looked almost gray in this low light, but they were blue—a beautiful, crystalline blue that contrasted with the black hair now hanging wetly over his forehead. Black Irish, he'd told her, and she'd laughed at him, never having heard of such a thing before. He'd grinned then, but he wasn't grinning now.

She gave a small sigh, trying to figure out the right way to talk to this man, this human who, despite their shared past, was a stranger in this place and time. He didn't seem to appreciate the danger he was in, and she suspected it was because he knew so little about vampires. What she'd said a moment ago was absolutely true. If Raphael's mate died, nothing would save any of them. That much power unleashed in a storm of grief would wipe out everything for miles before the vampire lord even knew what he was doing. He would kill friend and foe alike, not discriminating in his blind need for revenge.

But even if Cynthia didn't die, there would be consequences. Colin and this other human, Robbie, had been with her when she was attacked. By Raphael's reasoning that would make them responsible for failing to protect her. Robbie, certainly—he was some sort of bodyguard, after all. But Colin would be considered equally guilty by association. Raphael would remain with his mate through tonight at least. But when he finally emerged from his lair, he'd be looking for someone to punish. He'd hunt down those truly responsible, but his anger would begin with the first person at hand. And if she had anything to say about it, that person wouldn't be Colin.

But how to convince Colin of that?

Aware of her vampire audience, particularly Juro, she turned her back on them and touched Colin's arm, urging him away from the group and across the driveway. It wouldn't stop Juro from hearing every word she said, but he wouldn't be able to see her face when she said it.

Colin surprised her by not shaking off her touch. He walked with her a few yards off the driveway and onto the grass. There wasn't much moonlight, but there were security lamps above the gate. And Colin seemed untroubled by the dark, his footsteps sure on the uneven lawn.

Careful to keep her back toward the gate and its vampires, she smiled up at him, a genuine smile of warmth and affection. He gave a little jerk of surprise at the change in her demeanor. He controlled it quickly, but she saw it. "You have very good night vision," she commented.

His eyes narrowed, as if trying to figure out her angle. But she didn't have an angle. Finally, he shrugged. "Years of night ops. It stuck with me."

"Colin," she began, her hand still resting on his thickly muscled forearm, "there's something you need to understand about vampires, especially powerful ones like Raphael. Their—" She struggled for the word. "—aggression is very close to the surface. It's part of what makes them who they are, what they are. Their willingness to fight for what they want, to defend what is theirs. And nothing, Colin, *nothing* is more sacred to a vampire than his mate. I heard the report from the human doctor—"

Colin's expression brightened immediately. "You talked to him? What'd he say?"

Sophia smiled, marveling at the complexity of her human. Her human? Was that what he was? She sighed inwardly. "He told us she is very badly injured, that if she is to live, it will be Raphael who saves her."

Colin shook his head in denial, a pained look on his face. "I don't understand that, Sophie. Everyone keeps saying Raphael can save her, but how?"

A part of Sophia jolted with pleasure at his use of the nickname, but at the same time, she realized just how *very* little Colin knew about vampires. This wasn't just about the power and aggression of a vampire lord; it was the essence of Vampire itself. And how much could she share with him? The vampire community held certain truths close and for very good reason. One of the most tightly concealed, and most dangerous, of those truths was the healing power of vampire blood.

She studied the familiar face of the man in front of her, so clear to her vampire sight. He was a handsome man, her Colin, with a strong jaw and square chin. The slight creases around his eyes testified to his easy laughter, creases that hadn't been there ten years ago. She wondered if another woman had put those laugh lines on his face and felt a surge of jealousy.

The truth hit her like a jolt of electricity. She wanted him. Not for an hour or a night. She wanted him to be hers and no one else's. Despair followed close behind, the knowledge that she might have destroyed whatever affection he once held for her when she'd made the decision to deceive him all those years ago.

Her jaw tightened determinedly. She couldn't change the past. But if she hoped for a future with him, only the truth would do now. He was still looking at her, waiting for an answer to his question.

"Vampire blood is very strong, Colin, especially that of an old and powerful vampire like Raphael. A vampire mating is based on the exchange of blood. Cynthia's human blood feeds him, but *his* blood keeps her healthy and young for as long as they are together. This is why most matings are between vampire and human. They sustain each other."

Colin was utterly focused on what she was saying. He was listening to every word, visibly taking it all in and storing it away, and she was forcefully reminded that Colin Murphy was more than a strong body, more than a highly skilled warrior. He had a first-class mind, as well.

But Sophia didn't want to say anything more about the healing properties of vampire blood, not in front of Juro and the others. She would answer all of his questions, but later, when they were alone.

Something in her expression must have warned Colin, because he cocked his head just a fraction and smiled slightly. "So he *can* save her life?" he asked.

"If anyone can," she cautioned. "We won't know for some hours and probably not until after sunset tomorrow. He won't want to leave her side until she is completely stable, and perhaps not even then. I don't know them well, but even I can see how much he loves her, and she's important to these others, too," she added, indicating the vampires around the gate and especially Juro and Robbie. "Their loyalty speaks, at least in part, to their master's love for her."

"So what are you saying, Sophie? What do you want me to do?"

She smiled gently. "I'm asking you to go home. It's not safe for you here. If—if—the worst happens, Raphael will go a little mad, at least for a time. That's why the doctor sent you and Robbie away in the first place. It's not safe, especially for humans."

"But Juro told Robbie he could stay, that it was—"

"And Juro is correct. It is probably safe for tonight. But Robbie has friends here, powerful friends who will argue on his behalf, perhaps even protect him as much as possible. You only have me."

Colin stared at her.

"I will let you know immediately when we have news, good or bad," she quickly added. "Trust me this much."

He was still studying her. Finally, he blew out a breath and looked away, shaking his head. "Fine. I'll go home. But I'm trusting you, Sophie."

He met her gaze evenly. "I'm trusting you," he repeated.

"I know," she said softly. "Thank you."

He shook his head once and spun on his heel, walking over to where Robbie still waited. Resting a hand on the other man's shoulder, he said quietly, "I'm going home to shower and change clothes. You're more than welcome to come with me. I have plenty of room."

Robbie looked from Colin to Sophia and back again. "Thanks. But I think I'll bunk here. I'll call you."

"I'll be waiting." Colin's head swung around, pinning Sophia with those perfect blue eyes. "You know where to find me."

Chapter Thirty-One

Colin pushed away from his computer and checked the time, just as he had every ten seconds since he'd been back home. It was barely two a.m., but it had been hours since he'd left the vamp compound and he was going a little stir crazy.

He'd hosed down the inside of his Tahoe one more time, knowing if he left it as it was, it would attract every scavenger in the forest. He'd washed away the remaining blood, balling up wet paper and bandages and throwing them in the secure trash bin behind his house. It had eaten up at least an hour—an hour he hadn't spent sitting around waiting to hear from Sophia.

He used up a bit more time with a hot shower, but showers just didn't take as long as they had before he'd spent twelve years in the Navy. Unless he was showering with someone.

Which brought him right back to Sophia. And damn if he didn't still want her. It would have been easy if she'd maintained that cool vampire persona she'd thrown at him tonight. Or even if she'd become someone completely different in the years since they'd spent time together. But tonight, standing there in the dark with her hand on his arm, the years had fallen away and he'd been back in that Central American village, with the heat and humidity, the smells of the jungle all around him, and the ebb and flow of Spanish teasing his ears.

Maybe he should just do her. A quick roll in the sack for old time's sake to get her out of his system. But it wouldn't be that easy with Sophie. It never had been. He'd loved her. Hell, he'd been planning that white picket fence with her. And now here she was back in his life.

He heard a car in the driveway and turned, his bare feet slapping the wooden floor as he crossed to the front window. He snorted softly. Yeah, here she was. Back in his life.

Colin pulled the door open as the lights clicked off on the Lexus sedan she was driving. He was a little surprised Sophie knew how to drive at all. She hadn't when he'd known her before. Not that he knew of, anyway. He scowled, reminded that he hadn't known as much about her as he'd thought.

The light from the doorway spotlighted her as she closed the car door and started toward him. Her eyes caught the light at a weird angle, making them shine a rich amber gold for a moment. He blinked and it was gone.

He watched her face as she drew closer, searching for some sign of bad news. He didn't see any, but . . . "Leighton?" he asked quickly.

"No news. But in its own way, that's good. Duncan—you know him, right? The blond vampire who's Raphael's lieutenant?" She waited until he nodded. "Well, Raphael is Duncan's Sire, the one who made him Vampire. They've been together for more than two centuries, and they work very closely together. Duncan is also quite powerful in his own right, which means he is far more sensitive to Raphael's state of mind than anyone else, except perhaps Cynthia."

Colin nodded impatiently. He appreciated the vamp history lesson, but what he really wanted to know was how Leighton was doing.

As if she knew his thoughts, Sophia explained. "I tell you this so you'll understand the reliability of Duncan's assessment. He reports that Raphael has sunk into the depths of his power." She held up a hand, forestalling his next question. "It's a trance of sorts, a deep, almost meditative state. It permits him to block out all distraction, to focus only on the one thing he seeks, or in this case, the one thing he cares about, which is his mate. He is concentrating all of his considerable power on healing her, not just his blood, but the . . . magic you'd call it that makes him a vampire lord."

"How does it work?"

She gave a grim smile. "It's impossible to explain, Colin. I'm sorry, it just is."

Intrigued, he asked, "Do you have this magic?"

She looked surprised by his question. "Yes, of course."

"So, it's not just vampire lords, then."

"No, but it is directly proportionate to the individual vampire's power. Tell me, do you have something else to drive?"

Lost in contemplation of vampire magic, Colin frowned at her question, then realized she was talking about his truck. "Right," he said as his brain caught up with what he was seeing. He jumped off the porch, strode over to the Tahoe, and began slamming doors. "This baby is a total loss. I'll have to have it towed tomorrow and then go down to the city and rent something. Why?"

Sophia sniffed discreetly and winced. "It smells of her blood. It would be best if you didn't drive it at all, not even to move it."

Colin rubbed a hand over his hair. "Is the blood smell really that bad? Maybe I should tow it tonight, after all."

"Not bad," she assured him. "It's only because the blood is Leighton's that I mention it. Things are more unsettled than usual right now."

"Unsettled how?"

"Even if Raphael succeeds in healing her, she'll be weak for some time. It will make him more protective of her than usual, and far more sensitive to the scent of her blood, especially on another man or his possessions."

"Got it. That's kind of freaky, you know. The whole blood scent thing." As soon as the words left his mouth, he regretted them. "Oh, hey, I didn't mean to be offensive."

"I'm not offended, Colin. I haven't so thoroughly forgotten my human origins that I can no longer remember what it was like."

They stood in awkward silence for a very long moment until Colin caved like the craven he was. "So. You want to come inside?"

Her smile was big and full of gratitude. "I would, thank you."

* * * *

Sophia walked past Colin and into the center of his living room. She could feel the tension in his powerful body and knew that, for all their easy banter, his feelings toward her were still ambivalent. Still, she considered it a victory that he could have a casual conversation with her at all.

"I won't stay long," she assured him. "I just needed to get away for a while. Everything is so tense over there, everyone on tenterhooks waiting for word, and I'm a stranger to them. All of the vampires traveling with Raphael are of his own making, including his entire security detail and all of the additional troops he brought in once the murders were discovered. They're fanatically loyal and they've completely closed ranks around him during this tragedy."

"Is that usual?" Colin asked. "I mean, for a vampire lord to be surrounded by his own . . . you know, the vampires that he made?"

Sophia shrugged. "Vampire lords are not trusting of strangers, so, yes, the innermost circle is frequently composed of the lord's own children. But it's unusual for a vampire lord to have so many of his own children living so closely to him, especially since many of Raphael's people are quite powerful. I would guess that at least half of the vampires living at my Sire Lucien's headquarters in Vancouver were turned by someone else, although he does have an inner circle of his own progeny."

"What about the others? The regular vampires, the ones who aren't vampire lords. What about their—" He stumbled over the word. "—children?"

She cocked her head, smiling in amusement. "It's not like movies or television, Colin. Only a very few vampires are strong enough to sire another, and the vampire lords reserve that power to themselves, in any event." Her expression turned serious as she continued. "Any vampire siring a child without permission would be severely punished, perhaps destroyed, depending on his master's wishes. It's a form of population control, you understand. Vampires are virtually immortal. Without restrictions, the population would soon grow too numerous."

Since she had no intention of telling him *why* too many vampires would be a problem—because they'd quickly outgrow their food source, i.e., humans—she turned away, strolling over to sit on one of the bar stools drawn up to the counter between the living room and kitchen. "Anyway," she continued, "I'm not one of Raphael's children, and with everyone on edge, tempers are flaring. The last thing I need is to get into some sort of pissing contest with one of his vampires."

Colin crossed the room, coming close enough that she could feel the heat of his body, could smell the strong masculine scent of his skin. He had a shirt on, but it was unbuttoned and his faded denims hung low on narrow hips. Her fingers itched to stroke a line down his chest and over his abdomen, to feel the hard ridges of muscle there and drag her nails along the arrow of dark hair that disappeared beneath the waistband of his jeans.

For his part, Colin seemed unaware of how attractive he was to her at that moment, reaching past her to snag an open bottle of beer from the bar before sitting on the stool next to hers. "Ignoring the pissing analogy for now," he said, "could you take 'em?" He started to take a drink, then paused and said, "I mean if one of the vamps started something, could you, know, win?"

"Probably," Sophia said, frowning at his total obliviousness to her desire.

Colin grinned. "Really?"

Her frown deepened to a scowl. "Yes, really. And I know what you're thinking. It's what they all think. The little woman, so pretty, so fragile. I'd expect Raphael's people to know better, at least. They accept Cynthia for what she is, after all." She flicked a hand in disgust. "But vampires are like some sort of primitive throwback. Granted, some of them were born a very long time ago when women were little more than chattel, but many of them weren't, and still they're all testosterone and thumping chests."

"I'm personally rather fond of my testosterone," Colin commented casually.

Sophia laughed, her eyes going wide with surprise as her hand flew up to cover her mouth. She felt her cheeks flushing, which was something that rarely happened to her anymore.

She dropped her gaze, her hands brushing needlessly at her black denim-clad thighs. "Anyway," she said, still not looking at him. "I *could* take most of them. Although, probably not Duncan. And not if they ganged up on me, but one-on-one, I'd do all right. I am Lucien's most powerful living child, you know. I doubt that's what he intended when he turned me, but here I am."

She grew quiet, thinking about the missing Lucien and the very real possibility that she could be in battle for control of his territory before too long.

"Sophie?"

She looked up and realized she'd been quiet for too long. "Sorry. I was thinking about something. The point is," she said, returning to their conversation. "Even if I could win, I don't want to fight anyone. That's not why I'm here."

Colin took another sip of beer, then laughed. "Little Sophie, big bad vamp," he teased and then froze, staring at her.

Sophia didn't have to hear his thoughts to know he was remembering why he shouldn't be hanging around talking to her—or God forbid, laughing with her. She saw it in his striking blue eyes. But she also saw the tug-of-war going on behind them. He *wanted* to do those things.

He wanted *her.*

He stood suddenly, setting his beer bottle on the bar with a loud clunk. "I'm sorry. I'm being rude. You want a drink or something?"

"Colin," she said quietly.

"I've got pretty much everything," he continued, walking around the bar and into the kitchen. "Or I can make—"

"Colin," she said again.

He stood with his back to her, his hands flat against the refrigerator door. He was silent a long time and then he turned around and looked at her. "What?"

"We have to talk."

"No. I don't think we do, Soph."

"I'd like to. Please."

His mouth twisted into a scowl. "Give me a reason, Sophie. Tell me something that can wash away the lies and make me believe in you again, something to make me believe you're the woman I was in love with ten years ago."

Sophia's heart thudded in her chest. She could hear it even if he couldn't. He'd never told her he loved her, not back then. Although she'd known it anyway. It was difficult *not* to read a man's mind when you were making love to him, when he was buried inside your body, bringing you more pleasure, more joy, that you'd ever felt before.

And she'd already promised herself that she'd tell him the truth.

"I was frightened," she said simply.

Colin jerked back. "Bullshit. I never did anything—"

"Not of you, Colin. Never of you. That was part of the problem. You were . . ." She shook her head in amazement. "Perfect. Too good to be true. You were kind, generous, funny. A wonderful lover and so vicious in protecting me from the slightest threat." She smiled, her thoughts going back to the time they'd spent together.

Colin huffed a dismissive breath. "It probably seems stupid now," he said. "I mean, you hardly needed me to protect you, but I didn't know—"

Sophia looked up. "No," she said quickly. "No, Colin. It was never stupid. It was lovely." Her smile fell away. "And I knew it couldn't last. I was a vampire. Even worse, I was a vampire living alone. Lucien had sent me away. Not harshly, and not without affection, but I couldn't go back to Vancouver. Not then. So I moved from country to country. I was still pledged to Lucien, and no other vampire was going to let me live in his territory for long when I was pledged to another."

"So why not do whatever it is you all do? Find a new lord or whatever?"

"I loved Lucien. I still do." Sophia saw Colin's eyes narrow unhappily at this and felt a little thrill of hope.

"I don't get it," Colin snapped. "This guy throws you out and you still love him?"

"It's not like that. Lucien is my Sire. We were lovers once, centuries ago when he first made me, but not since then. It would be almost unnatural if we were to become lovers now." She shook her head. "I don't know if I can explain it. I don't know if I have the words for something that is ingrained in every cell of what I am, what he made me, what he *gave* me."

"And what's that, Soph?"

Sophia stared at Colin and wondered if she could go back to that horrible place even for him. Her chest ached at the thought of reliving those terrible times. Almost as much as it did at the thought of losing Colin forever.

She closed her eyes briefly. "My father was a very wealthy man," she began. "My older brothers had all fallen to disease or warfare before I was ten. I was his only living child, his heir. My only virtue, the sole reason for my existence in my father's eyes, was my ability to produce a grandson to replace his dead sons. By the time I was thirteen and starting to grow breasts, we were entertaining suitors every night of the week. I say *we,* but no one cared what I thought. I was trotted out like one of his show horses and then sent back to my rooms. I wasn't even permitted to eat at the table."

Sophia stood and began pacing. None of these were good memories, but the next part . . . the next part was so painful, so powerful, it could still bring her to her knees. She paused and glanced over to where Colin was watching her, waiting. She turned away and started talking. "I was married at sixteen to a man I detested."

* * * *

1755 – Southern Spain

"I'm hot, Mama."

Sophia turned from the doorway where she'd been enjoying the fresh scents of the garden, hoping for a cool breeze. It had been hours since the sun had set on yet another scorching day, and still the air was warm, the breeze almost nonexistent. She stepped carefully in the near darkness, making her way over to the makeshift bed where her two young sons lay next to each other.

"I know, Teo. I'm sorry." She sat down, hearing the wooden frame creak beneath her weight. Teo, the oldest by less than a year, gazed up at her, his dark eyes gleaming in the dim light of the single lantern.

"It should cool down soon." She smoothed sweat-soaked hair away from his forehead, high and elegant like his father's. Both of her sons resembled their father, which was only natural, she supposed. Although she would have liked to see something of herself in them, maybe around the eyes or the shape of their chins? But no, they were each the very image of their father. And he was a handsome enough man, for all that he was a pig.

"Where's Papa?" Her younger son's face popped up over his

brother's shoulder.

She smiled fondly. "He'll be home soon, Miguelito."

"Will you stay here with us?"

"Of course, *bebé*. I will never leave you. Now sleep. I'll sing you a song."

She sang softly, sitting with them until they'd drifted off to sleep, so tired from their busy little boy days that not even the heat could keep them awake for long. She only wished she was so fortunate. The heavy layers of clothing she was forced to wear, even here in the privacy of her gardens, were stifling. The lacings were so tight she sometimes thought she'd suffocate before the sweltering heat could take her. On a normal evening, she'd have retired to her rooms and removed the binding clothes by now. But her little ones were so uncomfortable with the temperature in the house, despite its thick walls, and the gardens were green and welcoming.

She stood with a long sigh, walking over to the doorway and its feeble breeze. A light moved on the second floor of the main house and her lips tightened in irritation. Her husband had come home at last, finally leaving the bed of that French whore Alberto Alejandro had married last winter. Unfortunately, Alberto had dropped dead soon after, leaving his young wife a penniless widow in a strange country, without even the money to go home in disgrace, which was all she deserved.

One might have felt sorry for the woman had she possessed a scrap of virtue. But having lost one husband, she'd set her sights on Sophia's husband Teodosio, who was far from penniless. Or so the whore thought. She was too stupid to understand that Teodosio would never leave Sophia, not even for a beautiful French whore. Not because he loved Sophia, but because he loved the money and lands she'd inherited from her father. An estate which was vested in her sons, not her husband. If Teodosio abandoned Sophia, he would be just as penniless as his whore.

She watched as the balcony doors opened and her husband stepped outside, clearly seeking the same nonexistent breeze as she had earlier. He glanced down at the summer cottage where his sons slept and paused. Perhaps his eyes met hers. It was too dark to know, but he knew she was watching him. He turned without a word or gesture and went back inside.

A wave of pure, bright hatred swept over Sophia, leaving her shaking in its wake. Hatred for her father who'd married her off to a man she despised. Hatred for her husband who hadn't touched her since the birth of their second son. Not that she cared about sharing a bed with him. Many husbands and wives lived separate lives, especially those with estates to consider. But most at least played the game of courtesy, keeping their affairs discreet. Not Teodosio. The French whore was only the latest of his indiscretions and would not be the last. He would tire of her as he had the others, while Sophia bore her embarrassment in silence.

She spun back into the garden cottage, a flimsy structure with open half walls and a thatched roof, meant for picnics and children's games. Her sons had thought it a great adventure to sleep out here these last few nights. She smiled, remembering. They were the joy of her life, her treasures. Not even their pig of a father could destroy that.

She crossed over to the pitcher of water she'd had a servant bring out before retiring. The water had been cool then, fresh from the well. She tipped it over, pouring out the last few drops and remembered she'd used much of it to bathe their little faces before sleep. She made an impatient noise, thinking they were very likely to wake again during the night, asking for water and she'd have none.

She could wake one of the servants to get it for her, but the well was only in the courtyard on the other side of the kitchens. It seemed pointless to wake them for such a small thing, especially when she was up and certainly strong enough to do it herself.

Sophia checked each of her sons one more time, smiling at Teo's sprawl of sleep, while Miguelito lay quiet and tucked in against his brother's back like a mouse. She picked up the pitcher and walked into the gardens, heading for the courtyard.

She met no one as she passed through the kitchens and back outside to the big well in the center of the courtyard. The wooden cover was half open, the bucket sitting on the edge. It made a flat slapping noise on the water when she dropped it inside, and she leaned over idly, staring down into the dark depths until the rope tightened, telling her the bucket was full. Straightening, she took hold of the crank and began turning it to bring the bucket back up again.

She heard the shouting first. Leaning over to grasp the bucket as it rose over the lip of the well, she frowned. With the heat, Cook had been waking earlier than usual and it was nearly time for the kitchen drudges to be up lighting the fires on the big ovens. Had they discovered mice in the flour again?

She picked up her pitcher and started back through the courtyard, only to be nearly bowled over by men racing past her with buckets hanging from every hand. And then she smelled the smoke.

She dropped the pitcher, jumping over its wet shards as she ran for the gardens, visible now through the open kitchen doors. Golden light flickered among the green shadows, as if a million candles danced at once. Sophia was screaming before she reached the doorway, clawing her way through the clusters of terrified servants, knocking aside any who tried to stop her.

The cottage was on fire, its straw thatch a torch in the night. She registered the image as she shoved through the chaos, her heart thundering in her chest, her brain shrieking at her to hurry, even as her heart told her God would not be so cruel, that she was a good Catholic who honored her Church, who donated generously and never missed an observance. God would not take her beautiful babies, not her boys.

She raced toward the conflagration, searching the huddled servants as she did so, looking for her children, listening for their voices. Someone called out and she turned, relief like a rush of wind blowing through her soul. She scanned the faces all around and found her husband, Teodosio, his face a stricken mask of grief that stole his handsome features and turned them into something grotesque.

"Sophia," he said, his voice breaking as he reached out to her.

She backed away from him, shaking her head, somehow believing if she never heard the words, she would never have to know the awful truth.

"Sophia," he repeated, grasping her arms, pulling her against his chest in a mockery of comfort.

"No!" She pounded his chest, pushing him away.

A loud whooshing sound spun her around in time to see the flames twist suddenly higher, sending a shower of sparks to catch on the trees. Sophia screamed and raced toward the fire. Her children were in there, why was no one saving them? Why was their useless father weeping instead of braving the flames in search of her sons?

The heat hit her like a wall, shriveling the small hairs on her skin, burning her hands and face before she'd come within ten feet of it. She would have gone farther, would have run into the fire itself, but strong arms grabbed her, holding her tightly, turning her away from the intense flames.

Sophia fought, shrieking, kicking, clawing at the hands that held her. "*Chérie*, Sophia, no. It's too late." His voice was a soothing murmur of foreign words, his hands never easing their grip no matter how hard she fought.

The roof caved in without warning. Embers flew and servants shrieked, running after the smaller fires, lest the house catch and the entire estate burn down. Not that Sophia cared. She watched in despair, her eyes cloudy with tears and ash, her breath coming in sobs as she fought to breathe in a world that had lost all meaning.

The arms holding her relaxed slightly, lowering her until her feet touched the ground. She twisted, looking up to see the face of a stranger, blackened with soot from the flames, tears carving pale streaks down smooth cheeks.

Overwhelming grief drove Sophia to her knees. Her heart seized in her chest and she welcomed the agony. She drew breath to scream, but her lungs couldn't find the air, and she welcomed that, too. Why should her heart beat, her lungs bellow when her children, her beautiful babies, were gone? She raked her nails down her face and felt warm blood welling, replacing the tears she couldn't shed. She found her voice at last, but it was only to keen like an animal, rocking back and forth, clutching herself against a pain beyond any other.

She heard nothing of the servants or the villagers who had come running to help fight the fire which threatened everyone should it get it out of hand. Their shouts and cries, the distant panicked screams of the horses, footsteps running as bucket after bucket of water was thrown into the greedy maw of flame—all of it was meaningless noise. Her mind was filled instead with the sweet voices of her children, with their laughter and songs. She saw no reason to listen to anything else . . . until a woman's voice pierced the night, shrieking curses.

Sophia froze, her head swiveling to one side to listen. Men's voices were shouting angrily, the woman's outraged screams rising above them.

"Don Teodosio," one of the men shouted. "We found this one running away!"

Sophia heard the gasps all around. She stood and saw her husband glaring down at his whore of a lover. The woman was blackened with smoke, her hair seared away in places, but it was her hands that drew everyone's attention. They were reddened and burned, covered in blisters.

Sophia raised her gaze to Teodosio's look of horrified realization. She shrieked wordlessly, running the short distance and grabbing the whore by her hair, yanking at it in great handfuls until the men pulled them apart. Teodosio wrapped his arms around Sophia, whispering her name over and over again like a prayer for forgiveness.

Sophia howled and spun on him, reaching up and slapping his face. She had no forgiveness to give. "You did this," she snarled furiously, her face crumpling in grief. "You murdered your own sons." Her voice broke on the last, sobs replacing her words as she turned away from him.

"No. No, Sophia, please, I had no—"

Sophia didn't hear the rest of his denials. She went back to the fire and dropped to her knees, not to pray, but to bear witness to the death of her children.

* * * *

They'd buried her babies the next day. Their small bodies had been taken from the charred hulk of the cottage and swathed in white linen while Sophia lay in bed, drugged into unconsciousness by a well-meaning physician who'd thought to spare her the sight of all that was left of her sons. She'd stood on the dry hillside, listening to the priests mutter their empty words in fervent voices of how her children had been called to God, how their great destinies had just begun. But Sophia had no use for a God who would do this, who would permit a worthless French whore to murder innocent children. She'd turned away from them and their prayers, turned away from her faithless husband and walked into the hills, waiting for death to find her.

Death hadn't come. But Lucien had.

Three days later the heat broke at last. Sophia stood once more over the graves of her sons and felt the night's cool breeze blowing across the parched hills. She thought how Teo and Miguelito would have laughed to feel it and smiled sadly. There would be no more little boy laughter in her life.

Shouts arose from the estate house behind her. She looked over her shoulder and saw lantern lights moving out of the gates, toward the hillside where she stood alone with the souls of her sons. Her piggish husband had discovered her absence again and was no doubt screaming at the servants to find her.

The lights were drawing closer. She turned her back on them, whispered a final farewell to her children, and walked into the darkness.

He was waiting for her there—Lucien, the stranger who had held her as the cottage burned, who'd saved the life she no longer wanted to live. He'd been waiting for her that first night, when she'd snuck up onto this hillside, intending to bleed out her own life onto the graves of her sons. He'd kept the knife from her wrist and held her while she wept, sobbing out her grief to a stranger in a way she hadn't until then. There hadn't been anyone else she'd trusted enough to do so.

And then he had told her he could make it go away—the pain, the awful, wrenching loss, the emptiness that would never be filled. They would have to leave, he warned her, to travel far away, farther than she'd ever gone before, than she'd ever dreamed of going. Sophia had begged him to do it. She'd been ready to leave immediately, that very moment, if necessary. After all, what reason did she have to stay? But Lucien had insisted she wait. She had to be sure, he said. Because, once accepted, what he was offering could not be undone.

Sophia had been certain from the moment he first spoke, but he would not be moved. Until tonight. This would be their third meeting and he'd promised her they would leave tonight.

"Sophia." His voice was warm and rich, like heated rum on a winter's night.

"Lucien," she said softly, her own voice full of relief. "Tonight?" she asked.

"Tonight, *chérie*. If you are certain."

"I am. Lucien, please."

He smiled, and he was beautiful. He held out his hand.

* * * *

"Sophie?"

Sophia blinked in surprise. She'd been so lost in the past that she'd forgotten where she was. She looked around blearily, as if she'd just awakened. She was still standing, her legs aching with tension, her arms crossed and hugging herself tightly. Colin was near the bar, half sitting on one of the tall bar stools.

Sophia closed her eyes again, her chest aching and hollow. Even now, after centuries had passed, her loss was as fresh as if it had happened yesterday.

Colin stood, coming closer. "Sophie?" he repeated.

She opened her eyes and looked up at him.

"You said Lucien took away the memories," he said, frowning.

She met his gaze for a moment, seeing the same warm compassion there that she'd seen in Lucien's eyes so long ago. And she thought neither man would be pleased with the comparison.

"He did," she said at last.

"Then how—"

"He gave them back to me after awhile. He told me the story, as if it had happened to someone else and asked me what I'd do. I told him I couldn't imagine a mother not wanting to remember her own children, and so he gave them back to me. Not only the memory of their deaths, but of their lives, too. All those wonderful moments."

"Did you leave Spain right away after that?"

"Eventually. For all his debauchery, Lucien is very practical about certain things. Most of the older vampires are, especially when it comes to retaining wealth. When my sons died, the estate came back to me, for my future children. My father was quite determined that only his blood would inherit. And Lucien had agents in place to handle such things.

"My father's entire estate—mine now—was sold, the investments liquidated. At a considerable loss, I'm certain, but we didn't care about that. Or Lucien didn't. I didn't care about anything at that point. It took several months, and I had to make a few appearances before the authorities, but eventually it was done."

"What about the Frenchwoman? How did they punish murder back then?"

"I don't know what they would have done," Sophia said dismissively. "I didn't leave it to them. I killed her. She was my first." She glared at Colin, daring him to dispute her right to exact revenge on her children's killer.

Colin's eyebrows shot up in surprise. "You mean your first vampire kill?"

"It was a long time ago, Colin. Things were very different than they are now, especially for vampires."

He gave her a knowing smile. "I'm guessing not everyone you kill becomes a vamp, then. I can't imagine you giving that bitch immortality."

Sophia met his smile with a grin of her own. "You're right. I killed the whore outright, and I made sure she knew I was the one doing it, too."

Colin gave a sideways tilt of his head. "Sounds good to me. What about your husband? What happened to him?"

"I have no idea. I wanted to kill him, too, but Lucien wouldn't let me. Teodosio had no part in the deaths beyond lust and stupidity. And few men would be alive if *that* were a killing offense."

"I think I'm offended," he said thoughtfully.

Sophie smiled wearily. The memories no longer had the power to make her weep, but the emotions were still powerful, the loss still keen, and it was exhausting to talk about it.

Colin stepped even closer, his body radiating heat like a furnace, the thump of his heart loud in the sudden quiet.

"I'm sorry I made you talk about it," he said. His hands hung loosely at his sides, fingers flexing over and over as if he didn't know what to do with them.

Sophia met his eyes. "I wanted you to understand," she insisted. "You asked for the reason I left, the reason I let you think I was dead that night." She reached up and gave into temptation, touching his cheek, letting her fingers linger on his lips when he surprised her by not pulling away. "Do you know, I still hear that café exploding in my dreams. I was blocks away and still the street buckled so hard I nearly fell. Everyone was screaming and I looked up and saw the flames and I *knew*. There were the rumors—we'd even talked about them, you and I—that certain people were unhappy with the government, unhappy with foreigners suddenly appearing all over the country, and I knew they'd attacked that damn café and that you were in it.

She shook her head, remembering. "I ran as fast as I could, not bothering to be discreet or to hide my vampire otherness the way Lucien had taught me. When I reached the café and I saw the flames . . . I was back in that garden all over again, watching fire take someone I loved. I nearly went in after you. I didn't know if I could survive it or not, but I didn't care. I just knew I couldn't live through that again. But then I saw you standing across the square. I saw your friend hanging onto you, dragging you away as you fought him, and I knew the Fates had given me a second chance.

"I had lost my precious children. There was nothing I could do about that. But you were alive, Colin. Your life had been spared, and I wasn't going to ruin the chance I'd been given, that *you'd* been given, by dragging you into the drama of my life. I was a vagabond, traveling from place to place. I couldn't go back to the United States with you. The U.S. vampire lords would never have tolerated my presence. And we were never going to have that white picket fence you'd talked about. There would be no children, no picnics on the beach in the sunshine. I had nothing to offer you but blood and darkness. So I let you walk away, and I told myself it was what the Fates wanted, that I'd done the right thing."

Colin reached out at last, his arms tightening around her, his breath brushing against her hair when he asked, "And what do you think now, Soph?"

She sighed and spoke without lifting her head, afraid of what she'd see in his face. "I think I might have been wrong about what the Fates were telling me back then. Or maybe I just don't care anymore. You're the only man I've ever loved, Colin Murphy, and I'm tired of living without you."

Chapter Thirty-Two

Colin swore softly under his breath, cursing himself for every kind of fool as his body reacted to Sophie's words. If what Leighton had told him about vampiric senses was true, Sophie probably already knew that his heart was thudding and his breathing was so fast he was almost hyperventilating. And she sure as hell couldn't miss the erection trying to bury itself in her soft belly.

"Sophie," he murmured.

She lifted her head to look up at him, her beautiful, brown eyes full of questions.

"I probably should have told you this earlier," he began. Her eyes grew wider and a little fearful, and he hurriedly added, "I love you, darlin'." He stroked the fingers of one hand down her soft cheek. "I loved you then, and I've never stopped."

He lowered his head, intending to kiss her gently, soulfully. Something appropriate to this special moment. But his body had its own ideas. His mouth touched her lips and raw desire swept over him, tightening his gut and hardening his cock like a steel rod. He'd missed this for nearly ten years, missed Sophie, with her lush curves and tender mouth, her gorgeous breasts . . .

She moaned softly, her fingers tugging his hair and forcing him closer. He grinned against her lips. And, yeah, he'd missed that, too.

His mouth never leaving hers, he swept her up into his arms, carried her into the bedroom and lowered her to the bed. Her fingers were scrabbling fitfully at his shirt and he shrugged out of it. She switched to his jeans, undoing the button and tugging at the zipper. He reached to unzip it himself, but paused to appreciate his Sophie, as she shimmied out of her tight jeans and tugged her sweater over her head.

He knew the fashion these days was for thin women with narrow hips and tiny asses. But that wasn't for him. He loved the feel of soft hips and a rounded belly beneath his fingertips, of succulent breasts crushed against his chest as he sank into a woman's warmth. In short, what he liked in a woman was Sophie.

She stretched out on his bed, preening beneath the heat in his eyes, proud of her curves and wearing nothing but lace, a matching set of panties and bra in warm pink that made her skin look flushed with health in the light of his single bedside lamp.

"Take them off," Colin growled, his hands on the zipper of his jeans.

Sophie gave him a wicked grin. "I will if you will," she purred, climbing up onto all fours and crawling across the bed toward him.

Colin watched her come, her large breasts threatening to spill out of their fragile confinement, her hips shifting enticingly with every movement. When she reached for his zipper, he grabbed her fingers.

his eyes flashing up to meet hers.

She laughed, a low, sultry sound that took his breath away. "I'll be careful," she promised and bent over to kiss his cock through the denim, giving him a tantalizing view of her perfect ass.

Colin fisted his fingers in the thick strands of her long hair as she slowly lowered his zipper. He groaned out loud when his cock was free at last, when Sophie's delicate hands brushed against his hips as she pushed his pants down to his thighs.

He twisted her hair in his hands, holding it back from her face so he could watch as she began licking him slowly, twining her tongue around his cock, her fingers reaching beneath him to cradle his balls. He sucked in a hard, fast breath when she took him in her mouth, when she tilted her gaze upward to watch his reaction as she began to move up and down, his cock sliding in and out between her plump lips. He began to move his hips slowly, going deeper into her mouth and throat with each thrust.

His cock touched the back of her throat and Sophie moaned hungrily, the sound vibrating along his shaft like a tuning fork. Colin closed his eyes and began thrusting harder, his sac tightening beneath the caress of her fingers, her tongue stroking him as her mouth sucked harder and faster.

Colin groaned. He wanted to fuck her, wanted to be inside her and he'd never—

Jesus Christ!

Sophie ran a fingernail along the taut skin of his sac, a sharp, intense pain that sent every one of his senses into overdrive. He gave a hoarse shout as all thought disappeared, as every nerve ending suddenly centered on his cock and the need to come *now*. His orgasm roared through his body, boiling out of his balls and down his cock in a rush of pure, heated pleasure. Sophie drank it all in, her fingernails digging into his ass as she held onto him, as she kept him from flying apart.

* * * *

Sophie twirled her tongue around Colin's softening cock, smiling as he shuddered one more time. His fingers were still wrapped in her hair, but they were massaging gently now as his big body relaxed one muscle at a time.

She pulled back with a final lick, coming up onto her knees. He wrapped his arms around her, burying his face against her neck, kissing gently, moving up her jaw to her mouth. His hands dropped to her bottom, squeezing softly.

"You have the most perfect ass," he murmured.

She laughed. "So do you." She kissed him lightly, biting playfully at his lips. "If you show me yours, I'll show you mine."

He lifted his head sharply, blue eyes hot and intent. "You first."

Sophie trailed her fingers across his broad, muscled shoulders and down his arms, loving the hard feel of him. She moved back a few inches and sank down onto her heels, caressing herself, her hands moving slowly over her lace-covered breasts, down past her narrow waist to the fullness of her hips, along the outside of her thighs. Colin's gaze followed every movement, narrowing as she dipped her fingers to the inside of her thighs and spread her knees wide, smoothing her hands sensuously along her tender skin and over the pretty triangle of lace covering her sex.

His eyes lingered between her legs, suddenly snapping up to meet hers. "I want you naked, Sophie."

She smiled lazily, gliding her tongue along her upper lip as she lowered first one bra strap and then the other, feeling the heat of Colin's rapt attention as he watched her breasts slowly begin to overflow the lacey cups. She reached behind her and unfastened the clasp, letting it fall forward, feeling the accustomed rush of pleasure as her breasts were freed, glancing up and gasping as the hunger in Colin's eyes tightened her nipples and left her aching with need.

Her hands were trembling slightly when she tossed the bra to one side, shaken by what she saw when Colin looked at her. He wanted her. She knew that. But the strength of his lust, the sheer intensity of it . . . that rattled her. She had grown accustomed to her young men in Rio, the human toys she played with for a while and then cast aside, lovers who were completely dominated by her needs and wants. And she realized abruptly that Colin was not that kind of man. He was alpha down to his core, and he was eyeing her the way a lion eyes a particularly tasty gazelle.

"Colin," she started, but he interrupted her.

"The rest of it, Sophie," he growled. "Take it all off."

She swallowed hard and hooked her fingers into her panties, tugging them down her hips. But Colin didn't wait. He shoved his jeans and underwear down his legs, stepping out of them and onto the bed in a single movement. She fell backwards as he stripped her panties down her legs and over her feet, his big hands stroking up her calves and between her thighs, spreading her wide. But he didn't stop there. He ran his fingers over the silky bare skin of her mound, humming to himself with a pleased smile as he slipped two fingers between her swollen folds and, tormenting her with her own slick heat, bared her completely beneath his gaze. He looked up then with a wicked glint in his eye.

"My turn," he said.

Sophia bucked as his mouth fastened on her clit, sucking until it throbbed hungrily, every stroke of his tongue sending a jolt of unbelievable desire through her body—a shock of electricity that left her trembling perpetually on the edge of climax. Had any man ever pleasured her so? Had she let them? She shrieked out loud as he drove the same two fingers he'd been stroking her with deep inside her at the exact moment his teeth grazed her tingling clit. His fingers began to thrust in and out slowly and she pushed against them, desperate for the orgasm she could feel building in every inch of her body, in her breasts which were full and aching, in her womb which seemed to throb with the need to orgasm. She grabbed Colin's hair, pressing his mouth against her more tightly, afraid she would die the true death if he didn't release her soon.

"Colin," she gasped, then groaned wordlessly.

His tongue swept lazily along her slit, teasing her with quick brushes against her pulsing clit. He slid his fingers out from inside her and sucked them noisily, drinking in her wetness and watching her the entire time. "You taste good, Soph."

"Colin!" she practically shrieked at him.

He laughed! But then he sobered almost immediately, becoming preternaturally intent as he raised himself up over her body, his hips spreading her legs even wider, his big, hard cock sliding back and forth in the aching wetness between her thighs. "Is this what you want, darlin'?"

"Yes." Sophia nodded, nearly sobbing with relief. "Yes."

She wrapped her legs tightly around his hips, her fingers digging into his arms, holding him close lest he think to torment her further.

Colin drew back slightly and reached down, positioning his cock at her entrance. He looked up and met her eyes, holding her gaze while he slammed his full, hard, wonderful length deep inside her.

Sophia screamed as she came hard, her vaginal walls convulsing around his shaft, the orgasm rippling up to her womb and into her breasts, tightening her nipples and sending ripples of exquisite eroticism throughout her body. She thrust against him almost violently, unable to control her need to feel more—the rough scrape of his chest hair against her sensitive breasts, the thickness of his cock as he stretched her wider with every thrust, the tautness of his arms as he held himself over her, his powerful thighs and ass pumping his hard shaft deep inside her like a piston.

Sophia wrapped her arms around him, raking her nails down his back, feeling the warm blood beneath her fingertips. Colin threw his head back, groaning as he thrust harder. She pulled him closer, wanting the touch of his mouth, his kiss.

Their lips met in a hard, hungry kiss, teeth clashing, tongues battling each other in a frenzy of mating. She bit his lip, drawing her first taste of his blood. Heat zinged through her veins, that tiny sip like molten lava, racing to her heart and sealing her fate. Colin Murphy was hers and she would kill anyone who tried to take him from her.

"Come for me, Sophie," he murmured against her mouth, his blood still fresh on his lips. "Let me feel you come all over my cock."

As if his words were a psychic trigger, Sophia's entire body shook with orgasm, every muscle, every nerve responding to his demand. She moaned, overwhelmed with sensation, crying out as ripples of pleasure rolled over her like a tidal wave, tossing her back and forth as she hung on to him for dear life. Her thighs squeezed his hips as she bucked beneath him, her inner walls caressing his cock, trapping him inside her until he surrendered, throwing his head back and roaring as he joined her in ecstasy, his climax a heated rush against her trembling womb.

* * * *

Colin collapsed against Sophie, her soft, full breasts a sweet cushion against his chest. The image of those breasts with their large swollen nipples, plump and straining for his mouth, sent a pulse of fresh desire straight to his groin, taunting his drained cock with impossible ideas. He groaned and shifted sideways, taking his weight off Sophie and pulling her against his side. She responded limply, one arm falling over his chest as if she didn't have the strength to lift it.

He smiled in what he recognized as pure, male satisfaction and dropped his arm down her back to cup that spectacular ass. Another shock of desire stabbed his groin, this one causing his cock to twitch weakly. The guy might be drained, but he was recovering.

"I can hear you gloating," Sophie murmured around a yawn.

"I'm not gloating," Colin responded. "I'm planning for the future."

"Oh my God," Sophie protested dramatically. "Is there no satisfying you?"

He laughed. "Eventually."

Sophie lifted her head to smile at him, kissing her way down his chest. He rolled slightly, wrapping her in both arms. Her hands slid around his back and she gasped.

"You're bleeding," she said tightly.

"Scratches, I think," he said, suddenly aware of the distant pain. "They'll heal."

Sophie sat up, staring intently at the blood on her hand. She shifted her gaze to meet his. "I can make them heal faster."

Colin swallowed hard. Her eyes had taken on that weird amber glow again, and his sex-addled brain finally clicked on what it meant. She was a vampire. And he was bleeding. "You mean—"

"My blood can heal you," she said, completely calm. "Not just the scratches, but all of these as well." She touched the nicks and cuts he'd acquired in the gun battle that had nearly taken Leighton's life. She met his gaze again. "And anything else, Colin. If you take my blood, you'll feel ten years younger."

Colin blinked. "Is that what you were talking about back at the compound? About Raphael healing Leighton? You mean he can literally *heal* her?"

"Yes."

"But . . . you didn't see how bad she was, Soph. She was gut shot. There was blood everywhere. I didn't really expect her to make it back to the compound alive. Can vampires heal something that bad?"

"If the vampire is powerful enough, yes."

"But if that's true, why isn't vampire blood the new wonder drug?

Every researcher in the country could use something like that."

"And what would happen to us? To the vampires?" Sophie asked gently. "I've seen what humans are capable of. What do you think your leaders would do if they learned about our blood? They'd lock us away in a heartbeat. Or they'd try." She brushed back his sweat-dampened hair. "No, Colin. This is one secret every vampire alive respects. Or they die. Simple as that."

"Then why are you telling me?"

"There are exceptions, *meu querido*. People we trust." She shifted, pushing him over onto his back and going up onto all fours as she bent to lick at the sweat on his chest, biting his flat nipples gently. He wound his fingers through her long hair and tugged her head back, meeting her eyes.

"Do you want to take my blood, Sophie?"

She stilled, studying him in that intense way a predator watches its prey. Her tongue swept out and across her upper lip and he saw the first hint of her fangs, white tips barely visible below her gums. Her eyes changed, their color once again a brilliant amber that left humanity behind. She drew a long, slow breath, her nostrils flaring as they took in his scent.

"I can smell it," she said in a low, sensuous purr. "The scent of your blood is intoxicating. Think of the most delicious aroma you've ever encountered, baking bread, chocolate, a bubbling stew—all of that and more. It's not just blood, Colin, it's *your* blood. And, oh, yes, I want it."

Colin drew in a deep, hard breath. Adrenaline spiked, but it wasn't fear. Or not only fear. He'd have to be nuts not to be a little intimidated by the idea of someone biting into him and drinking his blood. But it was more than that. It was lust, pure and simple. Damn if he wasn't turned on by the idea. And if that made him a sick fuck, then so be it.

"Okay," he said. "Let's do it."

The amber glow of Sophie's eyes amped up, like turning on a flood lamp. She opened her mouth and her fangs slid into full view, white and gleaming. "Are you certain?" she asked.

Colin nodded. "Do it."

She smiled slowly and stretched out on top of him, sliding her satiny smooth mound over and around his cock, enticing him, as if he needed anymore enticement. Her nipples scraped against his chest as she buried her face against his neck. Her breath was hot, her tongue a stroke of wetness along the side of his neck. His heart was racing faster than in the worst firefights he'd ever endured. He rebelled against the fear, reminding himself this was Sophie. He began to thrust gently beneath her and she groaned against his neck. He felt something hard and blunt scrape over the skin below his jaw, heard her indrawn breath.

Ecstasy. His cock hardened instantly, unbelievably. Sophie was straddling him, her legs on either side of his hips, her silky hair draped over his chest. He could feel the tug of her mouth, the slick glide of her fangs as she took his blood. And he felt a kick of desire like nothing he'd ever experienced. He wanted to throw her over, spread her legs and fuck her hard and long. He gripped her ass, sliding his hands over the firm mounds and dipping his fingers between her legs. She was soaking wet and still hot from her earlier climax. She moaned when he began pumping his fingers in and out of her, rubbing herself gently back and forth over his erection where it lay trapped deliciously beneath her. He guided the fingers of his other hand along the crease of her buttocks, teasing her tightly puckered star, and Sophie jerked in his arms, the tight walls of her sex clenching around his fingers.

There was a sting, a slight ache as her fangs withdrew from his neck, but it was quickly replaced by the warm caress of her tongue. Pushing against his shoulders she sat up, her beautiful breasts swaying tantalizingly close. Her eyes were almost completely amber as she stared down at him, glowing like jewels in the dark room. Without a word, she lifted her hips, her soft fingers wrapping around his cock as she sheathed him inside her once again and began rocking slowly back and forth.

She cupped her breasts, squeezing and releasing, scraping her fingernails around and around her nipples, until they begged to be suckled, until blood streaked the round perfection of her breasts and drops hung poised on their very tips. She leaned forward, her hands to either side of his head as she moved, sliding herself up and down his aching cock. Colin growled, grabbing her hips and holding her in place as he began to thrust upward, delving deeper inside her with every stab of his cock into her welcoming body. She leaned closer and he fastened his mouth over one breast, sucking hard, tasting her blood on his tongue, feeling it hot and slick as he swallowed. Sophie cried out, her inner walls shuddering around him in warning. Colin grinned, tightened his grip on her hips, and switched his attention to the other breast, taking it in his mouth and sucking until it was bright pink and swollen.

Sophie had closed her eyes, her body swaying above him as if in a trance. Colin could feel her orgasm building around his shaft, could feel the tremors in her belly, the tightening of her inner walls as they began to ripple along his cock, caressing him, urging him to give up his seed. He grunted softly, trying to hold out a little longer, wanting to feel her climax, her wetness soaking his cock and dripping out of her swollen sex.

"Colin," she gasped. "I can't . . . I can't last much longer."

"Then, don't, Sophie. Come for me."

As if waiting for his invitation, Sophie threw her head back, screaming as the climax roared over her. She collapsed on top of him, moaning as her entire body quivered in the throes of sexual release. Colin gritted his teeth, relishing the feel of her soft body trembling over his, her channel convulsing, shivering with the strength of her orgasm.

Groaning, he tightened his hold on her hips and rolled over, drawing her knees up and placing her legs over his shoulders as he shoved himself into her over and over again in a frenzy of need. Sophie's eyes flashed open. She snarled wordlessly and began to move, meeting his downward plunge with an upward thrust of her hips, flexing her inner muscles to grip his cock even tighter.

Colin felt the orgasm coming. There was no stopping it this time. He shouted uncontrollably as it rolled over him like an earthquake, shaking him down to his bones, every muscle in his body clenching as his cock pulsed over and over again, burying itself deep in Sophie's body until it was spent.

He eased her legs off his shoulders and rolled over, gathering her against his side.

"Jesus, Soph," he managed.

She responded with an unintelligible "mmph," her voice muffled by his chest.

Colin wasn't sure how long they stayed that way. He wasn't even sure when they'd started making love or how long they'd been at it. He did know they both fell asleep at some point. He woke when Sophia stirred restlessly and sat up next to him.

"I fell asleep," she fretted. "It's nearly dawn. I don't know if—"

"It's okay, darlin'," he soothed, pulling her back down into the warm bed. "These are blackout drapes and I'll stand guard. It's okay."

She smiled sleepily, reaching up to caress his face. "Colin," she whispered. "I can't believe I found you."

"We found each other, Soph. Now, sleep. I'll be here when you wake up."

* * * *

The ringing phone dragged Colin from sleep. A quick glance at the clock told him, it was just past two. He checked it again. Two in the afternoon, he clarified. Sophie lay next to him, curled up beneath the covers. If he didn't know better, he'd think she was asleep, but a closer look told him it was more than that. It wasn't like the vampires in the movies who were pale and gray, their hands bony with long, curving nails. His Sophie wasn't dead. But this was something more than sleep, too.

He thought about the others, the vampires who'd been murdered, and he understood for the first time how completely vulnerable they'd been when their attackers fell on them. There would have been no resistance. Their deaths had been brutal butchery, nothing less.

The phone rang again, and he jolted, thinking it might be Robbie with news about Leighton. But right on top of that thought was the realization that it was his house phone ringing. Not his cell, but the land line. Cell reception had been spotty up here for years, until the vamps moved in and paid to have a new tower installed. His broadband came in over the land line, so he kept the service, but hardly anyone called him on that number anymore.

He let it ring. It would go to the answering machine before long, and he could listen to see if it was someone he wanted to talk to.

He pulled the covers up over Sophie and climbed out of bed, careful to close the bedroom door behind him. As he'd told her, the curtains in his bedroom were heavy, with blinds underneath. After years of sleeping in all sorts of places and conditions, he liked a dark room and a comfortable bed when he slept.

The incoming call rolled over to the machine as he walked into the living room, his skin prickling with cold. He almost turned around to go back to the bedroom and pull on a pair of sweats when Garry McWaters's familiar voice rolled out of the machine.

"Yo, Murphy. You around?"

Colin's stared at the machine in disbelief. Jaw clenched, he strode over the phone and yanked it off the charger.

"You son of a bitch," he said growled.

"You didn't tell me the woman had a bodyguard, Murph," Garry chided. "Not nice of you."

It had been Garry's voice he heard at Babe's after the shootout yesterday. He hadn't wanted to believe it, but now—

"And you didn't tell me you'd taken to ambushing friends, you bastard."

"Hey, we weren't aiming at you, buddy. You wouldn't have been hurt at all if that bitch hadn't seen a couple of the guys moving around outside. I hate working with amateurs, you know what I'm saying? Anyway, *she* was the target. You were just supposed to open the door like you always do for the ladies. You're such a gentleman, Murph. I always admired that about you."

"Yeah, fuck you, Garry."

McWaters just laughed. "Yeah, well *you* fucked up the plan. And the boys aren't happy. Their trucks got all shot up and you know how they feel about their trucks around here. Besides, you looked fine to me when you drove away. The bodyguard, too, for that matter. What is he, Delta? Rangers? That boy definitely had some training somewhere. Hey," he said suddenly, as if it had just occurred to him. "How's the woman doing?"

"Go to hell."

"Come on, she was hardly helpless out there. Fine lookin' woman, and she knows her stuff. Too bad she's on the wrong side."

"The wrong side? Which one's that?"

All laughter fled and Garry's voice turned grim. "The fucking human side, Murphy. You're from the South. I thought you'd recognize a righteous cause when you saw one."

"Happy to disappoint, asshole."

"Oh, I'm not disappointed. We were hoping to take her out, but we hurt her bad enough. I hear those vamps are pretty attached to their women, kinda fall apart when something bad happens to them, like with Mariane. But this one, the big man nearly losing his girlfriend like that? That'll put a crimp in their *hunt,* won't it?"

Colin frowned. Where was Garry getting his information? How did he know how badly Leighton was hurt, or even that she was still alive? For that matter, how'd he know what Raphael's reaction would be to Leighton getting shot up like that? Even he wouldn't have known before he'd seen Jeremy's reaction to Mariane's injuries. Sure, everyone in town probably knew about the assault on Mariane by now, but no one outside the vamp compound should have known how badly it had affected Jeremy.

All this time, they'd been looking for a mole among the humans in town, but maybe the mole was inside the compound.

Garry had remained silent, waiting for Colin to react. Was he looking for confirmation of Leighton's death, or at least an update on her condition? Colin's lip curled. The son-of-a-bitch would wait a long damn time before he got any information out of Colin. He'd also made a huge miscalculation if he thought Raphael's reaction was going to be anything like Jeremy's. Jeremy was a fucking accountant. Raphael was—

Shit. Raphael was going to tear this town apart.

"Do you have *any* idea what you've done, Garry?" he asked instead. "Raphael's going to paint the town with your blood for this."

"Gosh, I hope so," Garry said with false enthusiasm. "Well, not *my* blood. But anyone else's will do." His voice hardened. "Why the hell do you think we targeted *her* instead of someone else? If those vamps start killing people, maybe the rest of you will open your eyes and realize we've got a bunch of monsters living among us and our fucking government isn't doing shit about it."

"So, you're making some sort of political statement with this?" Colin asked in disbelief. "There's not going to be any last stand here, Mac. No Waco, no Ruby Ridge, no media standing by to cover your glorious sacrifice. You're dead, pure and simple. You and all your crazy ass buddies. Those vamps are going hunt you down and tear you into pieces so small, there won't be enough of you left to bury."

Colin didn't wait for a response. He hung up, shaking with anger. That stupid SOB. He couldn't believe Garry would go along with that kind of ignorant bullshit. Hell, he couldn't believe Garry would turn on *him* like this, after everything they'd been through together, after they'd saved each other's lives more than once. But Colin couldn't save him this time. He'd be lucky to save himself. Once the vampire lord found out Leighton had been specifically targeted . . . Colin shook his head. He might not know much about vampires, but he'd been there when Raphael woke up at sunset last night. He'd seen that huge, damn building rattle like it was made of cardboard.

Hell. Forget Garry McWaters and his idiot friends. Colin would have his hands full trying to convince the vamps not to take out every human being between here and Seattle.

He ran a hand through his hair, rubbing it back and forth. He wouldn't get any more sleep today, not with this buzzing in the back of his brain. But as long as he was awake he might as well do something useful, and he could start with Leon and Ellen Pettijohn, the owners of Babe's bar. He'd be surprised if either of them was directly involved in this. They weren't going to win any citizenship awards, but he didn't peg them as murderers either.

He started back toward the bedroom, intending to take a quick shower, get dressed and head into town. Ellen worked a day shift at the market, but Leon would probably be home, still asleep. Colin figured to head over there first. He could call, but these things worked better in person, and If he had to rouse Leon out of bed all the better—

He hit the bedroom doorway and skidded to a halt.

Well, hell. He couldn't go over to Leon's today. He couldn't go anywhere. Sophia was sound asleep in his bed, completely helpless. Chances were no one knew she was here except him, but was he willing to take that chance? Hell, no.

He spun on his heel, going down the hall to his study and sitting at his computer. There was one more thing he could do, and he didn't have to leave the house to do it. Garry and his buddies had to be holed up somewhere nearby, and this was a small town. If Garry had been staying with one of the regulars, it would have leaked out by now. But if he was in hiding, maybe with those out-of-towners Hugh Pulaski had complained about . . . well, Garry's family had been in Cooper's Rest a long time. They probably had property way out in the back of nowhere that Colin didn't even know about.

But if he could find it before the sun went down tonight, he could give the vamps someplace to start looking, a focus for their hunt. And maybe, if he was very lucky, he could stop Raphael from turning Cooper's Rest into a bloodbath.

Chapter Thirty-Three

Sophia stretched languidly, feeling more sated and relaxed than she had in a very long time. Maybe ever. Her eyes were closed, but she knew Colin was nearby. She could feel him watching her and she arched her back, preening for him, sliding her hands over her breasts and down to her thighs before extending them over her head in a final stretch.

Colin swore softly and she opened her eyes with a grin. He was half-naked, his chest bare, a pair of black combat pants snugged low on his narrow hips, and he was eyeing her body like a starving man.

"Why are you way over there?" she purred, patting the bed.

"If I come to bed, we'll never get out of here and we have to leave. God knows I'm sorry, but we have to get back to the compound."

Sophia sat up, her mind already churning over the possibilities. "Did something happen?"

"I got a phone call today from an old friend. He wanted to know if Leighton was dead."

Sophia grew very still. "Why would he care?" she asked carefully.

"Because he's probably the one who shot her. He and his buddies killed Marco and Preston and attacked Mariane, too."

Her power rose unbidden, filling her with fire. She saw Colin's eyes widen and knew her own had begun to glow. "Who is he?" she demanded.

"Garry McWaters. We served together." His jaw tightened, and his eyes narrowed with something more than anger. She tasted his emotions and recognized it. Betrayal. And that was something Sophia understood very well.

"So we kill him," she said bluntly.

Colin met her gaze directly. "We kill him," he agreed. "And I think I know where to start looking. Get dressed and I'll fill you in on the way. We have to talk to Raphael before he starts killing the wrong people."

* * * *

Colin slid the truck to a halt, jamming it into park and shoving the door open without even bothering to take the key out of the ignition. There had been even more vampires on the gate tonight, and they'd all been jumpy with adrenaline, or whatever it was that made vampires jumpy. They weren't scared and they weren't nervous, they were . . . excited, like something big was about to happen and they could hardly wait. But that hadn't stopped them from searching him and his truck thoroughly, as if they'd never seen him before. As if Sophia wasn't sitting right next to him.

And they'd completely ignored his questions about Leighton. Either they didn't know anything or they weren't telling.

The main building was lit up like a damn party palace, lights shining through the big glass doors. He saw people standing inside—vampires. Lots and lots of vampires, all dressed for war. It was like being back on an op—everyone wearing head to toe black, combat pants and boots, with long-sleeved T-shirts—except that some of these soldiers had fangs showing.

Sophie came up behind him and gripped his hand hard, forcing him to stop and turn to face her.

"Sophie," he protested. "We don't have time for this."

"Listen to me," she insisted. "Leighton must have survived the night or the guards wouldn't be so relaxed."

"That was relaxed?"

"Believe me, Colin. If she'd died, you wouldn't have made it through the gate, at least not in one piece."

"Okay, great, let's get in there, and—"

"Listen to me," she repeated urgently. "You had a taste of what Raphael can do. Just a taste, Colin. If he lashes out at you—"

"I'm a big boy, Sophie. I can take care of myself."

She jerked his arm angrily. "Not from this. But I can. Do you understand what I'm saying? You have to let me protect us if it comes to that. Don't interfere and don't try to help."

Colin stared down at her. He wasn't an insecure man and he didn't feel the need to constantly prove himself. Twelve years with the teams had taught him the value of standing back and letting someone else take the lead when they could get the job done better. But there was a huge difference, a cosmic difference, between his buddies and Sophia. She wanted him to hide behind her while she fought Raphael? The guy who could cause small earthquakes when he got pissed?

"Colin," she said. "Please. I know what I'm asking, but it's the only way."

He looked away. "Fuck," he snarled. "All right, fine. But so help me, Sophie, if anything happens to you, I'll take you over my knee and—"

She placed her lips on his, silencing him. "Promises, promises," she whispered. She froze for a moment and then her head whipped around toward the building. "Raphael," she said.

Colin looked over her head and saw Robbie on his knees. "Let's go," he said.

Chapter Thirty-Four

Raphael opened his eyes and immediately reached for Cyn. He'd been aware of her lying next to him throughout the day, had listened to her heart growing stronger with every beat. She would live. He knew that now. And she would heal. But it would be a long, slow process, and most likely many months before she was back to full strength. As powerful as he was, there was only so much he could do. His blood could start the process, could keep her alive and accelerate the healing. But with these injuries, her body would have to do some of it at its own pace.

He wrapped her gently in his arms and leaned over to kiss her forehead. She stirred, but didn't wake. She knew he was there, though, and that was enough for him. He would rather she save her energy for healing than waste it on unnecessary words.

Lifting his arm, he used his fangs to slice a vein open and lowered the wrist to Cyn's mouth. She latched on eagerly, another sign of her increasing strength. One of her hands came up to hold his wrist as she suckled and Raphael noticed how fragile it looked, how she seemed to have lost weight just over the last few hours. Her body was using itself up. He was reminded of Dr. Saephan's words yesterday. His Cyn was still human. She needed human blood to replace what she'd lost, and she needed nutrition beyond what Raphael could give her.

Her grip on his wrist loosened as her suckling ceased and she seemed to be falling more deeply asleep. Raphael put his mouth to hers, kissing her, murmuring words of love against her lips. He lifted his head, stroking her hair back from her face.

"I need to leave you for a short time, *lubimaya*" he said quietly. "Doctor Saephan will be here with you and Elke will be up above. I need to know how this happened, why Robbie was—"

Her eyes flashed opened and she grabbed his wrist again. "Don't hurt them," she said in a strained voice that seemed to take all of her strength.

Raphael shushed her, twisting his wrist carefully to take her hand in his. He kissed the back of it. "Who is it you think I'll hurt, *lubimaya*? Softly now, I'll hear you."

"Robbie," she breathed. "Murphy. It wasn't their fault."

Raphael's mouth tightened and he kissed her eyelids, forcing her eyes to close so she wouldn't see the anger on his face. He wouldn't make promises he couldn't keep. Not to Cyn. "Sleep," he urged her and nudged her mind gently under, ensuring she would rest until he returned.

He waited until she was breathing evenly, then pulled the blanket over her and crossed to the desk, picking up his cell phone.

"My lord," Duncan answered immediately. "How is she?"

"She will live," Raphael said grimly. "Tell Doctor Saephan to gather whatever supplies he requires. I'll send the elevator up. No one but the doctor is to come down here, Duncan."

"Of course, my lord. Everything is already prepared, Saephan needs only to retrieve the blood from the storage unit."

"Once he is here with Cyn, I'll come upstairs. Where's Robbie?"

"He is here, my lord, and ready to accept your judgment."

"Is he? We'll see." Raphael disconnected, tossing the phone back on the desk. He went first to the vault door, keying it open and sending the elevator up for Dr. Saephan. While he waited, he pulled on a robe, then sat on the bed next to Cyn, holding her hand, knowing she would sense his presence and take comfort in it.

He heard voices down the elevator shaft, heard Saephan directing others as they loaded up the doctor's medical supplies. And then the door closed and he heard the motor's hum as the elevator descended. The doors opened and Peter Saephan stepped out, dropping immediately to his knees.

"My lord."

The doctor was a very smart man. He'd been around powerful vampires enough to know Raphael would be walking the very edge of temper with his mate lying so gravely injured beside him. Raphael stared at Saephan's bowed head, fighting the instinct to leap across the room and destroy this intruding male presence.

"Doctor," he ground out at last. "You said she needed blood. Did you bring it?"

"Yes, my lord." Saephan looked up quickly, his gaze torn between Raphael and Cyn, his expression that of a physician who saw nothing but a patient in desperate need of his care.

And that easily, Raphael relaxed. Saephan wasn't here to harm Cyn or to steal her away. He was here to help her. He stood and, knowing the doctor would be reluctant to approach with him standing so close, walked to the bathroom door, then turned back to say, "I need a shower. I will leave her to your care for now."

Saephan met his eyes for the first time. "I *will* take care of her, my lord. On my honor."

Raphael nodded, his gaze shifting away to rest on Cyn and then back to Saephan. "Thank you, Peter." He stepped backwards into the bathroom and closed the door.

Raphael stripped off the robe and showered quickly. Normally, he wouldn't have bothered since he intended to bathe in his enemy's blood before the night was over. But he was covered in Cyn's blood and she was his. Her *blood* was his, no one else's. So he let the soap and water sluice over his body, and he swore privately that the blood of those who had harmed his Cyn would run like water tonight.

He didn't bother drying off, just wrapped a towel around his hips and yanked the door open, suddenly needing to see for himself that she was well.

Saephan barely noticed the intrusion. He glanced up absently, but most of his attention remained on his patient. He'd already hung a unit of blood and was checking Cyn's IV, his dark head bent over her too-thin arm.

"You saved her life, my lord," Saephan said quietly. "If anyone else—" He drew a deep breath. "She is your mate, my lord, but she is also my friend and I feared for her."

Raphael stood there dripping wet, watching another male touch his mate, and realized he trusted this human more than any other. "My Cyn inspires loyalty in others," he observed.

Saephan glanced over at him. "As do you, my lord. Never doubt it." He turned back to Cyn and when he spoke next it was with the flat, dry delivery of a physician reporting on his patient's condition. "Her greatest need at this point is human blood. She lost—" His professional demeanor slipped for a moment and he swallowed hard. "She lost a great deal," he continued, his voice slightly rough. "But, I can replace that. We have plenty on hand, of course, and her type is common. Cross matching is not necessary, because she has your blood to offset any incompatibility. She's also dehydrated, so I'll run a second IV and provide some critical nutrition at the same time. Given the severity and type of her injury, I'm going to add some antibiotics to the mix. Again, with your blood working inside her, this is mostly a precaution. At best, it will be unnecessary, at worst, it will speed her recovery. But, my lord," Saephan turned and addressed Raphael directly for the first time. "Even with your blood, her injuries . . ." He drew a breath. "She will take a very long time to heal completely."

Raphael nodded. "I understand." He walked over to the closet, rubbing the towel briefly over his body before donning clothing for the night. Jeans, sweater, boots. Black for moving through the shadows; black for hunting his enemies.

Saephan had bent over Cyn once again. He spoke over his shoulder without turning. "With your permission, my lord, I will bathe her more completely while you're gone. She'll rest more easily once she's cleaned up."

Raphael froze in the act of pulling on his boots, once again fighting the instinct to protect his mate. He brushed it off with an effort, swallowing his snarl of frustration to avoid alarming the doctor. "Do whatever you feel is necessary," he managed, stomping the boot onto his foot and standing to his full height. "But," he added, "no one except you is to see her like this, Doctor."

"Of course, my lord. I would have it no other way."

"Elke will stand guard above. You will remain here until I return."

"Understood, my lord."

"Very well. I leave you to it, then."

Raphael crossed to the bed, stroking a hand down Cyn's cheek.

He leaned close enough to kiss her mouth again, whispering against her lips, "They will pay, *lubimaya*. Those responsible will die tonight."

* * * *

Elke looked up quickly when Raphael emerged from the elevator. "My lord?"

"She will live, Elke. Others will not be so fortunate. Doctor Saephan will stay with her until I return. You will guard this entrance. No one is to come or go from my room, do you understand?"

"Yes, my lord."

He lowered his voice, speaking to her alone. "I know you would rather join the hunt, Elke, but there is no one I trust more to guard her."

Elke's pale eyes turned pink with unshed tears and Raphael blinked in surprise. He'd never seen her exhibit a shred of emotion before, except for anger. "I will guard her with my life, Sire. My place is here."

Raphael tilted his head, smiling slightly. He knew Cyn and Elke were friends of a sort. They sparred together in the gym, and because Elke was the only female guard in his inner circle, she was frequently assigned to Cyn. But he hadn't realized until now the depth of that friendship.

"Good hunting, my lord," Elke said.

Raphael bared his teeth. "The ground will be black with blood tonight, Elke. I swear it." He clapped a hand on her shoulder and turned a sober gaze across the great room. Duncan was already there, walking toward him. They met halfway.

"My lord," Duncan began, but Raphael interrupted.

"Where is he?"

Robbie emerged from the large common room. "I am here, my lord." He took several steps toward Raphael and sank to his knees, his head bowed.

Raphael stared down at the big bodyguard's bare neck. "Tell me why you deserve to live," he growled.

"Because he didn't do anything wrong," another voice interrupted.

Raphael swiveled his head slowly, looking over his shoulder to where Colin Murphy stood in the open door with Lucien's child Sophia. Cold, wet air gusted around them, slapping against his legs.

"You," Raphael sneered. "Another who somehow survived unscathed while my Cyn was being torn apart."

"My lord!" Robbie protested, but Raphael silenced him with a sharp look, exerting just enough power to pin the human in place without harming him. "Be very careful, Robert," he warned. "The only reason you're still alive is that my Cyn pled for your life, though she had barely the breath to do so. Don't make her sacrifice in vain."

Raphael turned to face Murphy, giving the human his complete attention. He gathered his power casually, letting a tiny fraction of it swell out into the room, enough to scatter papers and rattle doors.

To his surprise, Sophia stepped forward, her own defenses rising sharply, expanding to encompass the human male. Her eyes began to glow slightly as her power built, and she stood directly in front of the much larger human, hands clenched at her sides, her chin raised in defiance.

Raphael blinked lazily and gazed down at her. "Your Sire may have anointed you his successor, Sophia, but never make the mistake of thinking you are *my* equal."

Her shapely jaw tightened angrily, but she gave a curt nod, acknowledging the truth of his words. And then her chin came up again and she said, "You would die to protect your mate, Lord Raphael. I will do no less."

Raphael studied her more carefully, noting for the first time the connection between her and Murphy. It was very new and very tenuous, but it was there. He frowned, glancing over at Duncan who was regarding the newly mated pair with open curiosity. Apparently, no one else knew about this either. It wouldn't stop him from killing her if he had to, but it made him willing to listen.

"Robbie," Raphael snapped over his shoulder. "Tell me what happened."

Over the next several minutes, Robbie told him in detail the events of the previous day. "We were almost away, my lord," Robbie said, coming to the end of his tale. He was still on his knees, but his eyes met Raphael's stern gaze with open honesty. "I had Cyn moving toward the truck door, covering her back, when they opened up on us from a new direction. You know Cyn, my lord. She could have dived into the truck, gone for her own safety, but instead she started firing, covering Murphy's back. I should have grabbed her, should never have let her go. That's when—" His voice broke for the first time and he looked down. "I'm sorry, my lord. I failed Cyn and I failed you."

"It's not his fault," Colin Murphy insisted again. "Dammit, Raphael, you have to listen to me!"

Raphael's vampires, already jumpy and ready for the hunt, bristled at the human's tone, and even Sophia had the good sense to place a cautioning hand on her mate's arm. Murphy drew a deep breath and continued more carefully.

"My apologies, sir. But someone I know called me today with information that you really need to hear."

Raphael gritted his teeth impatiently. This was taking too long. "Talk," he demanded.

"Leighton was specifically targeted," Murphy said intently. "They knew, or they thought they knew, that taking her out would weaken *you* personally. They thought your vamps would be leaderless and go nuts, or that you'd join them and start butchering humans indiscriminately. They *want* a bloodbath. They want headlines all across the television and Internet screaming about vampires prowling the night and slaughtering innocent humans."

Raphael flattened his lips thoughtfully. "Stand up, Robbie," he said without turning. He heard the human coming to his feet behind him.

"My lord," Robbie said.

Raphael turned. "The only words my Cyn spoke this morning were in defense of you . . . and him," he added, with a jerk of his head toward Murphy. "And your account of events was truthful." He regarded the bodyguard silently. Robbie had been with him a long time, and he was mated to one of Raphael's vampires. It was why he'd entrusted Cyn's protection to him. "We won't slow down for you," he told him now. "But you're welcome to join the hunt for these killers."

"Thank you, my lord."

"Sir," Colin Murphy spoke up again and Raphael turned to eye him darkly.

"They knew about Mariane," the human said urgently. "They knew what the attack on her did to Jeremy, how it weakened *him*. They knew where to find Marco and Preston—" He glanced quickly at Sophia before continuing in a quiet voice, "And they knew Leighton was still alive when we brought her here yesterday."

Raphael stared at him, slipping easily into the human's mind despite Sophia's newly established link. The man was telling the truth as he knew it. And that meant Raphael had a leak inside this compound. His own people, the ones he'd brought from Malibu, were loyal to the core. He would stake his life on it. He *did* stake his life on it every day. He looked around, noting who was there . . . and who was not.

"Get Loren on the phone," he ordered Wei Chen, watching the nest leader's eyes widen as he searched the surrounding faces and realized Loren was not among them. He pulled a phone from his pocket and paged rapidly through his call list.

"Loren," he said, surprise evident in his voice. "Where are you?"

Raphael took the phone from him in time to hear Loren's answer. "I'm at Marco's," he said. "I got word of a possible break-in."

Even over the phone line, Raphael could hear the lie in his words, and it only confirmed what he'd already begun to suspect.

"Would you like to try that again?" Raphael said coldly.

"Sire!" Loren gasped. "My lord, I—"

"Get back here now. And bring the woman with you." He hung up while Loren was still sputtering, trying to justify his duplicity. Stupid son-of-a-bitch. He exchanged a quick look with Juro who nodded and took several steps away, taking two of his security people with him.

As they began to confer in low voices, Raphael turned to Murphy. "Do you know who these killers are?" he asked.

"Some of them," the human replied. "And I think I know where at least some of them have been hiding out. But I don't know all the names. If we can take the ones I do know alive, we can—"

From behind Raphael, Robbie spoke up, "Wait a minute." He walked around Raphael to face Murphy. "Cyn took pictures of the license plates in that parking lot."

"That's right," Murphy agreed, snapping his fingers. He switched his gaze to Raphael. "We need her cell."

Raphael pulled his phone from an inside pocket and rang Peter Saephan, who answered on the first ring.

"Yes, my lord?" he said quietly.

"Cyn?"

"She is resting well, my lord. The fluids are helping already."

"Excellent. I require Cyn's cell phone. Her clothing from last night is in a bag in the closet. Could you check and see if her phone is there?"

There was a brief pause and then Raphael heard the closet door slide open and the sharp crackle of a plastic bag. "One moment, my lord," Saephan said, followed by a soft thud as he put the phone down. More rustling of plastic and then the phone was picked up again.

"I have it, my lord. Let me . . . I'm cleaning the blood off with a bit of alcohol."

Cyn's blood, Raphael knew and was grateful for the good doctor's hygienic impulses.

Saephan had continued, saying, "It looks okay, but the battery is low. Do you want me to—"

"That won't be necessary, Doctor, thank you. If you would put it in the elevator and send it up."

"Of course, my lord. Was there anything else?"

"No, thank you."

Raphael disconnected and turned to the others. "The phone is coming up in the elevator now."

Murphy stepped forward as if to retrieve the phone himself, but Raphael growled and Duncan stepped in front of the human, blocking his path.

"Elke will get it," Duncan said. His tone was calm enough, but his body language left no room for dispute.

Murphy opened his mouth as if to protest anyway, but it died unsaid when he swung toward Raphael and saw the look on his face. Duncan might be calm, but Raphael most definitely was not.

Murphy fell back to stand next to Sophia who placed herself slightly ahead of him and cast a hostile glance in Raphael's direction. Duncan, meanwhile, waited until they heard the elevator doors close once again and then sent one of the vampire guards over to get the phone from Elke who remained at her post.

The guard brought the phone over to Duncan. He looked to Raphael for permission, then accessed the phone's memory. "They're here," he confirmed, paging through several photographs. "There's a shot of the entire lot and then the individual plates. It looks as if . . . yes, she got them all," he said with a note of admiration.

"I can run those—" Murphy started.

"That won't be necessary," Duncan interrupted

He beckoned Maxime over from near the front office where she stood along with Wei Chen and some others, watching events unfold. None of those watching were hunters—Raphael's soldiers were specifically chosen and trained. But even among the vampires who wouldn't actively participate tonight, even to those who spent most of their waking hours in front of a computer, the excitement level was high and contagious.

Duncan turned the phone over to Maxime, and she flipped through the images, moving far more quickly than he had. She gave Murphy a smug look. "Give me five minutes," she said and headed for the nearby office.

"Most of those license plates are local," Murphy commented, watching Maxime walk away. He turned back to Raphael. "So I'm guessing the owners are, too. And I have a couple of possible locations for the guy who called to taunt me this afternoon—Garry McWaters. He was raised around here, but until yesterday I thought he was living in San Diego."

"Clearly not," Raphael observed dismissively.

"You're right," Murphy admitted. "But that's what he wanted me to think. I'd know if he was staying in town. You can't keep a secret in this place. But his family has a couple of old properties way the hell back of nowhere. I didn't even know they were there until I went looking for something like it."

"How do you know him?"

Murphy frowned, as if reluctant to speak. "He was a friend," he admitted grudgingly. "I thought I recognized his voice out at the bar yesterday, after Leighton went down, but now I'm sure."

"Then tonight he dies," Raphael said darkly.

Murphy shook his head, but didn't argue, which was a good thing, because Raphael wasn't in the mood to be contradicted by anyone, much less a human.

"Look," Murphy said impatiently. "You don't need us here. While you wait for Loren to show up, Sophia and I can swing by Leon Pettijohn's place."

"The owner of the bar where Cynthia was attacked, my lord," Sophia supplied. "He and his wife own it jointly, but only the man works there. She has a day job at the local market ."

"I don't think they're part of this," Murphy jumped in to add. "I tried calling Leon at the bar already, but there's no answer. He's probably running scared after yesterday's shootout, but if I can get him to talk, he'll know who else was there. It wasn't only McWaters shooting at us."

Raphael studied the human silently. He wasn't inclined to trust him, but Cyn had.

"Our hunt will begin at the bar, then," Raphael said. "By Robbie's accounting, it's likely one or more of the attackers were shot, which means they bled. We'll catch their scent and track them that way, if nothing else works. Sophia, you and Murphy go to this bar owner's house, and if you discover anything of worth from these people, let us know. If not, you may catch up to us later.

"Loren is at the gate, my lord," Duncan murmured.

Raphael smiled slowly, viciously. "Excellent."

Chapter Thirty-Five

"Well, that was intense," Colin commented as he held the door open so Sophie could climb up into the Suburban they'd borrowed from the compound's garage. Sophie had suggested they take the Lexus she'd been driving earlier, but there was no way Colin was going out on an op—even a civilian one—driving a damn luxury sedan. It would be too embarrassing. Since his Tahoe was pretty much totaled and, according to Sophia, stank of blood, he'd commandeered one of Wei Chen's fleet of SUVs.

He closed Sophie's door, hurried around the hood and settled himself behind the wheel, starting the truck with a quick twist of the key. He pulled out of the garage and started down the curve of the driveway, slowing as the gate opened and a gray BMW pulled through with Loren at the wheel. Colin caught a glimpse of the vampire's shaken expression as he drove by. There was a woman sitting next to him and she didn't look happy, either. Colin shook his head. He didn't envy Loren. Not one little bit.

It was a short drive to the Pettijohn's place. Their house was on the near side of town, down a narrow slice of dirt that barely qualified as a road. Like a lot of the other homes around Cooper's Rest, theirs was older and in a state of gentle disrepair. The wood could have used a good oiling and the eaves were clogged with pine needles, but the roof was sturdy and there was a brand new aluminum garage off to one side. The double doors were open and Colin could see Ellen's Honda sitting inside, but there was no sign of Leon's truck.

"Let's make this quick. Looks like Leon's left already and I'd like to get to him before Raphael does."

Sophie snorted delicately. "Only if you want him to keep breathing." She opened the truck door and slid to the ground, closing the door quietly behind her. "Maybe we should go directly to the bar and this Leon fellow. You said the woman's never there anyway. She won't know anything."

"Yeah, but Leon probably tells her stuff. As long as we're here, it's worth a five minute conversation."

Sophie shrugged. "It's your call. I don't know these people." She glanced around the yard and then at Colin, as if to say, *and I'd really rather not know them.*

Colin grinned, taking the steps to the front porch in two long strides. Before he could ring the doorbell, the door whipped open and Ellen stood there, rifle in hand and pointed right at his face.

Chapter Thirty-Six

Raphael felt Loren's fear long before the vampire entered the building with the human woman at his side. He looked awful, his face pale and his eyes wide as he scanned the vampires gathered around the entrance. He pushed his way through, took one look at Raphael and dropped to his knees.

"Forgive me, Sire," he sobbed.

Raphael gazed down on him dismissively. How had he ever thought this one was worthy of responsibility?

"In the other room," he said coldly.

Two of his vampires grabbed Loren by the elbows, hauling him to his feet. The woman wailed noisily and Duncan stepped up, cutting off her cries with a thought. At his signal, another of Raphael's guards escorted the now placid female after Loren.

"Duncan, you're with me." He turned to face Juro. "This won't take long," he told him. "We'll go directly to the bar and move out from there. Make certain everyone understands the rules of engagement. I want to be absolutely certain we catch every one of these animals in our net. Information first—" He lowered head and let a fraction of his power flow outward, swirling around him. "—and then we hunt," he finished.

His vampires roared. He gave them all a fierce grin, then spun around and strode through the double doors and into the nearly empty room. With just the few of them there, the lights were low, the night nothing but a black space beyond the windows. Loren was on his knees, hunched over, arms wrapped around himself miserably. The human woman sat on a chair nearby, although she didn't seem aware of anyone, much less her vampire lover.

Raphael walked over to Loren and stared down at him, hands on his hips. Raphael had given Loren life. He owned him body and soul. It was impossible for him to lie to his Sire, even if he'd thought to try.

"How long have you been fucking her, Loren?" Raphael asked flatly.

He swallowed dryly before speaking. "Almost a month, my lord."

"Who is she?"

"Deb Jenkins. But I've told her nothing, my lord. I swear—"

"Silence."

Loren's mouth closed and he dropped his head to his chest, his shoulders bowed and shaking with fear. Raphael hadn't yet decided what to do with him. Despite Loren's protests to the contrary, Raphael knew the vampire *had* been spilling secrets to the woman. The question was with what intent? It was one thing if he was simply a fool who let information slip while lying in bed with her. But if he'd intentionally dropped secrets to persuade her of his importance or to curry favor, that was something else. The next several minutes of Loren's life would depend on what he'd told the woman . . . and what she'd done with it.

"Deb." As Raphael said the woman's name, he wrapped a thread of power around it, ensuring her cooperation. If necessary, he'd rip the truth from her mind, but as he touched her thoughts, he knew it wouldn't be necessary. She was wide open to him.

She looked up, meeting his gaze with a smile. "Yes?" she said pleasantly.

"How long have you known Loren?"

"Just since I've been back from L.A. We met in town at the Post Office. I was in there makin' sure that old bat Mavis didn't fuck up my mail. I don't know why they keep her on there. Anyway, Loren was there. Gettin' his mail, too, I guess."

"Did you know who he was?"

"Oh, sure. My brother Curtis told me all about you guys as soon as I got here."

Raphael's gaze sharpened. When he'd scoured Hugh Pulaski's mind—after teaching him the folly of threatening Cyn—the human had identified someone named Curtis as one of those he'd overheard plotting against the vampires.

"Curtis said if I got the chance," Deb continued, "I should hook up with one of you. Loren was good-looking enough—"

Loren had turned to stare at her in horror, and she winked at him when she said this, unaware of his reaction.

"—and I'd heard the sex was mind-blowing," she added. "So I thought why not? I'll give it a try. It's not like Coop's is crawling with eligible guys, you know?"

"Sire, I swear—"

Raphael simply looked at Loren. The vampire shut his mouth with a whimper.

"You were saying, Deb?"

"Right, well, Curtis, him and his friends that is, wanted to know all about it. Not the sex so much—that would have been too creepy, him being my brother—but everything else. He used to grill me like a steak after I'd spent the night with Loren. Pissed me off sometimes, because all I wanted to do was sleep. You know what I'm saying," she said with a meaningful look.

Raphael sighed. "What sorts of things did you talk about?"

"Well, shit, there wasn't much to tell. I mean sex was pretty much all we did. At least until you showed up. Loren was pretty stressed about that, because you wanted everyone living in this place," she said, waving a hand around. "That would have meant no more sex, and neither one of us was too thrilled about that, I gotta tell ya."

"But then that poor girl got attacked," she went on, shaking her head. "I didn't know her, but that shouldn't happen to anyone. I asked Curtis was that him or any of his buddies—'cuz they might have a grudge against vamps, but that girl was as human as me or—" She grinned. "Well, not you, but you know what I mean."

"What did Curtis say to that?" Raphael asked curiously.

"He told me *no*. Honestly, I wasn't sure I believed him. I mean I believe *him*, but some of those boys he's hanging around with . . . well, I wouldn't wanna run into them in a dark alley."

"What about Loren?"

"Oh, Loren's sweet as can be. He'd never hurt a fly."

"No," Raphael said patiently. "I mean what did Loren tell you about Mariane's attack?"

"Oh, well, he told me all about her husband Jeremy and how upset he was. How it was a good thing you came when you did or she would've died and that would have been it for Jeremy, too."

"And you told your brother this?"

"Well, sure. It was the first real thing I ever had to tell him."

"The first? Was there more?"

"Well, last night Loren was pretty upset. I guess some woman got shot, so he couldn't stay over. Is she okay?"

Raphael ignored the question. He wasn't about to tell this woman *anything* about Cyn. Unlike Loren, apparently. "Did you talk to Curtis about this, too?"

"Hell, yes. He woke me up this morning with that damn phone."

Raphael turned away, walking over to the window and staring out, seeing in his mind's eye the bloody mess they'd made of his Cyn, hearing her cries of pain. And why? Because they wanted to weaken *him*. Because Loren had been so hungry to fuck this ignorant human that he'd run his mouth off like an eager-to-please child. He hoped the woman had been worth it, because Loren wouldn't be fucking anyone else for a very long time.

He remembered the other conspirator Pulaski had overheard in the bar, and he spoke without turning to look at her. "Tell me, Deb, are any of Curtis's friends called *Junior?* Maybe a nickname?"

"Oh, sure. That'd be Garry McWaters, but he hates that name. Pretty much hates his old man, or hated him. I think he's dead."

Raphael spun away from the windows, striding across the room, signaling his guards as he went by.

Two of them grabbed Loren who cried out, "Sire, please!"

Raphael ignored his cries. If he stopped now, he'd kill Loren without a thought. As for the woman, her mind would be wiped. She'd remember nothing of the last month—not Loren, not the post office, not anything. Certainly not Mariane or Jeremy, and especially not Cyn.

As for her brother, Curtis. He wouldn't be a problem after tonight.

Chapter Thirty-Seven

"What the hell you want, Murphy?" Ellen nudged the rifle to emphasize her question. It was an amateur's move, but at this distance, it didn't make much difference.

"Ellen," Colin said quietly, aware that Sophia had grown perfectly still behind him. He held his hands up where the woman could see them. "I'm not trying to cause problems. I heard there was some trouble at Babe's yesterday afternoon and I'm just trying to figure out what happened."

Ellen regarded him suspiciously down the long barrel of her Remington. It was a nice rifle and, amateur or not, at this range a blind man could hit him.

"Leon didn't come home last night." Her voice wavered when she said it, but the rifle didn't. "That's not like him."

Colin nodded. "I heard there was some trouble," he repeated.

Ellen stared at him, clearly trying to decide how much to say or whether she could trust him. She lowered the rifle a fraction.

"Someone said guns were fired, Ellen. If something has happened and—"

She snapped the rifle up again, glaring at him suspiciously. "Where'd you hear that? What'd you—"

That was all she managed to say before Sophia stepped deftly around Colin, wrapped her fingers around the rifle barrel and tore it from Ellen's hands, almost before Colin even saw her move. Holding the rifle out to Colin with her right hand, she held Ellen immobilized with her left and said, "Shall we take this inside?"

"Well, shit, Sophie," Colin drawled. "It was goin' so well, too."

"I can give her the gun back if you'd like?" she said, smiling sweetly.

"Maybe not. All right, let's see what Ellen has to tell us."

Sophie had wanted to use her vampire mojo to force Ellen to talk, but Colin had persuaded her to let him try talking with her first. Once Ellen stopped rubbing her neck and glaring at Sophie, it hadn't taken long to convince her that Colin had nothing to do with the men who'd shot up the parking lot yesterday. He'd been right about Leon telling her what went on at the bar, but he'd never mentioned Colin's name. Besides, Ellen was genuinely worried about her husband and had no one else to turn to.

"Leon didn't have nothing to do with them," Ellen insisted for the third time. "They met in the bar, but that was it. He can't turn away customers because he don't like their politics. He'd have no one at all if he did that. Besides, even if he knew they was planning something, what's he supposed to do about it?"

"If something was going on, he could have told me, Ellen."

She scoffed noisily. "Your buddy McWaters was right in the middle of 'em, Murphy. How'd we know we could trust you?"

"Fair enough," he ground out, still feeling the punch of Garry's betrayal.

Ellen shrugged. "I'll tell you this much, though. Those boys are bad news. If you're planning on taking 'em on, I hope there's a lot more than just you two." She eyed Sophia distrustfully. "Even if one's a vamp."

"Ellen," Murphy said, drawing her attention away from Sophie. "Did Leon mention anyone besides Garry?"

"Curtis Jenkins, who else? He's been trouble since day one."

Colin nodded. "Where's Leon now, Ellen? I'd like to talk to him."

She gave him a bleak look. "I told you, he didn't come home last night," she whispered. "I figured I'd find him here when I got home tonight, sleeping off a bender." Her eyes filled with sudden tears. "He'd have called me if he could, Murphy. He knows I'd worry."

Colin swore under his breath. "Okay. I'm going to the bar—"

Ellen stood. "I'll go with you. I can—"

"No," Colin said immediately, thinking of Raphael and his vampires who'd soon be overrunning Babe's and the woods around it. "I'll check it out and call you."

"You can't force me to wait here, Murphy. I'm a free—"

Sophia was suddenly there, her hand cupping Ellen's neck as she eased her onto the couch. Clearly after having zapped her unconscious, or whatever the hell it was that vampires did.

"Geez, Soph, could you warn me before you do anymore of that vamp shit?"

"You're too polite, and we don't have time to argue with her. Raphael will be on his way by now, and we don't want to miss the hunt."

Colin covered Ellen with a crocheted throw from the back of the couch. There was something in Sophie's voice when she talked about the hunt that made him turn and look at her. She was edgy and anxious to leave, already heading for the door. She glanced back at him impatiently and he saw the gleam of her eyes, not full-on amber the way they got sometimes, but like a rim of gold around her irises.

She met his scrutiny with a challenging stare. "What?" she demanded.

"You're excited," he said, realizing it as he spoke. "You're looking forward to this."

"Hell, yes," she agreed. "You've no idea what it's like to spend your life pretending to be ordinary. To tamp down your power, conceal your differences, lest the humans become frightened. Raphael will let his people run tonight. There'll be no holding back. You're damn right I'm looking forward to it."

"I'm human," he reminded her.

She moved faster than he could see. One second she was by the door and the next she was right in front of him, her arms around his neck, her lush body pressed against his.

"You may be human, Colin Murphy." She licked a long line up his neck and over his jaw until her mouth touched his. "But you're definitely not ordinary."

She pressed her lips against his in a quick hard kiss.

"Let's run the night, Colin. It's time to hunt."

Chapter Thirty-Eight

Colin and Sophie pulled into the parking lot outside Babe's on the heels of Raphael and his vampires. The bar was dark, the lot empty. Or it had been before they arrived and filled it with SUVs. And even then it remained dark. The vamps had traveled without headlights, apparently seeing as well or better in the dark than they did in light. Even Sophie had slipped on a pair of sunglasses to preserve her night vision from his headlights as they'd driven here.

Colin turned off the engine and flicked off the interior light, so it wouldn't come on when they opened the doors. Then he waited, although he didn't know what they were waiting for. The SUVs in front of him just sat there, presumably filled with vampires. He was about to ask Sophie what was going on when, as if some signal had been given, the doors all opened at once and Raphael's people piled out.

Colin did the same, going around to the back of the truck and gearing up, all the while watching warily as the vampires jostled each other, practically bouncing on their toes with anticipation. He wasn't sure how to feel about that. On the one hand, the adrenaline rush of going into battle was so familiar, it almost hurt to feel it again. He hadn't appreciated until that moment how much he missed this. But there was something a little creepy about being surrounded by vampires who were all juiced up at the idea of killing a bunch of humans.

"Don't let it get to you," a deep voice said next to him.

"Hey, Rob," Colin said, looking up to find the Ranger standing in front of him, armored up and ready to roll.

"And don't let their hyperactive behavior fool you either. These guys are trained within an inch of their lives. When it comes down to it, they're disciplined as hell."

"Good to know." Colin's attention shifted as Raphael walked over to the two of them.

"Tell, me, Murphy, do you think you managed to shoot any of these animals? Or was my Cyn the only one injured?"

Colin ground his teeth together, reminding himself the vampire was worried about Leighton. "We hit a few. I don't know how seriously."

"We can start with that, then. Duncan." His lieutenant half-turned toward the assembled vamps and nodded.

Like horses out of the gate, several of the vamps took off, rushing in among the trees so fast, they were little more than a blur of motion. And they didn't make a fucking sound, not even a whisper of movement despite the tightly packed trees and years of deadfall.

Sophia joined Raphael and Duncan in some sort of confab. Presumably discussing their plans for tonight, but who the hell knew? Not Colin.

When she joined him again, he gave her a dark look which she returned with a smile. "Patience, Colin."

"What the hell are we doing here?"

"Raphael's people are searching for a blood scent. You and Robbie both said some of the attackers were injured which means they bled. The scent will help us identify the guilty. It also has a . . . psychological benefit, I suppose you'd say. It motivates the soldiers, gets them ready for battle."

"Like these guys need more motivation," he muttered.

"Raphael knows his people," she said calmly, placing a hand on his arm.

A huge noise shattered the stillness. Colin looked up, expecting to see a tree falling nearly on top of them, but at the same time, his brain played the sound back in his head and he realized it wasn't a tree at all. One of the vamps had kicked in the back door to Babe's.

The vampires around Raphael all came to immediate attention, staring at the closed bar like dogs on point.

"I'm guessing they found what they were looking for," Colin said dryly.

Sophia stood quietly, her head tilted to one side, listening. "A body," she said. "In the freezer."

"Ah, fuck." Colin sighed deeply. "I should take a look."

Sophia walked with him into the bar. They went in the front door, held open by one of Raphael's vamps who directed them to the back. Not that Colin needed the assist. There was only one place a freezer big enough to hold a body could be.

It was a big chest model, maybe twenty-five or six cubic feet. A lot of the people around here had them. Coop's small grocery store was fine for day-to-day sort of stuff, but most of the residents made a monthly trip down the hill and stocked up on things like meat and anything else that could be frozen.

The lid was propped open, but Colin really didn't want to see what was inside. He looked anyway.

"Yeah, dammit, that's Leon." He glanced away. This was beyond the pale, completely unnecessary. It wasn't Leon's fault those jack-offs had decided to meet in his bar. But even so, the bar owner hadn't told anyone what he'd heard. And they'd killed him anyway.

He reached for the freezer lid and slammed it shut, careful to hold it by the edge and wiping his prints. "The cops'll have to be called on this," he said flatly. "Make sure there's nothing to say you were here."

He spun on his heel and strode back through the bar into the parking lot.

Sophia walked with him. She put a hand on his arm as they crossed the dirt lot. "I'm sorry, Colin."

"Yeah, well, it wasn't any of you that did it."

Sophie's grip on his arm tightened, pulling him to a stop. He waited while she listened to something only she could hear. "Raphael wants to speak with us," she said.

Colin didn't even ask how she knew that. He'd already figured out there was some sort of telepathy going on between the vamps. He just wondered how widespread it was.

"You were correct in your assessment," Raphael told him, once they'd drawn within human earshot. "There were no fewer than four blood trails. They begin among the trees, where the assailants concealed themselves, and they end here—" he said, indicating the parking lot. "—at which point the humans took to their vehicles. The human male in the freezer—"

Colin's head shot up and he glared at Raphael. "Leon," he snapped. "Leon Pettijohn."

Raphael gave a sideways tilt of his head, acknowledging the point. "Yet another victim of these killers. He died inside the bar, his neck was broken. With no blood and the body frozen, the scent was almost completely concealed by the air tight container."

Colin nodded. "So what happens next?"

"We go after them, beginning with McWaters," Raphael said. "He appears to be some sort of ringleader, maybe even the mastermind behind this scheme."

"I think we should split up," Colin suggested. "Ellen Pettijohn, Leon's wife—his widow now—gave us a name that came up on the vehicle list, as well. Curtis Jenkins—"

"Deb's brother," Raphael said, surprising him.

"Yeah," Colin agreed, puzzled. "But how do you know that? She just got back into town a month or so ago. Are you saying she's involved in this?"

"Not directly, no."

Colin waited for some sort of explanation, but it wasn't forthcoming. Next to him Sophie seemed as puzzled as he was, at least at first.

But then she exhaled a breathy "ahhh" sound and said slowly, "But she is involved. Perhaps with one of your vampires?"

Raphael gave her an unfriendly look, which was answer enough.

"She is most likely the one who told them how devastated Jeremy was after Mariane was attacked," Duncan provided. "Which is no doubt why they believed targeting Cynthia would incapacitate Lord Raphael."

"No doubt," Colin said dryly. "Okay, fine. So, one of us goes after McWaters and the other Curtis Jenkins."

"McWaters is mine," Raphael said flatly.

Colin nodded, trying not to think about what Raphael had planned for his old buddy.

"Then, Sophie and I will check out Jenkins and a couple of others on that list," he said. "Maybe we'll get lucky and they're all holed up together somewhere."

Raphael looked over at his lieutenant. "Duncan?"

"It makes sense, my lord. Sophia and Mister Murphy can reconnoiter Jenkins and the local citizenry. Several of your hunters can accompany them, while the rest of us take on McWaters and his allies. You have my cell number, Mister Murphy. In the event you require assistance, we can immediately dispatch additional people to your location. If the need is urgent," he added, anticipating Colin's next words, "we can abandon the vehicles and arrive in moments."

Colin's eyebrows shot up in surprise. He'd seen the vamps move fast earlier, but apparently they could do it over distance, too. Good to know.

"All right, then. Sophie?"

"That is acceptable. Good hunting to you, my lord."

"To all of us," Raphael growled, and his vampires responded with an eerie howl, a warning to all creatures that a far more dangerous predator was abroad in the forest tonight.

Chapter Thirty-Nine

Raphael strode into the yard in front of Garry McWaters's hideout, his vampires maneuvering silently among the trees to surround the house. This was the first of the two locations Murphy had suggested, but there was no doubt it was the right one. There were multiple trucks parked alongside and around the back, several of them showing signs of the gun battle, and at least one carrying a familiar and strong scent of blood. These were the men he sought, the men who had tried to kill his Cyn.

Next to him, Duncan was communicating quietly with the others, while Juro walked several paces ahead of him. They were all aware that the humans they hunted were armed and willing to kill. Cyn herself had taught Raphael and his vampires that even the most powerful among them could be destroyed by a human with the right weapon and the courage to use it.

Juro's twin brother was back at the compound tonight, overseeing security and protecting Cyn, which had taken on a new urgency in light of Murphy's information that she'd been specifically targeted. That same urgency fed Raphael's hunger for blood tonight. The best way to ensure her safety was to eliminate those who sought to harm her.

Duncan moved closer. "Two sentries, my lord," he said in a whisper that only another vampire could hear. "Both eliminated."

Raphael nodded. Around them, the night had grown utterly quiet. Any animals that might have been about earlier had taken refuge in their dens or nests, or what other safety they could find. The ultimate predator was afoot tonight, the top of the food chain on this planet, and the animals, even the human ones, knew it.

He focused on the house in front of him. It was a rough-made structure, fairly old, but well maintained and larger than he'd anticipated. Instead of a pitiful cabin along the lines of Hugh Pulaski's, this was more like the hunting lodges of old Europe—drafty structures with few private rooms designed to accommodate the lord and his retinue in what passed for comfort back then. The building in front of him had been expanded not too long ago, probably in anticipation of their killing spree. The additional wing was obvious and the sharp bite of fresh wood still stung his nose. The windows were covered with thick curtains, but there was light visible around the edges, and there were definitely people inside.

There was no music or television to be heard, and only muted conversation, which only made his task easier. He listened closely and isolated the beating hearts of—he cocked his head, counting—thirteen humans, one of whom was near death. With the two sentries whose hearts would never beat again, that made fifteen humans altogether. Raphael had himself and seven vampires, including Duncan and Juro.

It was hardly a fair fight. For the humans.

"Duncan?"

"Ready, my lord."

Raphael shrugged away the façade of humanity that he wore like a cloak, released the bonds that kept his power concealed and let it flow out of him like a river of molten silver. It warmed his veins and sped the pumping of his heart, pushing his lungs to expand more fully with every breath. It was a heady rush that had his lips drawing back in a vicious smile of pure exhilaration, his fangs emerging from his gums as he became the purest form of what he was . . . Vampire.

He lowered his head and focused on the flimsy structure in front of him. He could knock it down with a single brush of his power, could snuff out every living creature cowering within its walls. But that would be too easy, too kind to those who had dared harm what was most precious to him. And his vampires deserved to join in this hunt.

He let his power swell outward to touch the human dwelling, heard their cries of fear as the walls shook around them, tasted their terror as it drenched their cowardly minds.

"Garry McWaters," he whispered, sending his words lofting on a thread of power so that every being inside the dwelling would hear it as if spoken directly into his own ear. "Come out and face me if you dare."

Raphael waited, unconcerned. There was little possibility of his prey escaping. Even if the humans somehow managed to sneak out of the house, his vampires would catch them before they'd taken more than a few steps. And if by some completely unlikely stroke of luck they managed to take out one of his vampires, perhaps they deserved to live.

Or perhaps Raphael would wait until they believed themselves safe, and then he would hunt them down and kill them.

After a few moments, he heard low voices from inside, urgent words quickly hushed. The locks snapped back and the door opened. The lights within had been turned off, but that was more of a disadvantage to the humans than to him. They clearly had little understanding of whom they'd set themselves against when they'd taken on Raphael and his vampires.

Several men emerged finally from the shadows inside the house, edging slowly onto the narrow wooden porch where they spread out, shotguns and other weapons at the ready. Juro tensed, but Raphael watched impassively as one of their number separated from the rest, taking the steps down to the yard.

The human was a big man, nearly as big as Raphael himself. His head had been shaved bald and he wore clothing similar to that of Raphael's hunters, black combat gear with lace-up boots. There were two weapons visible, and more concealed on his person.

Juro started to step forward, no doubt intending to disarm the man, but Raphael stopped him with a thought. This one was his, no else's.

Raphael frowned. There was something draped around the man's neck and shoulders, crisscrossed over his chest.

He stared at it, then raised his gaze to the human's in disbelief.

"That's right, vampire," the human taunted. "Pure silver. Suck on that!"

Raphael exchanged a silent signal with Duncan, and then he moved. Faster than McWaters's primitive senses could detect, Raphael stripped away the man's guns and tossed them to one side, while Duncan hit the others with a mental blast that sent them reeling, dropping their weapons as they fell to their knees, one of them vomiting over the side of the porch.

Raphael took a single step back and paused intentionally, smiling at the look of shock in the man's eyes at finding himself all alone, face-to-face with the big, bad vampire, and weaponless. He recovered with admirable speed, however, puffing out his chest, confident in the protection of his silver talismans.

Raphael's smile took on a mocking edge as he reached out, grabbed one of the silver medallions studding the human's thick chest, and snapped the chain holding it in place. Flipping the hunk of silver in his fingers, he held it up in front of McWaters's face.

"Ssssst," he hissed and laughed when the man jerked in surprise, his eyes gone wide with fear.

Raphael grinned, revealing the full length of his fangs. All around the clearing his vampires roared as they reacted to the surge of vicious satisfaction emanating from their Sire.

"Garry McWaters, I assume," Raphael confirmed unnecessarily.

McWaters just stared at him, clearly terrified. And he had reason to be, because for him the terror was just beginning.

"Kneel," Raphael said calmly.

McWaters started to shake his head, but Raphael slipped the command straight into his brain. "Now," he added.

The human hit the ground with a soft grunt of pain. Raphael looked down and saw the silver glow of his own eyes bathing the man's face in light. He brushed back his leather coat and began flipping the bit of silver medallion back and forth over the knuckles of his right hand.

"You should know, human, that I am Raphael. It was *my* mate you targeted. My mate you bragged about trapping in your cowardly ambush. My vampires you murdered in cold blood."

Thinking of Cyn's pain, of Marco and Preston's terror, Raphael's vision washed out in a haze of red for a moment. Everything in him screamed for vengeance, urging him to squash this human like a bug. But he wanted him to suffer first.

Raphael's vision cleared and he contented himself with a small sliver of power, smiling in satisfaction as a series of sharp pops radiated from McWaters's right arm. The man grunted in shock at first and then screamed as every bone in his arm cracked in sequence, one at a time.

Raphael leaned closer and whispered. "What do you think, human? Am I weak? Am I huddled in a corner terrified by your brazen display of courage in sending a dozen men to kill a single woman?"

McWaters only stared up at him, his eyes wide and unfocused with pain, tears lost in the sweat soaking his pale face.

Not enough. Not nearly enough.

Raphael studied the man, pretending a curiosity he didn't feel. "Would you like to beg for your life? It probably won't help, but you never know, and I'm quite certain my vampires would find it entertaining."

Despite his fear, the human's jaw clenched and he shook his head. "Just don't make me one of you," he rasped. "I'd rather die."

Raphael reached down and grabbed the big man by his throat, lifting him effortlessly until his feet dangled several inches above the ground.

"That won't be a problem."

* * * *

Raphael crouched by what remained of Garry McWaters. The human's intestines had been shredded and were gushing poison into his system. Raphael had especially wanted him to experience the precise agony he had inflicted upon Cyn. Every bone in his body had been broken, as well, but the human was still alive, his spine still intact to ensure he felt every ounce of pain. Raphael had made sure of it. He'd also made sure to retrieve every bit of information the human possessed about this plot against his vampires.

"One last lesson before I send you to hell," Raphael said, pushing his coat back behind him to get it out of the way.

"Never, ever, touch what is mine."

He slammed his fist into McWaters's chest, grabbed his heart and squeezed. The human screeched feebly, the only sound he had the strength left to make. Raphael looked up and captured the man's gaze, and then he ripped the beating heart from his chest and stood, eyeing it dispassionately.

"Do you think my Cyn would like a souvenir?" he asked Duncan.

Duncan leaned sideways to study the dripping organ. "Probably not, my lord."

"No," Raphael agreed. He exerted a small amount of power and the heart went up in flames, turning to ash in seconds, soon joined by the rest of McWaters's body.

Raphael brushed his hands off briskly and looked toward the house. The remaining humans were huddled against its walls, rendered harmless by terror. They still had weapons, but were unable to muster the will to use them as long as Duncan and the other vampires filled their heads with nightmare visions of what awaited them.

"Shall we deal with these others now?" Raphael asked, flashing

Duncan a quick grin. "I didn't bring my hunters all the way out here only to watch."

He gave Duncan a nod and stood back, smiling in satisfaction as his vampires howled their release, as the shackles of civilization fell away and they were given free rein to hunt, to rip and tear, to drink blood flowing hot and fresh from the vein, as the heart of their prey fluttered beneath their palms. Willing donors were fine, far better than bagged blood, but nothing beat the viscous gush of heat as a vampire tore out the throat of his prey and reaped the reward of a successful hunt.

Raphael leaned against the SUV and waited, as the human killers were freed from their nightmares and the true terror began.

Sometime later, Duncan appeared from beneath the trees, strolling over to where Raphael sat in the open door of an SUV.

"Judging by the photographs in Cynthia's cell phone, my lord, I would estimate that the bulk of her attackers were here. The hunters with Sophia and Mister Murphy may be disappointed."

"Perhaps," Raphael said absently. His attention was on the distant compound where Cyn was beginning to stir from the deep healing trance he'd woven around her. He turned back to focus on Duncan. "Is that everyone?"

"Yes. Juro is cleaning up the last of them now. By morning, there will be no trace that anyone was here, other than their vehicles."

"Any blood traces?"

Duncan nodded. "Both inside the cabin and in two of the trucks. All human, none of them ours."

It was a delicate way of saying there was no scent of Cyn on the premises or in the vehicles. Raphael debated what to do next. He could leave things the way they were, or torch both the cabin and vehicles, leaving nothing but a blackened pile for anyone who came looking. But there would be no bodies either way.

A very few of the humans had invited death, cowering inside the cabin, believing they'd be safe there, that his vampires couldn't enter the dwelling. Unfortunately for them, once McWaters died, the cabin was no longer anyone's home, which made it akin to an office building where anyone could come and go—including vampires.

The rest, those who had come outside with McWaters in the first place, had at least fought back and provided his vampires with a good hunt. Not that any escaped. That was never even a possibility. And once the hunting was done, Duncan and Juro had incinerated the bodies, just as Raphael had disposed of McWaters. Not every vampire had the power to do so, but Raphael surrounded himself with power, not with weakness.

"Leave the cabin as it is," he said finally. "Have one of the vehicles dropped in the bar's parking lot. It will give the investigators something to think about when they discover the owner's body there. Leave the rest of the vehicles here. But make very certain the bodies are gone and any other evidence as well, Duncan. The human authorities may have their suspicions, but they'll have no proof we were here."

"Of course, my lord."

Raphael turned in the direction of the compound once again, drawn almost against his will. Cyn wasn't doing it consciously, but her need called to him and that was enough.

"I need to return," he said abruptly. He started around the SUV intending to drive himself, but Duncan issued a sharp command and two vampires appeared out of the darkness, their black combats reeking of blood and violence. Raphael glanced down at his own clothes. He would have to shower before seeing Cyn.

* * * *

Raphael leapt from the SUV while it was still rolling, his cell phone to his ear.

"My lord," Saephan's voice answered immediately.

"I'm in the building," Raphael said as Juro's twin held the door open for him. "I'll shower in the guards' quarters and be there momentarily."

He didn't bother asking his guards if anything had happened while he was out. If it had they would have contacted him. Instead, he took the left-hand hallway out of the great room, heading for the wing opposite the one where he had his private quarters, hitting the door to the basement stairs at a near run.

He slammed open the door of the first room he came to, noting absently that it was currently in use by one of his male vampires. The odds had favored him, but it was fortunate all the same, because he intended to borrow some clothes. Equally fortunate was the fact that this section was reserved for Raphael's personal security and those vampires tended to be bigger than average.

He tore off his bloodied and filthy clothing, dropping it into a pile. Someone would retrieve it later. What could be saved would be cleaned and returned to him. Anything else would be burned. He stepped into the shower while it was still warming up, soaping his body and washing his hair with quick economical movements. He could feel Cyn's restlessness. On some level, she knew he was near and she wanted him closer. And, although he'd been gone only a few hours, he needed to see her again, needed to see with his own eyes that she was well, before the sun rose and deprived him of his senses.

He rubbed a towel over his wet hair as he rummaged through the available clothing. A pair of sweats and a T-shirt came to hand, which was all he needed.

Two minutes later and he was back upstairs—barefoot, his hair still wet, towel in hand, heading across the great room to his private quarters in the opposite wing. Wei Chen stepped out of the office as Raphael strode by. The Seattle nest leader opened his mouth to say something, probably to ask about the hunt, but Raphael spoke first.

"The human woman you have working for you," he said. "Will she be here tomorrow?" He didn't slow down, forcing Wei Chen to hurry along next to him.

"Yes, my lord."

"Find an excuse to keep her tomorrow until after sunset. I'll have someone follow her when she leaves. And I'll want to meet with you privately first thing. Bring her records. Do you understand?"

"Of course, my lord. Is there anything—"

"Nothing." He turned his attention away from the Seattle leader, nodding instead to Elke who looked as if she hadn't moved the entire time he was gone. He hurried past her and entered the code to call his private elevator, waiting impatiently for it to arrive. The ride down was interminable and he shot through the opening doors as soon as they'd widened enough to accommodate his shoulders.

Dr. Saephan stood, calm despite Raphael's precipitous arrival. No doubt he'd heard the elevator's departure and known what it meant.

"Lord Raphael," he said, bowing slightly.

"She is well?"

"Very well, my lord. I've removed her IV for now. The bag would have needed changing during the day, and she'll be fine without it for those few hours. What she needs most she will have, and that is you, my lord. Speaking of which—"

Saephan paused as if gauging Raphael's mood before continuing. Raphael tore his gaze away from Cyn to give him an inquiring look.

"There is blood in the refrigerator, my lord, if you have need of it."

Raphael didn't move. Under normal circumstances, he took blood from his mate and no other. But that was obviously impossible in her current condition. So either Saephan feared that Raphael's hunger would drive him to take blood from her anyway, and thus endanger her life. Or he was honestly concerned that Raphael might be neglecting his own health in his preoccupation with healing Cyn.

Raphael chose to believe the latter.

"Thank you, Doctor," he said, his gaze meeting Saephan's without blinking. "We'll see you tomorrow evening."

"Yes, my lord."

Raphael waited until he heard the doors open upstairs and close again, confirming with a quick probe that the elevator was empty. He then called it back and locked it down for the night, pulling the vault door across the small vestibule and securing that as well.

Stripping off his borrowed clothes, he slipped into bed next to Cyn. She was wearing one of Raphael's t-shirts, obviously selected by Dr. Saephan after bathing her. Cyn rarely wore nightclothes of any kind and almost certainly had not brought any with her on this trip. Raphael experienced a surprisingly visceral pleasure at seeing her in his clothes and mocked himself silently. Perhaps he wasn't as far above primitive man as he liked to believe.

He slid closer, wrapping his body around her carefully. "I'm here, *lubimaya*," he said unnecessarily. Cyn's entire body relaxed as she turned into him, her breath running out in a long, slow exhalation that warmed the naked skin of his chest. Raphael closed his eyes in relief and placed a gentle hand beneath the shirt she wore, resting it against the bare skin of her lower back. They both needed the contact. But in this case, his need might have been greater than hers.

"I love you, my Cyn," he murmured. He fell asleep to the strong beat of her heart against his ribs, not even noticing when the sun began its daily ascent.

Chapter Forty

Colin sat in the front passenger seat, giving Robbie directions to the next address on the list Raphael's tech had provided. Sophie sat behind him. She didn't say anything, but he was exquisitely aware of her, almost as if she was touching him even though she wasn't. He wondered if it had something to do with the blood she'd taken from him. Had it linked them somehow?

Robbie made a turn and Colin looked up. They were heading for Curtis Jenkins's place, but several people on the list were on the way, so they were stopping at those addresses as they came up. They'd already checked a couple off and it had taken no time at all, since no one had been home.

There had been no word from Raphael and his party yet, but it was still too early to expect anything. After all, both of McWaters's old family places were pretty far out. Maybe he expected more because of Duncan's assertion that the vampires could come to his assistance in only minutes, no matter where they were. Or maybe it was because he was sure on some level that Garry was at one of those hidden cabins, and that his old buddy wouldn't survive the night if Raphael had anything to say about it. And Colin was pretty sure Raphael had a lot to say on that particular subject.

Not that Colin blamed him. Garry and his newfound friends had tried to murder Leighton. They'd killed Leon, as well as Marco and Preston. And Garry had all but bragged about what they'd done to Mariane. But after so many years of covering his back . . . Hell, maybe that was the real reason he'd suggested splitting into two groups. So he wouldn't have to face up to his friend's execution. Or, rather, his former friend. He might have mixed feelings about Garry's death, but he had none at all about the past tense of their friendship.

"Deep thoughts, dude," Robbie said, without looking away from the road.

Colin grunted and ran a hand through his hair, aware of Sophia listening to every word. She knew he was ambivalent about Raphael's plans for McWaters and the other humans. And she was watching him, probably wondering if he'd judge her, too, before the night was over.

Colin turned halfway around in the seat. "I'm surprised you didn't go with Raphael, Jeremy," he said to the vampire sitting next to Sophia.

Jeremy turned back from staring out the window. He'd grown tenser with every mile they'd driven away from the bar, and Colin recognized it for what it was. Fear, plain and simple. The vampire might be determined to seek revenge for his mate, but he'd never been in any kind of battle before. He was scared to death.

Jeremy darted a quick glance at Sophia before answering Colin. "I'm only an accountant. Lord Raphael and his people are accustomed to a level of violence that is completely foreign to me. Some of them have been with him for decades and have fought challenge after challenge. I would only be in the way."

Colin shrugged. "We're likely to get into some shit here, too, you know. If we find any of these old boys, they won't go down easy."

Jeremy jerked his head in a sharp nod. "Yes. And I won't hold you back. I may be an accountant, but I am also Vampire. And besides, I'm hoping at least one of those we find will be among the ones who attacked my Mariane. I owe her that much."

"I've got *no* problem with that," Colin assured him, aware of the morbid amusement in Sophia's dark eyes. He suspected it was over the fact that her very human lover was less nervous than a fucking vampire about going into a firefight.

And speaking of that, what the hell had she meant back at the compound when she'd called him her mate? It had sure made Raphael sit back and take a second look. Shouldn't somebody have asked *him* if he wanted to be her mate? Hell, wasn't there even a ceremony involved? He rolled his eyes, realizing he sounded like a reluctant bride. What was next, for God's sake? Was he going to start worrying about getting a nice ring? Shit.

He was relieved when Robbie took the final curve, bringing the next house into sight. Give him a clean fight any day of the week. It was a lot easier than trying to figure out what made a vampire tick.

Robbie slowed, stopping before they left the protection of the trees. Behind them, the second SUV, with a half dozen of Raphael's hunters inside, followed suit. There were lights inside the house, but no vehicle parked out front.

"What do you think?" Robbie asked, peering through the windshield.

"I think the wife's home. They don't have kids." Colin unbuckled his seat belt. "Stay here. I'm gonna knock on the door." Sophia's hand touched his shoulder as he climbed out and he gave her a reassuring wink as he quietly closed the truck door and headed for the house.

He took it slowly, his fingers stroking the butt of his gun. He checked both sides of the house, looking for a vehicle or even some sort of shed where one might be hidden. But there was nothing. Still, he took the steps cautiously and listened at the door for a moment before knocking.

The sound of a television immediately went silent. He knocked again. Someone cursed, and he heard what sounded like a recliner being lowered and then footsteps approaching the door. Whoever it was had on mule slippers. He could hear them slapping against a hardwood floor with every step. The door swung open.

"Colin." The woman standing there didn't look or sound happy to see him.

"Jan," he said politely. "Gordon home?"

"Does it look like he's home? You see a big, black truck out there anywhere?"

"No, ma'am, I don't, but it's always possible it's in the shop."

"Well, it ain't. You want Gordon, you best be heading over to Curtis's. The whole lot of 'em are cooking up something over there. And before you ask, I don't know what the hell it is and I don't want to."

When Colin didn't immediately react, she made a disgusted sound. "Is there anything else? I'm watching my shows."

Colin shook his head. "No, ma'am. That's it. I'll check out Curtis's like you said."

"Well, whoop-dee-doo. Jesus H. Christ," she muttered, already closing the door in his face.

Colin grinned in spite of himself. Before he'd gotten two steps down the stairs, he heard the clunk of a recliner slamming backwards, followed by a wave of canned laughter as Jan returned to watching her shows.

He was still smiling when he climbed back into the SUV.

"She looked right happy to see you standing on her doorstep, Murph," Robbie observed.

"You got that," Colin agreed. "She saved us a bit of time, though. Says her husband and his buddies are all over at Curtis Jenkins's place. Looks like these boys are hiding out in someone's rec room, after all."

"Saves us some time and ammunition."

"If you find them, we won't need much ammunition," Sophia chimed in, her sexy, low voice a sharp contrast to the bloodthirstiness of her words. "We vampires favor a more direct solution to this sort of problem."

"Yes, ma'am," Robbie agreed. "I've seen Lord Raphael in action and direct is definitely the word I'd use."

"I want blood," Jeremy said in a savage murmur from the backseat. He lifted his gaze and stared at Colin. "Human blood. I want the night itself to scream with their terror."

Colin met the vampire's intense gaze, noting the red glaze flickering over his eyes. "I hope you get what you need, Jeremy," he said. "For Mariane's sake."

Colin turned to face the front once more, watching the dark road disappear beneath them as they raced to Curtis Jenkins's house. He just hoped none of that human blood Jeremy was so hungry for would be his or Robbie's.

Chapter Forty-One

Sophia strolled down the center of the gravel road, or maybe it was a driveway. They all looked the same and really, what did it matter which it was? The only thing she cared about were the ruts to either side where the gravel had all but disappeared into the dirt, leaving a pitted, uneven mess. She'd worn her sturdy, flat-heeled ankle boots, anticipating there might be some mucking in the dirt, but that didn't mean she *wanted* to do any mucking.

She smiled, amused at herself despite the seriousness of the situation. She'd have to share that thought with Colin once this was all over and they were safely back in Vancouver. Because that's where she was going. No more hiding down in South America. If Lucien was dead—and it still grieved her to think so—but if it was true, then she intended to be the next Vampire Lord of the Canadian Territories. And if Lucien wasn't dead? If somehow he'd managed to thoroughly conceal himself while others cleaned up his mess? She frowned.

It might be better for him if he was dead.

A tiny sound brought her back to the present and the house at the end of the driveway. She eyed it curiously. All of the missing humans might not be hiding out here, but many of them were. She counted five trucks pulled up in front, like horses at a hitching post. And there was a glint of metal around the side of the house that could easily be one or two more.

Still within the cover of the forest, and camouflaged by her dark clothing, she paused, assessing the situation. She might not be as experienced in combat as Raphael and his people, or even Colin and his friend Robbie, but she'd fought her share of challenges over the years. And since vampire duels were frequently to the death, especially among strangers, she wouldn't be standing here in front of this dismal dwelling if she hadn't learned how to fight . . . and win.

The house in front of her was mostly dark. Perhaps they hoped to hide their presence from the road. Or maybe Colin was right and they were all gathered in the basement. Either way, they hadn't bothered with sentries. The vampires Raphael had sent with her and Colin had already surrounded the house and reported they'd found no one.

She identified Colin and Robbie as they came up behind her, their human heartbeats giving them away despite the fact that they walked nearly as silently as a vampire. They moved into position on either side of her, fading in among the trees. In response, she left the cover of the forest behind and took a single step into the yard proper. A loud click sounded and she winced, lowering her eyes against a flood of yellow light from above. Too late she recognized the scattering of ragged poles around the house for what it was. Security lights set on some sort of motion detector system which she'd just set off.

Not that it mattered. She wanted to be seen. The plan was to draw the humans out of the house and this would do as well as anything else.

Sure enough, another light snapped on over the front door just before it opened to reveal a skinny human standing behind the screen and peering out into yard. It was foolish of him to provide such an easy target. Fortunately for him, dropping him in the doorway wasn't part of their plan.

"Animals probably set the lights off all the time," Colin whispered from somewhere to her left.

Sophia nodded and took two more steps forward, making sure the human could see her.

The man jerked slightly when she appeared, freezing for just an instant too long. Further testament to his poor survival instincts. As if belatedly aware that he was spotlighting himself, the human reached back inside and snapped the light off, saying something to someone behind him before opening the screen door and stepping onto the porch. He carried a rifle of some sort, and he had it up to his shoulder. But while it was more or less pointed in her direction, even she could tell it wasn't quite aimed at her. She was, after all, only a woman and all by herself. What threat could she possibly represent to an armed man?

This was the part of the plan Colin had objected to. He'd hated the idea of her standing there in the open, just waiting to be shot. Sophia had assured him she could survive almost any gunshot wound, even one to the head as long as her brain remained largely intact. Colin had responded by enumerating the list of bullets readily available which could blow her brains out the back of her head quite handily. And although he'd pointed out that these were the same men who had tried to murder Cynthia Leighton, even he had admitted, when pressed, that most men would hesitate to shoot a lone, unarmed woman.

And just to sweeten the argument, Sophia had reminded him that even when they'd been *trying* to kill Cynthia Leighton, they'd shot her body, not her head. Of course, it was always possible they'd been *aiming* at her head and had simply missed, but she hadn't mentioned that to Colin. He had enough to worry about.

The skinny human from the house took another step forward, coming to the edge of his porch, the toe of one boot hanging over the first step. He lowered the rifle slightly and did a slow one-hundred eighty degree turn as he searched the grimy yard, snapping back to her when he found nothing there.

He grinned, revealing a mouthful of even, white teeth. "Hey, guys," he called back over his shoulder. "You gotta see this."

Dropping the gun to his side, he bounced down the four steps to the ground, landing on both feet in a puff of dirt. More men crowded out onto the porch behind him, all of them armed, some skipping the stairs to drop directly off the porch and fan out to the sides. Sophia counted quickly. Seven humans. She wondered how many Raphael had found.

"Is this what them vamps have come to?" the first man asked jeeringly. "Sending a human woman to do their dirty work? You got a message for us, sweetheart?"

Sophia shrugged. "In my experience, women have always done the dirty work."

"Not bad enough she's a fucking fangbanger," someone muttered. "She's a fucking femi-Nazi fangbanger."

"Just one more reason to off her, the way I see it," the skinny man said, his sharp gaze resting briefly on her face before continuing to search the trees.

"Good lookin' enough, though," another said, taking the four steps from the porch in two long strides. "Maybe we should have some fun before we get rid of her. How 'bout it, beautiful?" he called out. "You wanna fuck a few of your own before you die?"

Sophia cocked her head curiously. Interesting that they assumed she was human. Had they never seen a female vampire?

"I don't fuck animals," she said evenly.

Several of the men swore nastily, the last of them dropping off the porch and onto the ground, where they confronted her in a rough half circle, although they were still several yards away. For all their bravado, none of them were willing to leave the protection of the herd.

The skinny one took an aggressive step forward. "You watch your mouth, bitch, or I'll fill it with something useful."

"And what would that be?" she asked curiously.

"Hey, Curtis," one of the other men called out suddenly, "something's not right about this." Clearly the brains of the bunch, he backed toward the porch, looking around uneasily. "What's she doing out here all by herself?"

Behind Sophia, Colin's voice rang out, "Who says she's by herself?"

She smiled, letting them see her fangs, as all around the clearing grinning vampires stepped from the cover of the trees.

The humans turned almost as one, racing for the safety of the house. Sophia reached out with her power, slamming the door and cutting off their retreat, scattering them into the arms of Raphael's hunters.

All except the skinny human, Curtis Jenkins. Jenkins was hers.

Ignoring the sounds of battle all around her, trusting completely in the ability of her fellow vampires to handle a half dozen humans and knowing Colin would watch her back, she wrapped Jenkins in bands of power and pulled him slowly, inexorably, across the yard until he was standing a couple feet in front of her, bellowing curses as he fought to break free.

"Be quiet," she muttered irritably.

The human's mouth continued to move, opening and closing like a fish gasping for oxygen. When no words came out, his eyes widened and he stared at Sophia in shock.

"Curtis Jenkins," she said, smiling pleasantly. "I've decided I want to fuck you after all." She frowned. "Or wait, that's not right. My English . . ." she added, shaking her head in dismay. "Let me think. Ah. No. I don't want to *fuck* you. That's rather repulsive. What I *want* is to fuck *with* you."

Her smile disappeared and she slammed the human to his knees. Strangled noises filled his throat as he thrashed about, struggling to break the invisible bonds of her power. Sophia circled him slowly, amused by the way his head twisted as he tried to keep her in sight.

"Tell me, Jenkins, do you know where Lucien is?"

The human froze, clearly startled by her question. He stared at her in confusion.

Puzzled by his reaction, Sophia cocked her head quizzically. "Do you know who Lucien is?"

He shook his head frantically, eyes wide.

Sophia sighed. She didn't know why she'd thought it would be that easy. Throwing away all pretense of humanity, she delved directly into the man's mind, ripping it apart in search of the truth. His thoughts were a cesspool of hate and resentment and she felt sullied by the touch of them. Foremost in his mind was triumph over his gang's recent attack on Raphael's mate and Colin, too. He resented that Colin had been hired for the local law enforcement job, believing he was far more qualified, although what possessed him to think so was unclear.

But the brutal assault on Jeremy's young mate was there, too, surrounded by a savage lust that sickened her soul. She destroyed that memory without hesitation, not caring what damage she caused. Reeling with disgust, she was debating whether she needed to waste anymore time on this piece of trash when a familiar face flashed briefly—there and gone. Sophia dug around, trying to call it back, but it was lost in a jumble of recent memories, most of them hardly worth remembering.

Frustration made her clumsy and she shoved the human's mind away from her too quickly. The muscles in his body seized all at once and then released with an audible snap like the release of a spring. It sent him sprawling to the ground where he lay quivering as his brain recovered from her indelicate probing.

Sophia eyed him dispassionately. She lifted a hand to end it all, pausing when she heard familiar footsteps. She turned in time to see Colin emerge from the shadows under the trees. He was carrying some sort of shotgun in one hand, and as he drew closer she detected the distinct scent of gun powder on his clothing. She blinked, suddenly registering the fact that she'd heard gunfire a short time ago.

"Are you all right?" she asked, scanning him quickly.

Colin gave her a half smile. "Fine." He leaned around her, eyeing Jenkins with bored disinterest. "What about this one?"

Some remnant of Jenkin's brain recognized Colin's voice, and he grunted, drawing her attention. He was on his back in the dirt, unmoving but for his eyes which were wide open and fixed on Colin. Sophia watched him curiously, wondering if perhaps he retained just enough animal brain to think his fellow human would save him.

"You need any help here, darlin'?" Colin asked her.

"No, I've got this one."

"If you're sure, then I'm gonna track down Jeremy. He was looking pretty green a while back."

Sophia stood on tiptoes and pulled Colin's head down for a quick kiss. He blinked, clearly startled, but his eyes sparked with pleasure nonetheless. "This won't take long," she assured him.

Colin nodded and walked past her, heading for the rear of the house. She watched him go, admiring the way he moved, that loose-hipped grace of a powerful male. She sighed with pleasure. And then turned back to Jenkins.

"Now where were we?"

* * * *

Colin was surprised at himself. He had no qualms at all about leaving Jenkins back there with Sophie, even though he knew there was only one possible outcome. It wasn't a matter of whether the old boy would die, but how. And if Sophie wanted to do the honors, that was fine with him. Somewhere between the day he'd discovered Mariane ravaged nearly to death and the afternoon he'd raced Leighton's bloody body back to her vampire lover in a desperate bid to save her life, he'd decided these people didn't deserve to live. And he didn't trust the courts to serve up justice when it came to vampires or the human women who loved them.

He heard a soft grunt and brought his shotgun up, his eyes searching the shadows behind the house as he advanced slowly. He'd seen Jeremy disappear back here sometime ago. The vamp wasn't a soldier and it was entirely possible . . . He froze in mid-step, letting his foot drop slowly to the ground.

"Hey there, Jeremy," he said carefully.

The vampire lifted his mouth from the neck of someone Colin no longer recognized, spitting out a gob of blood and flesh before treating Colin to a gruesome grin. "Hi, Colin," he said cheerfully.

Colin stepped closer. The human was clearly dead, although his blood was still dripping, so it hadn't happened all that long ago.

"You know this guy?" he asked, glancing at Jeremy.

"Well enough," the vampire said darkly. "He was one of those who hurt my Mariane. I saw only glimpses of what happened that day, but his voice is one I recognized. I don't know his name. Do you?"

Colin studied the mess that was the man's face. He shook his head. "Nope."

"It doesn't matter," Jeremy said. "Sophia will destroy all the bodies before we leave here tonight anyway. Even I know that much about how things are done."

Colin nodded. He'd overheard Sophie saying something about that to the others, although he didn't have a clear picture yet of *how* it would come about.

"We should probably drag this one around front," he said. "You need any help with that?"

Jeremy stood with that surprising speed and grace that all vampires seemed to possess. He grabbed the dead human's arm and hefted him easily, tossing him over one shoulder in a fireman's carry, as if he weighed nothing at all. He grinned at Colin's look of surprise.

"Vampire, remember? Better get used to it if you don't want Sophia to run you ragged."

Colin watched the vampire march off with his burden like the eighth dwarf in a particularly gruesome fairy tale. And he had a feeling Sophia was going to run him ragged no matter what he did.

It was a while before they got everything cleaned up, but eventually Sophia was walking alongside him back to where they'd left the SUVs tucked into a narrow turnout on the main road. The bodies were gone, reduced to ash and scattered throughout the forest, so there wouldn't be any suspicious piles of ash for some industrious crime tech to sift through. Not that it was likely they'd find anything if they did. Sophie's power had produced a blaze that disintegrated flesh and bone more thoroughly than any regular flame could have done. The result had been something that more closely resembled the remains of a wood fire than any human cremation. It gave Colin pause to realize Sophie had that much power inside her, but it also made him a little proud.

He was quiet as they neared the SUVs, but he needed to know something and Sophie was the only one he could ask. "You saw what Jeremy did to that guy. I couldn't even tell who it was when he finished."

"Yes."

"Is that . . . I mean, do you think that's what Raphael did to Garry?"

She took his hand, pulling him to a stop so she could look into his face. "Your friend—"

"Not my friend," he insisted, meeting her gaze evenly. "Not anymore."

Sophia nodded slowly, acknowledging the distinction. "McWaters, then—he tried to murder Raphael's mate. You saw what Jeremy did, what his need for revenge drove him to do. And Jeremy is—" She shook her head, as if searching for a comparison. "Jeremy is a child's breath compared to the most destructive storm the world has ever seen, one that destroys everything in his path without regard. And that storm is Lord Raphael."

She took his other hand, squeezing gently. "McWaters is almost certainly dead by now, and there is no benefit to be found in trying to envision things which are quite beyond most people's imagination."

"Fuck." Colin looked away. "Mac wasn't who I thought it he was. He turned out to be about as low as a man can get. But he was a good soldier, too. And once an honorable man. It's hard. Feelings can't change on a dime, you know?"

"I do. Sometimes people disappoint us, but that doesn't change our memories of them."

"Yeah." He tightened his fingers on her hand and started walking again, looking up when they reached the road and Robbie called Sophie's name.

He started toward them in the dark, holding out a cell phone. "Duncan," he said and offered her his cell.

Sophie nodded her thanks and accepted the phone.

"This is Sophia."

Her mouth tightened in irritation as she listened, but her voice remained all business. "Yes, of course," she said. "The bodies were burned to ash and scattered at random, all blood trace eliminated. None of ours were injured."

She listened a bit longer, then raised her head and asked Colin. "How long before we arrive at the compound?"

"This late at night, we can make time. Half hour probably, forty minutes at the most."

She repeated the information and nodded in that automatic way people do on the phone. "Tomorrow night, then. I'll be there." She disconnected the phone and handed it back to Robbie with a murmured, "Thank you."

She looked up at Colin and said quietly, "We'll talk later."

He nodded, taking her hand again and continuing toward the SUVs. He figured whatever it was they had planned for tomorrow night involved the still missing Lucien. The humans responsible for the murders might have been taken out, but Lucien had something to do with it, too, and he was still an unknown. Was he dead? Or was he pulling the strings from somewhere in hiding? Colin didn't know. And it seemed no one else did either.

But Colin knew one thing. He wasn't leaving Sophie's side until Lucien was rounded up and neutralized. The vampire lord was her Sire and that gave him some sort of power over her. The bastard had also called Sophie back to Vancouver, letting her and the others risk their lives, paying the price for *his* stupidity and sheer cowardice. But now that the mess was cleaned up, now that Lucien no longer *needed* Sophie, he might view her as a threat. He might be looking to get rid of her.

But Colin needed her. Now and forever. He'd lost her once and he had no intention of losing her again. Jenkins and his buddies hadn't had the foresight to arm themselves with vampire killing rounds, but Colin wouldn't make that mistake. Not when Sophie's life might be on the line.

Chapter Forty-Two

The first thing Raphael heard when he woke, the first thing he listened for, was Cyn's heartbeat, still pulsing against his chest. He'd felt her there in his dreams, but that didn't stop the relief that squeezed his heart at finding her there in truth as night fell around them.

He touched his lips to her forehead, tightening his arms around her by the slightest degree.

"Raphael?" she said, sounding sleepy and confused, and far too weak.

"And who else would be lying naked in your bed, my Cyn?"

He felt her smile against his skin, and in the next moment felt her tense sharply. "Are you okay? Did you go—"

"They are dead, *lubimaya*. The ones who harmed you, who murdered Marco and Preston and attacked Mariane. All dead."

She pulled back a little, searching his face with eyes that were weary with pain. The sight infuriated him and for a moment he wished he had a hundred more humans to slaughter for her vengeance.

Some of that must have shown in his face, because she touched cool fingers to his cheek. "Are you sure you're okay?" she asked.

"I am well, my Cyn. As is everyone else, including your Robbie."

"And Murphy, too?"

Raphael felt a surge of jealousy that she would even ask about the human. She saw that, too, and her mouth softened into a gentle smile.

"I love you, Raphael."

He bent his head to touch his lips to hers and she responded for the first time since her injury, opening her lips and letting her tongue brush lightly against his.

Something broke inside him at that fragile touch, so unlike their usual lovemaking. He struggled to control the emotion, not wanting her to be upset by it.

"Mister Murphy is unharmed, as well," he told her. "And I believe he and Sophia are, as you would say, an item."

"They have a history," Cyn murmured, sounding tired, as if even this short exchange had exhausted her.

Raphael kissed her mouth once more, briefly. Then her cheek and her forehead, brushing her hair back with his fingers.

"I need a shower," she fretted.

"You're perfect as you are, my Cyn." *Alive*, he thought privately, which was all that mattered. She would regain her strength in time. Thinking of that, he lifted his arm and sliced his wrist with his fangs.

"You need to drink, *lubimaya*."

Her eyes flashed open. "What about you? If I keep drinking from you, won't—"

"I fed last night," he assured her. She didn't ask, and he didn't offer to tell her whose blood it was he'd dined on. But he and his vampires had all fed very well on the blood of their enemies.

"Okay," she said. "That's good, but I'm feeling a lot better tonight. I won't need—"

"Drink," he ordered, interrupting her. "We'll discuss the rest later."

She sighed, but surrendered to the inevitable. She was too weak to resist him in any event. Her mouth closed over his wrist and she began to suck. Raphael cupped the back of her head with his other hand, his thoughts drifting to the night ahead. The humans had been taken care of, but Lucien was still a problem. He needed to be found soon and dealt with permanently. Raphael could no longer tolerate the influence of a foreign vampire lord within his territory, particularly one who had brought such grief to Raphael's people.

Lucien would have to go, and Sophia would have to follow.

Chapter Forty-Three

Raphael was pulling a sweater over his head when Elke called down to say that Dr. Saephan had arrived. Cyn was asleep, but she woke when the phone rang, turning her head to watch as he opened the vault and sent the elevator up to fetch the doctor.

While he waited, Raphael called Duncan, letting him know he'd be upstairs shortly and verifying their arrangements regarding the human woman Wei Chen employed. Raphael wasn't certain she was involved in recent events, but he felt she was. He had no reason that he could put a finger on. It was instinct, nothing more, but he trusted his instincts. They'd brought him a long way from his father's dirt farm in Russia.

The elevator doors opened and Peter Saephan emerged, murmuring a brief greeting to Raphael while heading directly for the bed and Cyn. He was carrying a cooler under one arm and his black bag in the other hand.

"My Cyn seems much improved tonight, Doctor. She slept through the day and just woke a short time ago."

"Your Cyn is right here," she muttered.

Saephan laughed. "You *are* feeling better. I never thought I'd say this, but I missed your smart ass self."

"Nice bedside manner, Doc."

"I saved it just for you, darling." Saephan sat down and opened his bag. "Let's take a look."

Raphael watched quietly as the doctor checked her vitals, then listened to her chest and rolled up the t-shirt to examine her abdomen. Cyn winced more than once beneath his careful touch and Raphael frowned, but Dr. Saephan gave a satisfied nod.

"You're right, my lord," he said to Raphael and then to Cyn, "You're definitely better. But considering you were nearly dead two days ago, better is a relative term."

"Fuck," she whispered, with only a shadow of her normal vitriol.

Saephan laughed. "You're a terrible patient, but I love you. So come on, give me the arm."

Cyn glanced at Raphael as she stretched out her arm with a sigh. "Go on," she told him. "I'll be fine. And if I'm not, you can beat up the doc here for me."

Raphael crossed the room, leaning over to give her a careful kiss. "Not likely since he helped save your life, *lubimaya*. But be good and I'll tell you all the news when I return."

"News of what?" she asked, her voice already fading as she yawned tiredly.

"The new Lord of the Canadian Territories."

* * * *

Raphael nodded at the ever vigilant Elke as he came out of the elevator. She gave him an inquiring look and he stopped long enough to say, "She improves every day, Elke. When I left she was arguing with Saephan."

Elke knew Cyn well enough to laugh at this, knowing it for the good news it was. "Thank you, my lord," she said.

"Thank you, Elke, for guarding her so well."

Elke was still flushed with pleasure when Raphael left her to join Duncan who met him halfway across the great room, handing him the leather coat he'd left in the guard's room he'd used to shower in last night. It had been cleaned and he shrugged it on as he walked. Raphael liked the coat. It was comfortable and functional. But he wore it largely for Cyn's benefit. She loved the coat, saying it made him look *all vampirish and dramatic.* He'd actually replaced it more than once at her behest and now had several identical coats as backups.

"The woman left the compound shortly after sunset, my lord," Duncan told him as they walked. "Justin and Aaron are following her and Wei Chen is in the conference room."

Raphael nodded. "Sophia?"

"She spent the day at Mister Murphy's," Duncan reported dryly. "They're on their way here now."

"Excellent. Wei Chen first."

Raphael turned off the great room, heading not for the big meeting room where he'd greeted Sophia at the start of all of this, but for the smaller, more private conference room down the hall from Wei Chen's office.

The nest leader was waiting for him. A manila folder sat on the table in front of him and he was working busily on his PDA when Duncan opened the door. He set the device aside immediately and stood, giving a short bow.

"Good evening, Sire," he said. "I understand last night's hunt was successful."

Raphael nodded. "We eliminated the human threat." He sat, leaning back in his chair, gesturing for Wei Chen to resume his seat. "But Lucien remains at large," he continued. "And neither Sophia nor I found any knowledge of him amongst the humans."

Wei Chen cocked his head thoughtfully, then tapped the folder in front of him. "But you believe Sandra Koepke may have knowledge of this?" He nodded and opened the folder, flipping a few pages before turning the folder so Raphael could see. "Before coming to us, she worked in Vancouver, my lord."

Raphael passed the folder to Duncan who bent over the table to read it. Raising his eyebrows at what he found, he pulled out his cell and made a call.

"Justin," he said quietly. "What is your location?" He listened a short time, then said, "Whatever it takes, stay on her."

Raphael looked up at his lieutenant, and Duncan said, "Wherever she's going, it's definitely not the address she lists as her home."

Wei Chen looked from Duncan to Raphael in surprise. "My lord, I—"

"Did she have a vampire connection in Vancouver, or anywhere else before coming to work here?" Raphael interrupted.

Wei Chen seemed badly startled by Duncan's news and it took him a moment to process Raphael's question. "No, my lord," he insisted. "I would never have hired her if that were the case."

Raphael stood without warning, prompting Wei Chen to jump to his feet. "My lord?"

"I'm going to pay Ms. Koepke a visit. You are not to call her or communicate with her in any way."

"Of course not, my lord!"

Raphael strode through the door Duncan held open for him and down the hallway. Sophia and Murphy were coming through the doors as he reached the great room.

"Sophia," he said without pausing. "You and Murphy will want to join me for this. You have a vehicle, Murphy?"

"Yes, sir," Murphy said, frowning.

"Good. Take Sophia and follow us."

"Duncan, you and Juro. No one else."

"Juro is already waiting, my lord."

Raphael smiled grimly as he pulled the door open and headed down the stairs into the cold, wet air. His instincts were screaming louder with every step he took. He wasn't certain yet what this night held, but he knew he was on the right track.

And Lucien was waiting at the end of it.

Chapter Forty-Four

"Do you know where we're going?"

Sophia jerked her gaze and her thoughts away from the SUV in front of them. It was little more than square of black, with the red taillights gleaming like a demon's eyes on the dark roads. Colin had both hands clenched on the wheel and was every bit as tense as she was.

"I'm not sure," she admitted. "You heard everything I did. But it must have something to do with Lucien. He's the only string left dangling."

Colin gave her a quick glance. "This is the same Lucien who's your Sire, right?"

"There is only *one* Lucien, believe me."

"So, let's suppose we find him. What then?"

Sophia's lips tightened unhappily and she turned away from Colin, staring at the blur of dark trees as they sped by. She would never have said as much to Raphael—it shamed her to admit it even to herself—but she was fairly certain Lucien had intentionally led the killers away from his own territory and into Raphael's. She didn't know how he'd done it, but she understood Lucien enough to know why, especially now that she'd seen the kind of men who were behind the murders. For Lucien, it would have been quite simple. He was not a fighter, but Raphael was. So why not let Raphael deal with these vicious human thugs?

"Sophie?" Colin said, when she remained quiet. "You okay?"

She swallowed hard and nodded. "Those men were here because of Lucien. I don't know how, but I believe it. And I think Raphael does, too. He'll want to kill Lucien if he finds him, and he would be justified."

Colin gave her a long glance. "And you?" he asked quietly.

"If he did this, he *deserves* to die."

"That's not a good answer, Soph."

"I know, but I don't have another one right now."

Colin braked sharply and Sophia looked up to see the SUV ahead of them making a hard right turn. They drove along for several more minutes before Colin muttered, "Where the fuck are we going?"

He started playing with the GPS device built into the dash, punching buttons and swearing softly at whatever he found.

"Look at the GPS," he said tightly.

Sophia did, then shrugged. "All right. I've looked. Now tell me what I'm seeing."

Colin huffed impatiently. "A few more miles and we're at the Canadian border. Do vampire territories follow international lines?"

"Usually. It's easier that way. But there's no *checkpoint* here."

"Doesn't mean there's no border. There are places around here where you can walk back and forth pretty easily. This is the longest border in the world, you can't guard the whole thing."

Sophia got a sick feeling in her stomach. If they were that close . . . Her thoughts were interrupted as Raphael's SUV braked sharply, turning again, but onto a private road this time. The gravel here was thick, shifting smoothly beneath their tires as they drove a short distance and parked in front of a tidy little cabin. Lights glowed warmly from behind white lace curtains and tubs filled with flowers crowded a porch as wide as the cabin itself.

Colin turned off the engine. "What now?"

Sophia stared at the cabin.

"Sophie?"

She shook herself impatiently. Whatever, whoever, waited for them here, she would deal with it, because she had to. Because no matter what it was, she had dealt with worse and survived.

"We see who answers when we knock," she said matter-of-factly and opened the truck door.

She was struck immediately by the scent of all those flowers. It was lovely, the first truly pretty thing she'd seen since arriving in this rainy place. Whoever lived in this house had an appreciation for beauty.

Something whispered through her mind, a touch there and gone before she was even aware of it. She caught her breath and stared hard at the homey little cabin. Impossible.

Her attention shifted as a pair of dark shapes separated from the shadows and headed directly for Raphael and his party. Vampires. They were clearly Raphael's and had been set to watch this place until he arrived.

A light came on over the door. One would have to be deaf and blind not to notice their arrival. The door was pulled back and a vaguely familiar human female appeared in the opening. Sophia took a few steps to the side to escape the porch light's glare and get a better look. She was puzzled to discover it was the woman who worked for Wei Chen during the day.

Even more puzzling, the woman took one look at who was waiting for her and instead of sensibly slamming the door, she opened the screen and stood back, welcoming them into her home.

Sophie frowned. This was not the behavior of a guilty person. So why were they here?

Whatever qualms Sophia had, Raphael had none. He started toward the stairs, and Sophia smiled as both Juro and the two vampire guards jumped to get there ahead of him. Raphael's people were fanatically devoted to his safety. She could only hope her own— Sophia froze in mid-step. *Her own?*

"Sophie?"

She took Colin's offered hand, taking comfort from its solid warmth. "Let's see what Lord Raphael has in mind, Colin."

* * * *

The woman was unremarkable, Sophia thought. Although not unattractive. She might have been pretty if she'd taken the time to fuss. Her hair was a lovely auburn shade, but she had it pulled back into a tidy pony tail that did nothing to enhance her features, and her eyes were hidden behind sturdy wire rim glasses.

She was nervous, but who wouldn't be when confronted in the middle of the night by so many hulking vampires? It had to be terrifying to answer your door and find them waiting on your doorstep.

And yet, even knowing who Raphael was—and working at the compound, she had to know what he was—she smiled and invited them inside, as if she'd expected them.

"Ms. Koepke," Duncan said with his customary calm. "You have nothing to fear from us. Wei Chen has spoken highly of you and your work for him."

The woman nodded, her gaze flashing around once again, seeming to hesitate when it touched on Sophia before moving on. "How can I help you, Lord Raphael?" she asked.

"You know why Lord Raphael is here in Seattle," Duncan said. "You know about the murders."

"Of course. But I heard—" Her lips shut in a tight line.

"What did you hear?" Duncan asked gently.

Sophia watched the woman closely, wondering why Raphael was bothering with such gentle inquiries if he truly believed she had something to do with the murders. And if she didn't, then Sophia's question was the same as the woman's. Why were they here?

"I heard you found the awful men who did this," the woman said in a low voice. "The ones who murdered Marco and Preston and then attacked poor Mariane. And I heard that Lord Raphael and . . . that one," she added, giving Sophia a malevolent glare, "killed them all."

Sophia drew back in surprise. As far as she knew, she'd never met this human before, and the woman seemed to have no problem with the others. So why the hostility toward her?

Raphael was leaning against the cold fireplace, one arm resting negligently along the mantle, as if trying to seem less than he was. Privately, Sophia thought it would take much more than a casual pose to make Raphael seem harmless, and apparently he agreed with her. He straightened impatiently, giving up the pose.

"I'm tired of this," he said abruptly. "What do you know about the men who committed these murders? About their connections in Vancouver?" he demanded.

"She doesn't know anything about that."

Lucien! The abrupt awareness of her Sire drew Sophia's shocked gaze to the dark hallway. She stared as he walked slowly into the light, anger warring with relief that he was here and alive. She risked a quick glance at Raphael. *He* wasn't surprised. Clearly this was the reason they were here. That big bastard had known all along that they'd find Lucien with this woman.

"Sophie?" Colin said softly as Sophia tensed, facing her Sire.

But she was too stunned to answer, staring in horror as Lucien emerged fully into the soft lamplight of the woman's living room. If Sophia hadn't heard his voice first, she wouldn't have recognized him. He was bent and feeble, his fingers bony with knobby joints and yellowed nails. His black, wavy hair, once a source of shameless vanity, was now a dull gray that drank in the light and swallowed it, hanging as stiff and straight as dried twigs. And his face—his beautiful face—was parched and wrinkled, jowls hanging to his chin, his once sparkling eyes concealed beneath heavy lids and coarse brows.

Sophia wanted to weep. Concern radiated from Colin like a heat lamp as he moved closer, and she knew he was prepared to defend her even though he had no idea what was causing her distress.

Her fingers brushed against his. He was too much a warrior to take her hand in an unknown and possibly hostile situation, but his hand touched her lower back briefly in reassurance.

"Raphael," Lucien rasped. His head rotated slowly in her direction. "And Sophia, my treasure. I knew I could count on you."

His clouded eyes studied the other vampires in the crowded room. "Duncan, of course. But I don't know these others."

And then his gaze fell on Colin, standing so close to Sophia, and for one moment his eyes held their old sharpness. But then it was gone, and he smiled, baring discolored teeth.

"Yours, Sophia? I gave you my good taste, if nothing else, heh?" He chuckled dryly and then coughed, one hand hitting the wall as he staggered into it.

"Sandra love," Lucien said, beckoning the Koepke woman to his side. She hurried over, her face wreathed in joy as she gazed up at the vampire lord's ruined countenance.

"He's beautiful, isn't he?" she whispered, her fingers reaching upward to stroke his cheek, halting inches away as if not daring to despoil such perfection.

Lucien smiled and rested his hand on her arm as she guided him to a big upholstered chair in the corner as if he was a visiting prince.

"She doesn't see him," Sophia murmured, staring. The words were intended for Colin's ears, but she knew every vampire in the room caught it, too. "He's cast a glamour over her mind. She sees him in his glory, as he used to be."

Sophia tore her gaze away from the spectacle of Koepke fawning all over Lucien, and studied Raphael, wondering what would happen next. She could feel the hunger rising from every vampire in the room. It was only the fact that Lucien was her Sire that kept her own hunger from joining theirs. Vampires were predators, all of them. But among vampire lords, that instinct reached soaring heights. Raphael was the epitome of Vampire, the predator's predator. And Lucien had just shown himself to be prey.

"Why?" she asked suddenly, needing answers before Lucien died. She stared at him, demanding that he deal with her. "Why all this subterfuge? Why—" She struggled to find words for a concept she didn't really understand. "Why *diminish* yourself like this?" She gestured at their modest surroundings, although her words encompassed so much more.

Koepke twisted around to glare at Sophia once more, but Lucien touched the human woman's cheek, stroking it softly to pull her attention back to him. "I have spoken to her of you, Sophia," he said without looking away from Koepke. "I'm afraid she is somewhat jealous. Gently, *cherie*," he murmured to the human, and the familiar endearment on this *old man's* lips filled Sophia with fear and disgust in equal measure.

That was all he said for some minutes, but then he raised his head and met Raphael's gaze, as if asking for permission to tell his story. He had to know his situation was precarious, Sophia thought worriedly. But did he understand the extent of his danger? Did he know his actions had nearly cost the life of Raphael's mate? It was a miracle, an act of supreme restraint on Raphael's part, that Lucien still breathed.

Lucien was still staring at his fellow vampire lord, waiting. Raphael's jaw tightened perceptibly, but he nodded, a short, sharp jerk of his chin.

Lucien seemed to relax, his breath running out in a sigh. He leaned back in the chair, one gnarled hand stroking Koepke's head where she sat tucked up against his legs like a dog.

"It was a woman, of course," Lucien began. "I've always had a weakness for beauty, although it never mattered whether it was man or woman, did it, Sophia? Remember that young man—ah, my apologies. We shouldn't speak of such things in front of your human."

A soft growl, little more than an audible vibration, emanated from Raphael where he stood near the empty fireplace.

"Quite right, old friend," Lucien said quickly. "I am sorry for the deaths of your people. I never intended— Well, that's not quite true.

"But the woman was lovely, and I was vain. Little to be vain about anymore, I suppose," he added ruefully. "Although *ma belle* Sandra sees me as I was, don't you, *cherie?*" he said, stroking her head once more.

"My story goes back to before I became what you see. And the woman—so beautiful, so very human—was charmingly shocked to discover that I was Vampire, that such a thing really existed. I know now it was all a pose, but I was too blinded by her flattery to recognize it. She was intrigued by everything—what I was, what I could do. And finally, by all of the others I held in my grasp. I boasted like a fool. I told her about the vampires living among humans, while neighbors, friends, even coworkers were none the wiser. I told her of our houses, our wealth."

A pink tear rolled from his eye, losing itself in the deep creases of his cheeks.

"And I then I showed her. I showed her Giselle," he said in a barely audible voice.

Sophia jerked at the name. Giselle. It had been her face Sophia had glimpsed in Curtis Jenkins's dying memories. He'd been there when the Vancouver vampire and her housemates were murdered.

"You led them right to her," she said, horrified. "They murdered her, Lucien. They killed all three of them while they lay helpless in sleep!"

Lucien looked away, refusing to meet her gaze. "To my great shame," he said softly.

"What happened to the human woman?" Raphael demanded harshly.

"When I found out what she'd done, I stripped her mind and then I killed her," Lucien said calmly. "It was too late for my Giselle and her lovers, Damon and Benjamin. Such beauty gone forever," he said sadly, "and all because of me."

His voice ached with regret, but it only infuriated Sophie. What good was his regret to the vampires who had died, both here in and Vancouver?

"But killing the woman who seduced me wasn't enough," Lucien continued. "I knew she had told others everything I'd shared with her. I might be a fool, but not so big a fool that I thought she had the stomach to do the killing herself. I took the identity of the killers from her mind. I sought them out and charmed them. And I discovered how little they knew of what we are and what we can do. They were killers, certainly. But there was no subtlety in what they did. They hated and they killed.

"So I persuaded them to move their butchery out of Vancouver and into the U.S. Into your territory, Raphael, although they didn't know that. I let them believe it was simply a matter of convenience, why kill in Canada, when they could do their killing right here at home?"

Raphael had become frighteningly still, his silver-flecked eyes staring unblinking at Lucien, who seemed unaware of his danger.

"But why?" Sophia interjected, hoping he would redeem himself somehow, that he would tell them he'd done more than simply shove his murderous problem onto others—including her—to take care of. "Why send them here to kill even more, my lord? Why not stop them?"

Lucien looked up at her, his eyes sunken and shadowed, and yet there was a light of compassion there, as if he knew she was hoping for an answer he couldn't give her.

"Because I knew I couldn't defeat them," he told her gently. "They'd brought in someone new—this McWaters fellow. And where the others were disorganized and mindless in their killing, he was not. He was a strategist and more than just a killer—he was a highly trained, intelligent killer who hated everything we were. I had been hard pressed to deal with them before, but I didn't stand a chance once McWaters became their leader. Even worse, he brought more humans with him. Far too many for me to deal with alone.

"But it was painfully easy to turn McWaters's hatred back on the ones he despised most. It took so little encouragement on my part, just a few hints about where to look and what to look for. It was the reason he'd come to Vancouver in the first place, to learn how to find and kill the vampires who'd sullied his home town."

He shifted his gaze to Raphael and continued, "My vampires were so much easier to kill than yours. You know me well, Raphael. You used to chastise me for my lax ways back when we were both new to this continent, for not having even a pretense of security."

His eyes narrowed as he studied his fellow vampire lord, becoming shrewd and calculating. "But I know you, too, old friend. And I knew *you* could defeat them. Even more, I knew nothing would stop you once they'd killed one of yours."

Raphael moved faster than even Sophia's eye could follow, his eyes shooting silver sparks as he grabbed Lucien by the throat and ripped him from the chair. The human woman screamed, finding herself shoved aside where she huddled whimpering against the wall.

Raphael's rage filled the room in a rush, crushing Sophia's chest and hurting her ears as it threatened to displace every ounce of air in the small house. She raised a small cone of power, for Colin's protection even more than her own.

"They nearly killed my mate," Raphael growled, his voice so deep it rattled the dishes in the kitchen. "They *butchered* two of mine and nearly *raped* another to death."

His power grew along with his fury, becoming a storm of energy that sent furniture scraping across the floor to shatter against walls, pictures crashing to the floor with the chime of breaking glass.

"Wait," Sophia cried. "Wait. Please, Lord Raphael."

He turned to stare at her and she wasn't certain he could see her anymore. His eyes had gone solid silver, and even Duncan and the others had backed away.

Sophia was exquisitely aware of Colin standing next to her, of his terrible vulnerability if Raphael unleashed even a fraction of the power swirling around them. She tightened her own power ruthlessly. It was like knives of red-hot steel clawing at her insides, demanding to be set free, to respond to Raphael's overwhelming threat and defend what was hers. She wanted to scream in agony, to shred her own skin in a bid to release the unbearable pressure. But Colin's life, and probably hers, as well, depended on her ability to seem harmless, to offer no challenge to Raphael's execution of the vampire who had caused so much pain and loss to Raphael's children, and God save them all, to his mate.

"A question, my lord," she pled. "Please."

Raphael stared at her, unmoving. And then he blinked. "Make it fast," he grated out and dropped Lucien back into the chair.

Sweat was pouring from Sophia's skin, soaking her clothes as she turned to face her Sire. "Why me, Lucien? Why call me back here?"

Lucien gave her a gruesome smile. "You were always my favorite, child. I sent you away because I loved you, not because I didn't."

She nodded impatiently. "I know that, but why—"

Lucien stood abruptly, pushing himself up from the chair, flailing with one hand and grasping a nearby bookcase to remain upright. He shook himself slightly and then straightened to stand unassisted and look Sophia in the eye.

"I surrender to you, Sophia. All that I am, all that I have . . . is yours."

Sophia frowned. "What are you saying?"

He closed his eyes.

Sophia jerked as he touched her mind. She opened her mouth to protest.

Lucien shuddered once.

And Sophia fell to her knees, screaming.

Chapter Forty-Five

Sophia's head was full of voices, crying, screaming, demanding. Wanting answers, comfort . . . love. She fought to make sense of it, to understand what was happening. And suddenly Lucien was there, showing her how to quiet the tumult, to shuffle the pleas and silence the screams. To counter the demands with one of her own. *I am your lord. You will be silent.*

"Take care of them, cherie," Lucien whispered. *"Be better than I was."* And with a final wash of love, he was gone, the one constant in her life for nearly three hundred years vanished, leaving a gaping hole in her soul.

She opened her eyes, sobs choking her throat as she stared at the pile of thin ash that was all that was left of Lucien. He'd known Raphael would kill him. He hadn't even tried to defend himself, knowing it would be fruitless to try. Instead, he'd taken the easy way out. He was already diminished by his efforts to hide from Raphael, and if his appearance was any indication, he'd taken no blood nourishment for sometime. Rather than die in agony by Raphael's hand, he'd simply surrendered his life along with his power.

Lucien had been her parent far longer than the humans who'd given birth to her, had shown her more love and understanding, had taught her more of the world than those two strangers had ever dreamt of doing. But in the end, he'd been true to his selfish nature, leaving Sophia to deal with the carnage he'd left behind, to face the furious Raphael alone.

"Sophie." It was Colin's voice, harsh with stress and fear. For her. He was standing over her, his gun drawn, his strong legs bracketing her. And he was facing down Raphael and his vampires. For her.

She was not alone, after all.

"Colin," she croaked. "Don't."

He dropped down next to her, his voice deep and warm in her ear, one arm clasping her tightly to his chest. "I'm here, darlin'."

"He's gone," she whispered brokenly against his chest. "Lucien is gone."

"I know. I know, and I'm sorry."

"Take care of the human, Duncan."

Raphael's voice had her stiffening to attention, painfully aware of the target she made at this moment. A freshly minted vampire lord, overcome with the shock of transfer despite Lucien's efforts to ease the transition for her.

She crumpled Colin's shirt in her fingers, fighting for composure, for the strength she'd need. She loosened her hold and stood slowly, giving Colin plenty of time to adjust to her movements.

Raphael was still standing on the far side of the room. He was watching her closely, his power no longer evident but for the occasional flash of silver in his black eyes.

"Lord Raphael," she said, her voice still rough with emotion.

"Lady Sophia," he acknowledged meaningfully. "I propose an alliance."

Sophia's heart was pounding, but she met his gaze evenly. She couldn't afford to show weakness and yet she would do almost anything to get herself and Colin out of here alive. But an alliance? She'd never heard of such a thing. Not among vampire lords.

Her thoughts sped, trying to reason out Raphael's motives, to calculate her own benefit in such an arrangement. And wondering why he would propose such a thing and what he would expect in return. In all of this, however, one thing was certain. She would be vulnerable for some time as she built her power base essentially from scratch. The weaker vampires in the territory would simply accept her, grateful they had survived the trauma of Lucien's death and that someone had been willing to step up and keep them alive.

But Lucien's stronger children, few as they were, would have to be brought to heel, would have to swear loyalty to her in person one by one, and some of them would challenge her. Many of them didn't know her and even those who did hadn't seen her in decades and would assume she was weak because she was female and, frankly, because Lucien had chosen her. His preference for beauty over practicality was well known, even among his children.

But if Raphael supported her, if it was known that he at least would not oppose her and would not make a move on the territory as long as she was its ruler . . . That would go a long way toward smoothing her takeover, to soothing doubts and damaged egos.

"What do you have in mind, Lord Raphael?" she asked, making her voice as cool and controlled as she ever had.

Raphael smiled, as if he knew the effort it cost her, the arrogant bastard.

"You rule your territory and I rule mine. But when certain matters come before the Council, matters which are to our mutual benefit—" His black eyes turned flat and cold. "—you agree to be guided by my greater experience."

Sophia wasn't fooled by the polite language. Nor was she fooled into thinking he would let her live if she didn't agree . . . or if she tried to renege later on. But in the final analysis, it was still a good deal for her.

"I accept your offer," she said, with a formal little tilt of her head.

"Excellent." He paused for a polite few seconds. When he continued, his voice and manner were both inflexible. "Given the late hour, and *our newfound alliance*," he added deliberately, "you have twenty-four hours to leave my territory. I assume Mister Murphy will accompany you back to Vancouver. Arrangements will be made by my people to act as agents in the disposition of his affairs within my territory."

He didn't wait for her agreement, but strode for the door, pausing just before he exited into the night. "Congratulations, Lady Sophia."

And suddenly it was all over.

Lucien was a pile of ash on the carpet.

Raphael was gone.

And Sophia was Lord of the Canadian Territories. She shuddered, a hard, full-body jerk that had Colin wrapping his arm around her in concern. She permitted herself a moment to relish the heat and comfort of his big body, and then she straightened and said, "Let's get the hell out of here."

* * * *

Colin nodded as the two vampire guards followed him out onto the porch and locked the house door behind them. Raphael and Duncan were gone, so was Juro. They'd left right after the dustup and taken the Koepke woman with them. Justin and Aaron, the two vamps who'd followed Koepke home from work for Raphael, had stayed to clean up the house. They'd also disposed of what was left of Lucien after he fucking disintegrated—and *that* was something Colin could very happily do without ever seeing again.

The two vamps gave Sophie a wide berth as they circled around the yard and climbed into their vehicle. She was sitting on the passenger seat of the Suburban, turned around so she faced the open door. Which was right where Colin had left her after hustling her out of that house.

He waited in the yard, watching the vamps leave, and thinking about what to say to Sophie. Lucien had apparently passed his mojo—Colin refused to call it magic—to Sophie and then offed himself. Or maybe it was the transfer of mojo that killed him. Who the hell knew? It didn't really matter. If the old guy hadn't done himself in, Raphael sure as hell would have done it for him.

For a while back there, Colin had thought he was going to have to defend Sophie against that whole bunch of badass vampires. He'd figured he could take out a few before they got to him and had hoped it would be enough for Sophie to get away.

But it hadn't been necessary because his Sophie turned out to be a badass vampire all her own. He grinned, liking the idea, and suddenly he knew what to say to her.

He waited until the vamps' SUV made it down the drive and turned left onto the highway leading back to the compound before walking over to see what was up. Because something was definitely up.

"What's goin' on, darlin'?"

Colin took one look at Sophie's face when she raised her head to glance at him and amended that thought. Not up, down. Definitely down.

He edged in closer, resting his hands along the outside of her thighs and rubbing them slightly. "Talk to me, Sophie."

She didn't say anything for a few minutes, long enough that Colin was about to nudge her again before she finally pressed her hands against his and sighed.

"When I arrived in Vancouver," she said quietly, "and discovered Lucien was missing, my first desperate thought was that we had to find him. But my second thought was that if he was dead, I would do anything it took, fight and kill anyone who stood in my way, to seize his territory for myself."

"Nothing wrong with ambition," Colin said confidently.

"No, there's not. But now that Lucien *is* dead and the territory really is mine, I can't help wondering what the hell I was thinking." She shook her head, laughing softly.

"But you took it without a fight. That's gotta be good, right?"

"If only that were true. But the fight is just beginning."

Her fingers curled into fists against his, and he shifted, taking her hands in his and smoothing her fingers gently.

"Most of Lucien's people won't care if I'm the one who succeeds him, as long as I don't demand anything more from them than he did. But there are others who will only pretend to offer support while they wait for me to fail. They'll watch for every mistake, for any shred of weakness. And until I have a chance to create vampires of my own, people I can trust, I'll have to be on guard every moment, wondering whom I can trust and where the stake will come from. And then there are those who will point to every sign of anger, every tiny mood, every hint of indecision as proof that a woman simply doesn't have what it takes to rule. It exhausts me just talking about it."

"Well, then," Colin said, raising each hand in turn and kissing her fingers. "I'll tell you what, Sophie. Until you can make your own vamps, I'll be the one who stands guard and watches for that stake so you won't have to. And if you get angry, you can yell at me. If you get down or just need a sounding board, I'll be there. And at the end of the night, when we've locked the door and it's just you and me again, I'll strip you naked and we'll make love until sunrise, because I happen to love every womanly inch of you."

Laughing, Sophie slid off the seat to stand in front of him. She wrapped her arms around his neck and hugged him tightly. "I'm going to hold you to that."

Colin tugged her closer, pulling her into his arms while resting one hand on the curve of her delicious butt. "Hold me anyway you want, darlin'. I'm easy."

"Colin," she said, pulling back to see his face. "You do understand that if you go with me to Vancouver, if you continue to take my blood . . ." She paused, searching his eyes. "We will live a very long time together. You need to be sure—"

He laughed with relief, squeezing her tightly. "Is that all?"

"I'm serious."

"So am I, darlin'. And I *am* sure." He bent his head and kissed her, drinking in the sweet warmth that was his Sophie, feeling her soften in his arms.

"I love you, Sophie," he murmured against her mouth.

"Colin," she said breathlessly, her eyes wide open and staring into his from only inches away. "You'd really leave your home here and go with me to Canada?"

"Just try to keep me away. I do have one question, though."

"Just one?" she said, smiling.

"Just one. Who says we have to clear out on his high and mighty's timetable? There's plenty of hours left before sunrise and Vancouver's not that far. I say we blow this place tonight and the hell with Raphael."

Sophia fisted her fingers in his hair and pulled him in for a quick, hard kiss. "I like the way you think, *meu querido*. You drive."

"Damn straight I'm gonna drive. Don't let this vampire lord thing to go your head, woman."

Sophie was still laughing as they drove out to the highway and turned right, heading for Canada.

Chapter Forty-Six

"You didn't destroy Sophia," Duncan observed quietly, as they sped back to the compound.

It wasn't a question; Duncan would never have questioned him. But Raphael heard the curiosity in his lieutenant's voice. He considered the statement for a few moments, then said, "In the end, she wasn't really a part of this. Lucien played her just as he did the rest of us. But mostly, I want the Canadian territory stable, and she's strong enough to hold it. She's also indebted to me now. That will be far more useful in the coming days."

Duncan nodded thoughtfully. "The Koepke woman didn't know Lucien was using her."

"No," Raphael agreed.

"Lucien knew her in Vancouver. He'd never bound her to him, but he'd used her. It was easy for him to find her and use her again."

Raphael shook his head irritably. "Lucien might have pointed the killers at Marco and Preston, but they didn't need him for the addresses. They'd both been here long enough that people knew where they lived. They may not have gotten out much, but they did go out, and Marco's horses made it easier to identify his property."

"Even so, my lord, if they'd only upgraded their sleeping arrangements, this wouldn't have happened."

Raphael nodded. "When the new compound was commissioned, I authorized whatever expenditure was necessary to bring everyone's security up to modern standards. Loren was to have seen to it."

A few more miles went by as Raphael thought about everything that had happened since they'd arrived, all the details that had slipped his mind in his worry over Cyn. His hand tightened into a fist as he fought the urge to punch something. Or someone. But Loren wasn't here, and Lucien was no more.

"I want someone new brought in," he said abruptly. "Someone from outside the Seattle nest. Wei Chen can remain the nominal leader, but I want a strong head of security, someone more powerful than Wei Chen."

"I'll compile a list, my lord. Do you want it before we leave?"

"No. We're leaving first thing tomorrow night. Cyn will be able to travel by then and I want to take her home."

They pulled through the compound's gate, Juro guiding the SUV to a smooth stop below the stairs to the main building. One of Raphael's security contingent was waiting. He pulled the door open and Raphael climbed out, giving the vampire a nod of greeting.

As he started up the stairs, Duncan joined him. "How *is* Cynthia, my lord?"

Raphael gave his lieutenant a small grin. "Well enough to fight with

Doctor Saephan over his restrictions."

Duncan laughed. "I would expect nothing else. I will see you both tomorrow evening, then, my lord. I will make the arrangements."

* * * *

The next night came none too soon for Raphael, nor for Cyn, although for all her professed eagerness to return to the comfort and security of their home, there was something troubling her.

He didn't push her, though, knowing she'd eventually tell him what it was.

He glanced over to where she sat on the bed, resting after the exertion of her first shower since the shooting. She'd managed to pull on her underwear and a sweater, but her long legs were bare, and far too thin.

Doctor Saephan had finally permitted her to eat something this evening. Or rather to drink something. He'd arrived bearing a high protein liquid shake instead of the usual blood bags. He'd made it up for her himself, adding plenty of chocolate syrup, which testified to how well he knew his patient. Cyn hadn't even whispered a protest.

"Raphael."

He shook himself out of his thoughts and smiled at her, picking up the yoga pants she'd chosen to wear.

"Stay there, *lubimaya*. I'll put these on for you."

"I can stand."

"Of course you can," he agreed, standing in front of her. "Now, slide over here."

"Bossy," she muttered, but she did as he asked, sitting on the edge of the bed while he slipped the pants over her feet and up her legs. He held out a hand and she took it, letting him help her stand and then support her while she wiggled the pants over her hips.

"I look awful," she said miserably, stepping into her shoes.

"You don't. You look beautiful, as always."

But her eyes when they met his were shining with tears. "I don't want everyone staring at me," she whispered.

Ah, he thought to himself. *So that's what it is.*

"Then no one will," he told her and pulled out his cell phone. "I want the great room cleared, Duncan." He looked around, gauging their departure time. Everything was packed and ready, except for Cyn. "In five minutes. You, Juro and Elke. The rest of our security can wait in the vehicles outside."

"Thank you, Raphael," she said, then gave him a weak grin. "It's good to be the king, huh?"

"Only if you're my queen, *lubimaya*." He bent over and touched his lips to hers. "Come. I'll carry you."

"No!"

He scooped her up easily. She was too weak to fight him, but she didn't try very hard, wrapping her arms around his neck and resting her head on his shoulder. He touched his cheek to her freshly shampooed hair and smiled, remembering her almost orgasmic sigh when he'd washed it for her.

"You're thinking about the shower," she murmured, stroking one finger along the back of his neck.

"Be good," he scolded, carrying her to the elevator.

"Give me a few days," she said softly, switching her finger to the curve of his ear. "And I'll be very good."

"And now you're just toying with me."

Cyn nestled into the curve of his shoulder, her kiss soft and moist against the underside of his jaw. "Have I told you you're my very favorite vampire?" she murmured tiredly.

"Not often enough," Raphael said smoothly, fighting a tidal wave of emotion at how light she was in his arms, how very fragile.

He felt the curve of her lips as she smiled against his skin. "I'll have to remember that. I love you, fang boy."

Her body softened and Raphael knew she was close to falling asleep. He tightened his hold on her, the terror of almost losing her still too fresh and too horrible to remember. He didn't know what he would have done if she'd died. But he knew one thing . . . She wouldn't have died alone.

Epilogue

Malibu, California

Raphael settled the phone back on its cradle and shared a sober look with Duncan, who sat across the desk from him in one of the two visitor chairs.

"It's time, my friend."

"I know."

"I will miss you. Cyn will—" He lifted his head and nearly groaned. "Cyn will be joining us soon."

Duncan stood immediately. "I'll give you some privacy, my lord," he said and headed for the doors.

Raphael laughed grimly. "Coward."

Duncan grinned, bowed slightly from where he stood at the open door and disappeared down the hall.

Raphael sat alone, tracking Cyn's movements as she drew closer to his office, automatically gauging her mood and her physical well-being. She'd made considerable progress since coming home from Seattle, but she was far from her usual fighting form, and she still tired much too easily. He hated that he was about to upset her. Hated the news he was about to deliver almost as much as he hated telling her about it. But now that the decision was made, word would travel like fire through the household, and she would be angry and, even worse, hurt if she heard it from someone else first.

The doors pushed open and Cyn strode into the room. She'd come from her daily, and carefully monitored, workout in the gym and her lovely face was flushed with life, her green eyes sparkling as she smiled at him.

Raphael sighed and rose to meet her, walking around to take her in his arms.

She might be angry if he kept the news of his decision from her, but she would never forgive him if it turned out he had just sent Duncan to his death.

To be continued . . .

Acknowledgments

As always, my first thanks go to Linda Kichline of ImaJinn Books for her support and the incredible talent that goes into every single book. And to Patricia Lazarus for creating a beautiful cover for Sophia and Colin, despite my PITB messages.

There are so many people I lean on for advice and expertise when I'm writing a book. I can only list them here and hope they know how much I appreciate their contributions. My foremost thanks go to my critique partners Steve McHugh and Michelle Muto. I could never put out a single book if I didn't have these two incredible writers to tell me what works, to rein me in when I go a little nuts and to keep me going when I'm ready to scream. Someday we'll all be famous together!

To John Gorski once again for advising me on everything that goes bang or has a sharp edge, plus for keeping my characters from getting shot dead because they didn't follow basic police procedure! To Ken McDaniel for being "overly technical military guy." To Sophie of the OWG for her assistance with French and general wonderfulness, and to Carlos Looney and Elaine Villafane for helping my Sophia's Portuguese make sense.

I'm delighted to say that two of my readers contributed to this book very directly. Mary Walker (aka Amy) came up with the perfect name for a bar in lumber country. Babe's was her inspiration, the bullet-riddled sign was mine. (I'm sure that says something about me, but let's not go into *that*.) Another reader, S. C. Liu, gave me the character Maxime, whose scene was cut from Rajmund, but who finally made it on-screen in Sophia. Huge thanks go to all of the reviewers and bloggers who help get the word out about my vamps, and to my readers who let me know every single day how much they love Raphael, Cyn and all the gang. Your support means so much to me!

Thanks to Adrian Phoenix (writer of brilliant books) for her generosity and support, to Kelley Armstrong for hosting the OWG, the best online writing group ever, and to all of my fellow OWG members for their advice and enthusiasm. Special thanks go to Danielle Wegner for hosting me in the Book Club at KelleyArmstrong.com. Totally cool!

And finally, thank you to my enormous family for their continuing love and support, and to my wonderful husband for putting up with a wife who writes all the effing time!

Stop by my blog at http://dbreynolds.wordpress.com for the latest news, contests, and Vampire Vignettes!